Praise for
MARY JANE

"Delightful. . . . Blau is a deft hand with comic juxtaposition and domestic fantasy. She keeps it light, she keeps it moving and she's got terrific visuals. . . . You can watch the movie in your mind. Lady Gaga as Sheba? I'm already casting it."

—*New York Times Book Review*

"I LOVED Jessica Anya Blau's novel. *Mary Jane* is about an oppressed teenager being given a jolt of life and joy by an eccentric found family of therapists, a child, a rock star, and a movie star in the 1970s. . . . If you have ever sung along to a hit on the radio, in any decade, then you will devour *Mary Jane* at 45 rpm."

—Nick Hornby

"I dare you to find a more winning novel than Jessica Anya Blau's *Mary Jane*. Filled with humor and sharpness and so much light, this book introduces an amazing cast of characters, all so unique and finely observed, held together by the clarity of Mary Jane's voice. It evokes those rare moments when your world is on the precipice of change, almost a dream, and how thrilling it is to push your way toward something new."

—Kevin Wilson

"Blau's intelligent, witty novel captures the essence of the '70s with humor and immensely appealing characters. Highly recommended." —*Library Journal* (starred review)

"Blau's coming-of-age charmer will hit all of the nostalgia notes."

—*Parade*

"*Mary Jane* is that rare thing: an utterly charming, absurdly delightful novel that also makes you think deeply about the world around you. Jessica Anya Blau's clear-eyed wit reminded me of Curtis Sittenfeld and Laurie Colwin, and, of course, Jane Austen." —Joanna Rakoff, author of *My Salinger Year*

"The experience of reading Jessica Anya Blau's *Mary Jane* is a lot like eating quality candy: super enjoyable, crazy good. I am sad to have finished it." —Marcy Dermansky

"The best book of the summer." —*InStyle*

"A charming and poignant tale of desire, image, Americana, and chosen family."
—*Booklist*

"This novel is a week at the beach with rock stars, it's a three-part harmony at a kitchen table, it's finding a family where you fit in. Jessica Anya Blau is a smart, generous, sensitive storyteller, and *Mary Jane* is a loving, sexy, funny, and beautiful book."
—Gabriel Brownstein, author of *The Open Heart Club*

"Both poignant and tremendously funny . . . unendingly charming and fun."
—Shelf Awareness

"Wonderful. . . . A tale of clashing cultures and a slow awakening of ideas, hope and beliefs, this is one of those novels you'll be so glad to lose yourself to. It's also perfect for fans of Curtis Sittenfeld's books—and we can give it no higher praise."
—*Stylist* (UK)

"This may be the best book about an adolescent since *The Adventures of Huckleberry Finn*. Fourteen-year-old Mary Jane, straight as a ruler, gets a summer job as a nanny to sweet Izzy, whose psychiatrist father is providing live-in therapy to a recovering rock star. Mary Jane and her cast of characters will carry you to bliss on every page. It's Baltimore in the '70s and Jessica Anya Blau gets everything right. Buy it for someone you love." —Michael Elias, author of *You Can Go Home Now*

"With *Mary Jane*, we indulge in everything that makes Jessica Anya Blau one of my favorite novelists today: humanity, humor, compassion, utter transformation, and the irresistible tease of what might be. I loved this book."
—Greg Bardsley, author of *Cash Out* and *The Bob Watson*

"This novel is an absolute delight! Mary Jane is the best friend, sister, daughter we'd all love to have. A beautifully written and life-affirming coming-of-age tale."
—Jane Delury, author of *The Balcony*

"The novel *Mary Jane* gives us a fabulously updated female version of Holden Caulfield, a coming-of-age story of political and sexual awakening unlike any other. It grabbles with all kinds of dysfunction—prejudice, addiction, and, of course (if you know Blau's work), rock and roll. Unique, moving, and funny as shit."
—Paula Bomer, author of *Tante Eva*

mary jane

A NOVEL

jessica anya blau

MARINER BOOKS

Boston   New York

P.S.™ is a trademark of HarperCollins Publishers.

MARY JANE. Copyright © 2021 by Jessica Anya Blau. All rights reserved. Printed in the United States of America. No part of this book may be used or reproduced in any manner whatsoever without written permission except in the case of brief quotations embodied in critical articles and reviews. For information, address HarperCollins Publishers, 195 Broadway, New York, NY 10007.

HarperCollins books may be purchased for educational, business, or sales promotional use. For information, please email the Special Markets Department at SPsales@harpercollins.com.

A hardcover edition of this book was published in 2021 by Custom House, an imprint of William Morrow.

FIRST MARINER BOOKS PAPERBACK EDITION PUBLISHED 2022.

Designed by Paula Russell Szafranski
Interior artwork © blue67design / Shutterstock

Library of Congress Cataloging-in-Publication Data

Names: Blau, Jessica Anya, author.
Title: Mary Jane : a novel / Jessica Anya Blau.
Description: First Edition. | New York, NY : Custom House, [2021]
Identifiers: LCCN 2020047171 (print) | LCCN 2020047172 (ebook)
   | ISBN 9780063052291 (hardcover) | ISBN 9780063052307
   (trade paperback) | ISBN 9780063052314 (ebook)
Classification: LCC PS3602.L397 M37 2021 (print) | LCC PS3602.
   L397 (ebook) | DDC 813/.6—dc23
LC record available at https://lccn.loc.gov/2020047171
LC ebook record available at https://lccn.loc.gov/2020047172

ISBN 978-0-06-305230-7

22 23 24 25 26 LSC 10 9 8 7 6 5 4 3 2 1

For Marcia and Nick

1

Mrs. Cone showed me around the house. I wanted to stop at every turn and examine the things that were stacked and heaped in places they didn't belong: books teetering on a burner on the stove, a coffee cup on a shoebox in the entrance hall, a copper Buddha on the radiator, a pink blow-up pool raft in the center of the living room. I had just turned fourteen, it was 1975, and my ideas about homes, furniture, and cleanliness ran straight into me like an umbilical cord from my mother. As Mrs. Cone used her bare foot (toenails painted a glittering red) to kick aside a stack of sweaters on the steps, I felt a jolt of wonder. Did people really live like this? I suppose I knew that they did somewhere in the world. But I never expected to find a home like this in our neighborhood, Roland Park, which my mother claimed was the finest neighborhood in Baltimore.

On the second floor all but one of the dark wood doors were open. The bottom half of the single closed door was

plastered with *IMPEACHMENT: Now More Than Ever*
bumper stickers and a masking-taped poster of Snoopy
dancing, nose in the air. Everything was slightly angled,
as if placed there by a drunk on his knees.

"This is Izzy's room." Mrs. Cone opened the door and
I followed her past Snoopy into a space that looked like
it had been attacked by a cannon that shot out toys. An
Etch A Sketch; Operation game board; Legos; paper doll
books; Colorforms box and stickies; Richard Scarry books;
and a heap of molded plastic horses: No surface was un-
covered. I wondered if Izzy, or her mother, swept an arm
across the bed at night, pushing everything to the floor.

"Izzy." I smiled. Our neighbor, Mrs. Riley, had told me
her name was Isabelle. But I liked Izzy better, the way it
fizzed on my tongue. I didn't know anyone named Izzy,
or Isabelle. I'd never even met Izzy Cone. But through
the recommendation of Mrs. Riley, and after a phone call
with Mrs. Cone, I'd been hired as the summer nanny. I
had thought the phone call was going to be an interview,
but really Mrs. Cone just told me about Izzy. "She doesn't
like to play with kids her own age. I don't think she's interested in what other five-year-olds do. Really, she only
wants to hang out with me all day," Mrs. Cone had said.
"Which is usually fine, but I've got other stuff going on
this summer, so . . ." Mrs. Cone had paused then and I'd
wondered if I was supposed to tell her that I'd take the
job, or was I to wait for her to officially offer it to me?

A five-year-old who only wanted to hang out with her
mother was someone I understood. I, too, had been a girl
who only wanted to hang out with her mother. I was still
happy helping my mother with the chores in the house, sitting beside her and reading, or grocery shopping with her,
searching out the best bell peppers or the best cut of meat.

When I did have to socialize with kids my age—like at the sleepovers to which every girl in the class had been invited—I felt like I was from another country. How did girls know what to whisper about? Why were they all thinking about the same things? Depending on the year, it could be Barbies, dress-up, boys, hairstyles, lip gloss, or *Teen Beat* magazine, none of which interested me. I had no real friends until middle school, when the Kellogg twins moved to Baltimore from Albany, New York. They, too, looked like they didn't know the customs and rituals of girlhood. They, too, were happy to spend an afternoon by the record player listening to the *Pippin* soundtrack; or playing the piano and singing multilayered baroque songs in melody, harmony, and bass; or watching reruns of *The French Chef* and then trying out one of the recipes; or even just making a simple dessert featured in *Good Housekeeping* magazine.

The more Mrs. Cone told me about Izzy on that phone call, the more I wanted to take care of her. All I could think was how much nicer it would be to spend my summer looking after a little girl who had no friends than going to our country club pool and *being* the girl who had no friends. I barely listened when Mrs. Cone told me how much they'd pay. The money felt like a bonus. Before the call had ended, I'd decided I'd save everything I earned and then buy my own record player at the end of the summer. One I could keep in my room; maybe it would even have separate speakers. If there was enough money left over, I'd buy a radio so I could listen to American Top 40: the songs from the records that my mother would never let me buy.

Downstairs I could hear the front door open and then slam shut. Mrs. Cone froze, listening, her ear tilted toward the doorway. "Richard?" she called out. "Richard! We're up here!"

My stomach clenched at the idea that Dr. Cone would ask me to call him Richard. Mrs. Cone had told me to call her Bonnie, but I couldn't. Even in my head I thought of her as Mrs. Cone, though, really, she didn't look like a *Mrs. Anything* to me. Mrs. Cone's hair was long, red, and shiny. She had freckles all over her face and her lips were waxy with bright orange lipstick. Draped over her body was either a long silk blouse or a very short silk dress. The liquid-looking fabric swished against her skin, revealing the outline of her nipples. The only place I'd seen nipples like that was in posters of celebrities, or women in liquor ads. I'd never seen even a hint of my mother's nipples; the couple of times I'd entered her bedroom when she was in her bra, it was like seeing breasts in beige armor.

"What?!" Dr. Cone yelled from the bottom of the stairs.

"Mommy!" Izzy yelled.

"Richard! Izzy! Come up!"

It was more hollering than I'd ever heard in my own house. Once, just before bedtime, my mother had loudly said "Damn it!" when she'd stepped on a shard of glass from a plate I'd dropped in the kitchen earlier in the day. I had thought the world was about to cave in like a tar-paper shack being consumed by fire. It wasn't only the words; I'd never seen my mother barefoot before. My eyes must have been bugging out of my head as I watched her pull the shard from her heel.

"Mary Jane," my mom had said, "go upstairs and fetch my slippers so I can mop this floor the right way." She had stood over my shoulder and supervised when I had mopped up after breaking the plate. Obviously, I hadn't done a good job.

"Why are you barefoot?" I asked.

My mother only said, "This is why we should never be barefoot. Now go get the slippers."

"You come down!" Dr. Cone yelled up the stairs. "Izzy made something!"

"I made something!" Izzy yelled.

"Mary Jane is here!" Mrs. Cone yelled back.

"Who?" Dr. Cone shouted.

"MARY JANE! The summer nanny!"

I smiled nervously. Did Dr. Cone know I had been hired to work in his house? And how much hollering could go on before someone moved closer to the other person?

"Mary Jane!" Izzy's feet made a muted *thunk thunk thunk* as she ran up the stairs and into the bedroom. She had a face from a Victorian Valentine's card and the energy of a ball of lightning. I liked her already.

I bounced back and received the hug.

"She's been so excited for you to get here," Mrs. Cone said.

"Hey. So good to meet you!" I ran my fingers through Izzy's coppery-red curls, which were half knotted.

"I made something!" Izzy turned from me and hugged her mother. "It's downstairs."

Dr. Cone appeared in the doorway. "Mary Jane! I'm Richard." He stuck out his hand and shook mine, like I was a grown-up.

My mother thought it was nice that I'd be working for a doctor and his wife for the summer. She said that a house with a doctor was a respectable house. The outside of the Cones' house certainly looked respectable; it was a rambling shingled home with blue shutters on every window. The landscaping was a little shabby (there were dirt patches on the lawn and half the hedges were dead and looked like the scraggly arms of starving children), but still, my mother never would have guessed at the piles of things lining the steps or strewn down the hall or exploded around the room where we stood just then.

And my mother also never would have imagined the long sideburns Dr. Cone had. Tufty, goaty things that crawled down his face. The hair on his head looked like it had never been combed—just a messy swirl of brown this way and that. My own father had a smooth helmet of hair that he carefully combed to the side. I'd never seen a whisker or even a five o'clock shadow on his face. No human under forty would have ever called my father anything but Mr. Dillard.

If my father knew I was working for a doctor's family, he would have approved. But he didn't pay much attention to matters concerning me. Or concerning anyone, really. Each night, he came home from work, settled into his chair by the living room window, and read the *Evening Sun* until my mother announced that dinner was ready, at which point he moved into the dining room, where he sat at the head of the table. Unless we had a guest, which was rare, he continued to read the paper while Mom and I talked. Every now and then my mother would try to include him in the conversation by saying something like "Gerald, did you hear that? Mary Jane's English teacher, Miss Hazen, had a poem published in a magazine! Can you imagine?"

Sometimes my dad responded with a nod. Sometimes he said things like *That's nice* or *Well, I'll be*. Most often he just kept on reading as if no one had said a word.

When Dr. Cone stepped deeper into the room and kissed Mrs. Cone on the lips, I almost fainted. Their bodies were pressed together, their heads only an inch apart after the kiss as they whispered to each other. I would have listened in, but I couldn't because Izzy was talking to me, pulling my hand, picking up things from the floor and explaining them to me as if I'd grown up in Siberia and had never seen American toys. Of Legos she said, "You click the blocks together and voilà!" Then she threw the blocks she had just coupled straight into the air. They landed, nearly invisible, in a heap of Fisher-Price circle-headed kids that lay beside their upside-down yellow school bus.

Dr. and Mrs. Cone continued talking, their mouths breathing the same thin slice of air, while Izzy explained the buzzer in Operation. The twins had Operation and I considered myself an expert. Izzy held the tweezers against the metal rim, purposefully setting off the electric hum. She laughed. Then she looked up at her parents and said, "Mom, you *have* to see what I made!" Dr. and Mrs. Cone snapped their heads toward Izzy at the exact same moment. Their bodies were still touching all the way up and down so that they were like a single two-headed being.

Izzy led the charge down the stairs, almost tripping over a cactus in a ceramic pot. Mrs. Cone was behind her, I followed Mrs. Cone, and Dr. Cone was behind me, talking the whole way. They had to get going on the third floor. They needed a better mattress on the bed, and they'd need better lighting, too. It could be a very comfortable guest suite.

As we entered the living room, Mrs. Cone picked up the inflated raft and sailed it into the dining room. It hit the long junk-covered table and then fell silently to the floor. The four of us assembled in front of the coffee table, which was covered with books, magazines, and a package of Fig Newton cookies that looked like it had been ripped open by a wolf. Beside the Fig Newtons, on top of a teetering pile of paperbacks, stood a lumpy papier-mâché lighthouse. It rose about three feet high and curved to the right.

"That's beautiful," I said.

"Is it a lighthouse?" Mrs. Cone leaned to one side to get a better look.

"Yes! On the Chesapeake Bay!" Izzy had been at a sailing-and-craft camp down at the Inner Harbor. Today was her last day. Mrs. Cone had mentioned the camp in our introductory phone call. She described it as "a bunch of bratty private school kids who think nothing of excluding Izzy from every game."

"It's magnificent," Mrs. Cone finally said. She picked up the lighthouse and went to the fireplace. On the mantel were more books, wineglasses, bongos that appeared to be made of ceramic and animal hide, and what I thought was a ukulele but was maybe some other kind of stringed instrument. She set the lighthouse on top of the books.

"Perfect," Dr. Cone said.

"Sort of looks like a giant dildo." Mrs. Cone said this quietly, maybe so Izzy couldn't hear. I had no idea what a dildo was. I glanced at Dr. Cone. He seemed to be holding in a laugh.

"I love it!" Izzy took my hand and pulled me back upstairs. Maybe her instinct was right and I was like a visitor from Siberia. I had never met anyone like Dr. and Mrs. Cone. And I'd never been in a house where every space was crammed with things to look at or think about (could it be that all messes weren't evil and didn't need to be banished with such efficiency?). I'd felt instantaneous affection for Izzy and was happy that I was to be her nanny. But I was happy for other things too: that I'd be doing something I'd never done before, that my days would be spent in a world that was so different to me that I could feel a sheen of anticipation on my skin. Already, I didn't want the summer to end.

On my first full day at the Cones', I dressed in my red terry-cloth shorts and the rainbow-striped top I'd picked out as part of my new summer wardrobe. My mother thought the shorts were too short, but we couldn't find anything longer at Hutzler's downtown, at least not in the juniors section. Mom told me to put my dirty-blond hair in a ponytail. "You need to be professional. It's a doctor's home," she said.

I pulled my hair back, put on my flip-flops, and walked through the neighborhood toward the Cones' house. It was sunny and quiet out. I saw a few men in suits walking to their cars, about to drive to work. I only saw one woman: our new neighbor. My mother and I had driven by as the movers had been unloading the furniture, and my mother slowed the car to catch a glimpse of a chintz sofa being carried off the truck. "A bit too blue," she had said, once the couch was out of sight.

The new neighbor was in her gardening capris and a

checked shirt. In her blond hair was the thin triangle of a blue scarf. She was on her knees, leaning over a hole she'd just dug in the dirt outline of the lawn. Beside her was a wooden crate full of flowers.

She sat up straight and shielded her eyes as I approached. "Good morning," she said.

"Good morning." I slowed but didn't stop, even though I really wanted to. This woman had a face out of a Hitchcock film. She was pretty. Clean-looking. Did she have kids? Was she married? Had she grown up in town? Had she attended the all-girls Roland Park Country School, where I was a student?

Before I crossed to the next block, I looked back at the woman. Her rump was in the air, her hands were deep in the dirt, and the scarf on her head flapped like a bird about to take off. She sat up quickly, caught me watching, and waved. I waved back, embarrassed, and then hurried away.

Mrs. Cone opened the door for me, smiling and holding a cup of coffee. As she closed the door behind us, she splashed coffee on the floor of the foyer. She was wearing a nightgown that came to her knees and was unbuttoned down the front, revealing just about everything. I tried not to look.

"They're in the kitchen—go on in." She turned and trotted up the stairs, ignoring the spill.

"Mary Jane?!" Izzy shouted. "We're in the kitchen!"

Dr. Cone shouted, as if Izzy hadn't, "We're in the kitchen!"

"IN THE KITCHEN!" Izzy repeated.

"Coming." I couldn't bring myself to shout, so I announced myself again after I'd passed out of the living room, through the dining room, and into the kitchen. "I'm here."

Dr. Cone was wearing pajama bottoms and a T-shirt. Izzy was wearing pink pajama pants and no shirt. Her taut belly sweetly popped out.

"I'm coloring!" Izzy announced.

"I love coloring." I scooted in next to her on the blue-cushioned banquette. The window behind the kitchen table looked out into the backyard and toward the garage. There was a lamp on in the garage; it appeared to be sitting on a surface—a table or a desk—at the window.

Dr. Cone noticed me looking. He pointed past me and Izzy. "That's my office."

"The garage?" I imagined a nurse inside, hospital beds, IV bags full of blood, ambulances pulling into the alleyway.

"Well, it was a garage once. A barn before that."

"Ours, too." The neighborhood had been built about eighty years ago by one of the Olmsted brothers who'd designed Central Park in New York City. It was full of winding roads, already mature trees, and a horse barn behind every house. I loved that our neighborhood had a connection to New York City. I liked to imagine myself in New York City, walking beside all those towering buildings and among the people cramming the sidewalks, like I'd seen in movies and TV shows. But most of all, I wanted to go to a Broadway show. My mother and I belonged to the Show Tunes of the Month Club and received a new Broadway cast album every month. I had memorized every song from all the great shows, and the best songs from the bad shows. My mother adored Broadway songs but not New York City, which she said was full of thieves, drug addicts, and degenerates.

"What should we color?" Izzy was sorting through a six-inch-high stack of coloring books.

"Is there a nurse in there?" I asked Dr. Cone, nodding toward the window.

"A nurse?"

"Who helps you with the patients."

Dr. Cone laughed. "I'm a psychiatrist. I'm a medical doctor, but I just work with thoughts. Addiction, obsessions. I don't deal in bodies."

"Oh." I wondered if my mother thought psychiatrists were as big a deal as the doctors who dealt in bodies.

"Bodies!" Izzy said, and waved a coloring book in front of me. *The Human Body* was printed on the front.

"That looks cool." I gathered crayons from around the table and grouped them according to color.

"Let's do the penis." Izzy opened the book and started flipping through the pages. My face burned and I felt a little shaky.

"What color are you going to do the penis?" Dr. Cone asked, and I almost gasped. I'd never heard an adult say *penis*. I'd barely heard people my age say *penis*. The Kellogg twins were the two top students in our class, and they never said words like *penis*.

"GREEN!" Izzy stopped at a page that showed a penis and scrotum. The whole thing looked droopy and boneless; the scrotum reminded me of half-rotted guavas that had started to wrinkle as they shrunk. Words were printed on the side and lines directed each word to what it was naming. This penis was larger and far more detailed than the one I'd barely glanced at on the anatomy drawing we'd been handed in sex ed class last year. In fact, upon receiving that handout, most girls took a pen and rapidly scratched over the penis so they wouldn't have to look at

it. I was too afraid of the teacher to graffiti my paper.
Sally Beaton, who sat beside me and was afraid of no one,
saw my pristine page and reached from her desk to mine
to scribble out the penis. Izzy picked up a green crayon
and started frantically coloring the penis green. I wasn't
sure if I should color with her or not. If it hadn't been a
penis, I would have. *But it was a penis,* and Dr. Cone was
right there. Would he want a girl who colored a penis taking care of his daughter? Then again, his own daughter
was coloring a penis! And I had to assume he or Mrs.
Cone had bought her the book.

"Help me!" Izzy handed me a red crayon. I nervously
started coloring the tip.

Dr. Cone glanced over. "Jesus, looks like it's pissing
blood."

I froze. I felt like my heart had stopped. But before I
could say anything, or put the red crayon down, Dr. Cone
wandered out of the kitchen.

Izzy and I finished the penis. I was relieved when she
turned the page and we colored a uterus and fallopian
tubes. Orange and yellow and pink.

That day, neither Dr. nor Mrs. Cone appeared to go
to work. And they didn't get dressed till around noon. In
my own house, both of my parents were showered and
dressed by six thirty. My father walked out the door Monday through Friday at seven a.m. Dad was a lawyer. He
wore a tie every day, and only removed that tie at the
table after we'd thanked the Lord for our food *and* prayed
for President Ford and his wife. A framed color picture
of smiling President Ford hung on the wall just behind
my father's head. Ford's gaze in the picture was aimed
directly at me. His eyes were a feathery suede blue. His
teeth looked like short little corn nibs. An American flag

undulated behind his head. Sometimes, when I thought *father* or when people talked about their dads, I envisioned President Ford.

My mother's work was mostly in the home. I'd never seen anyone busier than Mom. She made the beds every day, vacuumed every other day, swept every day, grocery shopped every Friday, made breakfast and dinner every day, and mopped the kitchen floor each night. She also taught Sunday school at the Roland Park Presbyterian Church. And she was really good at it. Sometimes the kids colored pictures of Jesus while Mom read them Bible verses. Sometimes she played Bible bingo with them. But the best part of Sunday school was when Mom played the guitar. Her voice was thick and husky, like her throat had been carved from a hollowed-out log.

Mom said Jesus didn't care that she didn't have a pretty voice, but he did prefer it when I sang along. Harmony came naturally to me and it made my mother proud when I harmonized. So every Sunday, with an audience of eight to fifteen little kids (depending on who showed up), Mom strapped on her guitar and we stood together at the front of the church basement classroom and belted out songs about Jesus. The kids were supposed to sing along, but only half of them did. Some just played with their shoes, or nudged and whispered to their friends, or lay on their backs and stared at the water-stained ceiling. When they really started to lose attention, we sang "Rise and Shine," because all kids love that song.

There was a thirty-minute break between Sunday school and church services. During that time, Mom went home to drop off her guitar and fetch Dad, while I ran off to practice with either the youth choir (during the school year) or the summer choir (during the summer). I preferred the summer choir, as it was made up mostly of adults and only a few teenagers—the majority of whom rarely showed up. I didn't feel self-conscious with the adults as I did the youth choir. Singing with my peers, I never let my voice go too loud, as I didn't want to be teased for my vibrato, or for slipping into a harmony when my ear told me that it would be right to do so.

We were always home before noon on Sunday. After lunch, Mom either did prep work for the meals she would serve during the week, or worked in the garden. Our lawn looked like a green shag rug. In front of the house were blooming azaleas, all trimmed to the exact same height and width. In the backyard were more blooming trees, and flower beds that curved around rocks and outlined the property like a plush purple-and-pink moat. Gardeners came once a week, but no one could keep it as neat as my mother. Weeds that dared to poke their pointy green heads out from the soil were immediately snatched from life by my mother's gloved hand.

Every spring, a team of men showed up to wash our house's white clapboard, repair the loose black shutters, and touch up the paint where necessary. It was only after this touch-up that my mother planted the window boxes that hung below each window on the front of the house. When I was around Izzy Cone's age, my mother hired an artist to paint a picture of our house. That painting now hung above the sofa in the living room. Sometimes when I helped pull weeds or water the flower boxes or plant new annuals in the beds, Mom would say, "We're obliged to live up to the painting, Mary Jane. We can't let that painting be fiction!"

The Cones seemed uninterested in how their house or yard looked. The only thing that appeared to concern them was turning the third floor into a guest suite, which they were discussing every time they passed me and Izzy—in the TV room, in the kitchen at lunch, and on the front porch, where Izzy and I played with her Erector Set.

At five, when it was time for me to go, Izzy and I wandered around the house, looking for her parents.

"Mom! Dad!" Izzy yelled.

I was growing accustomed to the yelling but couldn't bring myself to do it. I quietly sang out, "Mrs. Cone? Dr. Cone?"

On the second floor, the doors except for Izzy's were open.

"Why is your door the only one that's ever shut?" I asked her.

"To keep the witch out," Izzy said. "Mom! Dad!"

"What witch?"

"The one that haunts the house. If I shut my door, she doesn't go in when I'm not there." Izzy walked straight into her parents' bedroom. I stood in the hallway and waited.

Izzy came out a minute later. "They're not in there. I'm hungry."

We went downstairs, through the living and dining rooms, and back through the swinging door into the kitchen. In my own house, the kitchen belonged to my mother and it was up to her if it was "open" or "closed." Most days, it closed at two p.m., as she didn't want anyone to lose their appetite before supper. Though sometimes it closed right after lunch.

I wondered if Mrs. Cone planned to make dinner that night. There was nothing in the Cones' oven, nothing defrosting in the sink, nothing in a saucepan on the stove.

There was no indication that plans had been made to feed the family.

I had a feeling that Dr. and Mrs. Cone wouldn't be angry if I made dinner for Izzy. "Lemme call my house," I said. I looked around the kitchen for the phone. I'd seen one somewhere earlier but couldn't remember where. "Where's the phone?"

Izzy found the cable plugged into the wall below the counter and followed it with her hands as high as she could reach. "It's here somewhere!"

I pushed aside the bathrobe that was on the counter, and found the phone.

"Can I dial?" Izzy climbed up onto the orange wooden stool and balanced on her knees. She removed the handset from its cradle and rested it on the counter.

"Four." I watched as Izzy carefully examined the holes in the number dial, found the four, and inserted her chubby little finger. There was a line of black dirt under her nail and I made a note to myself that I'd give her a bath after dinner, if I ended up staying that long.

"Four!" Izzy rotated the dial until it hit the silver comma-looking thing, then released her finger as the dial clicked around back to the start. We went on like this for six numbers. On the seventh number, I glanced away and looked back, only to see Izzy had inserted her finger into the 9 instead of the 8. When the dial finished its slow *click-click-click*, I picked up the handset, placed it back in its spot to disconnect the call, then took it out again so we could start once more.

When we finally got the numbers dialed, I put the phone to my ear. Izzy leaned in and I tilted the receiver toward her.

"Dillard residence," my mother said.

"Hey, Mom, I need to stay and feed Izzy dinner."

"Oh?" Mom's voice screeched up.

"She needs to feed me dinner!" Izzy shouted. I stood up straight and pulled the handset from Izzy's ear.

"Is that Izzy?"

"Yes," I said. "She's a goofball."

"Sounds like it. Why do you need to feed her dinner? Where is her mother?"

I didn't want to admit that I couldn't find Dr. or Mrs. Cone. I turned away from Izzy so she wouldn't hear, and whispered, "Her father is stuck with a patient and her mother is sick in bed." It was, as far as I could remember, the first time I had lied to my mother.

"Oh," my mother said. "Oh no. Okay. Well, maybe I should come down there and help."

"No, it's okay," I whispered. "Everything Mrs. Cone was going to make is out on the counter. The oven's already turned on too. I just need to stick the casserole in the oven and then—"

"Cereal!" Izzy shouted. I turned and saw she had opened a cupboard and pulled out four different boxes of cereal.

"I'll call after dinner to let you know what time I'll be home," I said.

"You have Dr. Cone walk you or drive you if it's after dark," my mother said.

"Okay, Mom. Bye!" I hung up quickly before Izzy could shout again.

"I want cereal for dinner," Izzy said.

"Have you ever had cereal for dinner?" I asked cautiously. It seemed as unimaginable as using a banana for a telephone.

"Yes."

"Well . . . let's look in the fridge and see if there's something in there that might be a better dinner. Do you usually have a bath before dinner?"

"Nah, no bath." Izzy opened the avocado-green fridge before I could get to it. I edged her aside and peered in. The door shelves were crammed with mustards, oils, and grease-stained bottles of things I didn't recognize. In the body of the fridge, standing out from the crowd of scantily-contained unidentifiable blobs, were two pots covered in tinfoil, a carton of eggs, a hunk of unwrapped cheese balanced on a Chinese take-out carton, and an unbagged head of iceberg lettuce. Everything, even the lettuce, had an odd, oily sheen. A smell created a wall that kept me from getting too close. Maybe the cheese?

"Where's the milk?" I asked. Izzy shrugged.

Item by item, we unloaded the refrigerator, placing things in whatever space we could make on the orange linoleum counter. I finally found the milk in the back. When I pulled it out, the contents sloshed with an unusual weightiness.

Izzy stood on a stool and took down two bowls.

"Let me check the milk." I opened the triangular pour spout of the carton and then jerked my head back from the slap of stink that hit me. It smelled like an animal had died in there.

"Peeee-ewww!" Izzy screamed, still standing on the stool. I put the milk down on the counter and put my hands on Izzy's tiny legs, which were covered in a downy blond fuzz. The idea that she'd fall on my watch was more horrifying than the smell of the milk.

"Izzy?!" Dr. Cone shouted from the entrance hall. My stomach felt as if a string had pulled it shut like a drawstring bag. I lifted Izzy off the stool and placed her on the ground. I wondered if Dr. Cone would fire me for allowing her to climb up there.

"Here!" Izzy shouted.

Dr. Cone walked into the kitchen. "What are you two up to?"

"We were gonna make cereal for dinner," Izzy announced. "But the milk stinks."

"I think it soured." I pointed at the carton on the counter.

"Oh yeah, that one's from last month. I don't know why no one's thrown it out." Dr. Cone laughed and so did I. What would my mother think of milk that had grown chunky and putrid with age? It was unimaginable. Though, now that I was seeing it, it was very imaginable.

"What about we go to Little Tavern and get some burgers and fries?" Dr. Cone offered.

"Little Tavern!" Izzy shouted.

Dr. Cone moved things around the kitchen counter, looking for something. "Where's your mom?" He patted his pockets—front, back, front again—and then pulled out his keys and held them in the air for a moment as if he'd performed a magic trick.

"Don't know." Izzy shrugged.

"We haven't seen her," I said.

"Let's go!" Izzy marched—knees up, like she was in a band—out of the kitchen. Dr. Cone put his hand out for me to step ahead, and I did, following Izzy down the hall and out the front door to the wood-paneled station wagon waiting in front. Dr. Cone didn't lock the front door behind us. I wondered if Mrs. Cone was somewhere in the house. If she wasn't, wouldn't Dr. Cone have locked the door?

"How many burgers can your mom usually eat?" Dr. Cone asked as Izzy opened the door to the back seat.

"She's a veterinarian this week." Izzy climbed in and pulled the door shut.

"Is she? I thought she got over that *veterinarian* phase." Dr. Cone winked at me and stared up at the open window on the third floor. "BONNIE!" Dr. Cone cupped his hands around his mouth and shouted. I looked up and down the street to see if anyone was witnessing this. "BON-NIE!"

Mrs. Cone stuck her head out the window. Her hair was blown around her shiny face. "What?"

"Do you want something from Little Tavern?"

"WHAT?!"

"DO YOU WANT SOMETHING FROM LITTLE TAVERN?"

Mrs. Cone paused as if she really did want something. Then she shook her head. "I'M TRYING NOT TO EAT MEAT!"

"SHE'S A VETERINARIAN!" Izzy shouted from inside the car.

"FRIES?!"

Mrs. Cone nodded and gave a thumbs-up. Then she disappeared into the attic room.

"You'll eat Little Tavern, won't you?" Dr. Cone asked me.

"Yes." The truth was, I'd only been there once. My family didn't often eat in restaurants. We did eat out of the house once a week, but always at our country club. Sometimes, when we had visitors from out of town, we'd take them to a restaurant. But my parents would never eat at the Little Tavern, whose slogan was *Buy 'em by the bag!* The single occasion I'd been to the Little Tavern was the twins' birthday, when we went with their parents.

"Okay then, get in!" Dr. Cone nodded at the front seat of the car. The passenger side was covered with piles of paper and a brown file folder. I stacked them neatly and slid them down the bench seat toward Dr. Cone so I could sit.

Izzy immediately scooted up and leaned her head over the front seat. She talked the whole way to Little Tavern and I tried to listen, but my brain was stuck on question after question. Had Mrs. Cone been in the attic all day, and was she converting it into a guest room? Why hadn't she come downstairs to make dinner? How did the Cones eat dinner normally? Who went grocery shopping and why wasn't there fresh milk in the fridge? Did they not get their milk delivered like everyone else in the neighborhood? We got two cartons of whole milk every week. My mother said one was for baking and cooking and the other was for her and me. My father was never poured milk at dinner and instead had a glass of orange soda. I was allowed orange soda on weekends, and only at lunchtime. My mother said that sugary drinks were less harmful if they were consumed before the dinner hour. In the Cone house there wasn't even an option of soda. Just clotted milk.

We drove into Hampden, a little neighborhood of narrow row houses with marble stoops and dogs chained in front yards that were either dirt or cement. Dr. Cone parked the car at Little Tavern, and Izzy and I followed him in.

Dr. Cone ordered two bagfuls of burgers and four boxes of large fries. "What do you want to drink?" he asked Izzy.

"Orange soda," Izzy said.

"Mary Jane?" Dr. Cone asked.

"Orange soda," I repeated, and then I glanced behind me to see if my mother was somehow there.

Once we had the food, we returned to the station wagon. Izzy ran ahead of me and Dr. Cone. She opened the passenger-side door and climbed into the front seat.

"We'll eat in the car," Dr. Cone said. "It's more fun that way and we can all fit up front!" He placed the burger bags and his soda on the roof of the car, opened his door, and then pulled out all the papers and the folder and moved them to the back seat. Then he waved his arm at me to slide in.

We handed the bag of burgers back and forth. The burger was oily and salty, and sweet, too, from the ketchup. It was one of the best things I'd ever eaten.

"So, we've got some big stuff coming up. . . ." Dr. Cone chewed down his burger and swallowed. Izzy had emptied her orange soda and was sucking out the last bits with a bubbling sound.

"Do you want the rest of mine?" I asked, and she kissed me on the cheek and took it.

"One of my patients and his wife are going to move into the house this weekend." Dr. Cone unwrapped another burger and lopped off half in one bite.

I nodded. I wasn't sure why he was telling me this and if I was allowed to ask questions.

"Can I trust you, Mary Jane?" Dr. Cone asked.

I nodded again.

"Doctor-patient confidentiality is very serious in psychiatry. No one can know who I'm treating or why or even where."

"I understand." I was no longer hungry, but I was nervous, so I reached into the bag and removed another burger. If Dr. Cone was treating someone, didn't that mean *that someone* was crazy? So would a crazy man and his wife be in the house where I was working all summer? And did I have to turn my face away and not look at the crazy man to preserve doctor-patient confidentiality? The whole thing felt big and scary and as much as I enjoyed Izzy Cone, the barefoot and sideburn nature of Dr. and Mrs. Cone, and the cluttered kaleidoscope of the Cone home, I wondered if maybe this wasn't the job for me.

"So, this patient, well, he's an addict—even the press knows by now, which is why I'm telling you." Dr. Cone tossed the other half of his burger into his mouth and took a big swill of his orange soda. Izzy handed my orange soda back to me and I took a sip and then returned it to her. "And the wife needs lots of support too. You know, it's hard when your spouse, or anyone in your family, is addicted."

Why would the press know this man was an addict? Did the *Baltimore Sun* print lists of local addicts? I swallowed hard and said, "Will it be safe for me and Izzy to be in the house if an addict is there?"

Dr. Cone burst out laughing, releasing a small spray of food. "It's entirely safe! He's a smart, interesting, creative man. His wife is too. Neither of them would ever harm anyone. No one chooses to be an addict, and my job is to help out those who are unfortunate enough to be struck with it. I treat drug addicts, alcoholics, sex addicts . . . the whole shebang."

My face burned. I shoved two fries into my mouth. Izzy didn't seem to notice that Dr. Cone has used the word *sex*. With the word *addict*! I didn't even know you could be a sex addict. A slideshow started in my brain: images of people kissing, naked, pushing themselves against each other hour after hour. Would the sex addicts ever get hungry? Would they eat *while* doing sex things?

"In this situation," Dr. Cone continued, "it seemed better that the patient and his wife just move in and stay with us until everything's more under control. They live in New York City and he's been taking the train down for twice-weekly visits with me. He's actually detoxed now; we're just working on ways he can stay sober."

"Oh okay." I took the drink back from Izzy, swallowed another strawful, and then handed it to her again.

"The thing that's tricky here," Dr. Cone said, "is that they're both very, very famous."

"Movie stars?!" Izzy asked.

"Yes. The wife's a movie star. He's a rock star."

"A rock star!" Izzy shouted. "I want to be a rock star!" She held the drink in front of her face as if it were a microphone, and started singing a song I'd heard a couple of times but didn't really know. Izzy had it down word for word, so I assumed the Cones had the record.

"A movie star and a rock star from New York City are going to move into your house?" I asked, just to be sure I was understanding this correctly.

"Who who who who who who who?" Izzy asked. "Is it the Partridge Family?"

"You'll see when they get here." Dr. Cone reached out and mussed up Izzy's hair.

I had many more questions but didn't dare ask. What was the rock star addicted to? Would I ever see him or his movie star wife, or would they be in Dr. Cone's office all day? Were they bringing maids with them? Did they have a limousine and a driver?

If Izzy didn't know who they were, I doubted I would. I barely knew Little Tavern burgers! The records in my house were all cast albums from Broadway musicals or the Mormon Tabernacle Choir. Kids at school talked about bands and rock music, but the names of the singers and bands were as foreign to me as the neighborhoods and streets east, west, and south of where we lived. For all I knew, the rock star and the movie star, the drug addict and his wife, might be less recognizable to me than Dr. and Mrs. Cone.

All weekend long, I thought about the Cones and the addict rock star/movie star couple who would be moving in. On Saturday, I walked up to Eddie's market and flipped through *People* magazine to see if there was any mention of a rock star/movie star couple dealing with an addiction. I wondered if the addict would look like the addicts I'd seen downtown from the window of the car. Skinny people in dirty clothes, leaning against doorways. Or the man with only one limb who pushed himself around on a wide skateboard. I'd seen him many times. Once, I asked my father if we could roll down the window and give him money. Dad didn't answer, but my mother said, "We can't roll down the window here."

That Sunday night, my mother was serving ham, peas with bacon, coleslaw, succotash, and corn muffins and a trifle for dessert. I always stood by and helped while she made dinner. Step by step she'd narrate what she was doing so that I could do it myself when I grew up. If she handed me a knife, she showed me exactly where on it I should place my fingers. If she handed me a whisk and a bowl, she showed me the angle at which I should hold the bowl in the crook of my left arm, and the speed and force with which I should use the whisk with my right hand. But that night she let me prepare the trifle all by myself. Mostly.

When it was time to eat, after I'd set the table, my mother and I sat in our padded-seat chairs, waiting in silence for my father. He finally arrived, still wearing the tie he'd had on at church that morning. The Sunday paper was tucked under his arm.

Dad sat, placed the paper on the table, and put his hands together for prayer. Before he spoke, he dropped his forehead onto the pointed tip of his first fingers. "Thank you, Jesus, for this food on our table and for my wonderful wife and obedient child. God bless this family, God bless our relatives in Idaho, God bless President Ford and his family, and God bless the United States of America."

"And God bless that man with no legs and only one arm who hangs out near the expressway," I said.

My father opened one eye and looked at me. He shut the eye and added, "God bless all the poor souls of Baltimore."

"Amen," my mother and I said.

"Mary Jane," my mother said, forking ham onto my father's plate, "what country club do the Cones belong to?"

"Hmmm." I chugged from my cup of milk. "I don't know. They haven't gone to one since I've been babysitting."

"Certainly not Elkridge." My dad removed his tie, placed it on the table, and picked up the newspaper. My mother loaded succotash onto his plate.

"How do you know they don't belong to Elkridge?" I asked. That was our country club.

"It's spelled *C-O-N-E*," my mother said. "I looked it up in the Blue Book." The Blue Book was a small directory for our neighborhood and the two neighborhoods that abutted us on either side: Guilford and Homeland. You could look up people by address or by name. Children were called *Miss* if they were girls and *Master* if they were boys. The Blue Book also listed the occupation of every man, and any women who worked. Sometimes, when I was lying around the house doing nothing, I flipped through the Blue Book, read the names, the children's names, the father's job, and tried to imagine what these people looked like, what their house looked like, what food they'd have in their refrigerator.

"The Cones are Jews," my father said. "Probably changed the name from *Co-hen*." He turned the page and then folded the paper in half.

"Well, then not L'Hirondelle, either. What are the names of those two Jewish clubs?" My mother stared at my father. My father stared at the paper. She was holding a corn muffin aloft.

"Are you sure the Cones are Jewish?" I didn't know any Jewish people. Except now the Cones. And Jesus, who, if I were to believe everything I heard at church, knew me better than I knew him.

"Jim Tuttle told me they're Jews," Dad said without looking away from the paper.

"I should have known sooner. A doctor." My mother placed the muffin onto my father's plate and picked up the coleslaw.

"They haven't said anything Jewish," I said. Though I had no way of knowing what Jewishness might sound like. I knew there was a neighborhood in Baltimore where they all lived—Pikesville—but I'd never been there and

I'd never even met someone who'd been there. I'd just heard my parents and their friends mentioning the area in passing, as if they were talking about another country, a country far, far away, where they were unlikely to ever travel.

"I'm sure they're just being polite." My mother was onto the peas and bacon. "But being a doctor makes up for being a Jew."

"What do they have to make up for?" I asked.

My father put the paper down on the table. "It's just a different type of person, Mary Jane. Different physiognomy. Different rituals. Different holidays. Different schools and country clubs. Different way of speaking." He picked the paper back up.

"They look normal to me. And they sound the same to me." Well, there was the shouting. Did all Jews shout? And there were Mrs. Cone's breasts, which usually seemed on the verge of being exposed. Was that a Jewish thing? If so, it would be interesting, though maybe embarrassing, to travel to Pikesville.

"Look at their hair. It's often dark and frizzy." My mother served herself now. I would serve myself after she had fixed her plate. "And look at their long, bumpy noses."

"Mrs. Cone has red hair and a little button nose like Izzy," I said.

"Probably a nose job." My mother held the serving spoon over the coleslaw, stared at it, then dumped half back into the bowl.

My father put the paper down again. "It's another breed of human. It's like poodles and mutts. We're poodles. They're mutts."

"One breed doesn't shed," my mother said.

"So Jesus was a mutt?" I asked.

"Enough," my father said, and he snapped the paper in the air as he turned the page.

After dinner, I stood at my closet and looked for the best outfit to wear when I met the rock star and the movie star. Everything was so contained, tidy, new-looking. My mother even ironed my blue jeans.

I pulled out a pair of bell-bottoms. The hem was above my anklebone, what the kids at school would call *floods*. They had fit last time I'd worn them.

Mom and Dad were in the TV room watching the news. I quietly went down the hall into my mother's sewing room. On the wall was a rack with hooks on which hung various-size scissors. I took down the heaviest pair and then leaned over and cut up the seam of the jeans. When I got above my knee, I paused. I wanted to go shorter, but would I dare? No, I wouldn't. I stopped about four inches above my knee and then turned the scissors sideways and cut off the leg. When that leg was done, I did the other, then returned the scissors to their rightful spot.

Back in my bedroom, I stood in front of the door mirror and examined my work. The cut had left a toothed, uneven edge, and one leg was longer than the other. I rolled up the bottoms until they were even.

For my top, I picked out a red-and-white-striped tank top that covered my bra straps. I'd wear the rainbow flip-flops my mother had agreed to buy me after she'd seen the other girls at Elkridge pool wearing them. She didn't like me to be out of sync almost as much as she didn't like me to appear dirty or unladylike.

On Monday morning I put on the outfit, rolling up the

shorts as little as possible. When I came downstairs my mother looked me over. "Where did you get those shorts?"

"I made them from my bell-bottoms that were too short."

"You can't wear them to Elkridge."

"I know."

"What if the Cones want to take you to their Jewish country club?"

"I'll run home and change."

"And they would be okay with that? It's not very professional of you."

"I don't think they go to a country club, Mom. Izzy and I stayed home all last week. And when she wanted to swim, we walked to the Roland Park Pool."

"I see." My mother stared at the cutoffs as if she were looking at a bloody body.

"Please?" I asked.

"It's your choice. I'm simply trying to lead you down the correct path." My mother turned her head toward the brewing coffeepot as if she couldn't bear the sight of me dressed this way.

"I really don't think they'll mind if I wear cutoffs." There was no way I was going to tell her that Izzy spent half her day naked and that Mrs. Cone never wore a bra. And of course I'd never let on that the rock star and the movie star (the addict and his wife) were moving into the Cones' house. There was the issue of confidentiality; the promise I'd made to Dr. Cone. And the issue of my parents, who would never allow me to set foot into a home where an addict was staying.

"Hmm." My mother continued to stare at the coffeepot, and then she sighed and almost whispered, "Maybe it's a Jewish thing."

I slipped out of the house before she could say anything else. The pretty blond woman was gardening again; she waved as I passed, and I waved back.

I'd been instructed last week to just walk into the Cones' house without knocking. Still, I stood for a moment on the porch and smoothed my hair back. I looked down at my shorts and felt panicky about the length. Surely a movie star and a rock star would think they were too long. I rolled them up a few more times, until they were binding my thighs like rubber bands.

I put my hand on the doorknob and walked in. The house was silent. Things were slightly tidier than they had been last week. Nothing had been removed, but the stuff that was around had been amassed, stacked. So instead of scattered magazines, there was now a small tower of magazines sitting on the bottom step of the stairs. I headed straight toward the kitchen, which was where I usually found Izzy. When I got there, I almost screamed.

Sitting in the banquette, alone, was Sheba, the one-named movie star who'd once had a variety show, *Family First!*, on TV with her two singing brothers. I'd watched the show the very first night it aired and never missed an episode. Each week in the opening, Sheba and her two brothers sang three-part harmonies about love, rock and roll, and family. There were always great guest stars like Lee Majors or Farrah Fawcett Majors or Liberace or Yul Brynner. Sheba went through about eight costume changes each show—she played Indian maidens, mermaids, cheerleaders, and even an old lady in one recurring skit.

Family First! was canceled shortly after Sheba had a falling-out with her brothers. The twins and I had read about it in *People* magazine. Sheba said her brothers thought they were the boss and she was sick of it. It turned out no one wanted to watch the show without Sheba; only two episodes aired without her before *All Hat, No Cattle* replaced it in the time slot. And Sheba didn't need the show anyway—she was busy making movies with sexy costars or with horses, and on ranches in Africa. I'd only seen some of her movies, as my mother thought most of them were too racy.

On TV, Sheba had long black hair that hung like a curtain almost to her waist. Her eyes were giant circles with lashes that hit her eyebrows. And her smile flashed like a cube on a camera. As she sat in the Cones' banquette, I could see that Sheba's hair was just as long and beautiful. Her eyes were just as big. But her lashes were missing. She was wearing cutoff shorts and a tank top, no bra. Her feet were bare and tucked under her bottom. Her golden skin was as shiny and smooth as a piece of wet suede.

I couldn't speak.

Sheba glanced up and saw me. "You must be Mary Jane," she said. "Izzy's been talking about you."

I nodded.

"I like your cutoffs." She smiled and I felt my knees wobble.

"I made them last night. Maybe they're too long."

"Well, hell, we can fix that, can't we?" Sheba scooted out from the banquette and started rummaging around the counter. "How do they find anything in this house?"

"Izzy can usually find things. What are you looking for?"

"Scissors!"

I opened the drawer I'd sorted through one day last week when I had been looking for a vegetable peeler. Scissors had been there, nestled among bottles of nail polish, toenail clippers, a AAA map of Maryland, paper-wrapped (and ripped) chopsticks, sticky loose coins, Wrigley's gum, rubber bands, and other odds and ends. Magically, the scissors were still there. I pulled them out and handed them to Sheba.

"Go stand on the bench," Sheba said.

I went to the banquette and climbed up. My hands were shaking. I hoped my legs weren't shaking.

"Let's unroll them first." Sheba unrolled one leg of my shorts. Her hands felt cool and gentle. I unrolled the other.

She laughed. "Were you drunk?!"

"What?"

"When you cut these? Looks like you were drinking!"

"No. I don't drink."

"I'm teasing." Sheba winked at me, then inserted the scissors into the edge of one leg and started cutting upward. "Turn slowly."

I rotated and Sheba glided the scissors, cold against my skin, around my thighs until I was facing front again. The shorts leg was barely longer than my underpants. My mother would die.

"Good?"

I nodded. Sheba dug the scissors into the other leg. I turned slowly. When I came back around, the Cone family had entered the room with a man who looked familiar but whose name I didn't know. The addict, I presumed. He held a heavy hardcover book in one giant hand.

"We're fixing her shorts," Sheba said.

"Hurrah!" Mrs. Cone said, and she winked at me.

"Mary Jane!" Izzy shouted. "Sheba lives here now but we can't tell anyone!"

Everyone laughed, even the rock star whose identity was coming back to me. I remembered reading about

Sheba marrying him shortly after *Family First!* was canceled. Her brothers disapproved and her family disowned her. He was the lead singer of a band called Running Water. The cool girls at school loved Running Water, but I couldn't name a single song of theirs.

"I'm Jimmy," the rock star said, and he stuck out his hand. I put out mine, as I assumed he wanted to shake as Dr. Cone had done that first day. Instead Jimmy just held on. I paused, unsure as to why he was grasping my shaky hand, and then realized he was helping me down from the bench. I took a quick breath and stepped down, my eyes on the floor so no one could see my red face.

"I'm Mary Jane," I almost whispered. I glanced up and then away again. Jimmy didn't look like an addict. But he did look like a guy in a band. His dyed-white hair was spiked up all over his head. His shirt was open to his navel, revealing a flat surface of curly black hair with two nipples popping out like tiny pig snouts from a bramble. He wore a leather cord around his neck, three blue feathers hanging off it. He, too, was barefoot and wearing cutoff shorts.

"You know what we need," Sheba said. Everyone looked at her expectantly.

"Popsicles?" Izzy asked.

"Well, those, too. But look at us. We're a six-pack and only three of us have on cutoffs."

"We all need cutoffs!" Izzy shrieked, and ran out of the room. Normally, I would have followed her—being with Izzy was my job, after all. But I was disoriented by Sheba in the room and the fact that I was now wearing shorts so small, it felt like there was wind blowing on my bottom. I went silent and still, as if that might make me invisible, and listened to the grown-ups talking. They were smiley, energetic, and happy. No one seemed insane or addict-y.

Mrs. Cone went to the freezer, pushed stuff around, and pulled out a single half Popsicle. The white paper looked like it had been ripped open with teeth; the Popsicle itself had the white acne of frost over it. "Mary Jane," she said. "Maybe you and Izzy can walk up to Eddie's and get some Popsicles."

"Sure," I said. Izzy and I had walked up to Eddie's every afternoon last week except the first day, when we'd gone to the Little Tavern. It turned out that no one in the Cone family cooked. At the deli counter of Eddie's, Izzy and I had picked out dinner, to be served after I went home to have dinner with my parents. I picked out pasta salads, bean salads, roasted chicken and fried chicken, steamed corn and peas, and cheesy twice-baked potatoes. Also, because Izzy loved them, we always got bags of Utz barbeque potato chips. Dr. Cone had given me the number to their account, and told me I could get whatever snacks and foods I wanted too. So far, I had been too scared to use it for food for myself.

Izzy tumbled into the kitchen, holding a heap of jeans. "Cutoffs!" she shouted. "One for me, one for Mommy, one for Dad."

Sheba began singing a made-up song about cutoff jeans. *"Cut them off, little Izzy, cut them off. . . ."* She picked up Mrs. Cone's jeans and held them out to Mrs. Cone. Mrs. Cone slipped them on right there under her flimsy cotton dress. Sheba got on her knees and started cutting. She was still singing the "Cut Them Off" song.

Dr. Cone examined his own jeans. "This is my only pair."

"I'll buy you new ones," Jimmy said, and then he started singing the "Cut Them Off" song too.

Dr. Cone unbuttoned his chinos and I turned around

before he dropped his pants. No one else turned around, though, so I went to the refrigerator and said, "Does anyone want some milk?" No one responded, but I took out the milk anyway. Izzy and I had bought it last week. It was good. Smooth. No chunks.

By the time I turned around again, Dr. Cone was wearing his jeans, waiting beside Mrs. Cone, who had one leg cut off and one leg long.

"Me next!" Izzy stripped off her dress and underpants so she was completely naked. I put the milk back and went to her.

"You can wear your underpants." I picked them up from the kitchen floor and held them open while she stepped back in them. "I'll go get you a shirt."

I picked up Izzy's dress and rushed upstairs. Her door was shut, keeping the witch out. Last week I'd spent a little time each day putting things in order, and I was pleased to see that her room was still tidy and organized. All her shirts were in one drawer, folded and arranged by color. I was wearing a rainbow-striped tank, so I pulled out Izzy's rainbow-striped tank. It seemed like a fun idea to match.

When I returned to the kitchen, Sheba was cutting Izzy's jeans and Mrs. Cone had tied her dress around her waist like a shirt. "Do you want me to get you a shirt?" I asked.

"Maybe there's one in the laundry pile," Mrs. Cone said.

The laundry pile was on the couch in the TV room. Last Thursday, Izzy and I had watched *Match Game '75* while I folded and sorted everything. The piles of folded clothes remained where I had left them, lined up on the floor. But the couch now held a new pile of clean clothes.

I ignored the heap, went to what I'd folded, and pulled out Mrs. Cone's only clean shirt, a white tank top. I'd seen her in it before, and it was embarrassingly see-through. Would Mrs. Cone worry about her nipples showing with Sheba and Jimmy in the room? Maybe not, as Dr. Cone had just removed his pants in front of everyone. And no one even noticed when Izzy was completely naked. I liked the idea of all the girls being in tank tops, so I took a chance and hurried back with it.

I handed Mrs. Cone the tank. She took it and then lifted her dress straight off her head so she was completely nude on top. My breath left my lungs. I tried not to stare, but I didn't know how to stop. I quickly glanced around the kitchen. No one else was looking at Mrs. Cone. Not the rock star, who was monitering how Sheba cut the second leg of Izzy's pants. Not Sheba, who had her eyes focused on the scissors. Not Izzy, who was staring at me, grinning, as if getting her pants cut into shorts was the greatest fun a kid could have. And not Dr. Cone, who stood with his hands on his hips, waiting.

At Sheba's urging, Dr. Cone took a Polaroid picture of all of us in our cutoff shorts. How strange it was to see myself, Mary Jane Dillard, in a photo wearing shorts the size of underpants, standing with Sheba and her furry-chested rock star husband; Mrs. Cone, whose white circular breasts had recently been flashed at me; Dr. Cone, with his goaty sideburns; and sweet Izzy, who was pushed up against my torso like we were two Legos snapped together. I looked so happy. So in place. I looked like there was nowhere in the world I'd rather be. And, really, that was true just then. There was no place I'd rather be.

There was so much chatter and excitement around the new shorts that I'd forgotten that Jimmy was there for therapy. The moment ended when Dr. Cone gave Jimmy a little pat on the back and said, "Time for work, my friend."

"Let's go to Eddie's for Popsicles," I said to Izzy. I went to the drawer that had held the scissors and pulled out two rubber bands so I could put a couple of braids in Izzy's hair before we left.

"Maybe we have to put a wig and sunglasses on you and get you to Eddie's one day," Mrs. Cone said to Sheba. "The customer-to-employee ratio is one to one. It's a trip, man!"

"Are we south of the Mason–Dixon Line?" Sheba asked, and the two of them drifted out of the kitchen. I started braiding Izzy's hair as Dr. Cone and Jimmy made their way out the screen door to the backyard, a package of Oreos dangling from Dr. Cone's right hand. Before he crossed the lawn, Dr. Cone came back, opened the screen door, and said, "Mary Jane, will you get some sugary sweets at Eddie's too? And bring them and one box of Popsicles to my office?"

"How many Popsicle boxes should I get?" I fastened a rubber band over Izzy's braid.

"As many as you and Izzy can carry."

"I can carry a lot!" Izzy lifted her soft little arm and made an invisible muscle.

I wanted to ask Dr. Cone exactly what sugary sweets he wanted, but he turned and followed Jimmy across the weedy lawn to the garage-barn-office.

Izzy dropped to the floor and shoved her tiny fingers between her tinier toes. She picked out fuzzy black dirt while singing Sheba's cutoffs song. I had a feeling she hadn't been washed since I'd scrubbed her Thursday afternoon.

"Do you want to go swimming after we go to Eddie's

or do you want to take a bath?" I squatted beside her and braided the other half of her hair.

Izzy shrugged and kept picking.

"We can decide after we get Popsicles." I scooped up Izzy in my arms. She wrapped her legs around my waist and I hobbled out of the kitchen. In the entrance hall I found two flip-flops, each from a different pair. I searched around for the mate to either and then decided, what difference did it make?

I put Izzy down near the front door and placed the mismatched flip-flops in front of her feet. "Look, it's like two different Popsicles." I could hear Mrs. Cone and Sheba on the second floor and wondered what they were doing there. What would they do all day while Jimmy was being cured?

Normally, to get to Eddie's, Izzy and I would walk past my house. That day we had to take an alternate route lest we run into my mother, who would disapprove of my short-shorts.

"Let's go up Hawthorne," I suggested. Hawthorne was one street over and ran the same direction as our street, Woodlawn, meaning my mother rarely had any reason to drive on Hawthorne (though she always made it a point to do so on any holiday so she could see how people had decorated).

Izzy took my hand and skipped, while I took bigger steps to keep us side by side. We looked at the big clapboard and shingle houses, most with a front porch of some kind and painted shutters. The colors were all Colonial, dictated by the neighborhood association. The white houses had black shutters; the ocher-colored houses had burgundy shutters. The yellow houses had green shutters, and the green houses had black shutters. The blue houses had either darker blue shutters or black shutters.

Front doors were either black or red lacquer. And many of the porch ceilings were painted a sky blue.

Izzy spotted a plastic Barbie van on a front lawn and stopped to play with it. I figured if the owner had left it outside, she shouldn't mind if Izzy pushed it around a bit.

"Do you think Sheba and Jimmy own a van?" Izzy asked.

"Maybe," I said. "They might have lots of cars."

"I bet they own a limousine."

"We can ask them."

"We're not allowed to tell *anyone* they're here."

"I know."

"What's an addict?" Izzy scooted the van up the cobblestone walkway toward the steps of the wraparound porch.

"Mmmm, it's a person who does something that's not good for them, but they can't stop doing it."

"Like when I pick my nose?"

"No. Because you stop. You pick and then stop."

"But Mom keeps yelling at me, *STOP PICKING YOUR NOSE!*" We were back at the sidewalk now. Izzy placed the van on the grass and took my hand.

"But picking your nose isn't bad for you. Addicts use drugs or alcohol." I didn't mention sex, though the idea of a sex addict had poisoned my brain since Dr. Cone had mentioned it. The words *sex addict* came to me at the strangest times. I never said them, but they hovered behind my lips like a mouthful of spit that I wanted to hock out. Like when my mother asked me to iron the napkins, I wanted to shout, "Yes, *sex addict!*" And when Izzy and I went to the Roland Park Pool and the lifeguard had blown her whistle and told Izzy to walk, I wanted to say, "Don't worry, *sex addict,* I'll make sure she walks!" Maybe I was addicted to the words *sex addict.*

Izzy talked for the remainder of the walk. She named all her repetitive habits and activities so we could try to figure out if she was an addict. Right when we got to Eddie's, she asked, "What about closing my door because of the witch?"

An old man with dark brown skin that looked more cracked than wrinkled opened the door for us. He winked at me. I smiled and said thank you as we passed. That man had been working that door my whole life. He always said hello or smiled, though I was never sure if he recognized me.

"Do you believe in the witch?" I asked.

"What do you mean?"

"Maybe the witch is just in your imagination." I led us toward the freezer aisle.

"Nah. Mom and Dad never said it was imagination."

Why would a psychiatrist let his daughter think there was a witch in the house? I wondered. But I said: "Then closing the door is a good thing."

"Do you believe in the witch?"

"Uh, I don't think so. I've never seen a witch."

"Do you believe in God?"

"Yes, of course."

"Have you seen him?" Izzy smiled. I wondered if she'd heard this argument elsewhere and was repeating it. Or maybe she was just that smart.

"Okay, I'll believe in the witch. Let's get a cart so we don't have to carry the cold Popsicles in our arms." On the way back to the entrance, we passed a man in a green apron stocking a shelf. A celery-stalk-shaped woman stood talking to him. I thought of what Mrs. Cone said to Sheba about the employee-to-shopper ratio being one to one. "I have an idea for a game, Izzy. You count the people shopping and I'll count the people working."

The carts at Eddie's were smaller than the regular grocery store ones. Izzy climbed on the far end, clasped her tiny fingers through the metal-cage edge, and rode backward. This gave me a small, interior thrill, as it was something I'd always wanted to do. Cart-riding was forbidden by my mother, who thought it was the childhood equivalent of racing a motorcycle without a helmet.

"Okay." Izzy's head bobbed as she started counting. "Why?"

"So we can find the employee-to-shopper ratio."

"What's a ratio? I forgot my number."

"Let's start at the far aisle. We won't shop yet; we'll just walk and count, and then we'll go through the aisles all over again and shop."

"OKAY!" Izzy excitedly lifted a fist. "But what's a ratio?"

"It's one number compared to another. So the ratio of me to you is one to one. The ratio of you to your parents is one to two."

"Because I'm one girl and my parents are two girls. Or a girl and a boy."

"Yes, exactly. There are two of them and one of you. Two to one."

"The ratio of me to the witch is one to one."

"Yeah, but I'm on your side, so the ratio of me and you to the witch is two to one."

"We're a team."

"Yeah."

"The ratio of Sheba and Jimmy to me, you, my mom and my dad is two . . ."

"Two to four."

"I was gonna say that."

We'd reached the far right aisle. "Okay, let's start counting, and then we'll walk along the checkout area and you count people in line and I'll count checkers and baggers."

"Yes!" Izzy pumped a fist again and almost fell off the cart.

"Ready?" We were poised at the far end. "No talking until we're done with the count. And don't get distracted by food you see."

"Okay." Izzy nodded enthusiastically. She was taking this task very seriously. "Wait!"

"What?"

"Do you think any of these people are addicts?"

Only a day ago I would have said, *No way, not in Roland Park.* But now that I'd met Jimmy and he appeared to be so normal—well, rock star normal—it seemed like anyone could be an addict. I mean, the more the words *sex addict* popped into my head, the more convinced I was that I was a sex addict. One who hadn't yet kissed a boy.

"Maybe," I compromised.

"Maybe," Izzy repeated. She seemed unbothered by the possibility.

"Ready?"

"Ready."

I pushed the cart and we carefully started through the narrow aisles. When we turned down the canned goods aisle I sucked in a huge breath. My mother was standing in front of the stacked Campbell's soups, running her pink fingernail along the cans. Her blond hair was in a blue headband and she wore a knee-length blue dress with a white scalloped hem. I had a similar dress, which I often wore to church.

Izzy looked at me and I put my finger against my lips to make sure she didn't speak. Slowly, I backed out of the aisle, turned, and went to the next aisle.

"Mary Jane—"

I violently shook my head and put my fingers to my lips again.

Izzy half-whispered, "Mary Jane, what about the ratio?"

I pulled Izzy's head toward mine, put my mouth against her ear, and whispered, "We're hiding from someone in the next aisle."

"The witch?!" Izzy said loudly.

I wondered if anyone in the Cone house ever fully whispered. They yelled so much that it had started to feel like plain old talking to me. And when they talked, it felt *almost* like a whisper.

"Witches hate grocery stores." I turned the cart around so I was facing the checkout counters. I couldn't see each cashier, but would see if my mother went to the middle one.

And then my mother turned up on the far end of the aisle we were on.

I jerked the cart and dashed around to the canned soup aisle. What was my mother doing in the store *now*? She went shopping every Friday morning. Today was Monday! She'd already gone shopping for the week!

I considered pulling Izzy from the cart and running from the store. We could wait behind the newspaper boxes, spying to see when my mother walked out.

Then I remembered the gift corner. There wasn't much there: packaged candies, boxed chocolates, and some coffee mugs and aprons that had EDDIE'S printed on the front. The wheels of the cart wobbled and clacked as I almost sprinted toward the gifts and then came to a jerking stop.

"What are we doing?" Izzy whisper-shouted. "What about the ratio?!"

"Let's pretend we're chefs!" I pulled two aprons off the rack and put one on myself quickly. I put the top loop of the other apron over Izzy's head and then tied it around her waist. It was like a maxi dress on her. I was double knotting it behind her back when my mother strolled up.

"Mary Jane?" My mother's body was stiff, upright, an ironing board on end.

"Mom! This is Izzy."

"Hello, dear." My mother nodded down once at Izzy, who stared at her, openmouthed and bug-eyed, as if my mother were the witch. "Is it safe to ride on the cart like that?"

"What are you doing here?" I ignored my mother's question, and Izzy didn't answer either. She must have intuited that my mother's words were a statement of disapproval disguised as a question.

"Your father called from work and said his stomach was upset. I need to change the dinner menu tonight."

"Oh, poor Dad."

"Why are you in aprons?" Mom's head tocked to the side. I could almost hear her thoughts. She didn't like dilly-dallying and obviously didn't approve of what appeared to be dangerous game-playing in the grocery store.

Quickly, I blurted out, "Mrs. Cone asked me to buy some for them and I thought it would be fun to wear them while we shopped."

"Are you doing the grocery shopping for Mrs. Cone?" Now she actually showed her disapproval on her furrowed brow. To my mother, shopping for one's home was serious business.

"We need Popsicles," Izzy said. Her voice wasn't as jumpy and high as usual.

"I thought we'd start with the aprons, you know. To make the shopping more exciting."

"Hm." My mother nodded, examining me. "I suggest you don't wear them until you pay for them."

"But it's so much fun for Izzy." I held my mother's gaze and smiled.

"I'd think twice about that if I were you." Mom turned her head toward Izzy, balancing on the end of the cart. "And you need to be safe, too."

"Okay. Yeah, maybe we'll hang out here a few minutes, just for fun." I finally glanced at Izzy, who was now staring at me. She seemed confused but also appeared to know that she shouldn't say anything.

"See you tonight, dear." My mother turned abruptly and walked to the closest checkout counter. She didn't look back at us. I could feel my heart like a drum in my chest and knew it wouldn't stop until my mother was entirely out of the store.

"Your mom is scary," Izzy actually whispered.

"Really?" It never occured to me that she looked or seemed scary to anyone but me. Her voice was always in a steady, calm middle tone. She was tidy. Clean. Not many wrinkles. Her hair was blonder than mine. If she colored it, she didn't let me know.

"Does she spank you?"

"No, not often." She'd whacked me across the head many times. But she'd never pulled me over her knee. My father had never spanked me either, but he did have a big fist that balled up in silence when he was angry. Usually his anger was directed toward the newspaper, or the news. He disliked many politicians, and he particularly hated the heads of most foreign countries.

When my mother finally walked out of the store, my body relaxed, my blood felt like warm milk. I turned the cart and Izzy and I went down the nearest aisle.

"Uh-oh." Izzy looked up at me, her mouth held in an O

from the word *oh.* "I don't remember my number for the ratio."

"I do."

"You remember my number?"

"Yes. Well. No." It was one thing to lie to my mother; it was another to lie to Izzy. "We'll start from this end and we'll count all over again. Okay?"

"Okay."

I returned the aprons before we checked out. Izzy had counted fifty customers and I had counted twenty-six employees.

"So our ratio is twenty-six to fifty," I said.

"And the ratio of me and you to the witch is two to one."

"Yes. And the ratio of me and you to my mom is two to one."

"Because we're on the same team?"

"Yeah." I tugged one of Izzy's braids. "We're on the same team."

I held a brown paper bag in each arm and Izzy held one with two hands in front of her. Nothing was too heavy, but we had bought a lot: five boxes of Popsicles, six bags of M&M's, five boxes of Screaming Yellow Zonkers popcorn, five Chunky bars, five Baby Ruth bars, three rolls of candy buttons, six candy necklaces (one for each person in the household), and handfuls of Laffy Taffy and Bazooka bubble gum. I hoped that I had bought neither too much nor too little. Dr. Cone's instructions had been so vague that failure seemed highly likely. When my mother sent me to Eddie's to get something for her, the instructions were specific: *one shaker of Old Bay Seasoning in the small rectangular shaker, not in the larger cylinder; one white onion the size of your father's fist, no brown spots; and three carrots, each the length from your wrist bone to the tip of your middle finger.* All Dr. Cone had said was "some sugary sweets."

Once we had passed my cross street, we cut back over to Woodlawn. The blond woman was out gardening again. As we approached, she sat up on her knees, pushed her hair out of her face with the back of her gloved hand, and said hello.

"We got lots of sweets!" Izzy said, and we both paused.

I put down my bags and Izzy put down hers as well. The woman stood and walked to the edge of her lawn so she was standing right beside us.

"What did you get?" She peered at the bags.

Izzy pointed. "Popsicles and candy and popcorn and bubble gum and . . . what else?"

"Holy moly! Lucky you!" The woman smiled at Izzy. "Are you the summer nanny?" she asked me.

"Yes. For Dr. and Mrs. Cone."

"I'm Izzy." Izzy pulled out a box of Screaming Yellow Zonkers. "Can we have this?"

"Sure." I took the box from her and opened it, then handed it back.

Izzy stuck her little hand into the box and pulled out a fistful of shellacked popcorn with peanuts frozen in the gaps like insects in amber. "Want some?" she asked the woman.

"Sure." The woman removed her gloves and stuck her hand in the box. "What's your name?" she asked me.

"Mary Jane Dillard."

"Oh, you're Betsy and Gerald's daughter." She plucked a piece of popcorn from her palm and stuck it in her mouth. "I met your mom at the Elkridge Club. My husband and I are thinking of joining."

"Do you know my mom and dad?" Izzy asked.

"Mmm . . . what are your parents' names again? I'm new here, so I'm just getting to know people."

"Mommy and Daddy!" Bits of popcorn flew from Izzy's mouth as she spoke.

"Well, I'll have to walk over and introduce myself."

"Dr. and Mrs. Cone are very busy this summer," I said quickly.

"My dad is Richard." Izzy handed the box back to the woman, who took another handful and then passed the box to me. "And my mom is Bonnie."

"I'm Mrs. Jones. But there are three Mrs. Joneses in this neighborhood, so you can call me Beanie."

"Beanie?!" Izzy laughed.

"That's what my parents called me when I was little. I was so skinny, I looked like a string bean. And then it stuck and now everyone calls me Beanie."

"Does Mr. Beanie call you Beanie?" Izzy asked.

"Mr. Jones calls me Beanie. Yes."

"Do your kids call you Beanie?"

"Mr. Jones and I haven't been blessed with children yet." Beanie Jones smiled. When my mother's friend, Mrs. Funkhauser, talked about not having kids, she seemed sad, but this wasn't a sad smile. Beanie Jones turned her head toward the house and then I could hear it too: through the wide-open front door, the phone was ringing. "Oh, I have to get that! You girls have fun." She ran toward the phone.

"Should we leave her the rest of the box?" Izzy asked.

"Yeah." I folded down the wax paper and closed the box, then set it on the cobblestone walkway.

"What if a dog eats it first?"

"Run it up to the porch."

Izzy picked up the box, ran up to the wide blue-floored porch, and placed the box on a little glass table that stood between two cushioned wrought-iron chairs.

When Izzy and I walked in the house, the Cone phone was ringing. No one seemed to be answering, so I rushed into the kitchen, put the bags down on the table, and looked for the phone. I found it between a stack of phone books and a Hills Bros. Coffee can that held pencils, pens, and a dirty wooden ruler.

"Cone residence, this is Mary Jane."

"Mary Jane! You're back." It was Dr. Cone.

"Yeah, we got lots of sweets."

"Great. Can you bring some out to my office?"

"Okay. Popsicles and—"

"You pick an assortment. Just lots of sweets."

"Okay."

Dr. Cone hung up and I looked at the phone for a second before setting it in the cradle. My stomach churned. I was still worried about bringing the correct sweets to Dr. Cone and Jimmy.

"Can I have a Popsicle?" Izzy asked.

"Just a half. Don't want to spoil your dinner."

Izzy ripped open a Popsicle box and sat on the floor, removing Popsicles one by one. I could tell she was looking for the right color. The Popsicles had started to melt during our walk, so the colors were printing through the wrapper.

"Purple." Izzy handed me a purple Popsicle. I placed

the gully between the two sticks against the edge of the kitchen table and then slapped the top one with the heel of my palm. The Popsicle broke into two perfect halves. I ripped off the paper, gave one half to Izzy, and stuck the other in my mouth. I held it between my lips, melting, as I unloaded the sugary treats onto the kitchen table.

Next, I opened the freezer door and looked inside. A warty, hoary frost covered all the contents, like the Abominable Snowman had vomited in there. Few things could be identified past a shape: rectangle, edgy blob, carton. "How about we clean out the freezer today?"

"Okay!"

I took out a few boxes of unknowns and placed them on the dirty dishes in the sink to make room for the Popsicles. Then I shoved in all the boxes of Popsicles but one, which I placed in the bottom of an empty Eddie's bag. On top of the Popsicles I put two boxes of Zonkers, and then two of each of the other candies.

"I'll be right back." I headed out the screen door as Izzy flipped over to her stomach and continued sucking her Popsicle. I was nervous about getting the sweets order right. But, I realized, far less nervous than when I'd run into my mother at Eddie's.

I paused in the middle of the lawn, looked up toward the sun, and shut my eyes for just a few seconds. My heart wasn't even beating hard. In fact, I felt wonderful.

4

I learned two things that first week that Sheba and Jimmy stayed in the Cone house. The first was that addicts ate a lot of sugar to replace the drugs and alcohol they'd been taking. The second was that being married to an addict seemed harder than being an addict.

Most mornings I arrived to find Sheba and Izzy waiting for me in the kitchen. Sheba didn't like to cook and both she and Izzy thought I made the best breakfasts. I started making a daily trip to Eddie's with Izzy, where we'd stock up on ingredients for a good breakfast the next day: eggs, flour, sugar, baking soda, bacon, real maple syrup, butter, and loads of fresh fruit and berries. Also, I'd pick up more sugary treats, particularly Screaming Yellow Zonkers, which Jimmy had declared essential to his recovery.

Sheba talked a lot when there were adults in the room. She gossiped about other celebrities, and once complained at length about a particular director who wanted her to take off her top for a horseback riding scene in which "there was no logical reason this character would ride without a top on!" More frequently, she talked about how hard it had been living with Jimmy the past year. There was the Oscars party where he "nodded off" at the table and his head fell on his plate; the intimate dinner party at a famous producer's house where he disappeared into the bathroom for two hours and then stumbled out and fell asleep on the couch, his head falling into the lap of the sixteen-year-old daughter of the producer; and numerous flights on airplanes—private and public—where he vomited all over the bathroom, peed in his pants, and/or had to be carried off once they'd landed. I wondered how she had stayed with him through all that. And then my sex-addict brain wondered if it had to do with attraction and if she was a sex addict like me, and just couldn't pull herself away from his body. Jimmy was muscly and lean. And he had a smell to him that made me want to stick my face into his chest. It was almost an animal smell, but sweeter, softer.

Sometimes Sheba relayed stories of addicted Jimmy right in front of Jimmy. When that happened, Jimmy just shrugged, apologized, and more than once looked at Dr. Cone and said, "I need you, Doc."

When it was just me, Izzy, and Sheba, Sheba became quiet and curious and asked questions about us. It was like Izzy and I were foreigners from another country. Sheba had been a celebrity since she was five years old, so, really, we were foreign to her, people from the country of non-stars.

The Monday of Sheba and Jimmy's second week, Sheba sat with Izzy at the banquette, coloring. I was at the stove making "birds in a nest" as my mother had taught me.

Once I had flipped the pancakes, I would cut out a center hole (with a drinking glass, as the Cones didn't have the circular cookie cutter my mother and I used at home), into which I cracked open and fried an egg. The key to making it work was putting lots of butter in the pan and cooking at a super-high heat so that the egg would cook before the pancake burned. Also, I covered the bird in a nest with salt. When you added butter and syrup, it was the perfect salty-to-sweet ratio.

"Who colored this bloody penis?" Sheba asked.

My face burned. Izzy leaned over the coloring book, looked at the penis, and said, "Mary Jane."

"Do you hate penises?" Sheba asked me.

"Uh . . ." I felt breathless. "Well, no. I don't think so. I've never seen one."

"I've seen lots." Izzy focused on coloring the parrots from the nature coloring book.

"You have?" I slid the three birds in a nest onto three different plates. The syrup and butter were already on the table, as were three place settings and batik napkins I'd found when Izzy and I had cleaned out and organized the pantry.

"Yeah, I see my dad's penis ALL THE TIME!" Izzy kept coloring. I knew enough about the Cones now to know that Izzy likely saw Dr. Cone's penis as he walked out of the shower or downstairs to the laundry room to find clean clothes. No one in this house closed doors, except Izzy, who needed to keep the witch out of her bedroom. I had almost seen Dr. Cone's penis once as he walked past his open bedroom door toward his bathroom when I was in the hall. I turned my head quickly, but I could barely speak for the next half hour, as I was fairly certain Dr. Cone had seen me, and I worried he thought I had deliberately been looking toward their room because I was, maybe, a sex addict.

Sheba laughed. "I never saw my dad's penis, but I used to see my brothers' penises all the time. Boys are ridiculous. Every single one of them thinks that every person in the world wants to see his penis."

Of course I knew her brothers from their TV show. Sheba's brothers were wholesomely clean-looking with giant white teeth and hair that was so thick, you could lose a thimble in there. How odd to think of them with their penises out.

I carried the three plates, waitress style, to the banquette and slid in next to Izzy.

"Does Jimmy want every person in the world to see his penis?" Izzy asked. She leaned closer to the parrot picture. Her face was three inches from it as she pressed hard with a purple crayon.

"Jimmy doesn't even have time to think about that, because as soon as he walks into a room, women—" Sheba looked down at Izzy. She must have realized she was talking to a five-year-old kid, because she sat up straight and pulled her mouth tight.

I wondered what women did when Jimmy walked into a room. Did they *ask* to see his penis?

I stood and went to the fridge. Changing the placement of my body might change the subject. I opened the door and looked inside for inspiration. "Anyone want orange juice?" Izzy and I had been buying freshly squeezed juice at Eddie's. The charge of pulpy taste had shocked me when I'd first tried it, and now I couldn't imagine drinking anything else.

"Me." Sheba raised her hand.

"Me." Izzy raised her hand too. They both still stared at the coloring books.

"I guess since you don't have brothers," Sheba said as I handed her a glass of juice, "you never had to deal with boys the way I did."

"No." I scooted in next to Sheba on the banquette. "But I'd always thought it would be fun to have siblings." In my fantasy, my brothers and sisters and I would sing together, like Sheba had with her brothers on TV.

"Me and Mary Jane are snuglets," Izzy said.

"Singlets."

"That the word for it?" Sheba dug into the bird in a nest.

"Well, it's what the mother of my best friends, they're twins, calls me."

"Her best friends are at sleepaway camp." Izzy liked hearing about the Kellogg twins and what the three of us did when we hung out (they played piano, I sang; we had chess tournaments with the three of us and their mother; we walked around on stilts; we sewed halter tops, which my mother wouldn't allow me to wear; and we rode our bikes to the Roland Park library, or Eddie's, and mostly just looked at things).

"Do your parents dote on you?" Sheba asked. "Since you're the only one around."

"Hmm. No." Was what my mother did called doting? "My dad doesn't seem to notice me; he rarely talks to me. And my mother likes me to help her with things. You know, cooking and stuff." In my mind, my family was like all the other families in the neighborhood, except the Cones, of course.

"So your dad ignores you? That's awful! How could

anyone ignore you, Mary Jane? You have so much charm."
Sheba kept coloring, as if she hadn't said anything unusual. But everything she'd just said felt startling and
unusual. It had never occured to me that there was something awful about my father ignoring me. I'd thought that
was just how fathers were. And the idea that I had charm
was equally startling. Other than my teachers praising
my work, I'd received very few compliments in my life.

"Uh . . ." I couldn't find words to respond. Fireworks
were exploding in my brain.

"Do you like going to church?" Sheba asked, relieving
me from further thought on my possible charm and my
possibly awful father.

"I love church," I said. "I sing with my mom when she
teaches nursery school, and I sing in the choir."

"Oh, I'm going to come hear you sing," Sheba said. "I
love church singing. I used to sing in church."

"I know." One of the reasons I had been allowed to
watch Sheba's variety show was that she and her brothers
always closed with a church song. They told the audience
the song came from their hometown church in Oklahoma.
I always wondered when they were ever in Oklahoma. As
far as I knew, the family lived in Los Angeles.

"I could put on a wig," Sheba said. "I brought about
seven of them."

"I want to wear a wig and go to church," Izzy said.

The conversation stopped when Mrs. Cone came into
the kitchen wearing what looked like genie pants and a
red lace bra. "Mary Jane, do you know where my pink
blouse is?" she asked.

"Oh, Izzy and I ironed it." I scooted out from the banquette and went to the TV room, where I had left the
ironed clothes in two neat piles.

"We ironed everything!" Izzy shouted. Ironing had been one of our Friday activities. Izzy was as happy doing housework as anything else, so it seemed like I was taking care of two needs, or maybe three, at once: keeping Izzy occupied and stimulated, teaching Izzy how to take care of a home and family, and organizing the Cone household.

When I returned with the blouse, Sheba was talking to Mrs. Cone about a woman she called "that bitch."

". . . giving a known addict junk!" Sheba said.

"Terrible." Mrs. Cone was in my seat, eating the rest of my bird in a nest. Her eyes were fixed on Sheba.

"And he just can't say no. He pleases any woman in his sphere as if each one is his mother. Who he was absolutely never able to please."

"I can see that." Mrs. Cone finished my breakfast.

I handed her the blouse and then went to the stove and said, "Does anyone want another bird in a nest?"

"Oh, sweetheart, Mary Jane, I ate yours!" Mrs. Cone was so nice about it, I couldn't be mad. "Do you mind making more? Another for you and one for me."

"And me," Sheba said.

"I just want the nest." Izzy was frantically coloring a picture of sunflowers.

I was proud of my ability to cook for everyone. At home, I never prepared food unsupervised. I hadn't realized how much I could do on my own until I came here and did it. The past few days I'd been thinking that maybe I should cook dinner one night for the Cones so they wouldn't have to eat takeout or whatever I'd picked up for them at the deli counter at Eddie's. But I feared that the offer would be ridiculous: a fourteen-year-old girl preparing a family meal. Still, breakfast had seemed a success, so I took a chance and said, "Should I cook you dinner tonight so you don't have to eat already prepared food?"

"Oh, Mary Jane, I would love it if you made dinner," Sheba answered, as if the decision were all hers.

"That'd be fabulous!" Mrs. Cone slipped on the blouse and began buttoning it from the bottom up, the opposite of how my mother had taught me (*Start at the top to preserve your modesty and then work your way down*).

"And you'll stay and eat dinner with me, right, Mary Jane? 'Cause I miss you at dinner."

"Of course she'll eat with us." Mrs. Cone fastened the last button. "Do you mind preparing dinner?"

"No, I'd like it. I mean, I think Izzy and I need to clean out the refrigerator first, but if we do that, I'll know exactly what you have and then I can plan."

"Maybe you could cook all summer," Sheba said. "I really think Jimmy needs fresh vegetables, and a meat that hasn't been fried on a grill or in a wok."

"Are you still a vegetarian?" I asked Mrs. Cone. We'd added Slim Jims to our daily Eddie's run. Jimmy loved them and said he liked to alternate a sugary treat with a Slim Jim. Mrs. Cone, upon hearing that, had ripped open a Slim Jim and then a Chunky bar so she could alternate bites. I wasn't sure if a Slim Jim counted as meat or not. It didn't look like meat any more than Screaming Yellow Zonkers looked like corn.

"You're a vegetarian?" Sheba said. "No. Stop. Now is not the time to be a vegetarian."

"Okay! I'm easy!" Mrs. Cone laughed.

Jimmy walked in the room wearing only boxer shorts. "Hey." He ran his fingers through his shaggy hair. There was a tattoo of Woody Woodpecker on the inside of his thigh. I tried not to stare at it, as it was so close to his penis.

Sheba stood, went to him, and hugged and kissed him like he'd been gone a month. "Hey, baby, you good? Mary Jane can make you some eggs in a blanket—"

"Birds in a nest!" Izzy shouted.

"Yeah, yeah, sure," Jimmy said. "Are there any Zonkers left?"

I rushed to the pantry and got a new box of Screaming Yellow Zonkers. Jimmy sat where Sheba had been. I handed him the Zonkers. Sheba scooted in beside him, so Izzy scooted down too. I went back to the stove, flipped the pancakes, and cut out the center of three. Jimmy stared at me as I cracked eggs into the holes. I nervously smiled at him and tried not to look at the fuzz all over his chest or the tablecloth-patterned tattoo running down one arm.

"What about coffee?" Jimmy asked.

"Yep, right here." I'd found the coffee maker when Izzy and I cleaned out the pantry, and had been making a fresh pot every morning. The first day I did it, I didn't know if anyone drank coffee, but since the pot was mostly empty by noon, it seemed like a task worth doing. I poured a cup for Jimmy and brought it to the table.

"You are a living doll, you know that?" Jimmy stared at me so intensely that I couldn't speak for a second. It felt like his eyes shot out electricity.

"Mary Jane Doll." Izzy sighed, coloring away.

"Does anyone else want coffee?" I wrenched my eyes from Jimmy. Was I a sex addict? Is that why I kept looking at his nearly naked body?

Dr. Cone walked into the room. "Are you the one who's been making the coffee?"

"I stopped drinking coffee when I stopped eating meat," Mrs. Cone said.

"Enough." Sheba pointed at Mrs. Cone. "From now

on, you drink coffee and eat meat. Got it? No alcohol and drugs, but lots of coffee and meat."

"And sugar," Jimmy said.

"Okay!" Mrs. Cone laughed again. "I'll eat meat and drink coffee!"

"HURRAH!" Izzy lifted two crayons in the air.

After Dr. Cone and Jimmy had gone to the office and Mrs. Cone and Sheba went upstairs, Izzy and I started in on the refrigerator.

"I'll say *good* or *bad*," I said. "If it's bad, you put it in the Hefty bag. If it's good, stick it on the table."

We both looked over at the table. It was stacked high with coloring books, crayons, dishes, coffee cups. Izzy read my face and went to the table, where she started stacking coloring books. I followed.

"Fast motion!" I wanted this cleanup done quickly so I could get to the fridge, figure out what to make for dinner, and get to Eddie's and buy what was necessary.

Izzy laughed as she fast-motion shoved crayons into the box. I moved the dishes straight into the dishwasher, which I had emptied earlier in the morning. There were books on the table too: Freud's dream analysis and *The Diary of Anaïs Nin*—five editions, each with a different-colored cover. I stacked the books in my arms and took them into the living room, where the built-in bookshelves were full. I had been collecting books from all over the house and stacking them in front of the shelves the past few weeks, with the eventual plan for me and Izzy to organize and alphabetize them. I figured the alphabetizing would help Izzy be ready for kindergarten in the fall.

Once the table was clear, I returned to the fridge. Izzy stood by, holding a Hefty bag open with two hands.

The first thing I pulled out was a foil-wrapped, thick, semi-gelatinous brown blob. "Bad." I dropped it in the bag.

Izzy looked in the bag. "Bad."

Next I pulled out a saucer that had a shimmery slab of what might have originally been a meat but was now covered with a mossy green fuzz. "Bad."

"Bad," Izzy repeated.

I jumped to the vegetable bin, as it was a smaller space and would sooner give me a sense of accomplishment. There were several loose onions, half the skin gone, with divots of black and crumbs and dirt embedded in the exposed flesh.

"Bad. Bad. Bad. Bad. Bad."

"Badbadbadbadbad," Izzy said.

With my thumb and forefinger I removed three different bags of half-deteriorated mushy lettuce. "Bad. Bad. Bad."

"Baaaaad," Izzy brayed.

The oranges were as soft as Silly Putty. The apples had wrinkled skin. And there was a bagged, flowering, multidimensional green entity that could not be identified.

When nothing remained in the bin, I returned to the shelves. I pulled out an oily glass jar that appeared to have detached gray toes floating in murky brownish water.

"What is that?" Izzy asked.

"If we don't know what it is, it's bad." I handed the jar to Izzy so she could examine it further.

"It looks like thumbs."

"Ah! I thought it looked like big toes. But I think you're right."

"Do you think the witch put the thumbs here?"

"No."

"I think the witch put it here." Izzy placed the jar in the bag.

"Bad." An opened chocolate bar that was chalky white.

"Bad." A brick of cheddar cheese that was green except for the corner farthest from the gaping-open clear wrap.

"Bad." Carrots (they should have been in the vegetable bin) that were as loose and droopy as overcooked spaghetti noodles.

"Good." I held up a jar of Grey Poupon and handed it to Izzy.

"HURRAH!" Izzy put down the Hefty bag and ran the mustard to the table.

"Bad." Empty orange juice carton.

"Bad." Unopened Knudsen yogurt that had expired three months ago.

"Bad." A half-eaten taco half wrapped in tinfoil, with white cauliflower-looking mold erupting in spots.

"Good." I held up a jar of maraschino cherries.

"What is it?"

"Maraschino cherries. They're really sweet."

"Can I taste one?"

"Yes." I opened the jar and pulled one out. "You know, maybe the witch put the cherries in the fridge. Maybe she's a good witch."

"Are there good witches?"

"Yes." I placed the cherry in Izzy's open mouth. She chewed thoughtfully.

"I like the cherry."

"It's definitely a good witch food. Good witches eat lots of maraschino cherries."

"How do you know?"

"I read about it in a book."

"Can I have one more?"

"Last one." I dropped another cherry in her mouth and then stuck the jar on the table.

Back at the fridge, I pulled out three deli containers of wet mush in colors varying in shade from green to brown. The Eddie's price stickers on top were smeared out by oil and time. "Bad, bad, bad."

Izzy opened one container and sniffed. She jerked her head back and then sniffed again.

"Close that," I said. "The stink is filling the kitchen." It was the smell of fishy garbage in summer, magnified.

Izzy sniffed once more, her eyes crinkled up as if in pain. "Mary Jane! It's so bad, I CAN'T STOP!"

I understood the urge. The twins and I often dared each other to smell their mother's limburger cheese, which was usually stocked in their fridge. Still, I took the container from Izzy, snapped the lid shut, and dropped the container in the Hefty bag.

It wasn't long before the Hefty bag was nearly full and the refrigerator was nearly empty.

I had bought cleaning supplies and gloves earlier in the week. My mother wore gloves to protect her manicure. I didn't have a manicure, and neither did Izzy, but it seemed like fun to wear gloves anyway. We scrubbed the cleared shelves and drawer until the inside of the refrigerator looked almost brand-new. And then we stood back, the door open, and stared in admiration.

Mrs. Cone and Sheba walked into the kitchen. Sheba was wearing a short blond wig and giant sunglasses. Her body looked both slim and curvy in a tight floral jumpsuit. I'd never seen anyone dressed like that in Baltimore. If she was trying to go out unnoticed, she was failing.

"I don't think I've ever seen the refrigerator look like this." Mrs. Cone stood at the door, smiling. She was wearing the pink blouse and genie pants, and had tied a pink floral scarf around her head so she looked sort of like a dancer.

"You both look so pretty."

"Ah, thanks." Mrs. Cone leaned in and kissed the top of my head. No one had ever kissed me like that. Not my mom and not my dad. Sometimes I'd get a little pat on the back, or a squeeze from my mom that might resemble a hug. But a kiss on the head was totally new to me. What were you supposed to do when someone kissed you like that? Just stand there? Say thank you? I blushed, then grabbed Izzy and pulled her in close to me because my hands suddenly needed something to do.

"We're going to lunch," Sheba said. "You think anyone will recognize me?"

"I don't think anyone would ever in a million years expect that you'd be in Baltimore, so they probably won't recognize you. But I bet they'll stare at you, just, 'cause . . ." I was too embarrassed to go on.

"We're going to make dinner!" Izzy said.

"I know." Mrs. Cone leaned over Izzy and kissed her head three times, before turning up Izzy's face and kissing her fat cheeks.

Just as all this kissing was taking place, Dr. Cone rushed into the kitchen, his hair a scrambled mess on his head. He left the door open and I watched out the window as Jimmy ambled across the lawn, eating from a box of Screaming Yellow Zonkers.

"The Apollo-Soyuz docking is on TV now!" Dr. Cone went into the family room as Jimmy entered the kitchen.

"We gotta see this, man." Jimmy talked with his mouth

full of Zonkers. "Russia and the US coming together in space. It's fucking historical shit." Jimmy walked into the TV room and Sheba, Mrs. Cone, and Izzy followed. I paused at the threshold of the kitchen, looking into the family room.

"What is fuckinghistoricalshit?" Izzy climbed onto her dad's lap. None of the adults seemed to notice that Izzy had just used a swear word.

Dr. Cone clicked the thick brick-size remote control and turned up the volume. Mrs. Cone dropped onto the couch next to Dr. Cone. Jimmy sat on the other side of Dr. Cone, their shoulders touching. Sheba tucked herself down at Jimmy's feet and wrapped her arms around his calves. They looked like a litter of pups.

"Mary Jane!" Jimmy called. "Get your butt in here. This is his-to-ry!"

"Here. Mary Jane." Sheba patted the shag rug beside herself. I walked in and sat down, my back perilously close to Dr. Cone's calves. Izzy climbed off her father's lap and nestled into mine; her weight pushed my back against Dr. Cone's legs. I looked up and saw that Mrs. Cone had tucked herself under her husband's arm. Sheba put her hand on my knee, and at that moment every single body in the room connected into a single fleshy, leggy, arm-entwined unit. We stared silently at the TV as an American astronaut leaned out of his spaceship and shook the hand of a Russian astronaut who was leaning out of his.

"I still don't understand what is going on," Izzy said. "Are they on the moon?"

"No, they're just connecting," Sheba said. "The space-ships connected and now the people are connecting."

"Like us," I whispered in Izzy's ear, and she nodded and pushed herself deeper into my lap.

No one stayed to listen to the newscasters discuss the moment. Dr. Cone and Jimmy returned to the barn-garage-office; Sheba and Mrs. Cone left to have lunch downtown. Izzy and I returned to the kitchen, where I picked up the phone and called my mother. She answered on the first ring. I knew she was in the kitchen doing prep work for supper before she left for the club.

"Mom, I need to stay at the Cones' for dinner tonight."

"But I'm making meatloaf with pan-fried potatoes."

"They want me to cook. Mrs. Cone can't—"

"She can't make dinner?"

"No, not for the rest of the summer. They asked me to make dinner."

There was silence for a moment. I wasn't sure if my mother was doubting my lie, or if she regretted that I wouldn't be home to help her prepare the meatloaf and fried potatoes. Or maybe she'd miss my company at the dinner table. After all, my father rarely spoke.

Finally my mother said, "Can you do that? Can you make dinner on your own?"

"I think I can, Mom."

"Why can't Mrs. Cone cook?"

"An illness," I said. "I'm not sure what." My second lie to my mother.

"Oh." My mother gasped. "I hope it's not cancer. Maybe this is why they hired you in the first place."

"Yeah. Maybe." I had never lied to my parents until I'd started working at the Cones'. And though I felt bad that I was transforming into someone different, a girl who would hide things from her parents, the payoff seemed worth it. I'd get to eat dinner every night with Sheba and Jimmy. And Izzy! How could I *not* lie?

"I'll come down there and help you."

"No, Mom. They're not letting anyone in the house."

"Oh. Oh no. Okay. Now, you call me if you need help. What does she want you to prepare tonight?"

"She didn't say. She just said meat and a vegetable."

"Oh, Mary Jane. She must be very ill."

"How about I just make what you're making?" I suggested quickly, to distract her.

It worked. "Meatloaf, pan-fried potatoes, and iceberg wedges with tomato slices and ranch dressing."

"Okay. And dessert?"

"Orange sherbet. Just one scoop with three Nilla Wafers, each broken in half, and then stuck in the center like a blooming flower."

"I can do that."

"Remember to sauté the meatloaf filling before you mix it into the hamburger and bread crumbs. That way it's more savory."

"Onion and . . ." I tried to remember exactly what we added to the hamburger for meatloaf.

"Onion, diced celery, garlic powder, salt, and pepper."

"Okay, I can do that."

"And fry the potatoes in Crisco, not butter. They're better in Crisco."

Izzy loved helping with dinner preparation. She sat on the kitchen stool and stirred the meatloaf filling in the frying pan. She whisked the buttermilk ranch dressing and arranged the cut tomatoes over the iceberg wedges. She salted the potato wedges as we fried them in Crisco. And she assembled the Nilla Wafer flowers in the sherbet bowls, which we made ahead of time and then kept in the newly roomy freezer.

While the meatloaf was cooking, we went to prepare the dining room. The table was so heaped with things, there was no visible surface. "Let's do this methodically," I said.

"What does that mean?" Izzy put a hand on each hip, just like me.

"Let's be organized in how we put away all this stuff."

"Should we do 'bad/good' again?"

"Yes, that's a great idea. Get a trash bag."

Izzy disappeared into the kitchen. I was starting to understand that one of the values of having a kid around was that they could always do things like run off and fetch a trash bag. I did things like that for my mother and now Izzy was doing them for me.

Izzy returned with a trash bag and two pairs of gloves.

"I don't think we need the gloves."

"Maybe we do?" She put on a pair. They were floppy at the ends, the fingers drooped like melted candlesticks.

"When I hand you books, put them in stacks in front of the bookshelves in the living room. Any dishes or kitchen things go to the kitchen counter."

"And trash goes here." Izzy shook the garbage bag.

"Yes. But you can't hold on to the bag. You have to be willing to run stuff around the house. Clothes can go on the steps to take upstairs later. Shoes, too. Okay?"

"Okay." Izzy looked at me with an intense little stare. Like she was going to be graded on this task.

I circled the table and gathered books, which I handed off to Izzy in stacks of three or four. Each time she returned from dropping them off, I gave her another pile. When the books were gone, we started in on the trash: empty take-out containers, receipts from the grocery store, candy wrappers, old newspapers, two empty pizza boxes, and lots of junk mail. I found the matching flip-flop to one of the two that had been in the entrance hall, and also Izzy's orange bathing suit she had been wanting the week before when we went to the pool one afternoon.

Finally all that was left on the table was an unplugged record player, a dozen records, and a large collection of Izzy's arts and crafts projects. I picked up the records and shuffled through them. Three of them were Running Water records, all of which had a picture of the entire band, Jimmy always in the middle. On one cover, his shirt was open to the top button of his pants. On the other cover, he wasn't wearing a shirt at all and it looked like he wasn't wearing pants, either, though the photo ended before you could really know. He stared the viewer in the eye, the way he had stared at me this morning during breakfast. Like he was daring you to look away. Like he was asking a question with his eyes. Like you should know what the question was and be able to answer it with your own eyes. But I didn't know how to answer any questions with my eyes. I didn't even know people could stare like that. Until I met Jimmy.

"Should we play a record while we finish cleaning?" I asked.

"Yes." Izzy put her fist below her chin as if it were a microphone and began singing a song that was vaguely familiar. Maybe I'd heard it on the radio at the twins' house?

"You pick." I held up the Running Water records. Izzy pointed to the one with naked Jimmy.

"While I'm setting this up, you pick up all your art projects and divide them into two piles, one pile we can keep in the TV room and one pile can go in storage in the basement." I wouldn't dare suggest that some of Izzy's art

projects be thrown away, but that was what I was thinking. It seemed like one or two samples from each category
would be fine. Did we really need five ceramic pinch pots,
each one looking like the crumpled glazed shell of a spiny
tide pool animal?

Izzy climbed onto a ladder-backed dining room chair
and reached around for her paintings, drawings, tinfoil
and macaroni art, and the pinch pots. I put the record
player on the floor and went into the TV room, where I
had seen two unplugged speakers, each the size of a cash
register. I brought the speakers into the dining room and
plugged them into both the wall and the record player.
Between the speakers, I stacked the records, like books
between bookends. I had seen other records around the
house. Maybe tomorrow Izzy and I would do a scavenger
hunt for the house's record collection.

I threaded the record hole onto the silver prong, lowered it, and turned the knob to 33⅓. I lifted the needle
and blew on it only because I'd seen someone do that
once in a movie and then I set the needle down on the
outer edge of the record. The music startled me when it
started—I hadn't realized the volume was so high. I didn't
turn it down, but instead backed away from it and took
Izzy's hand as if to steady myself. After the twangy guitar sounds, the song erupted with Jimmy first shouting
and then singing in a voice that reminded me of walnuts
mixed in maple syrup: both crunchy and sweet. Izzy sang
along. She knew all the words.

Jimmy grumbled out, *"Thundering shudders from my
head to my—oooh baby, yeah—to my head. . . ."*

I loved the thumping of the music, like a heartbeat
on the surface of my skin. And I loved that raspy-sugar
sound of Jimmy's voice. It was like the way he spoke but

more forceful, more alert, like he had woken up from a death nightmare and just realized he was actually alive.

I figured out the melodies pretty quickly, and started humming harmony to every song. I nudged Izzy and we continued singing as we appraised and then put away her art. Next we sorted through the remaining things: Sears and JCPenney catalogs, Chinese food take-out menus, instructions to assemble a shoe shelf I'd never seen, and costume jewelry that I assumed belonged to Mrs. Cone.

Once the table was completely bare, Izzy and I stood facing the turntable as Izzy belted out the last song on the A side of the album. She sang directly into her fisted gloved hand, her tiny hips jerking around. I moved my body a little, following the music, pretending I was someone who danced.

When the song ended, I lifted the needle, flipped the record, and started the B side. The first song was slow and quiet. Izzy wasn't singing along. "Izzy, below the sink in the kitchen is lemon Pledge. Bring me that with those dusting rags we made."

"Lemonplige?"

"Lemon Pledge. It's a yellow spray can. I bought it at Eddie's last week, remember?"

"Yes. You said we were going to clean wood."

"Exactly. But first we had to find the wood to clean it. And look." I stood and pointed to the dusty and dull wooden table. It was big enough to seat ten or twelve.

"Got it." Izzy ran out of the room and returned seconds later with the Pledge and a stack of cleaning rags I had made from an old ripped Brooks Brothers shirt Dr. Cone had thrown in the trash.

"You're going to love this." I handed Izzy one of the rags. "I spray, and then you rub the rag in circles on the spot where I've sprayed. The table will shine and it will smell so good, you'll want to lick it."

"Can I?"

"What?"

"Lick it. Can I lick the table after I wipe it?"

"No. It's probably poisonous."

Izzy's eyes popped wide. "Do you think the witch wants to poison us?"

"No. I bought the Pledge, not the witch. And I think the witch is good. She put the cherries in the fridge."

"Yeah. Maybe." Izzy squinted, then started growl-yelling the chorus of the slow song.

I waited for the chorus to end and then sprayed. Izzy climbed onto a chair, leaned over the table, and wiped. I sprayed a new spot. Izzy lifted her knee high, as if she were crossing a stream rock to rock, and stepped onto the next chair. She wiped. I sprayed; she moved down to another chair and wiped again. In this way, we circled the table, with Izzy singing and me humming the whole way. We were just at the end of the table, or at the beginning—we were where we'd begun—when Jimmy and Dr. Cone walked in.

My hands started shaking. I worried that Jimmy would be angry that we were listening to his record. But he just smiled, and then he took a step toward me, took the Pledge from my grip, placed it on the table, and started dancing with me while singing along with his own record. Izzy clapped and screamed and jumped into her dad's arms. He, too, sang, Izzy hanging on his chest as they danced. Jimmy held my hands and pulled me toward him, and then away, and then around. At the last line, Jimmy dipped me down and hovered over me. I'd taken lots of ballet and could easily arch so I was like a lowercase letter *h* one foot on the ground, the other kicked in the air. I could smell the sugary treats and coffee on Jimmy's breath. I could smell his skin, both sweet and musky, like something warm, maybe melted candle wax with wet autumn leaves. I had a strange urge to bite into him. The words *sex addict sex addict sex addict* swirled like an eddy of letters in my brain.

When that song ended, a faster song came on. Dr. Cone, Jimmy, and Izzy started fast dancing as if it were no big deal. I stood, leaning forward as if I were about to take a step but couldn't. I'd never danced to rock and roll before. I watched the others, my mouth open with a half-nervous, half-happy grin. Dr. Cone bounced up and down, his head hanging like a bird with a broken neck, like when the *Peanuts* characters danced. Izzy flung her arms around and jumped as if she were trying to fly. Jimmy swayed his hips a little, forward and back, as if he were dancing inside a phone booth. He never used both the top and bottom halves of his body at the same time. Each movement was isolated, on beat, with the flow of the music. Izzy grabbed my hands and pulled me into the circle of the three of them.

"MARY JANE, YOU HAVE TO DANCE WITH ME!" She shook my arms until I moved on the other side of them. I glanced over at Jimmy and tried to mirror him. He looked straight at me and nodded. When he moved more broadly, I moved more broadly. Izzy still had one of my hands and was as wild at the end of my arm as a scarf blowing off a neck. I followed the pace of Jimmy's steps and shoulder shakes. I sensed he was directing me with his eyes.

The longer I danced, the more I got used to Jimmy eye-directing me, the less I thought about dancing. And the less I thought about dancing, the more I danced. Eventually it felt *right*. Like it was something I already knew how to do that was coming back to me.

We kept on dancing as the next song came on. Izzy screamed at the opening chords and then started singing along, louder than the record. Jimmy laughed and then he sang too. Dr. Cone sang during the chorus. I figured out the words pretty quickly and desperately wanted to sing at the chorus too, but I was afraid to sing aloud with a famous professional singer—the person on the record, no less!—within hearing distance. At the final chorus, Izzy put her face real close to mine and was hollering along with the record. Right then, before I lost my courage, I started singing the harmony. Quietly at first, but then I went a little louder, because I knew I had it right. When the chorus picked up, I went louder still, almost as loud as Izzy and Jimmy. Finally I stopped dancing so I could really sing. I shut my eyes, let the words fly, and I heard my voice vibrating along with Jimmy's like intertwined electrical currents that were creating a stream of sparks.

The song ended and Dr. Cone and Izzy clapped. Jimmy nodded, smiling. He clapped his hands three times slowly and then said, "Well, fuck me, Mary Jane, you got some pipes on you!"

The *fuck me* part of that sentence caught in my brain like a piece of cotton in a briar patch. I finally said, "I sing at church," but I don't think anyone heard, as the next song was playing and Sheba and Mrs. Cone were dancing into the dining room. Sheba was blasting her voice so beautifully that I felt goose bumps from the roots of my hair all the way to my toes. Her voice was pure and solid, and sounded like an instrument I'd never heard played before.

Jimmy snaked his arms around and danced over to Sheba. She did a circle in the streamers of his arms and then they went hip to hip. Sheba jumped into harmony while Jimmy stayed on melody. Izzy was still outsinging everyone volume-wise, and Mrs. Cone was singing along too. Everyone danced together in a big bouncy circle, smiling, moving, swaying, singing, smiling, laughing, singing, dancing. . . . As the song got faster, Sheba started spinning in circles. Izzy threw her arms out to the sides and spun too. Sheba unfastened her wig and threw it up in the air. Dr. Cone caught the wig and placed it on Izzy's head. Izzy climbed onto a chair, and then onto our freshly polished table. She stood on that table in her dirty bare feet, wearing Sheba's wig, and she hollered out the song like she was onstage in front of a stadium. Everyone laughed and danced and kept singing, and no one—no one!—told her to get her dirty feet off the table.

In the background, I heard a faint beeping. I ignored it. I couldn't stop dancing, couldn't stop singing. Though I tried not to stare, I couldn't pull my eyes away from Sheba and Jimmy. How could anyone look away from them? How could anyone shut their ears off to them? How could anyone not stare at these shimmering, gyrating people who created a power of sound that ran through my body and filled me up so I was laden with it? Sated with it. Happy.

When the song ended, I could hear the beeping more clearly. It was the kitchen timer. The meatloaf was ready.

5

I'd never heard so much conversation at a dinner table. Mrs. Cone told everyone about her first kiss, and then Sheba told everyone about every boy she'd dated up to Jimmy. Jimmy told a story about a rock star friend (Dr. and Mrs. Cone knew who he was, but I only barely recognized his name) who'd joined him on his last tour. The rock star cried and played sad songs on his guitar every single night because he was heartbroken over a woman Jimmy and Sheba swore was a real live midget who was mean as anything. Izzy was very interested in this story and had lots of questions about midgets, the first one being if a midget could drive a bus. Then Sheba, right there on the spot, made up a song about midgets that was so good and catchy, everyone sang the chorus the second time she hit it. The opening line was *Midgets, they're just like us, / they drive in their cars and they can sure drive a bus.* . . . I was a little worried that people were being mean about midgets, but the song made it seem like the grown-ups, or Sheba, really, wanted Izzy to know that the only difference between most people and midgets was their height. When we were done singing, Dr. Cone explained to Izzy that just because that particular midget was mean, it didn't mean all midgets were mean. She was an aberration (and then Dr. Cone had to explain the meaning of *aberration*). Every now and then Sheba—who was sitting beside me—reached out her hand and squeezed my shoulder or arm, as if to make sure I knew I was included.

When it was time for dessert, Izzy and I put all the sherbet bowls on a blackened cookie sheet as a tray (I had tried but failed to unblacken it). I carried the cookie sheet and circled the table as Izzy pulled off a bowl and placed one in front of each person, saying *Madame* or *Monsieur* as she did so. I had taught her how to say this when we were getting the dessert out of the freezer. She only had to repeat it three times before she had it memorized.

Over dessert, the conversation shifted to Jimmy's treatment, with Sheba recapping what he'd gone through and what the future might bring. Izzy was deep into her sherbet and no longer paying attention. I was rapt, as I'd never heard anyone discuss a private issue so openly.

"Richard," Sheba said, "I just think if he's going to eat *so much* sugar, which can't be good for him, he should be allowed a little Mary Jane as well."

My back stiffened. My heart pounded and I felt burning in my cheeks. I looked from Jimmy to Sheba to Jimmy again. What did she mean?

Jimmy glanced over at me. I felt like his eyes were shooting lasers at mine. Then he burst out laughing. Everyone looked at him.

Jimmy dropped his head over his sherbet. He couldn't

stop laughing. Izzy said, "Jimmy! Why are you laughing?"

"Mary Jane!" Jimmy gasped at last.

Sheba looked at me. "Oh, Mary Jane! Did you think I was talking about you?!"

"Is there another Mary Jane?" I asked.

Sheba leaned over her chair and hugged me. She smelled like lemon and lilac. My heart calmed. The heat left my face. "It's another word for marijuana."

"Oh!" I laughed nervously. Was Sheba actually asking a doctor if her husband could smoke marijuana? What about the law? Wouldn't Jimmy go to jail if he got caught? Didn't Sheba worry about Jimmy doing something that was against the law?

Dr. Cone said, "Some people find marijuana relaxes them, Mary Jane. It isn't the terrible drug your school may have made it out to be."

"Oh okay," I said automatically. I must have looked confused, because Sheba patted my leg as if to comfort me.

She said, "It's illegal, but the government doesn't know best about everything. Marijuana can be a lifesaver for someone like Jimmy, who needs to find some way out of his whirly-twirly-creative-genius brain." Sheba spun both her pointer fingers in the air, like sign language for *Jimmy's brain.*

I nodded. It had never occured to me that something that was against the law might actually be okay to do.

"It's better than lithium," Jimmy said. "The lithium makes me feel like my head is stuffed with wet cotton batting."

Dr. Cone looked at Jimmy. "Maybe we can try a control test. You can't do it alone."

"What do you think, Mary Jane?" Sheba asked me, as

if I should have an opinion. As if I knew anything about marijuana or drug addiction or getting sober. As if I'd ever even heard people discuss marijuana outside of the don't-do-drugs talk at school once a year.

"Uh." I felt a little shaky, but everyone was looking at me so kindly, I knew there couldn't be a wrong answer. "I trust Dr. Cone. But, also, I just think it's strange that marijuana is called Mary Jane. My name."

Everyone laughed and my head went floaty and loose with feelings of foolishness. But foolish moments like this seemed worth the thrill and unexpected intimacy of being in on things with the adults.

After dinner, Mrs. Cone took Jimmy into the TV room, where there was a big, fluffy shag carpet. She wanted to show him a meditation technique she'd learned in California at a place called Esalen. I started to clear the table, but Dr. Cone said he'd clear and do the dishes if I'd put Izzy to bed.

Izzy climbed up onto my lap like a giant cat. She was sleepy and soft. And a little bit smelly. "Do you mind if I give her a bath first?"

"No, no, please do. That would be lovely."

"I'll go with you." Sheba put her hand on my elbow and helped me stand. Izzy clung to me, her legs wrapped around my back. The three of us walked up the stairs together, Sheba humming the midget song.

In the bathroom, I put Izzy down on the floor, then turned on the faucet. Sheba sat on the closed toilet and started singing. *Midgets, they're like you and me. Some go to church, some spend Sunday free. . . .* " The bathroom had a black-and-white tiled floor and black-and-white wallpaper of swirling 3-D balls. Sometimes they looked convex and sometimes they looked concave and I was never sure if I was looking at the balls or at the space between the balls, which also looked like balls. If I moved my head around too fast, I felt a little dizzy.

While the water was running, I removed Izzy's clothes and put them in the black wicker hamper. I suddenly realized I was singing along with Sheba, harmonizing. She sang a little louder, and so did I, and our voices echoed and reverberated through the bathroom. *"Your doctor might be a midget too. Of course there are plenty of midget Jews. You know they buy teeny, tiny midget shoes. And the Black ones sing the midget blues. . . ."*

Once the bath was ready, I picked up Izzy and placed her in. She splashed around, playing with the bucket of foam alphabet letters. When she stopped moving so much, I poured a palmful of Johnson's baby shampoo into my hands and washed her hair.

Sheba sang, *"I'm gonna wash that man right outa my hair . . ."*

I joined in. I knew the song from *South Pacific*, which was one of my favorite albums from the Show Tunes of the Month Club.

Izzy tilted her head back so the foam wouldn't get in her eyes, and tried to sing along with us.

I pulled Izzy's foamy shampoo hair into a horn on her head. "Look, you're a unicorn."

Izzy shook her head back and forth. "Do I look real? Like a real live unicorn?"

"Yup."

"I've really been wanting a baby," Sheba said.

I turned the unicorn horn into two horns that curled. "Now you're a ram." To Sheba I said, "Will you have one?"

"What's a ram?" Izzy asked.

"A big male goat." I thought of Dr. Cone and his side-burns. He would look perfectly natural with forceful curved horns.

"If Jimmy stays sober for five years, I'll have a baby," Sheba said. "You can't have a baby with an addict."

"Can witches have babies?" Izzy asked.

"Yes, but it's mostly the good witches who do," I said.

"Who are the mamas of bad witches?"

"Shut your eyes." I laid a washcloth over Izzy's eyes. She leaned her head back. I filled a dented saucepan that was lying next to the tub and dumped the water over Izzy's head to rinse out the shampoo.

"I bet good witches are the mamas of bad witches," Sheba said. "And even though they're good mamas, their babies just turn bad."

I filled the saucepan again and did a second rinse.

Izzy removed the washcloth and set it on her head like a scarf. "Mary Jane says the witch in this house is a good witch and that she gives us makarino cherries."

"Maraschino," I said.

"How do you like that?" Sheba said. "You've got a witch who leaves maraschino cherries."

I took the washcloth from Izzy's head, soaped it up, and then handed it to her. "Stand and wash your private parts."

Izzy stood and dug the washcloth into her butt and then her vagina, scrubbing back and forth with a crin-kled little concentrating face. She sat and rinsed herself.

"My mom is a bad witch," Sheba said.

"Really?" Izzy and I both looked at Sheba.

"God, yes. An awful witchy, witchy woman. She only loves my brothers."

I wanted to ask questions but wasn't sure if that was

allowed. Instead I grabbed a towel and held it open for Izzy. Izzy stepped out of the tub and into the towel. "Why does she love your brothers?" Izzy asked, like she was reading my mind.

"She's an old-fashioned witch who thinks boys are good and should get all the money and all the attention and girls are bad. Especially girls who like to kiss boys."

"Do you like to kiss boys?"

I tucked the towel up at Izzy's neck so she was wrapped like a burrito. I wanted to run and get her clean pajamas but didn't want to miss Sheba's answer.

"Yes. Especially Jimmy. I love to kiss Jimmy!" Sheba laughed, leaned over, and pulled the Izzy burrito into her arms. I went to get Izzy's pajamas.

When I came back, Sheba was singing "There Is Nothin' Like a Dame" to Izzy. I sang along while I unwrapped the towel and put Izzy in her pajamas. She peed and brushed her teeth and then I picked her up and the three of us marched into her bedroom, which was still clean, as Izzy and I spent a little time each day straightening it.

I tucked Izzy under the covers and then sorted through the stack of books we had laid by the bed.

"*Madeline!*" Izzy said. I dug out *Madeline*.

"I want to hear too." Sheba climbed onto the bed and lay on Izzy's other side, against the wall. I lay on the outside and opened the book.

I read the book and also floated above the three of us and watched myself reading the book. I was snuggled in close to warm, soapy-smelling Izzy, who fit against my torso like a foot in a slipper. Sheba was stretched out long with her arms flung over her head, her black hair pooled behind her like an oil spill. A steady current of contentment ran through me like a tuning fork humming deep in my bones.

I hoped that I would be a mom one day and the person I loved to kiss would lie on the other side of our kid while I read stories. It seemed like a simple desire. The twins both wanted to be the first woman president. They had agreed that one would be president and the other would be vice president the first four years, and then they'd swap.

When the book was finished, Izzy was asleep. We lay there in silence. I could feel that we three were breathing in unison, our chests rising and falling as one. Then Sheba leaned up onto her elbows, looked over at me, and nodded toward the door. I slipped out of the bed and then reached my arm out to Sheba so she could stand on the bed and step over Izzy without waking her. Just as Sheba was straddling Izzy, her legs in a long upside-down V, Izzy popped open her eyes and said, "Wait."

Sheba stepped off the bed and said, "What?"

"Is your witch mom a pretty witch or an ugly witch?"

"She's pretty if you look at her picture. But when you talk to her, the bad witchiness comes out and you can see that she isn't really pretty at all."

"Can we see a picture of her?"

"I don't have one with me. I'll draw one tomorrow."

"Okay. Good night."

"Good night," I said. "See you tomorrow."

"Close the door all the way."

"I will."

"I never heard of a five-year-old wanting to sleep with the door closed," Sheba said.

"The witch can't get through my door."

"Ah. I see. The maraschino cherry witch?"

"Yes, Mary Jane says she's good, but until we're ONE HUNDRED PURCHASE SURE, we have to close the door."

"One hundred percent," I said.

"ONE HUNDRED PERCENT."

"Sounds like a good plan," Sheba said. "Good night."

"Wait," Izzy said again. Sheba and I both stood still, looking at her round little face crowned in red curls. "If Sheba joins our team, then the ratio of us to the witch is"—Izzy pointed at us and then herself as she counted—"three to one."

"Okay, I'm in," Sheba said.

"That's a good ratio," I said. "Good night."

Sheba sang, *"Goooood niiiiight,"* like the kids from *The Sound of Music.*

"Gooood niiiight," I sang one octave higher.

"Good night. I love you," Izzy said. I wasn't sure which of us she was speaking to, but the words suspended me in motion. I stood halfway to the door, wondering if I should say it back. I'd never said that before, not to anyone. And no one had ever said it to me. But when I thought about it, I did love Izzy. And I kinda loved Sheba, too.

"Looove, looove, looove," Sheba sang as she walked out the door. I knew it was the beginning of a Beatles song, because the twins had those records.

"Looove, looove, looove," I sang after her, and then I went out the door and pulled it shut behind myself.

"How do you get home?" Sheba asked.

"I walk."

"In the dark?" Sheba looked out the window on the hall landing. Tree branches moved in the thick blackness, like a giant's waving arms.

"Well, I've never gone home in the dark before." The sun set fairly late, but we'd had a long dinner, and then the bath.

"I'll drive you. I want to see your house. Where exactly

does Mary Jane, the harmonizing, churchgoing summer nanny live?"

I followed Sheba down the stairs and then into the kitchen, where Dr. Cone, Mrs. Cone, and Jimmy were sitting at the banquette. Jimmy was forearm-deep into a box of Screaming Yellow Zonkers.

"Richard, where are the keys to your car?" Sheba asked. "I want to drive Mary Jane home."

"Over there on the . . ." Dr. Cone pointed his finger from left to right. He lost his keys every day and I found them every day. I had been putting them in the same place, on the covered radiator in the entrance hall, with the hope that he would understand that when he came in the house, he should just drop them there. So far he hadn't. Understood or dropped the keys.

"I know where they are," I said.

"I want to come." Jimmy shoved a handful of Zonkers into his mouth and then dropped the box onto the table so it fell sideways. He scooted out from the banquette and picked up Sheba's hand. "Let's go!" Jimmy took my hand too and pulled me and Sheba toward the swinging kitchen door.

"Can you find your way back?!" Mrs. Cone shouted.

"Yes!" Jimmy shouted. Sheba and I were laughing as he hurried us out of the kitchen.

"Do you want me to come with you?!" Mrs. Cone shouted.

I heard Dr. Cone say, "She's just down the street, Bonnie!"

"We'll be right back!" Sheba shouted.

In the entrance hall, I handed Sheba the keys and she ran out the door with them. Jimmy ran after her and then I ran too, as if we were fleeing something. When I was halfway to the car, I ran back and closed the front door. Then I doubled my speed to catch up to Sheba and Jimmy.

Jimmy was in the car and Sheba was standing at the open driver's side. She banged on the roof twice and shouted, "C'mon, c'mon!"

I hurried into the back seat as Sheba was starting the car. She pulled away from the curb before I had the door shut. I felt like we were in an episode of *Starsky & Hutch*. One of them was always jumping into a moving car.

"We made it!" Jimmy shouted.

Sheba did a kind of a yodeling yell, and then we all started laughing. I knew it was a game, that there was no one chasing us and no one to run from. Still, it felt exciting, exhilarating, like we really were on the lam.

Sheba and Jimmy rolled down their windows, so I rolled down mine. Sheba wasn't driving too fast, but we were moving at the speed of someone who knew where she was going.

I scooted up and put my hands on the back of the bench seat. "Um. My house is the other way."

Jimmy turned so he was looking right at me. In the darkness, with only the glow of the streetlight, he appeared to be made of spun sugar. I looked at Sheba. She, too, was shimmery.

"Ah, the other way." Sheba pulled the car into a driveway, then backed out and turned the car in the right direction.

"Mary Jane," Jimmy said.

"Yeah?" I hoped he was going to ask me something I could answer easily without being embarrassed.

"Mary Jane." Jimmy was twirling a hand-rolled cigarette between his thumb and first finger. He stuck the cigarette into his mouth and then leaned forward and poked his big pointer finger into the lighter.

"Is this doctor-approved?" Sheba asked.

"You were there."

"But did you discuss it further? Does he know you're going to do some tonight?"

"I'll confess when we walk in the door."

"Wait." I jerked upright, like my spine was being pulled on a cable. "Is that marijuana?!"

The lighter popped out. Jimmy took it and touched the glowing red coil to the tip of the cigarette. He inhaled deeply, held it, and then hissed out a long conic cloud of smoke. "Mary Jane, meet Mary Jane."

"Just call it a joint." Sheba reached out her hand and took the joint from Jimmy. Then she put it to her mouth and inhaled.

I felt like my brain was short-circuiting, like my hair might burst into flames. What if the police found us? Would Sheba and Jimmy go to jail? Would I go to juvey hall? But this was Roland Park. The only time I ever saw the police here was when someone called them. Which was very, very rare. The twins' parents never even locked their doors. The Rileys, next door, kept their car keys on the floor of the car.

"Mary Jane?" Sheba reached her long arm back over the seat, offering me the joint. I shook my head. I did like the smell, though. It was sort of like a school eraser, but sweeter. A green and rubbery smell.

Jimmy took the joint from Sheba and inhaled again. We were at a stop sign now, on the corner in front of Beanie Jones's house. Sheba punched in the emergency brake with her foot, put the car in park, and turned off the engine.

"Are you in a hurry?" Sheba turned so she was side-

ways in the seat. She pushed her hair back and I could see
that some of it had fallen out the window.

"No. I don't think so." I knew my mother would be sitting
in her chair in the living room working on something—
her dinner menu for next month, the needlepoint pillow
she was making for the TV room sofa, her lesson plan for
Sunday school—while waiting for me.

Sheba took another hit, and then offered the joint to
me again. Jimmy took it from her hand before I had time
to say no.

"Tell me more about your parents." Sheba took the
joint from Jimmy.

"Hmm. They're both from Idaho."

"Do they like rock and roll?" Jimmy asked.

"No. My mom and I love show tunes. And the Mormon Tabernacle Choir. And my dad has one Marine Corps
band record that he'll play every now and then."

"That's cool. Like a lotta horns and shit. That stuff's
totally cool when you sit down and really listen to it."
Jimmy sucked on the joint again, shutting his eyes as if he
needed to concentrate. I watched his face relax; the folds
in his forehead melted. Maybe he really did need Mary
Jane to calm his whirly-twirly-creative-genius mind.

"Mary Jane sings in the choir at church," Sheba said
to Jimmy. "And at Sunday school."

"Ah, that's where you trained that gorgeous voice."

"I guess." No one had ever used the word *gorgeous*
when talking about any part of me. I could feel the word
inside me like a warm liquid. *Gorgeous.* I knew I was
blushing but figured it was too dark in the car for Jimmy
and Sheba to notice.

Jimmy took a smaller hit, handed the joint to Sheba,
and then started singing. *"Jesus loves me, this I know. . . ."*

Little tufts of smoke puffed out with each word. *"For the Bible tells me so. . . ."* He took the song at a slower pace than it was usually sung. With his twangy, cello-sounding voice, he made it feel sad and lonely. Like a love song Jimmy's rock star friend might have sung about the midget who broke his heart.

Sheba joined in, and the song filled out. Now it sounded so beautiful and pure that I could feel the notes landing on my skin like feathers. My eyes teared up and I worried I'd start crying.

"Take the third part of the harmony," Sheba said to me, and this stopped me from crying. I cautiously entered the song—slowly and wistfully—in the next verse. *"Jesus loves me, this I know, as he loved so long ago. . . ."*

Crickets were chirping in the trees and even that felt like part of the song. Jimmy and Sheba each leaned toward me, so our heads were together in a triangle that almost touched as our voices braided together. We sang slowly and deeply until the moment was sliced open by another voice.

"Hello?" It was Beanie Jones. She stood just outside Jimmy's window.

Sheba threw the joint to the floor of the car and Jimmy turned in his seat.

"Hi, Mrs. . . . uh, Mrs. Beanie." I lifted my hand and nervously waved.

"Mary Jane, what are you doing?" Beanie's head was moving from side to side like a bird's. She had an enormous tense smile on her face. I could see that she was as confused as if Jesus Himself had been parked in front of her house.

"These are my friends from out of town," I said quickly. "We were practicing for church."

"Are you—" Beanie started.

"Pleasure to meet you," Jimmy said.

Sheba started the car. "So nice to meet you!" she called. Then she hit the gas and pulled away from the curb, running through the stop sign. Jimmy stuck his hand out the window, his first two fingers open in a V. "Peace!" he yelled out.

There was silence in the car for about five seconds and then we all burst out laughing. I laughed so hard that tears streamed down my face. Sheba screamed and hooted with laughter and Jimmy was actually wiping tears away from his eyes.

"Beanie? Her name was Mrs. Beanie?!" He laughed some more.

"Beanie Jones," I said. "Her first name is Beanie."

"Jesus, who names a daughter Beanie?" Sheba asked, and I wondered, *Who names a daughter Sheba?*

We were on my block now. "Up there," I said. "The one with black shutters and window boxes."

Sheba stopped the car one house before mine, at the Rileys'. This seemed safe, as my mother, like Beanie, would walk out to see what was up if she noticed a car parked in front. The Rileys were at their place on the Chesapeake Bay most of the summer, so they wouldn't be coming out to check on us.

"Dang, Mary Jane. That's a damn pretty house." Jimmy craned his neck and leaned his head out the window.

"It's like a storybook," Sheba said.

"So you're a rich girl, huh?"

I'd never thought of whether we were rich or not. Everyone I knew had more or less the same, though I was certainly aware of the less fortunate. But rich? Rich seemed like people who wore long sequined gowns, smoked cigarettes from alabaster holders, and rode in limousines driven by a man in a flat, black cap. I assumed Sheba and Jimmy were rich. Weren't all movie stars and rock stars rich?

"I dunno. My dad's a lawyer. We don't go on fancy vacations. I've never been to Hawaii."

"Are you working for the Cones for fun or for the money?" Sheba asked.

"Well, it is super fun. But I agreed to do it at first because my best friends went to sleepaway camp and I didn't want to go to camp and I didn't want to stay home all day and help my mother. And I don't love hanging out at the club."

"Why didn't you want to go to camp?" Jimmy asked. "I would have loved to have gone to sleepaway camp."

"I went one summer and it wasn't fun. There were so many people and it never got quiet and you could barely read. The only part I liked was when we sat around the campfire and sang."

"Sweet Mary Jane," Sheba said.

"Why didn't you go to camp?" I asked Jimmy.

"We were dirt-poor. Poorer than poor." Jimmy shook his head and smiled. "I'd never even met anyone who went to sleepaway camp. I spent my summers riding an inner tube down a rain gully—not even a goddammned river but the fucking culvert that ran through town. After a heavy rain, the water was black and there was trash bobbing it in like ice cubes in a glass of Coke. But it was fun as hell. Stole cigarettes from our parents. Rode that inner tube. Tried to find girls who'd let us touch their boobs. The usual."

My sex addict brain repeated the words *touch their boobs* three times, rapidly.

"I couldn't go to camp, because I was famous," Sheba said. "But I might have loved it too."

"Why didn't you want to hang around and help your mother?" Jimmy asked.

"Um, well." I shrugged. I'd never said anything bad about my mother.

"I don't suppose your mom smokes pot," Jimmy said.

"My family is very patriotic," I said, as if that would preclude pot-smoking. "We love our president."

Jimmy and Sheba both looked at me with gentle smiles on their faces.

"We'll talk you out of that soon enough." Sheba leaned forward and kissed me on the cheek. "Good night, doll."

"Good night." I had lifted my hand to feel the heat in the place where she'd kissed me when Jimmy leaned over and kissed my other cheek.

"Good night, sweet Mary Jane," he said.

"G'night." I barely had the breath to say it.

I stepped out of the car, pushed the door shut, and then walked toward my house. Sheba and Jimmy both watched out the front window. I turned, waved, walked. Turned, waved, and then, finally, entered the house.

My mother was exactly where I had expected her to be. "Did Dr. Cone drive you home? I didn't hear a car."

Just then the station wagon cruised by our front window. It was impossible to see Sheba's and Jimmy's faces in the dark. "That's him," I said.

"How was the meatloaf?"

"I think it was perfect."

My mother laid her needlepoint on her lap and looked at me, smiling. "That makes me very happy."

"Maybe I'll just use our menu for their dinners this month?" My mother worked so hard on planning our family dinners, I thought it would please her that more than just our small family would enjoy them.

"Excellent idea. Do you think she has any dietary needs? With her illness?"

"Um . . I don't know," I said.

"I have a feeling it's cancer. Especially because no one knows—I tried to pull it out of a few women at the club today. People are very secretive about cancer. No one wants their neighbors to know about the hardships in their home."

"Oh. Okay." I wondered how many hardships were going on in the houses around me—hardships I'd never before imagined.

"Did they pray before dinner?"

"Yes," I lied. The third lie. I would start losing count if there were too many more.

"In Hebrew?"

"No. In English."

"Hmm." My mother nodded once, decisively. "Well, good for them."

6

Beanie Jones was standing on the front porch holding an angel food cake on a glass platter. She hadn't knocked. Izzy and I had opened the door for our daily walk to Eddie's market and there she was, a too-big smile smeared across her face like a cartoon drawing.

"Hey, Beanie!" Izzy said.

"Hello!" Beanie said.

"Hey." I blushed. "I'm sorry about the other night. I'm sorry we were parked in front of your house." It was Thursday and I hadn't seen Beanie since Monday night, when Sheba and Jimmy had driven me home. Driving me home had become a ritual, one that began with Sheba taking off and Jimmy and me jumping into the moving car. We called it "Doing a Starsky and Hutch." Sheba critiqued our performance each time. *Mary Jane, you should have jumped in deeper! What if I had been going faster? You would have ended up under the back wheels!* I took

Sheba's critiques seriously, and put real effort into being a better car-jumper.

We took a different street to avoid Beanie Jones. And we only parked in front of houses whose owners I knew were out of town. Jimmy always lit a joint, and then the three of us sang church songs, with Sheba on melody and Jimmy and me harmonizing—him low and me high. Turns out that Sheba and Jimmy had both been in their church choirs, Sheba because she liked it, Jimmy because his grandmother forced him to. (Of his grandmother, Jimmy had said, "She was a warty old hag who loved Marlboros and Old Crow bourbon almost as much as she loved Jesus.")

"No need to apologize," Beanie said. And then she lowered her voice to a whisper and said, "But tell me. That was Sheba and Jimmy, wasn't it?"

Izzy looked up at Beanie with huge, blinking eyes. "NOPE!"

"Uh, it was just some people who looked like them. Old friends of the Cones. They're gone now." The words came out so smoothly that I almost wanted to laugh. The more I lied, the easier it was. And instead of feeling guilty about my lies, I was starting to feel guilty that I didn't feel so guilty.

"Mary Jane." Izzy tugged my hand. When I looked at her, she quietly said, "Secret."

Beanie's eyes ticked like a cat clock, back and forth. "Huh. Amazing resemblance. Why don't I bring this cake in? Mr. Jones suddenly decided he was watching his 'girlish figure,' and I thought, with you here all summer, there were enough people in the house to need an angel food cake."

"Oh, I'll put it inside for you." I took the cake and turned to go. Izzy followed me, and Beanie followed her.

There was no one to see; Jimmy and Dr. Cone were in Dr. Cone's office, and Sheba and Mrs. Cone had gone to the Eastern Shore for the day. They both wore wigs this time, long and blond, like Swedish sisters. Still, I felt a bolt of panic with Beanie in the house.

I put the cake on the kitchen table, then turned to Beanie. "Thank you so much." I wasn't sure what to do. How to be good, polite, and kind while still getting Beanie out of here?

"Is Bonnie home?"

"No, she's gone."

"And my dad's in his office with a patience," Izzy offered.

"A patient," I said. "We're on our way to Eddie's."

"Oh, I can drive you!" Beanie held up her car keys.

"Thank you so much," I said. "But we need the walk."

"We sing," Izzy said. "And we talk about the witch. And we look at things. Sometimes we play with toys that kids leave out front. Oh, and we buy Popsicles."

"How nice," Beanie said, making no effort to leave.

"Thank you again for the cake." My voice sounded airy and strange. I took Izzy's hand and walked toward the hall, hoping Beanie would follow. Eventually she did.

"Maybe I'll stop in again later. I'd really like to meet Bonnie," Beanie said, once we were out the door and on the sidewalk. She took a few steps toward her car, which was white and shiny.

"She'll be out all day," I said. "But I'll tell her you came by." I smiled real big; my cheeks hurt and my palm started sweating against Izzy's.

"Bye, Beanie!" Izzy waved with her free hand and tugged me down the sidewalk. My heart was still pounding as Beanie drove by us in the car.

"Let's cut over," I said, and we took the parallel street early to avoid Beanie Jones.

"That was scary," Izzy said.

"Yup. A close call."

"Can we have that cake for dessert tonight?"

"We sure can. We could add sliced strawberries and whipped cream."

"Hurrah!" Izzy lifted a tiny fist.

We walked in silence for a minute until we came upon a skateboard sitting alone on a lawn.

"Can I try it?" Izzy asked.

I looked up at the house. No one on the porch. No one in the windows. "Okay, but I have to hold your hands."

Izzy picked up the skateboard and placed it on the sidewalk. She put one flip-flopped foot on it. I took both of her hands and then she stepped her other foot on. I pushed her up the sidewalk to the edge of the property, then turned around, so she was backward and I was forward, and pushed her the other way.

We went back and forth like this several times, until my body, mind, and heart calmed. Beanie was gone. Everyone was safe. We'd eat the cake after dinner and then I'd return the glass plate on the way home. I'd have to run up to the porch and leave it so Sheba and Jimmy wouldn't be spotted. But I could do that. And Sheba and Jimmy seemed to like the sneaking around, as if it made their lives in Baltimore just a little more thrilling.

Each time we shopped at Eddie's, Izzy liked to find the ratio of employees to customers. She missed people, but I didn't point them out. And she often lost count, so I'd make up a number and give it to her. It was as inexact as pulling random numbers from a sack. The ratio that Izzy liked to talk about the most, however, was that of the witch. With Sheba now on our team, that remained three to one.

That day, we did our usual shopping. Izzy knew what to grab: Screaming Yellow Zonkers, Popsicles, and Slim Jims, which Jimmy and Mrs. Cone were eating with equal fervor, alternating a salty bite of Slim Jim with a sweet bite of something else. Yesterday I had tried it with candy orange wedges. There was something explosively wonderful about tasting salty, grainy meat stuff followed by chewy, gelatinous sugar stuff.

For dinner, I had a list of ingredients copied from one of my mother's index cards. Tonight was going to be the most complicated meal yet. Chicken breasts roasted in orange sauce. My mother went over it with me in the morning, giving me tips on how to know when the chicken was properly cooked, and how to spoon the sauce over every few minutes to keep the breasts moist. The more she told me, the more nervous I got. Mom must have seen this on my face, because she stopped her instructions and said, "Mary Jane, now is not the time to lose confidence. There is an ill mother in that house and a hardworking doctor who needs to be fed." She had stared at me until I nodded, and then she gave me even more directions.

"How many breasts do you think Jimmy will eat?" I asked Izzy. We were standing at the butcher counter. The butcher, whose long rectangular head reminded me of a cow's, waited patiently.

"Seven?" Izzy said.

"You think Jimmy alone would eat seven?"

"Jimmy a football player?" the butcher asked.

"Just a man."

"Two," the butcher said. "Prepare two breasts for each

man, one for each woman, and maybe a half for half-pint there." He winked at Izzy.

"Okay, seven breasts." I figured Izzy and I would split one if the men really did have two each. And I wasn't sure Sheba really would eat a whole breast anyway. I noticed that she sat down and ate at every meal, just like everyone else, but she left half of everything on her plate. It didn't matter what it was, or how much she claimed to love it; only half went in her mouth. Usually, when everyone appeared to be finished, Jimmy—though once it was Dr. Cone—would reach over and take her uneaten portion.

Mrs. Cone had noticed how Sheba ate as well. The past couple of dinners, she had tried to leave half of her meal on her plate. But with little success, as just as someone—Dr. Cone, usually—made a play for her food, she would come back to it with a few quick stabs. And last night, when we were clearing the table, I found Mrs. Cone in the kitchen, using her hands to shove down the half piece of lasagna that she had left on her plate. I'd never really thought about food, or how much to eat or not to eat, until these meals with the Cones. In my own house, you ate everything you took. If you weren't going to eat a whole chicken breast, then you sure as heck didn't put a whole chicken breast on your plate.

In addition to eating, or trying to eat, like Sheba, Mrs. Cone had been dressing like Sheba too. They were about the same height, but Sheba was more of a curvy line while Mrs. Cone wasn't a line at all. Her hips jutted out, her breasts jutted out, and lately they all had been jutting with greater enthusiasm as she wore tight pants, jumpsuits, and clingy maxi dresses. They were clothes that demanded you look at her, something that was virtually impossible when Sheba was nearby. Sheba sparkled. My eyes trailed her from room to room, as if she were a rocket sailing across a night sky. Mrs. Cone, in her snazzy outfits, was the contrail from that rocket, her breasts, behind, and flaming red hair streaking by in Sheba's wake.

Sheba and Mrs. Cone came home a few minutes before the chicken was ready. They both oohed and aahed over the way the house smelled and I could see that this made Izzy proud. I prayed the chicken would taste as good as it smelled.

Sheba helped Izzy set the table while Mrs. Cone stood in the kitchen with me as I finished preparing the rice and the string beans I had steaming on the stovetop. She leaned over to see exactly what I was doing when I spooned sauce over the chicken, and when I sliced off a hunk of butter and melted it into the beans.

"How do you know how to do this?" The long locks of Mrs. Cone's blond wig fell over her shoulder. She pushed them back with the side of her dangling hand, the same way Sheba pushed her long hair out of her face. It was a gesture I had tried to copy many times when I watched Sheba push her hair away during the opening monologue of her variety show. In person, she didn't do it as often as I'd seen her do it on the show. I wondered if it was a nervous habit.

"I help my mother with dinner every night." I wanted to ask how she *didn't* know how to do this, but I felt that it might be rude.

"I've never cooked," Mrs. Cone said.

"Your mother didn't teach you?" I spooned the rice into a serving bowl, then melted a pat of butter on top and garnished it with parsley.

"Oh, she tried, but I just wasn't interested. I was

boy crazy, and I loved rock and roll. There wasn't time to care about things like cooking." She laughed. "Nothing's changed!"

I blushed. It was odd to think of Mrs. Cone as *boy crazy*. She was married! "But you ended up with a doctor, not a rock star."

"Richard was in a band in college—he was at Johns Hopkins and I was at Goucher. When he started medical school, he quit the band and I quit school to marry him."

"Were you disappointed that he didn't stay in the band?"

"Not as much as my parents." Mrs. Cone pulled a string bean from the pan and bit off half.

"They wanted you to marry a rock star?"

"No, but they didn't want me to marry Richard. Medical school or not." She shrugged.

"Why not?" I needed to take out the chicken, but this news seemed important and I didn't want to turn away.

"Because he's a Jew!" Mrs. Cone laughed.

I tried to laugh with her, but I didn't understand why that was funny. I busied myself by putting on the oven mitts. Then I opened the oven and took out the chicken. "So you're *not* Jewish?"

"No way. We were Presbyterian. I grew up in Oklahoma."

"Oh. Wow." Oklahoma seemed exotic. I'd never met anyone from Oklahoma. And what about a Presbyterian marrying a Jewish person? Would my parents think a half-Jewish family was easier to take than a whole Jewish family? Did Mrs. Cone's parents, like mine, think Jewish people had a different physiognomy? Dr. and Mrs. Cone seemed more like each other than my parents. If I really thought about it, it was my parents who appeared to be different breeds (my mother the talker, the doer; my father the silent newspaper reader). And the Cones seemed happy and in sync. They were different versions of the same model.

"Yup, wow." Mrs. Cone smiled at me.

"We go to Roland Park Presbyterian. I'm Presbyterian."

"I know. Sheba told me. She thinks we all should go to your service on Sunday."

"That would be so fun!" I smiled, but Mrs. Cone just gritted her teeth. Like maybe it would be painful for her to go. "I mean, if you want."

"I try to avoid church. But if Sheba really wants to go . . . we'll see." She shrugged again.

I tried to imagine Sheba and Mrs. Cone in their long blond wigs in my church. It seemed impossible. No one looked like that at Roland Park Presbyterian. I took down the serving platter Izzy and I had washed a few days ago when we cleaned out some kitchen cupboards, and then moved the chicken from the pan to the platter, placing each piece with the bronzed meaty side up. The orange slices were hot, but I could still lift them from the pan with the edges of my fingers so I could arrange them artfully. I thought it looked like something out of *Sunset* magazine, and Mrs. Cone might have agreed because she stared down at the platter and looked happy again.

"What are the herbs?" Mrs. Cone poked a piece of chicken with her finger and then stuck her finger in her mouth.

"Rosemary, garlic, thyme, and salt. Izzy sprinkled all of it on top." Just like I did for my mother, though my mother premeasured the portions before handing them over.

"Mary Jane," Mrs. Cone said, "you are a gift to us all." She leaned in and kissed me. I was starting to get used to all the kisses around here.

I picked up the chicken platter and carried it out to the dining room table. Izzy was standing on a chair, with Sheba behind her. They were holding a match together, lighting candles in tall silver candlesticks.

"We're doing candles tonight!" Izzy said.

"That's beautiful." I placed the platter on the table. Mrs. Cone followed behind with the bowl of rice in one hand and the green beans in the other.

Sheba looked down at the chicken. "No, *that's* beautiful."

"Izzy did the spices."

"I put on the mary rose," Izzy agreed.

"Rosemary."

"ROSEMARY!"

"Go get your dad and Jimmy." Mrs. Cone put Izzy on the ground and gave her a little pat on the bottom to help her get moving. Izzy ran out, and then Mrs. Cone moved in closer to Sheba. The two of them started talking about something that had happened earlier in the day, the town they had visited, the little inn they had seen, a restaurant they both liked. Their voices were low and humming, like they were talking during the opening credits of a movie. I pretended to be straightening the place settings on the table, but really I was just listening in.

Dr. Cone, Jimmy, and Izzy came in. Izzy and Jimmy were making screeching monkey sounds, as if they were in the jungle and could only communicate with long-held vowels: *eeee oooo eeee!* Dr. Cone's brow was furrowed. He looked tired and maybe angry.

Jimmy lifted his hands in the air above the chicken,

like a preacher, and said, "Lord have mercy! What hath Mary Jane and Izzy made for us tonight?!"

"Chicken with mary rose!!" Izzy shouted. She clapped her hands and jumped up and down.

"Chicken with mary rose! Well then, this needs a song of praise." Jimmy left the room and Izzy ran behind him. The rest of us sat at our usual places at the table.

Dr. Cone reached for the chicken and Mrs. Cone said, "No, dear! Wait until everyone's seated."

Dr. Cone huffed out a breath but withdrew his hand. He leaned back in his seat, looking for Jimmy and Izzy to return.

"Do you like our hair?" Sheba asked.

"Isn't it the same hair you two had on this morning?" Dr. Cone asked.

"Maybe." Mrs. Cone threw her hair over her shoulder, Sheba style. She winked.

Dr. Cone didn't seem in the mood to play games. "I'm hungry," he said.

"Lighten up," Mrs. Cone said.

"Or light up," Sheba said, and she and Mrs. Cone laughed.

I didn't get the joke, and Dr. Cone didn't seem amused by it. "How long do we have to wait for this song?" He drummed his fingers on the table, and as if that movement were magic, Jimmy marched into the room with Izzy sitting on his shoulders. He had a guitar strapped across his chest, hanging on his back, and his hands on Izzy's ankles.

"We're going to sing for our supper!" Izzy said. Still, Dr. Cone seemed hungry, or angry. I worried I had done something wrong.

I stood and helped Izzy off Jimmy's back. Then I pulled her into my lap.

Jimmy put one foot on his chair, laid the guitar across his knee, and started strumming and singing. It was a Cat Stevens song, I knew, because we had learned it in choir at school. *"Morning has bro-ken. . . ."*

Sheba jumped in and sang with him. Then she reached over and pinched my arm to get me to sing. I looked at Dr. Cone, who had his arms crossed over his chest and a half frown on his face.

"Come on, Mary Jane. We need you on harmony," Sheba said, and I looked away from Dr. Cone and jumped in. *"Praise for the singing . . ."*

Mrs. Cone turned her head in my direction. Dr. Cone looked up. His face relaxed a little.

When the song was over, everyone clapped. Jimmy set the guitar against the wall and then sat down. "I just feel so grateful. I'm grateful for you, Richard."

"I feel grateful for Mary Jane's voice." Sheba put her hand on my leg and said, "If I weren't me, I'd be jealous of you."

I smiled and worked through the puzzle of that compliment. Did Sheba mean she was so content with herself that the only way for her to be jealous of another person would be if she already were another person? Maybe being famous like Sheba gave you so many advantages that you knew there was no point in wishing you were someone else. I spent a lot of time wondering what it would be like to be someone else. At school, I watched the cool girls with tube-curled hair and Bonnie Bell glossed lips and thought it would be thrilling to be one of them, clumped together in the dining hall, laughing and tossing their hair around. But now that I knew

Sheba, those girls seemed as human and normal as . . . well, as me.

Dr. Cone was talking. I tuned in just as he said, "Jimmy, you need to tell everyone what happened."

"What happened?" Sheba's voice was sharp.

"Wait. Richard, what happened?" Now Mrs. Cone's voice was sharp too.

"Can we eat first?" Jimmy said. "We skipped lunch today."

"Didn't you have Screaming Yellow Zonkers?" Izzy asked.

Jimmy took a chicken breast and placed it on his plate. "No Zonkers today. Today was BONKERS, so we had no ZONKERS!"

Everyone was serving themselves, but suddenly nothing felt right. Dr. Cone seemed angry, Jimmy was overly cheerful to make up for it, and Sheba and Mrs. Cone both looked tentative and concerned. Izzy climbed off my lap and went to her seat across the table, beside her mother.

I tried to separate from whatever was going on. I reminded myself that it probably had nothing to do with me. Instead of watching the adults, I focused on Izzy. First, I cut a breast in two and put half on Izzy's plate and half on mine. Then I put a spoonful of rice on her plate, on top of which I placed three string beans. We had negotiated the eating of the beans while preparing them. Dr. and Mrs. Cone never seemed to pay attention to what Izzy did or didn't eat, but I wanted her to be as healthy as possible, so I made it a point to get something green inside her body every day.

There was tense, sporadic chatter once everyone started eating. It seemed to take a lot of effort to *not* talk about whatever Dr. Cone had been referencing earlier.

And then there was a second of silence in which Dr. Cone made a long hum, like he was holding a note. I looked up at him. He was chewing the chicken and humming and moving his head as if it were the most spectacular thing he'd ever eaten. Jimmy took a bite and started humming too, but in a more exaggerated way so that we knew it was intentional. Then Sheba and Mrs. Cone took bites, and they, too, did moaning hums—chewing, humming, smiling. Izzy picked up her half breast with her hands and bit into it and she started humming, imitating the *mmm, mmm, mmm* sounds from the adults. I hadn't even tasted the chicken yet, but the group stared at me for a reaction, smiling, humming.

"Is it really that good?" I asked, and they all broke apart laughing. It was like a bubble had popped and released something that created relief, lightness. Dr. Cone no longer appeared angry; Mrs. Cone no longer appeared worried; Sheba appeared to have forgotten there was something to worry about.

"Dang, Mary Jane," Jimmy said. "It is *that* motherfuckin' good."

"Holy moly, Mary Jane." Dr. Cone took another bite.

"Incredible," Sheba said.

"Incredible!" Dr. Cone repeated.

Mrs. Cone nodded in agreement, her mouth full.

Izzy and I were serving the angel food cake with strawberries and whipped cream when Sheba said, "So what happened today? Why was it so rough?"

Dr. Cone wiped his lips, put his napkin on his lap, and looked at Jimmy.

"You make this cake?" Jimmy asked Izzy.

"Beanie did," Izzy said. "She brought it over today."

"Beanie Jones?" Mrs. Cone's brow knit into folds. She suddenly looked ten years older. "Is she that new woman who moved in down the street?"

"Yes," I said. "She dropped it off. I tried to keep her out of the house, but she barged right in."

"Beanie?" Jimmy said. "We met Beanie."

"Oh yeah, Beanie," Sheba said.

"When did you meet Beanie?" Dr. Cone looked unhappy again.

"We were dropping Mary Jane off one night and Beanie popped her head in the window. Nosy little thing," Jimmy said. "But pretty as a picture."

"Hush!" Sheba said. "Stop looking!"

"She's not as pretty as you," I whispered to Sheba, but I didn't think she heard me.

"Christ, I hope she doesn't start spreading the word," Dr. Cone said. "It's hard enough as it is."

"Exactly what happened today?" Sheba asked.

Jimmy had a huge hunk of cake in his mouth. He spoke around it. "I relapsed."

"What do you mean you relapsed?" Sheba turned in her chair so she was facing Jimmy.

"I used."

"What do you mean you used? How did you use?"

"I got some junk."

"WHAT THE FUCK, JIMMY!" Sheba slapped Jimmy's upper arm with the back of her hand. "WHAT THE FUCK?!" She slapped him again. Harder.

I knew I should pick up Izzy and take her upstairs for her bath, but I couldn't bring myself to walk away from this scene. Also, I was just as angry as Sheba. It felt like Jimmy had betrayed *me* by relapsing.

Mrs. Cone pushed her half-eaten cake away, and watched Jimmy and Sheba.

"Don has a friend who has a friend who has a friend." Jimmy shrugged.

Dr. Cone said, "He met someone in the back alley when we were taking a break, got a bag of heroin, and snorted it."

"Didn't have a needle," Jimmy said.

"What the fuck, Jimmy?!" Sheba's eyes were flooded, though no tears fell. "I thought we were isolated! I thought you didn't know a soul in Baltimore! How can you do this?! After all everyone's done! Richard canceling all his other patients for the summer! Mary Jane making fucking dinner every night! Fucking chicken à l'orange, you ungrateful fuck!"

I looked at my lap and replayed Sheba's words in my head. This was more yelling than even Dr. and Mrs. Cone had ever done. And Sheba had used the term *chicken à l'orange*, when all night long we'd been calling it orange chicken, as was written on my mother's recipe card. Also, she called Jimmy a *fuck*. I couldn't imagine ever calling another human, or even a dog, a *fuck*. I didn't even know the word could be used that way. Yet it seemed effective. Jimmy appeared to be shrinking into his skin. He was too small for his casing, like a Ping-Pong ball in a bowling ball bag.

"Are you in trouble?" Izzy asked Jimmy.

Jimmy smiled at Izzy. It was a sad smile. "Yeah. I'm in trouble."

Everyone was silent. Sheba dropped her head into her hands. Her back bumped up and down and I wasn't sure if she was breathing heavily or silently crying. Mrs. Cone pulled her plate back toward herself and finished the half slice she had abandoned only a few minutes ago. Dr. Cone had that scowl again. And Izzy stared at me with giant circular eyes.

"Let's clear," I said.

Izzy clambered out of her chair and helped me clear the table as the adults sat in silence. Jimmy stared at Sheba like he was waiting for her to look up at him, but her head remained in her hands.

Izzy and I moved most of the dishes into the kitchen and stacked them on the counter. Then I picked her up and headed upstairs. That was when the shouting started. Sheba mostly, with Jimmy shouting back in short barking sentences of two or three words. Izzy pushed her head into my neck and clung to me like I might drop her.

"You okay?" I asked.

"I'm worried about Jimmy."

"Jimmy will be okay."

"But Sheba's so mad."

"Yeah, but your dad's taking care of him. He'll be okay again."

"Was he doing his addict?"

"Yes. He was doing his addict."

The shouting continued as I put Izzy in her pajamas. Dr. Cone's voice appeared like parenthetical words inserted between Sheba's and Jimmy's bursts of yelling. He wasn't shouting, but his voice carried up in a steady, stern grumbling. Mrs. Cone was either remaining silent or had left the dining room. After Izzy peed, when she was brushing her teeth, we heard the sound of something crashing: the thick clunking sound of ceramic breaking, rather than the tinkling shrill of glass.

Izzy held her toothbrush with her teeth. Foam dripped down her chin and into the sink. We stared at each other

in the mirror, waiting for the next sound. There was absolute silence for ten seconds, and then Sheba began yelling
again.

"Finish up. Let's go to bed." I stroked Izzy's hair while
she spit and rinsed, and then I picked her up and carried
her to her room. Just as we were in the hallway, another
sequence of crashes began. This time it did sound like
glass. Or a series of glasses being thrown against a wall.
My stomach clenched and I felt my heart beating in my
throat. The crashing went on. And on. And on.

I carried Izzy into her room and kicked the door shut
behind me. The yelling was more muted now, but we could
still hear it, punctuated every now and then with another
crash.

"Will you stay with me tonight?" Izzy asked.

I put Izzy in bed and got under the covers with her. I
didn't know what to say. I couldn't spend the night. My
mother expected me home.

"Please. I don't want to be alone here. What if the witch
comes?" Izzy blinked rapidly. She'd rarely cried since I'd
started taking care of her, but the couple of times she
had—when she fell on the sidewalk once, and when we
couldn't find her favorite stuffed animal—she'd blinked
like this before bursting into tears.

"The witch won't come." I leaned over the edge of the
bed and picked up *Madeline*.

"But the witch will know that the grown-ups are angry and that the grown-ups aren't watching out for me, so
she'll come and—"

"I'll stay." Her panic fed my panic. I may have needed
Izzy then just as much as she needed me. "Let me go call
my mom. I'll shut the door behind me so the witch doesn't
come in while I'm on the phone."

"Hurry back." Izzy blinked and tears painted her cheeks. But she didn't cry. She didn't make a noise.

When I opened the door, I heard a *chuk-chuk-chuk* sound of things being thrown but not breaking. The adults had moved to the living room; their voices were louder and closer.

"Stupid fucking fuck!" Sheba screamed. I rushed into Dr. and Mrs. Cone's room and closed the door behind me, dulling the yelling sounds.

The bed was unmade and the Cones' clothes were heaped on the quilted blue love seat at the end of it and on the armchair in the corner. The nightstands on either side of the bed were covered with books, drinking glasses, a small jade Buddha, and magazines. There was a red telephone sitting next to the Buddha and an issue of *The American Journal of Psychiatry* on what I assumed was Dr. Cone's nightstand. I picked up the receiver and waited for more screaming. It seemed safer if I called in the silence right after a session. Jimmy was hollering now, so I dialed all the numbers but the last. Sheba picked up where Jimmy had left off. And then I could hear Dr. Cone's voice chopping through.

I stretched the phone cord and crawled down to the ground. The sound only seemed louder there; it was coming up straight through the floor. I stood again, and then looked at the Cones' bed. Dr. and Mrs. Cone kissed often, on the lips, and sometimes I could see their tongues. And they touched each other in ways that made my brain think of sex even when it was only Dr. Cone's fingertips on Mrs. Cone's lower back. I didn't want to get in their bed. I didn't want my body to touch their sheets. I couldn't stop myself imagining them having sex on and beneath those sheets. Still, I had to muffle the noise somehow. If my mother heard anything suspicious, she would get in the car and drag me home.

I picked up the body of the phone and held it against my belly. Then, as if I were about to go underwater, I took a deep breath and got in the Cones' bed, under the quilted orange bedspread. I pulled the bedspread over my head. It smelled loamy and warm, like a wet towel that had been left in a closed-up car. There was quiet for a second, and then faint grumbling from Dr. Cone. I dialed the last number and said a prayer, *Please, God, may no one yell while I'm on the phone.*

My mother answered on the first ring.

"Mom," I whispered.

"Is everything okay?" I imagined my mother standing up straight in the kitchen, the white floor mopped so clean you could see your reflection in the tile, the avocado-colored appliances gleaming from a spray-down with Windex.

I made myself speak in a regular voice. "Mrs. Cone is really sick and Dr. Cone asked if I could stay the night. Izzy seems scared and upset." Lie four. The most complex and complete of the bunch.

"Is she vomiting?"

"Yes."

"Chemo," my mother said.

"I don't know. They don't tell me."

"I'll drive up and bring you an overnight bag with a nightgown and a toothbrush."

"Dr. Cone gave me one of Mrs. Cone's clean night-gowns. And he gave me a brand-new toothbrush and my own tube of toothpaste, too." When my best friends slept over, my mother asked them to bring their own tooth-paste, as she didn't think it was sanitary for people to slide their brushes over the same spot on the tube.

"But what will you wear tomorrow?"

"I need to throw a load of wash in the laundry anyway."

"Because of the vomit?"

"Yes."

"Add just a couple of tablespoons of bleach to help sanitize everything."

"Okay."

"It won't bleach your clothes if you use less than a quarter cup."

"Okay." I heard muffled yelling and covered the mouthpiece with my hand, shut my eyes, and prayed again. God must have heard, because my mother didn't seem to.

"How was the chicken?"

"They loved it. They said it was the best meal they'd ever had." Finally I could speak the truth.

"Very good, dear. I'm glad you succeeded with that."

"Mom, I've got to go. I have to take care of Izzy."

"I understand. I'll see you tomorrow at the end of the day."

"Okay. Good night, Mom."

"Good night. And remember, just two tablespoons of bleach. And look closely at the labels on their clothes before you put anything in the dryer."

"I will."

"And you know to clean the lint filter before each dryer load, right?"

"Yes, Mom."

"Okay, Mary Jane. Good night." My mother hung up before I could respond.

I pushed the quilt down and breathed in the cool, clean air. Then I rolled out of the bed and returned the phone to the nightstand.

I paused in the hallway. The voices were calmer now. Sheba and Jimmy weren't yelling. And even Dr. Cone's voice sounded less grumbly. I wanted to make sure that Dr. and Mrs. Cone were okay with me spending the night. And maybe I could borrow a nightgown from Mrs. Cone. I had laundered two of them earlier in the day.

Mrs. Cone's voice floated for a second before Sheba started up again. I moved to the top of the stairs and slowly made my way down. My legs were watery and my heart felt like a Slinky flipping down an endless staircase inside my chest.

As I approached the living room, the four of them looked up at me. Sheba was on the couch. Her wig was off and her face was streaked with black mascara. Dr. Cone was sitting in the leather chair. He looked calm but still had that half-angry scowl. Jimmy sat on the floor, his head resting on the coffee table. And Mrs. Cone was beside Sheba on the couch. Her wig was still on. Surrounding them, on the floor, the table, the couch, everywhere I could see, were all the books from the shelves. Izzy and I had been discussing alphabetizing the bookshelves but hadn't started yet. I had a moment of thinking that maybe this disshelving would make that task easier.

"Uh, Izzy wants me to stay with her tonight. She's scared."

"Excellent idea," Dr. Cone said.

"May I borrow a nightgown?"

"Absolutely!" Mrs. Cone started to stand up, but Sheba took her hand and pulled her back down to the couch.

"Mary Jane," Sheba said very seriously. "Go in my and Jimmy's room, go in the closet, and find the prettiest nightgown you see. Whatever one you like, you can have. But you have to choose the prettiest one. Do you understand? It's very important that you take the *best night-gown there*. Can you do that?"

"I think so." I wanted to ask which one was the best, but I knew I was inserting myself, interrupting, and if I didn't leave the room soon, an emotional explosion might happen right before me.

"Good. Only the best one."

"Okay. Good night." I turned to walk away.

"Good night, Mary Jane," Sheba said.

"Good night, Mary Jane," Mrs. Cone said.

"Good night, Mary Jane," Dr. Cone said.

And then Jimmy shouted, "Mary Jane, you are a saint and I fucked up! I'm a stupid fucking shit—"

Before he could say more, Sheba was outyelling him. I rushed up the stairs, my heart thumping, and hurried into Izzy's room.

Izzy sat up. "Did your mom say yes?" Her eyes were like night-lights, catching the glow from the streetlamp outside her window.

"Yes. I'm going to grab a nightgown and brush my teeth."

"You can use my toothbrush."

"I'll just use my finger."

"Okay."

"I'll be right back and then I'll get in bed with you and we'll shut the door and we can sing a song if you want. Or we can read *Madeline*. Or we can just go to sleep."

"And the witch won't come in. The ratio is two to one."

"Right, the witch won't come in. The ratio is too big for the witch to get in."

Sheba and Jimmy's room was tidy and organized. Dr. and Mrs. Cone hadn't managed to empty it, but they had managed to stack all their stuff in boxes pushed against one wall. The bed was made with a bright pink batik bed-spread. There were mismatched nightstands on either side. One held the books I'd seen Jimmy reading in the banquette in the morning: *Play It as It Lays* and *Fear and Loathing in Las Vegas*. The other had hand cream and face cream. On the ceiling, over the bed, hung another pink batik bedspread. I wondered if Mrs. Cone had done that, or if Sheba had.

I took a few steps into the bathroom and looked around. There was a giant claw-foot tub and a separate walk-in shower. The tile was Tiddlywinks-size pink and black circles, like what I imagined might be in a diner in the 1950s. On the pink marble vanity a framed mirror lay flat, like a tray. Two perfume bottles and many face creams sat on the mirror tray. I picked up Chanel No. 5. I'd heard of it, but had never seen an actual bottle. I sprayed it on my wrists and sniffed. It didn't smell like Sheba. The other bottle was cut glass with a stopper in it. I lifted the stopper and sniffed. That sort of smelled like Sheba, but not quite. I dipped the stopper and dabbed each of my wrists where I had sprayed the Chanel No. 5. I lifted my wrist to my nose. Now I smelled like Sheba. I sniffed again. Breathing in Sheba's scent made the world momentarily fall away.

I left my Sheba-scented bubble and hurried to the walk-in closet. The bar on one side of the closet held Jimmy's clothes. The bar on the other held Sheba's. Her clothes were arranged by type: dresses, tops, jumpsuits, night-gowns, and robes. Within each group they were arranged by color, lightest to darkest, left to right. I ran my hand along everything, feeling the variegated textures—satin, silk, leather, cotton.

When I got to the nightgowns and robes, I pulled them out one by one. Some were so sexy—with see-through lace bra tops and thigh-high slits—that I was embarrassed looking at them. My sex addiction roared, tingling through my body, and I hushed it down sternly.

Even the not-as-sexy nightgowns were beautiful. I worried I'd disappoint Sheba and pick the wrong one. And then my hand stopped on a white nightgown with lace straps and lace on the hem. The cotton was so soft, it felt like thick water running between my fingertips. I took off my shorts, T-shirt, and bra right there in the closet, and slipped the nightgown over my head. The breast panels were baggy on me, but other than that it fit me well. The cotton was so smooth against my skin, I wanted to roll around on the ground just to feel it more.

I folded my clothes and carried them out of Sheba and Jimmy's room and then down the stairs to the second floor. The shouting had stopped, and the conversational voices of the four grown-ups floated up like sound clouds. Also, the smell of marijuana wafted up. I wondered if Dr. and Mrs. Cone were smoking too. Or was it just Sheba and Jimmy?

I walked into Izzy's room and shut the door behind me. It took a second for my eyes to adjust and see that Izzy was still awake, her glowing eyes flashing on me.

"Everyone's calm," I said. "They worked it all out."

"Okay. Can we sleep now?"

"Yeah." I climbed into bed. Izzy's sheets were clean and stiff. We had washed and starch-ironed them only two days ago.

"I love you, Mary Jane." Izzy scooted in closer to me and pushed her head between my breast and my armpit. She breathed deeply and slowly, as if she were releasing something from far inside her body.

"I love you too," I whispered.

7

When I woke in the morning, I was surprised that I had slept so solidly and easily. At school we went on camping trips every year and I always came home exhausted and ready to sleep for a week straight. And when I slept at the twins' house, we stayed up late and then got up early. But in Izzy Cone's bed I slept better than I did in my own house.

Izzy was still pressed up against me, her mouth gaping open like a fish's. Her thick eyelashes looked wet and shiny and her red curls were plastered behind her head. I slipped out of the bed slowly, carefully, and dressed in my OP shorts, bra, T-shirt, and flip-flops.

I put the nightgown to my face and sniffed. It smelled like Sheba's perfume combination and not like anything I recognized as myself. With the nightgown in my hands, I left the room. The door to the third floor was closed. Dr. and Mrs. Cone's door was ajar and I could hear ocean-sounding snores coming from it. I went down the stairs slowly, sticking to the wall edge, where there was less creaking.

The living room floor was covered with scattered books. The air still smelled like a rubber eraser. On the coffee table was half of a broken dinner plate, the edges chalky white and craggy. On the plate were three stubbed-out joint ends. *Roaches,* Jimmy had told me in the car one night before he swallowed a lit one, just to make me and Sheba laugh.

I stood for a minute surveying the damage. I could start shelving the books then, or I could wait until Izzy woke up. We'd been talking about it so much that she might be hurt if I started without her. But I was slightly worried that if I didn't start systemizing the books soon, someone else would jump in and shelve them willy-nilly. Certainly not Dr. and Mrs. Cone; they were blind to chaos and disorder. Sheba, however, had a neat streak in her as strong as mine. No one did anything in the Cone house before breakfast, however, so I knew I had time. Maybe Izzy and I would start shelving when she woke up.

The dining room looked fine. Even the candlesticks with the white nubs of melted candle in them were exactly where they'd been last night. The record player was on the floor where Izzy and I had set it up. The records were still lined against the wall, now held up by two stone carvings I had found on the washing machine. One was the shape of a woman's torso and one the shape of a man's.

I tried to push open the swinging door to the kitchen, but it was stuck. I walked around the back way: dining room, living room, entrance hall, TV room. When I got to the open doorway to the kitchen, I gasped.

The kitchen was like a crime scene. Or like the kitchen on *The Poseidon Adventure* after the boat sinks. The floor was covered with broken dishes: plates, bowls, glasses, even the serving platter I had used for the chicken. On top of the glassware and crockery was food from the pantry: cereal boxes, graham crackers, Screaming Yellow Zonkers, oatmeal, flour, sugar, raisins. Everything. The cupboard doors were open and the shelves were mostly emptied. In some places the debris was heaped two or three feet high.

I tried to imagine the scene in my head. Sheba had been doing most of the hollering. But would she break all the dishes? And how did Mrs. Cone feel, watching her dishes get destroyed? What was Dr. Cone doing? Was he trying to medicate or calm or stop whoever was doing the breaking?

My mother entered my head. *Not in Roland Park,* she often said, as if all the ills of the world were contained in a cloud that just refused to hover over this little nook of northern Baltimore. But there I was, in Roland Park, and a big, heavy shattered-glass storm had landed. I imagined my mother's face, seeing this scene, her head pulled back, eyes widened, the nearly invisible scratches of her eyebrows lifted almost into her hairline. I remembered the single broken plate in my kitchen at the beginning of the summer and how serious that crime had seemed.

I looked at the closed kitchen door and envisioned Izzy forcing it open, just a bit, and then squeezing through and stepping into a pile of broken glass. Very carefully, I high-knee-stepped through the debris. I picked up a cookie sheet from the floor and used it to push aside the crackling heap that was blocking the door. Then I swung the door open, and pushed debris against it so it would be held that way.

I turned and went back to the TV room, and then to

the laundry room, where Izzy and I had organized mops and brooms, rain boots, snow boots, raincoats, umbrellas, roller skates, and a bike pump. I pulled on Mrs. Cone's orange rubber rain boots. They were too big, but I could walk easily enough in them. With a bucket, a mop, a broom, and a dustpan, I returned to the kitchen. Izzy was standing in the doorway on the dining room side, her mouth open in the shape of the letter O.

"Mary Jane! I woke up and you weren't there!"

"I'm right here."

"WHAT HAPPENED?!"

"I don't know. When the grown-ups wake up, they can tell us what happened."

Izzy lifted her arms. I waded over to her, picked her up, and walked her to the kitchen table. There were a few cracked and broken glasses on the bench seats, so I placed her on top of the table, which was miraculously clear.

"Everything is broken."

"I know. I'll clean up."

"What will we eat?"

"Hmmm." I went to the refrigerator and checked inside. Untouched. "Milk straight from the carton? And some Laughing Cow cheese. Okay?"

"Yes!"

I took out the entire circular container of Laughing Cow and the carton of milk and placed them on the table beside Izzy. "Have you ever had milk from the carton?" The twins drank milk like that in their house. When I tried it once in my own home, I was swiftly whacked on the back of my head by my mother. The milk spilled, of course, and I had to mop the whole kitchen floor as punishment.

"I can do it if my mom holds it for me. She does it all the time."

I knew this already, as I'd seen Mrs. Cone stand at the refrigerator and drink milk from the carton. I'd also watched her dip rolled slices of cheese into the mustard jar with the fridge door still open. I opened the cardboard corner of the carton and held it to Izzy's lips. She guzzled the milk. A bit dripped down her chin. Finding a napkin seemed too labor-intensive, so I wiped her mouth with my thumb. "Can you open the cheese yourself?"

"Yes." Izzy wiggled out a wedge from the box. "You pull the red string." She made her concentrating face and went to work.

I waded to the sink cupboard and got out a trash bag and gloves. With my gloved hands, I picked up the food items one by one. If it wasn't canned or sealed, I threw it away. If it was boxed, I examined it closely for any possible openings where shards of glass could have entered. The idea of Izzy taking a bite of oatmeal and swallowing a nearly invisible sliver of glass made me feel a little panicky. Izzy ate cheese and talked to me while I worked. Every now and then I returned to the table and fed her more milk. She seemed entirely untraumatized by the night before and I thought, *If she can handle this, then surely I can too.*

It was easy to scoop up the broken dishes with the dustpan. I dumped them into a trash bag. There were more *unbroken* dishes on the floor than I would have guessed. Probably the second layer, cushioned by what had already been thrown down.

I picked up a white coffee cup and turned it around to make sure there were no cracks. "Coffee mugs have the highest survival rate."

"What's a survival rate? Can I have more milk?"

I put the cup in the sink with the other whole dishes

and then went to Izzy and fed her milk. "It means they lived through the crash. Through being thrown."

"Are coffee cups alive?"

I laughed. "No. I'm using *lived* metaphorically. Or maybe anthropomorphically." I tried to remember the lessons from English class.

"What does that mean?"

"I'm pretending the coffee cups were alive when I say they weren't killed. But really what I'm saying is that of all the thrown dishes, they were the ones that most often landed without breaking."

"Why do you think the coffee cups weren't killed?"

It was a good question. I went back to the sink and pulled up an unbroken mug. Then I rinsed it to make sure there were no shards of glass in it, and brought it to the table. "Don't drink out of it until we really wash it. But let's look at it and see if we can figure it out."

Izzy took the cup and turned it in her hand. "Maybe a circle is harder to break?"

"Yeah, I bet that's it. You're so smart!" I leaned in and kissed the mop of Izzy's curls.

"But why?" Izzy asked. "Why is a circle harder to break?"

"Hmmm." I recalled something from school about an arch being the strongest shape. That was why all those old Roman bridges shaped like arches were still around, even though they were two thousand years old. But I couldn't remember why. Something about force, all sides pushing into each other and creating tension that binds. "When one of the grown-ups wakes up, let's have them explain it."

"Okay." Izzy got down to business on another wedge of cheese and I went back to my task.

At last four Hefty bags were full and lined up in the dining room. The benches around the table were clean, but I kept Izzy on top of the table. I swept the kitchen floor, twice over.

"Can I go on the floor now?" Izzy asked.

"Nope. I have to mop. You can sing to me while I mop."

"What should I sing?"

"Your number one absolute favorite song." I loaded the unbroken dishes into the dishwasher and then placed the mop bucket in the sink and poured in some Mr. Clean. Izzy tapped a beat on her forehead with one finger. She was quietly singing the beginning of many songs, like flipping through a card catalog, trying to find the right title. I turned the faucet to the bucket and filled it with water.

"Mary Jane! I have my song!"

I heaved the bucket out of the sink and onto the floor. "Should I count you in?"

"Yes! Wait. What's that mean?"

"You'll understand when I do it."

"Okay. Do it." Izzy gave me a very serious stare, anticipating the count-in.

"A one and a two and a three and a—" I pointed at Izzy and she belted out one of Jimmy's songs from an album that we'd now listened to many, many times. At the parts where Jimmy's voice turned to tossed gravel, Izzy tried to make her voice gravelly too.

I mopped the floor and sang along at the chorus. When the song ended, Izzy took a deep, shoulder-rising breath and then started all over again. She sang the song once more as I poured out the water and refilled the bucket for the second mop. Everyone walked barefoot in this house—double-mopping was essential.

We were singing Jimmy's song, I was harmonizing with Izzy's gravelly chorus, when Jimmy came into the kitchen. He wore his cutoff shorts and no shirt or shoes. I tried to look away from the Woody Woodpecker tattoo on his thigh, but then found myself staring at the leather-and-feather necklace nestled into the fur on his chest. I moved my head up higher to Jimmy's electric stare.

Jimmy was a tattooed drug addict who had used heroin just yesterday, and maybe destroyed this kitchen. Still, all the great things about him—including his handsomeness and charisma—remained as powerful as always. It was easy to see why Sheba loved him so much.

"Oh Jesus Christ, Mary Jane." Jimmy turned his head away from me and stared at the floor. Then the sink. Then at Izzy on the table. And finally back at me and then to the mop in my hand. His eyes were more sad than electric now. Even his bleached hair looked sad; it hung, as if windblown, over his eyes.

"Are you okay?" I asked.

"Christ almighty, Mary Jane. Izzy. Ah fuck!" Jimmy slapped his hand into his head.

Izzy stared at him, her big eyes moving from me to Jimmy and back to me. I put the mop in the bucket and leaned the handle against the counter. I didn't know what to do. Or to say. All this: the drugs, the breaking-things fight, and now the clear remorse were brand-new to me.

"Oh, Mary Jane." Jimmy was crying now. Real crying, tears tumbling down his cheeks. He stepped into the kitchen and pulled me into him and sobbed with his face buried into the top of my head. I'd never seen a man cry in my life. Not even in a movie.

Jimmy's shoulders shook and he made actual noises.

He was trying to talk, but the crying kept pumping out of him. Izzy hopped off the table and ran to us. She put one arm around me and one around Jimmy and buried her head between our thighs.

"I'm so sorry," Jimmy sobbed.

"It's okay, Jimmy, it's okay. We're not mad!" Izzy said.

I tried to speak, but it felt like there was a rolled ball of Wonder Bread stuck in my throat.

"You shouldn't have had to see this." Jimmy's words stuttered out through his tears.

"JIMMY! We're not mad! We love you. We're not angry." Izzy spoke for the two of us. I still couldn't get out a word.

Jimmy started crying harder and then tears were rolling down my face too. I tried not to make a sound, but I could feel little hiccups coming out of me.

"It's okay. It's okay." Izzy rubbed our legs with her tiny hands.

"It's fine, I swear," I finally said.

Jimmy pulled his head from mine, and held my face in his hands. "Oh Jesus, now I made you cry too."

"I'm fine." I sniffed. "I don't know why I'm crying." I laughed a little.

Jimmy stared at me, shaking his head; he wasn't crying now. Izzy rubbed our legs and studied our faces. I was sniffing and laughing and still crying too.

"I'm just so sorry. I really lost control."

"JIMMY, WE'RE NOT MAD AT YOU!" Izzy shouted. "Eat Laughing Cow with me, and Mary Jane will feed you milk too."

Jimmy looked down at Izzy and laughed. And then I really laughed. He picked up Izzy, kissed her cheeks, and carried her to the table. "Let me finish the mopping," he said to me.

"I'm almost done. I swear it's fine." I quickly grabbed the mop and went over the last corners while Jimmy and Izzy sat at the banquette and ate Laughing Cow. What had happened last night seemed so horrible. But after that cry, and then the laugh, I felt ridiculously happy.

"Do you want Mary Jane to hold the carton? She holds it good."

"Oh, little Izzy, carton is the only way we ever did it in West Virginia. I'm a pro." Jimmy picked up the milk carton and chugged. Then he held the carton to Izzy's mouth, at just the right angle so it wouldn't spill down her chin.

I emptied the bucket in the sink and took off my gloves, and then I scooted onto the bench next to Izzy. I picked up the carton of milk, held it to my mouth, and chugged and chugged and chugged.

"Look how good Mary Jane is!" Izzy pointed at my face. I nodded and kept chugging. I felt like I was breaking the law. And it made me smile.

Over the next hour, everyone drifted into the kitchen. Sheba said since I had cleaned the kitchen, I wasn't allowed to cook for anyone that day. Izzy wondered how'd we eat if I didn't cook, which made Dr. Cone say, "Don't you remember how we ate *before* Mary Jane joined the family?" The words *joined the family* pulsated in my head. In my heart. Sheba got up and made omelets with onions, cheddar cheese, and green peppers. I knew I'd be copying that recipe soon. Everything was served on pink paper plates that were left over from Izzy's birthday party last May.

There was some discussion about the broken dishes. Dr. Cone brought up Buddhism and detachment and the idea that they were just things and had no spiritual value.

I wondered if he still counted as Jewish since he really seemed to believe in Buddha more than God. Mrs. Cone said she hated all those dishes anyway, as they had been given to her by her mother and symbolized her mother's need to impose her value system on Mrs. Cone. I tuned out of the conversation for a while as I thought over those ideas. It had never before occurred to me that sometimes dishes weren't just dishes, that things could represent ideas in more powerful ways than the ideas themselves.

When I tuned back in, Sheba was insisting that she pay to replace all the dishes. She asked Mrs. Cone where she should buy the new ones.

"Oh." Mrs. Cone shrugged. "It's not something I've ever done. I don't get into that kind of stuff."

Dr. Cone said, "I'd be happy if we used paper plates for the rest of our years. Or ate off newspaper to create less waste."

"Mary Jane," Sheba said. "Where does your mother buy things like dishes?"

"I think most people in Roland Park go to Smyth," I said.

"Of course!" Mrs. Cone nodded. "I feel like a hippie-alien every time I walk into that place. But yes, we can find dishes there."

Jimmy said, "When I was growing up, all of our glasses were from the gas station."

Gas stations still offered free glasses when you filled up, but my mother and father never accepted them, no matter how much I begged. I'd given up wanting them.

"I have gas station glasses with Bugs Bunny on them!" Izzy said, and then her face changed as she remembered that all the glasses were now broken.

"I'm so sorry," Jimmy said. He looked pained.

"No one needs gas station glasses," Dr. Cone said.

"JIMMY!" Izzy shouted. "I'M NOT MAD!"

Everyone laughed and then Jimmy said, "So, uh, I'll clean the living room."

Dr. Cone said, "Yes. I think . . . Well, I think it will make you feel better."

Izzy said, "Mary Jane and me were gonna do the alphabet with the books."

"We were going to alphabetize the bookshelves," I clarified.

Mrs. Cone shook her head and smiled. "Mary Jane, I don't know what to make of you!"

Sheba leaned over and wrapped her arm around me. "You sort of remind me of myself."

"Really?" Sheba was so glamorous. And I couldn't have described what made any human sexy, but I knew that Sheba was exactly that. Sexy. I wasn't, as far as I could tell, glamorous or sexy in any way. Though maybe I was a sex addict. Would that make me sexy?

"Yeah. Your desire for order. Clarity," Sheba said. "The need to wrangle chaos into something that can be managed."

"What's chaos?" Izzy asked.

"The books on the living room floor," Dr. Cone said.

"The kitchen when we went to bed last night," Mrs. Cone said.

"The shit swirling in my brain," Jimmy said.

After breakfast, Izzy, Jimmy, and I went into the living room. I brought a spiral notebook and a red crayon. I was going to write out the alphabet for Izzy, so she could see the order without having to sing through the song.

"The letter A comes first." I wrote a giant red A on the first page of the notebook.

Izzy dropped down to the ground like a marionnette who had just had her strings cut. "How do you say *A* in French?" Izzy asked. In our nightly reading of the book *Madeline,* I sometimes replaced English words with French ones (like all the girls at Roland Park Country School, I'd been studying French since kindergarten) and this thrilled Izzy.

I pushed some books aside and kneeled on the floor. "*Ah,* like the doctor put a tongue depressor in your mouth and said, *Say ah.*"

"*Ah,*" Izzy said.

"I've got an idea." Jimmy nudged away a few hardcovers with the side of his bare foot and then sat on the ground beside me. "For each letter, we take turns coming up with a song that starts with that letter. And if you can't think of a song, you get a point. The person who has the most points loses."

"*A, B, C, D,*" Izzy sang. "I won."

"Not yet," Jimmy said. "Wait till we start working. When we played this as kids, we couldn't begin until the car was moving."

"Did your mom and grandma play too?" I asked.

"Yeah. Granny only sang church songs. She just loved when it was her turn on the letter *J.*"

I worried Jimmy would see me as out of touch like his granny. The only songs I knew were from church, Camp Fire Girls, the twins' house, or the Broadway soundtracks in my house. Of course, I knew some of Jimmy's songs now that Izzy and I had played his records so many times. But I figured he wouldn't want to hear me sing Running Water songs in this game.

"Okay. Let's start NOW!" Izzy held a book above her head like a trophy.

"Hold on!" I raised my hand like I was in school. Jimmy winked and pointed at me.

"Mary Jane?"

"Before we put the books on the shelves, we need to put them in alphabetical piles on the floor. All the *A* authors, all the *B*s, etc. Then we'll alphabetize each pile. After that, we'll shelve them."

Izzy lowered the book and held it before her face. She squinted as she examined the cover "*S*. Right?" It was by Saul Bellow.

"That book's great," Jimmy said. "But *Augie March* is even better."

"*S* was a good try," I said. "But you have to look at the first letter of the last name. I put my pointer finger on the last name.

"*B?*"

"Excellent! Now put all the *B* books"—I wrote a giant *B* on a piece of paper, then stood and cleared a spot on the far wall—"here." I laid the *B* down on the ground.

Izzy stepped over the books and placed *Henderson the Rain King* in front of the paper with the *B*, and then she started singing "*A, B, Cs*" again to get Jimmy's game going. Jimmy sang along, poking through books and making a separate pile of his favorites that he said I should try to read. I promised I would, but didn't look through any of them just then as I was busy writing out the alphabet and finding space for the lettered papers around the room.

When it was Jimmy's turn, he sang "Bye Bye Blackbird." I harmonized and Izzy just bopped her head as she didn't know the words.

I paused nervously at my turn. Then I remembered "Chantilly Lace," a song from the '50s that I knew from

an album the twins had. If Jimmy could sing "Bye Bye
Blackbird," then "Chantilly Lace" wasn't so bad. Izzy
didn't know this one either, but she continued to bounce
her head to the beat. Jimmy sang with me, in a cartoony,
low voice, just like the Big Bopper—the guy who sings it
on the album.

We were at songs that started with the letter *R* when
Mrs. Cone and Sheba came into the living room.

"I want to help," Sheba said.

"Look at the last name," Izzy said. "When you find
the last name, you read the letter, okay? And then you
look for the EXACT same letter on the paper and you put
the book there. We're alphabetting. Get it?"

"I think so," Sheba said.

"Me too." Mrs. Cone rubbed Izzy's head and then
started picking through the books.

Jimmy explained the song game and Sheba immediately said "Rhinestone Cowboy."

"Ah, c'mon! No Glen," Jimmy said.

"He was before your time, baby. You know I don't love
him anymore." Sheba was staring Jimmy down. They
both looked very serious. Had Sheba been a couple with
Glen Campbell and did Jimmy hate him because of that?
I was scared for a second that they were going to fight
again, but soon enough, Jimmy smiled and crossed the
room so he was standing right in front of Sheba. And
then they locked their faces together, like they had noses
made of magnets, and they kissed, deep and wet.

I turned my head and looked away. Izzy didn't
seem to notice. Mrs. Cone watched them with a yearn-
ing but slightly anxious look in her eyes. I wondered if
she wanted to be Sheba kissing Jimmy. Or maybe she

wanted Dr. Cone to kiss her that way. Kissing like that seemed so advanced. Maybe one day I'd just stand lip to lip with someone. For starters.

The longer the kissing went on, the more my face burned. Finally Izzy broke the silence by singing "Rhinestone Cowboy." I knew the words too, because the twins' mother owned all of Glen Campbell's records. When we got to the chorus, Sheba and Jimmy finally stopped kissing and joined in. Mrs. Cone was singing too, but her mind seemed elsewhere. Her face went from the books to Jimmy to the books to Sheba.

We were on the letter *V* when I had to sing again.

"Uh . . . uh . . ." All I could think of was *"My Victory"* from church. This pained me so much that I considered taking the point and passing my turn.

"No church songs!" Izzy said, as if she could see into my head.

"Oh! Wait. What about 'Kumala Vista'? We'll go by the last word in the title, like the last names on books. V for *Vista*." I was so relieved to *not* sing a church song that I didn't mind singing a Camp Fire Girls song.

Everyone stopped what they were doing and looked at me. I kneeled on the ground and slapped my knees twice and then my hands together to get the beat. In my head it sounded like *cha-cha, pop, cha-cha, pop. . . .*

Izzy kneeled and clapped along. And then Jimmy, Sheba, and Mrs. Cone did too.

"Well, shit, Mary Jane, give us the words, will ya?" Jimmy said, smiling.

"You have to repeat after me," I said. "And follow my hand motions, too."

"Oh, I love this," Sheba said. "Is this from that one time you went to sleepaway camp?"

"It's from Camp Fire Girls. Ready? Repeat after me: *FLEA!*"

"*FLEA!*" they all repeated.

"*FLEA FLY!*"

"*Flea fly!*"

"*FLEA FLY FLOW!*"

"*Flea fly flow!*"

"*Kumala!*"

"*Kumala!*"

"*Vista!*"

"*Vista!*"

"*Kumala, kumala, kumala vista!*" I sang in the melody.

"*Kumala, kumala, kumala vista!*"

"*Oh, no, no, no not sevista!*"

"*Oh, no, no, no not sevista!*"

When we got to the end, where you pretend to scratch your body all over, Dr. Cone came into the living room. He sat on the couch and watched us as if we were monkeys in a zoo, his head tilted.

Everyone laughed when the song ended. It was Izzy's turn to pick the next song and she said, "I want to do 'Kumala Vista' again." And so we did.

Mrs. Cone, Sheba, and Jimmy all wore wigs that night to go out to dinner at Morgan Millard, the only restaurant in Roland Park. Jimmy put on one of Dr. Cone's suits. It was blue and had wide lapels and bell-bottom pants. He didn't wear a tie, but he did wear a starched button-down, with the top three buttons open.

"What do you think?" Jimmy asked me as we walked to the car. "Anyone gonna recognize me?"

"No." But I did think people would look at him. His

wig was black and straight, with bangs across the front. And he was wearing leather sandals. I'd never in my life seen anyone wear leather sandals with a suit.

Mrs. Cone and Sheba were wearing the Swedish sister wigs again. Dr. Cone looked just like himself with his fuzzy, irregular sideburns eating up half his face. I put Izzy in a flouncy pink dress and white patent leather shoes. Just for fun. And Sheba gave me one of her dresses to wear. Also just for fun. It was red with a pattern of black spiderwebs all over it. The dress wasn't cut low, but the straps were thinner than my bra straps, so it felt like I was being a bit risqué. Sheba was so much taller than I was, the dress probably fell to her upper thigh. On me, it modestly hit my knee.

Dr. and Mrs. Cone got in the front seat, and the rest of us got in the back. Sheba sat by one door, Jimmy sat by the other. Izzy and I squished in the middle. Everyone was talking at once, happily, excitedly. We had finished the bookshelves. Jimmy had recommitted himself to sobriety. And we were going out to a restaurant so no one would have to make dinner or clean up after it.

The car was warm and dark; streetlights cast moving shadows over us like ghosts dancing across our laps. Sheba leaned in close and whispered in my ear, "I think you should just take off the bra."

"I've never done that," I whispered, even lower. I really didn't want Dr. Cone or Jimmy to know what we were discussing.

"The dress will look better. Here. Lean forward."

I leaned forward and Sheba reached down the back of the dress and unhooked my bra. I quickly slipped my arms out of the straps and then pulled the bra out from the neckline. I was definitely being risqué now, though no one seemed to notice. Jimmy and Izzy were singing "Kumala Vista" again, and Dr. and Mrs. Cone were talking about what to do if they ran into someone they knew.

Sheba grabbed the bra and shoved it into her shiny pink handbag. I bit my lip and tried not to laugh. It felt funny to be braless in public: loose and airy. For a second I imagined my nipples having mouths, breathing in oxygen for the first time. I giggled. Sheba did too.

"Our secret." She pinched my knee.

Beanie Jones and Mr. Jones were leaving Morgan Millard just as we were walking in. He was as handsome as she was pretty, but there was a waxiness to his skin and a rubberiness to his lips. Even his thick light brown hair looked fake. It was parted to the side and as neat as a wig.

"Hi, Beanie Jones!" Izzy said. And then she gasped and turned her face into my belly as she remembered the secret of Jimmy and Sheba.

"Hi!" I nervously waved.

"Hello, hello!" Beanie Jones had a too-big smile and she nodded as she examined wigged Sheba, then wigged Jimmy, and lastly, wigged Mrs. Cone.

"Tommy Jones." Mr. Jones stuck out his hand and shook Dr. Cone's hand.

"Richard Cone. We're up the street from you," Dr. Cone said. He seemed stiff, uncomfortable. Jimmy wandered away and stood at the maître d' podium with his back to us.

"I'm so glad to finally meet you in person!" Beanie

Jones said. "It's taken a while to meet all the new neigh-bors, what with people gone for the summer."

"Thank you so much for the angel food cake!" Mrs. Cone's voice was higher and more singsong than usual. As if she were overacting in a church play.

"Are you neighbors too?" Beanie Jones put her face so close to Sheba's, she could have licked her.

"Jenny Johnson. We're visiting from Newport, Rhode Island." Sheba's voice was nasally, low, and filtered through pinched lips. It reminded me of Thurston Howell III's voice on *Gilligan's Island.* Izzy's head bopped and her lips made a little *pfft* sound as she tried not to laugh.

"Jenny Johnson, so nice to meet you!" Beanie Jones grinned. Mr. Jones was talking to Dr. Cone, who kept glancing away at Jimmy. "And your husband is?"

"Johnny Johnson," Sheba said.

The maître d' approached us with menus. Jimmy lurked behind him. Sheba said to Beanie Jones, "Dah-ling, it was lovely to meet you and your husband. Do let us know if you're ever in the Newport area."

"Yes, I'd love to visit—"

"See you around the neighborhood!" Mrs. Cone cut off Beanie Jones with her overacting voice.

Izzy and I both waved and Dr. Cone shook Mr. Jones's hand before he followed the rest of us to the table.

After being seated, we looked at each other with pursed lips or big, gaping smiles. No one spoke for a few seconds as Mrs. Cone leaned toward the window and looked out to make sure Beanie and Mr. Jones were gone. When she sat back in her chair and started giggling, we all fell apart laughing. Izzy laughed so hard, she began hiccuping and that made us laugh even more.

Sheba kept the joke going all night. By the time dessert was being served, everyone was talking like Jenny Johnson of Newport, Rhode Island, using words no one in the household used, like *trousers* and *de rigueur* and *on the contrary, my dear.*

When Dr. Cone pulled up the station wagon in front of my house, I thought I might weep. I wanted to stay with everyone, put on that water-soft nightgown, and sleep in Izzy's plush bed. I wanted to wake up in that house, where I felt like I existed as a real person with thoughts and feelings and abilities.

Mrs. Cone leaned over the seat and gave me a kiss goodbye on the cheek. Then Jimmy leaned over Izzy and kissed the top of my head. Sheba kissed my cheeks and Izzy climbed onto my lap and kissed me all over my face. "Mary Jane, I'm going to miss you SO MUCH!"

"I'll be back before breakfast on Monday!" I said cheerfully. But I wanted to kiss Izzy all over her face and say the same thing to her.

Sheba got out and stood by the open door. "See you Monday, doll."

"Can I have my bra?" I whispered. I'd have to put it on before I entered the house.

"Yes!" She dug into her purse and handed it to me.

"I left your nightgown on top of the washing machine, but I never started a load because we were so busy with the books and everything."

"No, you have to keep it! Take it home with you. It's yours now!" Sheba leaned in and held me for a second before kissing me again on the cheek.

I watched the car drive away, then I walked to the darkness at the side of the house, out of reach of the porch light. My hands shook as I lowered the straps of the dress and put on my bra. It took a few seconds to get the hooks latched in the back. Once they were fastened, I pulled up the straps of the dress and then walked inside.

8

On Saturday, I helped my mother in the garden. She talked about the neighbors: who she'd seen, who was away at the Eastern Shore or Rehoboth Beach, and who had played in her tennis foursome. This reporting was interrupted periodically by instructions on how to properly deadhead flowers and pull weeds. I listened to all of it, the stories and the directives, but my mind was on the Cones, Jimmy, and Sheba. I felt like the outline of a fourteen-year-old girl pulling weeds and nodding at her mother.

At four o'clock my mother and I changed into dresses. We were due at the Elkridge Club at four thirty. She was meeting friends on the porch for tea and lemonade before our six o'clock dinner reservation with my dad, who had been at the club all day playing golf.

As we were about to walk out the door, my mother looked me up and down. "Mary Jane, is there something you can do with your hair?"

I pushed my hair behind my ears. "Should I put on a headband?"

"Headband, ponytail, braids. Just don't walk around as if you're a child with no mother looking after you."

I ran upstairs, went into my bathroom, and opened the drawer that held my brush, comb, and hair bands. I put on a blue floral headband that matched my light blue dress, and examined myself in the mirror. With my hair pushed back like that, my forehead looked broader, and my dark eyebrows stood out. Just then, I could see that maybe someone might notice me someday: my smooth skin, my wide mouth, my orangey eyes.

"Mary Jane!" my mother called from downstairs. "Do not dillydally!"

My mother and I were silent in the car on the way to Elkridge. Just as we pulled into the lot, she asked, "Have you figured out which club the Cones belong to?"

"Well, Mrs. Cone isn't Jewish. And Dr. Cone is Jewish, but he's really a—" I stopped myself before I said *Buddhist*. My mother might think a Buddhist was worse than a Jew.

"Really a what?"

"Well, he prays but he doesn't seem so Jewish. And she's Presbyterian, like us."

"How do you like that! I wonder how their families deal with that."

"I'm not sure. Their parents both live in other towns. No one's around to help."

"Maybe they don't want to because it's a mixed marriage."

"Yeah, maybe." I didn't want to betray Mrs. Cone's

trust and tell my mother that Mrs. Cone's parents didn't talk to her specifically because Dr. Cone was Jewish.

"So what is Izzy? Presbyterian or Jewish?"

"I guess she's both."

"Does Mrs. Cone take her to church?"

"Mrs. Cone is sick, remember?" The lies came out so smoothly now, I barely thought about them.

"Before. Did she take her to church before?"

"I don't know, Mom. Right now no one is going to church."

"Hmm. You'd think with her sick, now would be the time to go to church."

"I guess."

"We'll pray for her tomorrow."

Lately all my prayers had been for Jimmy to get better and for me to not be a sex addict. "Okay. That would be nice. I'll tell her on Monday."

While my mother and her friends drank iced tea and lemonade on the porch, I stared out at the vast green lawn and watched the men play golf. I'd been coming to the club my entire life and had never seen it the way I did that day. What in the past had seemed normal suddenly felt abnormally hushed, quiet, and contained. It was like we were in a play that went on forever and ever without any dramatic tension. The waiters and waitresses, bartenders and busboys at Elkridge were Black men and women. I'd seen and known many of them since I'd first started walking. But it wasn't until this day with my mother that I could see myself, my mother, and her friends the way the employees might. What did they think of all these quiet white people? What did they think of the pastel-colored dresses and pants and the hairdos that were frozen in place with Aqua Net and hair bands? What did they think about working in a place that wouldn't accept them as members?

We'd learned about the civil rights movement in school. It made me feel hopeful, like change was happening all around us. But sitting at Elkridge that day, I felt stuck in a time-warp atrium of segregated politeness.

At dinner that night, my mother told my father about the Cones' mixed marriage.

"Hm." My dad sawed off a thumb-size bite of steak. "How can he play golf?"

"How can he play golf?" I repeated. I didn't understand what golf had to do with it.

"The Jew clubs won't take him because of his wife. And the normal clubs won't take him because he's a Jew."

When I didn't answer quickly enough, my mother said, "Your father is speaking to you, Mary Jane."

"I don't think Dr. Cone plays golf," I said. In all my organizing and searching of the Cone house, I'd never seen golf clubs. Even though this was a deflection, it wasn't a lie.

My dad shrugged. Chewed. Stared down his steak. I forced in another bite of lasagna.

"We're going to pray for Mrs. Cone on Sunday." My mother trimmed off a rim of fat from her steak. It looked like a thick white worm.

"Why are all the people who work here Black?" I asked, not looking up from my lasagna.

My mother's face shot toward me with the speed of a bullet. "What kind of a question is that?"

"Good employees." My dad put another thumb of steak in his mouth.

"I just mean, well, don't you think it's strange that

Black people work here but aren't allowed to join? Why don't white people work here?"

My mother put down her fork and knife and laid both her palms on the table. "Is this appropriate dinner table talk?"

My dad sawed away at a bloody center bite. "Ted is white."

"He's your caddie."

"Yes, he is." Dad spoke while chewing.

My mother picked up her fork and knife and went after another worm of fat. "I don't think this is appropriate dinner table talk."

"Why don't you have a caddie who's Black? Why is the bartender Black but not your caddie?"

My mother put down her fork and knife again. "Mary Jane! What has gotten into you?"

My father stabbed his fork and knife into the meat. He looked directly at me. It was so unusual that I could only look back for a couple of seconds before I turned my head toward my lap. Finally Dad said, "The bartender, Billy, makes the best Manhattan this side of the Mississippi. *That's* why he's the bartender. And Ted is a damn good caddie. If you can find me a Black man who can caddie like Ted, I'll take him. And if you can find me a white man who can mix a drink like Billy, I'll take him." It was the most I'd heard my dad say in a long time, maybe ever. Perhaps it was because we'd never discussed golf or drinks before.

"If Billy wanted to join the club, would you let him?" I looked up from my lap.

"Not up to me." My father started sawing again. "But the club rules say that no, he can't join."

"I don't approve of this conversation." My mother had

lowered her voice and slitted her eyes. I could tell she was worried someone might overhear us.

"But I will tell you this, Mary Jane"—Dad put another bite in his mouth—"if we had to let another race into the club, I'd rather have a Black than a Jew."

"Can we *please* change the topic?" my mother asked.

My father pushed his chair back and sat straighter. "Most Black men know their place. They don't assume anything. They're a pleasure to be with. The Jews, now. The Jews think they're smarter than everyone else. And that makes them unpleasant, untrustworthy, and unreliable."

I looked back and forth between my mother and father. If you had asked me at the beginning of the summer if I knew my parents well, I would have said yes. But these two people sitting here were utterly foreign to me. In school we'd learned about anti-Semitism, the Holocaust, racism, and the civil rights movement. What we'd never learned was that sometimes ideas of racism and anti-Semitism were sparked to life by the very people you lived with.

"I don't think it's right that Black men should have *a place to know* when they're around you," I said. "And Dr. Cone is none of those words you used to describe Jewish people." My lips quaked. This was the first time I'd ever voiced a disagreement with my father.

Dad turned his head toward me. "You don't know him, Mary Jane. You work for him." He went back to his steak.

What my father said about my knowing Dr. Cone stuck in my mind. I did think I knew him. Was I wrong? Was I just an employee to the Cones, and was their affection for me something like my father's affection for Billy the bartender? Did they only like me when I *knew my place*?

"Are you done?" my mother asked. She meant was I done talking. And, really, she wasn't asking.

"Yes," I said. "I'm done."

The kids were restless at Sunday school, so my mother started playing "Rise and Shine" on the guitar. I wondered if the Cones would mind if I taught the song to Izzy. Mrs. Cone seemed disapproving of the church and Dr. Cone was a Buddhist Jew. But Izzy would love the rhymes and naming all the animals on Noah's ark. And Jesus never even got a mention, so maybe they'd think it was okay.

After Sunday school my mother walked home to drop off her guitar and I hurried to choir practice. Mr. Forge, the choir director, rapidly clapped his hands together as I approached. "Hurrah!" he said. "Our greatest voice is here!" He was an enthusiastic man who smiled often and bounced on his toes when he conducted. When I saw Liberace on television, I thought of Mr. Forge. They had a similar exuberance. A like-minded festiveness.

When it was time for the service, I put on my red robe, waited for the other choir members to sit, and then took the empty front-row choir chair beside the pulpit. I watched my mother chat with other mothers as she made her way down the aisle to the second pew from the front. My father slowly stepped behind my mom. His tie knot bulged at his neck.

Usually I listened carefully at church, but that day I drifted in and out. When it was time for the first song, "Dona Nobis Pacem," Mr. Forge put his pitch pipe to his mouth and played G, the first note. He pointed in order to me, Mrs. Lubowski, and Mrs. Randall. He meant that we three were to sing the opening lines. The song was a canon, a round, and with each additional verse, more voices would be added in until the entire choir was singing.

Mrs. Randall put her hand on her throat and shook her head. She'd been complaining of a cold when we'd first sat down. Mr. Forge nodded at her, and then looked at me and waved his hands upward. I stood, as did Mrs. Lubowski. When directed, I shut my eyes and sang: "*Dona nobis pacem pacem, dona nobis pa-a-a-a-cem. . . .*" I thought of Jimmy as I sang, and the peace he would feel if his addiction faded away, left his body.

Just as the song was picking up, I looked out at the congregation. My father was staring off into space, as usual. My mother was staring up at me, her head tilted, her mouth closed with a thin-lipped smile.

I looked past my parents, down the aisles, and then my heart flipped around and I almost spit out a burst of laughter. Seated in the back row, in matching black pixie-cut wigs, were Sheba and Jimmy. They had huge smiles painted across their faces and were moving their heads to the music. I could see that Sheba was singing along. She looked far more pleased with me than my mother did. And Jimmy looked totally relaxed and joyful. Like this was a space where he didn't think about doing drugs or breaking dishes or throwing books.

When the song was over, I smiled at them. Sheba lifted her hands and gave me a silent applause. Jimmy lifted one fist and mouthed, *Right on!*

Sheba and Jimmy snuck out before the service ended. As I walked home with my parents, I couldn't stop thinking about the way they had looked at me while I sang: as if I mattered, as if I were *seen*. My father wasn't talking, as usual, but I didn't feel the weight of his silence. My mother was talking, as usual, but I could barely hear her palaver.

Mom was making a pork roast for dinner that night. I paid close attention so I could make it for the Cones on Monday. I wondered if they had a meat thermometer; I couldn't recall seeing one during my many organizing and cleaning sprees.

After I set the table, I stood alone in the dining room and looked at President Ford on the wall. The words *sex addict* knocked around my head, like my brain wanted to put the worst thing I could think of in front of the face of our president.

"Mary Jane!" my mother called.

I went to the kitchen and put on the yellow quilted oven mitts I'd gotten for Christmas last year. Together, my mother and I placed all the food on the table: pork roast, mashed potatoes, buttered peas and carrots, Bisquick rolls and butter.

My mother sat and put her napkin in her lap. I sat and put my napkin in my lap. We both looked in the direction of the living room, where my father was in his chair, reading the Sunday paper.

"I don't know why they sing songs from that *Jesus Christ Superstar.*" My mother was referring to the third song we'd sung, "Hosanna." She didn't like *Jesus Christ Superstar,* though she'd never seen it. I hadn't seen it either, but we had the record from the Show Tunes of the Month Club. When I played it, I had to turn the volume real low.

"I think if you heard the whole record, you'd like it."

"*Godspell, Jesus Christ Superstar.* What are people thinking? They don't show respect for the church."

I remembered Sheba's and Jimmy's faces one night when we sat in the car and sang *Godspell* songs. They both knew all the words to every song. Jimmy was so into it, he lifted his foot and stubbed out the joint into the tread of his sandal. And I could tell by the way Sheba shut her eyes at certain lines that she respected the church.

My father entered the room. He folded his newspaper in half, set it on the table beside his plate, and sat. As always, he surveyed the food before putting his hands in the prayer position. My mother and I put our hands in the prayer position too. I shut my eyes.

My father said, "Thank you, Jesus, for this food on our table and for my wonderful wife and obedient child. God bless this family, God bless our relatives in Idaho, God bless President Ford and his family, and God bless the United States of America."

"And God bless everyone in the Cone household and may all their illnesses be"—I paused as I tried to come up with the best word—"eradicated."

My father glanced at me for just a second. And then, as if my voice weren't strong enough to reach God's ears, he abridged my prayer with, "Health to the Cones. Amen."

"Amen," my mother and I both said.

My mother stood and served my father while he removed his tie. "Is someone else in the house sick? I don't want you going over there if everyone is sick."

"I just want to make sure we cover everyone under that roof."

"If you make the pork roast tomorrow, be sure it's cooked all the way through. Her body likely can't handle undercooked meat."

"Okay."

"I'll come up and check the roast before you serve it."

"They have a meat thermometer. She really doesn't like visitors."

"Peanut farmer," my father mumbled to the paper.

"Is she losing her hair?" my mother asked.

"She has been wearing wigs."

"Are they tasteful?"

"Yes."

"I would wear a wig that looked just like my hair so that no one would know it was a wig." My mother's blond hair was shoulder-length, thick, and stiff. It was like a cap. Or, really, like a wig.

"She's been wearing a long blond wig mostly."

My mother shook her head in disapproval.

On Monday I ran to the Cones', my flip-flops making a slapping sound. When I got to their house, I stood on the porch a minute and caught my breath. I didn't want anyone to know I'd run all the way; it was embarrassing to think of how badly I wanted to be there.

When I finally opened the front door, I found Izzy and Jimmy sitting at the banquette in the kitchen. Jimmy had a guitar in his hands and was making up a song about Izzy. Izzy was bouncing her head around like she was at a concert.

"Izzy! Izzy!" Jimmy sang. *"She makes me dizzyyyyyy with LOVE!"*

"MARY JANE!" Izzy jumped off the banquette and climbed up into my arms. "Jimmy's singing a song about me!"

"I heard." I kissed Izzy's curls. Her head smelled loamy and dank. Her last bath must have been Friday, before we went out to dinner.

"Now sing about Mary Jane!" Izzy monkeyed out of my arms and returned to the banquette. I went to the refrigerator and took out the eggs. Jimmy plucked out a tune on his guitar. He was humming.

"Oh!" I turned to Jimmy. "Thank you for coming to church."

"I hate church." Jimmy kept plucking. "But Sheba loves it. And I have to admit, it was worth it just to hear you sing. You were motherfuckin' beautiful, Mary Jane. I could pick out your voice above the others. Totally gorgeous."

I swallowed hard and blushed, then mumbled a thank-you and turned to the cupboards to busy myself. When I opened the upper cupboards, I found new dishes—white with a painted blue pattern of onions and leaves—and new glasses. The lower cupboards where I had put mixing bowls and roasting pans were still pretty empty, though a set of metal mixing bowls and some metal roasting pans had survived the purge.

Jimmy started singing. *"Mary Jane, she ain't so plain, my dear sweet Mary Jane."*

My heart banged. When I felt steadier, I turned to look at Jimmy. He smiled and did some picking, his fingers moving fast on the strings. Then he continued, *"That down-home girl, Mary Jane, makin' eggs, on her two strong legs."*

"BIRDS IN A NESSSST!" Izzy sang, and I laughed.

"MARY JANE!" Jimmy belted it out like he was sing-

ing to a stadium. *"She feeeeds us, but she ain't never, ever, ever, ever, ever tried to bleeeeeeed us."*

I cracked an egg into a metal bowl to start the pancake batter. Izzy clapped her hands and bounced around. She fed Jimmy lines for his song that he enthusiastically sang back to her as if she were Stephen Sondheim.

When Dr. Cone came down, I got up to make him a bird in the nest. "I like the new dishes," I said.

"Ah. Yes." Dr. Cone smiled. "Sheba and Bonnie picked them out. Mary Jane, has anyone told you about the beach house?"

"We're going to the beach for a whole week. That's seven days!" Izzy shouted.

"Oh yeah?" My body felt like it was an old, deflating party balloon. I had just spent a tortured weekend at home. What would I do for a week without the Cones and Jimmy and Sheba? How could I take seven full days with my mother?

"Yeah, we're borrowing the Flemings' house on Indian Dunes in Dewey Beach. It's a big place, lots of bedrooms and bathrooms. Right on the ocean."

"That so nice," I pushed out the words.

"It's a private stretch of beach too. And, you know, I don't believe in the privatization of certain areas—everyone should enjoy the sand, the water, the dunes—and it's better for us as people if we don't attach to things." Dr. Cone put down his fork, as if to rest for a minute. "But Jimmy and Sheba do need privacy, so I'll accept the private beach in honor of them."

"Jimmy can't addict on a private beach. Right?" Izzy looked up at her dad.

Dr. Cone smiled at her, then leaned over and kissed her several times on her cheeks and forehead. "Right.

And we can meditate there. Take long walks. Really incorporate some mind-and-body unity into the therapy."

"That sounds perfect." I blinked back my grief and started another bird in a nest.

As if on cue, Mrs. Cone came into the kitchen, wearing cutoff shorts and a tank top. "Mary Jane! Did you see the new dishes?"

"They're lovely." I could barely muster a smile. I put the bird in a nest on a new plate and slid it onto the table for Mrs. Cone, then started another batch.

"Oh, everyone's favorite! Birds in a nest." Mrs. Cone sat and started eating.

"Jimmy wrote a song called 'Mary Jane.'" Izzy climbed over her father's lap and nestled between her parents. Mrs. Cone kissed her all over her face, just as Dr. Cone had done.

Jimmy was singing softly, strumming out chords, picking out little rifts. Mrs. Cone stopped kissing Izzy and watched him closely. She looked like she wanted to kiss him the way she'd just kissed Izzy.

"Jimmy, do you want another one?" I asked.

"MARY JANE!" Jimmy sang. *"'Cause one bird in a nest will never, ever, ever, ever do, Mary Jane makes a second one tooooooo. . . ."*

I picked up Jimmy's plate and refilled it. Sheba came into the kitchen wearing a red terry-cloth romper, white knee socks, and red tennis shoes. In her hair was a thick red elastic hairband. She looked like she'd popped out of a magazine. Or off a record cover. "Mary Jane, how was your weekend?" Without waiting for me to reply, she added, "Did you hear about the beach?"

"Yeah. You all will have so much fun." I put the last bird in a nest on a plate for Sheba.

"Well, you'll come, won't you?" Sheba asked. Everyone looked at me.

"Oh," I said. My shriveled-up heart started to inflate. "I didn't know I was invited."

"Of course you're invited," Dr. Cone said. "You're part of the family now."

I felt my eyes tear up, and quickly turned to the stove so no one could see. "Oh okay, yes, I'd love to come." My mother's face flashed in my mind and I felt slightly ill. Almost dizzy. What if she wouldn't let me go?

"Mary Jane, I don't want to go anywhere without you!" Izzy climbed off the banquette and hugged the backs of my legs. Her grip steadied me. My mother vanished from my thoughts.

Later that day, when Izzy and I were home from Eddie's, I braced myself to call my mother and ask about the beach.

"I'd like to speak with Dr. Cone about this." My mother's voice was sharp. I could tell she wanted to say no but couldn't come up with a logical reason.

"He's working. Can I pass on a question?"

"I'm concerned about his wife being sick and your having full responsibility for a child near water."

"We've gone to the Roland Park Pool many times."

"There are lifeguards there."

"There are lifeguards at beaches, too."

"Mary Jane. Do not get fresh with me. You are asking to go away for a week with a family your father and I don't know. I'd like to speak to Dr. Cone to make sure this is a safe and wise decision."

"Okay."

162 jessica anya blau

"I'll come up just before dinner."

I looked around the kitchen. If my mother walked in, she wouldn't approve of the Cones' taste—antiques, Buddhas, framed etchings with naked people in them. Also, if she saw Sheba and Jimmy, I'd be imprisoned at home. And of course, Mrs. Cone was supposed to be ill. For just a minute I imagined her meeting my mother at the door, her nipples pushing out through her tank top. "Mrs. Cone doesn't like visitors."

"Then call me before dinner tonight and put Dr. Cone on the phone."

"Okay, I will."

"And, Mary Jane, if you're working around the clock like that, you need to be paid more."

"Okay, I'll ask if they're going to pay me more." I would not.

"Do they have a proper meat thermometer for your pork roast?"

"Yes." I'd bought one at Eddie's.

"Are you doing the berries and whipped cream for dessert?"

"Izzy's never had s'mores, so I bought the ingredients for them."

"That's not a proper dessert for adults."

"I can make the berries and whipped cream, too."

"What kind of butter do they keep in the house?"

"Land O'Lakes." This I had also purchased at Eddie's.

"Salted or unsalted?"

"Salted."

"Don't put too much on the peas and corn. Just enough to lightly coat them."

"Okay."

There was silence for a moment. I felt something coming across the phone line. Loneliness, maybe. Could it be that my mother missed me?

"I'll talk to you tonight when you make the call for Dr. Cone."

"Okay, Mom." I wanted to say *love you,* as Izzy and I now said every night when I put her to sleep. But my parents didn't say those words. Instead I just hung up.

The rest of the afternoon as Izzy and I prepared dinner and folded and ironed two loads of laundry, I worried about my mother's conversation with Dr. Cone. How could I make sure Mrs. Cone's make-believe cancer didn't come up? If I told Dr. Cone about the lie, would he still want me to watch his child and go to the beach with them? Could he abide a liar in his house? If I were a mother, would I let a liar (and maybe a sex addict) take care of my child?

As the roast was cooking, and Izzy and I were setting the table, Dr. Cone and Jimmy entered the house. Jimmy went straight to his guitar in the kitchen. Dr. Cone came into the dining room and said, "Smells wonderful."

I smiled and my face burned. My heart was beating so hard, I thought I might collapse right there. "Dr. Cone?" I managed.

Dr. Cone squinted at me. "Mary Jane, you okay?"

"May I speak with you privately?"

"Mary Jane, are you okay?" Izzy hugged my legs and looked up at me.

"Yes. I just need to talk to your dad a minute."

"Izzy, go help Jimmy."

Izzy squeezed my legs and then ran off to Jimmy. Dr. Cone pulled out a chair and put his arm out, indicating I should sit. I did. He sat next to me. "Just breathe. In and out. Slowly."

I took an inhale and then exhaled slowly. It did make

me feel better. "My mother wants to talk to you before she agrees that I can go to the beach."

"Okay. That's okay."

"But I told her something I shouldn't have." I took another deep breath and when I exhaled, I started crying. It surprised me as much as it seemed to surprise Dr. Cone.

Dr. Cone pulled the napkin from the place setting in front of him and handed it to me. "Did you tell her about Jimmy and Sheba?"

I shook my head. "Worse."

"Worse? It's okay, Mary Jane. You can tell me."

"I told her . . ." I startled myself by crying too hard to speak. Harder than I'd ever cried in front of my parents, who didn't allow crying. I couldn't help but think how different I was these days. I was growing into someone new, new even to me.

"Breathe in, breathe out."

I took a breath in. "I told her . . ." My voice hitched and I breathed out, firmly. "I told her Mrs. Cone has cancer."

"Why?" Dr. Cone tilted his head and looked at me. His brow was furrowed. His bushy eyebrows almost met his sideburns.

"That was the only way she'd let me cook dinner."

"I'm sorry. I don't understand."

"She thinks a mother should always cook dinner. And so the only way to explain why Mrs. Cone wasn't cooking dinner was to say that she was sick. And I actually never said she had cancer. I just said she was sick. And then my mother thought she had cancer and I never told her she didn't." I squeezed my eyes shut hard. When I opened them, Dr. Cone was staring at me.

"So your mother wouldn't let you stay and prepare dinner unless Bonnie was incapacitated?"

"Yes."

"So when I talk to her about the week at the beach she might mention Bonnie's cancer?"

"She probably won't," I said. "Because she thinks cancer is very private. But I don't know. If you said something about Mrs. Cone swimming in the ocean, she might . . ." I swallowed hard and squeezed back tears. "I'm sorry I lied. I bet you didn't think you had a liar as a summer nanny."

Dr. Cone laughed. "No, I understand why you lied." He reached out and rubbed my shoulder. "It's okay. This isn't a crime. You were trying to manage two different households with two different value systems. And, yes, it's not good to lie. But I can see that was the only way you could find to make the situation work. I appreciate it, Mary Jane. I think you can let yourself off the hook here."

Mrs. Cone and Sheba came into the dining room. They were in the matching black pixie wigs.

"What happened?" Sheba pushed a chair next to me, sat, and then pulled me against her chest. I started crying again.

"Richard, what is it?" Mrs. Cone hovered over us. Dr. Cone stood and then Mrs. Cone took his seat and leaned in close so she, too, was hugging me.

"Richard! Why is she crying?" Sheba said.

"Her mother wouldn't let her cook dinner for us unless Bonnie was incapacitated. So Mary Jane told her mother that Bonnie has cancer and that's why she has to stay and make dinner each night."

"I'm so sorry I lied!" I cried, and Sheba hugged me deeper. Mrs. Cone was at my back, hugging me too. I'd never been so close to two human bodies before, and I was surprised that it didn't feel closed in and claustrophobic. It felt nice. And warm. And safe.

"Oh, honey! You don't have to feel bad! I would have had to tell my own mother the same thing," Mrs. Cone said.

"Mary Jane, no one cares that you lied about *that!*" Sheba said, and kissed my head the way everyone kissed Izzy.

Mrs. Cone started laughing. "Cancer! Because only something as horrible and deadly as cancer would relieve a woman from the tedium of having to make dinner for her family every night!"

Everyone gathered in the kitchen near the phone as I dialed the number for my house. Sheba put her finger to her lips and made big eyes at everyone after I'd dialed the last number.

My mother answered the phone on the second ring. "Dillard residence."

"Mom, Dr. Cone can talk to you now."

"Thank you, Mary Jane. Put him on." I could see her so clearly. Standing in the kitchen near the beige wall phone. Holding a pen and a pad of paper so she could write down any important details, like the address of the home where we'd be staying.

"Mrs. Dillard, what a pleasure to finally speak to you!" Dr. Cone sounded more formal, more upbeat than he did in the house. Jimmy put an arm around me and pulled me into him. I could feel the fuzz of his chest hairs through his shirt and wondered if that was a sex addict thought or just a thought.

Mrs. Cone picked up Izzy. Izzy put her finger to her lips like Sheba. Sheba smiled and put one arm around Jimmy.

"Mary Jane has been a lifesaver this summer. I don't know what we would have done without her." Dr. Cone nodded as my mother spoke on the other end. "I'm not the least bit worried about her ability to mind Izzy at the beach. Also, Izzy loves cooking with her, so a large portion of their afternoon is spent in the kitchen." Dr. Cone looked over and winked at the group. "Yes. Yes. Of course . . . we'll be leaving first thing tomorrow morning and we'll return the following Tuesday morning. I could have her call each evening if you'd like. We'll pay the phone charges. . . . Yes, yes, I understand. Thank you and please give my regards to Mr. Dillard."

When Dr. Cone hung up the phone, we all looked at him.

"She asked that I give you a ride to church on Sunday and sends her best wishes to Bonnie."

"So I can go?"

"Yes, you can go."

"HURRAH!" Izzy shouted, and everyone cheered and hooted as if something truly spectacular had just gone down.

9

Jimmy sat in the front seat with Dr. Cone. The rest of us bumped around in the back, Izzy and myself framed by Mrs. Cone and Sheba. No one had on a seat belt and the windows were open, blowing my hair into my face. Mrs. Cone's and Sheba's blond wigs barely moved, as if the hair were too heavy to be pushed around.

"When I was a kid, my family always sang in the car," Sheba said.

"Can I have a Lorna Doone?" Izzy asked me, though her mother was the one who had packed the cooler with snacks and placed them in the wayback of the station wagon.

"Yes. Anyone else?" I flipped around in my seat and leaned into the wayback.

"Bring out the whole pack," Mrs. Cone said.

"We sang mostly school songs," Sheba said. "Like 'My Country, 'Tis of Thee.'"

"My country 'tis of thee—" I started the song as I sat

back in my seat and opened the box of cookies. I handed
one to Izzy and tried to give one to Mrs. Cone, who waved
her hand to mean *no, thanks.*

"*Sweet land of liberty—*" Sheba joined in.

I sat forward and handed Dr. Cone and Jimmy each a
cookie. Sheba and I kept singing. When Jimmy twanged
in with his rumbling voice, it suddenly sounded beautiful.

"*Land where my fathers died, land of the pilgrims'
pride, from ev-ryyy mountain side, let freedom ring!*"

"Why did the fathers die?" Izzy asked.

Mrs. Cone reached over my lap, took Izzy's unfinished
cookie, bit into it, and then handed it back. "I guess they're
talking about the dads who died in the Revolutionary War."

"What's that?"

"When Americans decided they didn't want a king or
a queen." Sheba reached over, grabbed the box of cookies,
and pulled one out. Mrs. Cone took the box from Sheba and
pulled out a cookie for herself.

"Maybe Izzy knows this one," Jimmy said. "*If I had a
hammer, I'd hammer in the morning, I'd hammer in the
evening. . . .*"

Jimmy sang and everyone joined in. Izzy made hand
motions as she sang, her fist bumping up and down for a
hammer, her hands over her head and her head tocking
back and forth for a bell. By the time we were on the last
chorus, everyone was doing the hand motions.

We sang "The Star-Spangled Banner" and then "Row,
Row, Row Your Boat" in a round. Next Dr. Cone sang us
a song he had learned at camp as a boy. It was about a
cannibal king playing the bongos under a bamboo tree
and kissing his girlfriend. Izzy loved the song, especially
the part where you made big kissing sounds. It went
Boom boom (kiss kiss) *Boom boom* (kiss kiss). It only took

a couple of minutes for Dr. Cone to teach the song to everyone, and soon we all sang it with as much exuberance as Izzy.

"Again! Let's sing it again!" Izzy said.

We did as Izzy requested, only this time everyone turned to someone beside them and kissed. Jimmy even kissed Dr. Cone's cheek. I'd never seen a man kiss another man like that, and it seemed so funny that I was still laughing as I kissed Sheba's cheek.

We all sat in the car and stared at the low, long white clapboard house. The shingles and shutters were old-looking, faded pea green. The house seemed lonely against the beach. The neighboring houses were so far away, they reminded me of the little green homes in Monopoly.

"It looks like a Hopper painting," Mrs. Cone said.

Jimmy sang, *"Starry, starry night, paint your palette blue and grey —"*

"Isn't that song about Van Gogh?" Dr. Cone asked.

"I'm about to pee my shorts," Sheba said.

"Really you will? Sheba, will you pee your shorts?" Izzy asked.

"Where did I put that key?" Dr. Cone was searching his pockets. He leaned past Jimmy and opened the glove box.

"I have to go NOW!" Sheba burst out of the car and ran to the sand dunes. The rest of us got out of the car, Dr. Cone still patting down his pockets. Sheba turned around to face us, then pulled down her shorts, squatted, and peed. I looked around. No one seemed to be paying attention, except Izzy.

Izzy ran to Sheba. "I want to pee in the sand!"

"Got it!" Dr. Cone pulled the key from his breast pocket. He unlocked the house and propped the front door open. Jimmy and Mrs. Cone started unloading the car.

I looked over at Izzy squatted at the base of the dune. "Mary Jane!" she shouted. "Come pee in the sand!"

Suddenly I did want to pee in the sand. Just for fun. Just because the nudest I'd ever been in public was two weeks ago when I put on my bra in the dark beside my own house. I looked toward the car. Dr. and Mrs. Cone were pulling out suitcases and placing them on the driveway. Jimmy was carrying a brown-and-mustard-patterned suitcase toward the house. He looked back at me and said, "Go for it, Mary Jane!"

Before I could think it through, I ran to Sheba and Izzy. They were both standing now, with their pants pulled up.

"Do you have to pee?" Sheba asked.

"Yeah."

"It's like being a cat. You just kick sand over it when you're done." Sheba kicked sand over the big, wet oval near her feet. Even though I had gotten used to being with Sheba, my brain dinged a little alarm that said, *You're looking at Sheba's pee.*

Izzy tried to kick sand over her wet circle. She was barefoot and her toes kept hitting the pee spot.

"Can you barricade me from their view?" I asked.

"Yes!" Izzy shouted. "What does that mean?"

"Stand in front of her so no one can see." Sheba moved so she stood between me and the house. Izzy positioned herself beside Sheba.

I backed up a bit so I wouldn't pee on their feet, and then pulled down my shorts. The hot sun on my bare butt was a totally new feeling. When I was done, I quickly pulled up my shorts and then kicked sand over my spot.

"Can we poop?" Izzy asked.

"No!" Sheba and I said together.

The house was mostly on one floor, with a small second floor that had only a bedroom with a sitting room. The five remaining bedrooms were on the first floor, lining a long hallway. Some of the bedrooms shared a bathroom and some had their own bathroom. Mrs. Cone told Sheba and Jimmy they had to take the second-floor room, and they did. She and Dr. Cone took the front-most bedroom, facing the beach. This left four bedrooms for me and Izzy.

Izzy took my hand. "Will you share a room with me?"

"Sure." I had been wondering what I was supposed to do after Izzy went to sleep. Was I to join the adults, or stay in my room? Even if Izzy and I shared a room, I could go in another bedroom to read.

Izzy pulled me into the room next to Dr. and Mrs. Cone's. "Do you think there's a witch here?" She dropped my hand and turned in a circle. The room had two single beds with anchor-print bedspreads that matched the wallpaper.

I turned in a circle too. Then I dropped to my knees and flipped up the bed skirt on the first one, and then the other bed. "No. There's definitely no witch here."

In the next room we looked again for the witch. This room had rowboat-and-fish wallpaper that matched the rowboat-and-fish bedspreads. The bedside lamps each had a copper rowboat for a base.

The next room had a double bed with daisy-print wall-paper and a solid white bedspread with lacy scalloped edges.

"Witch?" Izzy asked.

"Hmm, I dunno. But I don't like this room. Don't you think we should be in a beachier room since we are, actually, at the beach?"

The last room had beach-ball-and-beach-umbrella-print wallpaper with matching bedspreads. Izzy and I agreed that although it was beachy, it was too colorful to be peaceful.

"Rowboats or anchors?" I said.

"Rowboats," Izzy said.

Once Izzy and I had finished unpacking, I took the week's worth of recipe cards I had brought to the dining room table and read them to Izzy. She wanted to pick the order of meals. The dining room was open to the kitchen, where Mrs. Cone and Sheba were unpacking the bags of groceries—mostly snacks—we'd brought. They were talking about Jimmy and his progress. The way they spoke made Jimmy sound like a little boy—*taking responsibility, learning to be alone, figuring out how to sit still with his thoughts, stopping himself and thinking before he takes action.* I was glad Jimmy wasn't around to hear them.

Dr. Cone walked onto the screened porch off the kitchen. "BONNIE!" he shouted in.

"WHAT?!" Mrs. Cone shouted back.

Dr. Cone lowered his voice. "What if we worked here?"

Mrs. Cone and Sheba walked into the screened porch. Izzy and I watched. Sheba thought it was too public and the rest of us would feel banned from the house.

Jimmy came downstairs, wearing his jean shorts and nothing else, and sat at the table with me and Izzy. Hanging from his neck was the leather-and-feather necklace. In his hand was a wide-brimmed straw hat with a red bandanna-print scarf tied around it. The hat looked like it belonged to a woman. "What are you two up to?" he asked.

"We, uh . . ." I blushed. We were eavesdropping, but I didn't want to admit it.

"We're making the order of the dinner. Here." Izzy stood on the chair and spread out the index cards like a train in front of Jimmy. "First, mac 'n' cheese! Which one's mac and cheese?"

"Find the letter *M* and then *A*," I said. "*M,* ma ma ma. And *A,* ah, ah, ah."

"Ma, ma, ma." Izzy ran her finger along the cards.

Dr. Cone, Mrs. Cone, and Sheba returned to the kitchen. "What if you worked on the beach?" Mrs. Cone asked. "I saw a stack of chairs in the garage."

"Not a bad idea." Dr. Cone looked over at the three of us.

"MAC AND CHEESE!" Izzy waved the correct recipe card.

"We're gonna make an office on the beach?" Jimmy asked.

"What do you think of that? It could be productive to feel connected to the ocean, the sky, the sand."

"It's cool. I like it." Jimmy nodded and then he stood. "I'm going for a walk."

"Alone?" Sheba sounded nervous.

"Yeah. Just wanna clear my head."

"Maybe I should go with you," Sheba said.

"I'm fine. Relax."

"Why are you getting defensive? Why can't I go with you?" Sheba's voice was tightening. Her face was as pointed as an arrow.

"I just want to be alone for a few minutes! What's the fucking crime?!" Jimmy verged on yelling.

"Did you phone someone?! Tell me you didn't phone someone!" Sheba was yelling now.

"Who the fuck am I going to phone?! We're in a fucking shithole town in Maryland!"

"We're in motherfucking Delaware!" Sheba walked to Jimmy and stood so that her face was only inches from his. With her mouth drawn shut like that, she looked ten years older.

"HOW THE FUCK WOULD I CALL SOMEONE IF I DON'T EVEN KNOW WHAT FUCKING STATE I'M IN?"

Izzy climbed on top of the dining room table. She rearranged the index cards as if nothing unusual were happening. But I could see that she was anxious: her barely noticeable eyebrows were pulled together, and her mouth churned as she quietly spoke to herself.

"It's okay." Dr. Cone put up both hands, fingers spread. "Jimmy, I feel your frustration. I can see that it pains you that Sheba doesn't trust you."

"THE FUCK I DON'T! HE SCORED IN THE ALLEY BEHIND YOUR FUCKING HOUSE!"

"Sheba," Dr. Cone said. "I feel your anxiety. You love Jimmy. He had a setback. You're carrying a lot of fear. And I can see that you feel responsible for him."

Izzy whispered, "Mac and cheese tonight."

"She's not my fucking mother," Jimmy said.

"Yeah, I'm not an alcoholic chasing you around the house with a lethal wrought-iron fire poker!"

"The FUCK, Sheba! It was an ash shovel!"

"Why don't we do this? Let me check Jimmy's pockets, make sure he has no cash, and we'll put a time limit on the walk. You okay with that, Jimmy?" Dr. Cone put his hand on Jimmy's shoulder and rubbed, as if he were trying to warm him up.

Jimmy nodded, stuck his hands into his front jean shorts pockets, and pulled out the linings. He turned and Dr. Cone patted his back pockets.

"Don't forget your hat." Izzy stood on the table and held out the straw hat.

Dr. Cone took the hat, then looked inside it and ran his finger under the scarf. He handed the hat to Jimmy. "An hour okay?"

"What about ninety minutes?"

"What direction are you going?" Sheba asked. "To the left or the right?"

Jimmy shrugged.

"Pick one."

"Right."

"Nope," Sheba said. "Go left."

"Okay, left."

"You're fucking playing with me, aren't you? You knew I'd switch it, so you gave me the opposite direction."

Dr. Cone looked flummoxed. Mrs. Cone was leaning against the kitchen counter, watching. Izzy had crouched back down and was rearranging the cards again.

"Fine. You tell me what direction to go and that's the direction I'll go." Jimmy's chest was heaving. I worried he'd start throwing things or shouting again. But he didn't. Sheba did.

"YOU SNEAKY MOTHERFUCKER! IF YOU MEET ONE PERSON ON THAT BEACH, I'M FUCKING CUTTING OFF YOUR BALLS! YOU HEAR ME?!"

"What are Jimmy's balls?" Izzy whispered to me. "Do I have balls?"

"It's another word for testicles," I whispered back. "You know, like in your coloring book?"

"YOU CANNOT FUCKING POLICE ME LIKE THIS! YOU HAVE TO GIVE ME SPACE TO BREATHE YOU GODDAMMED—" Jimmy stopped and shook his head. I quickly assessed the throwable breakables in the room. There wasn't much. He'd have to open a cupboard.

"Breathe in, breathe out," Dr. Cone said. "Sheba, you too. Just breathe in and out. Let's have a quick meditation moment."

Dr. Cone, Jimmy, and Sheba turned so they were standing in a circle facing each other. Mrs. Cone joined them. Sheba still had on her old lady face and Jimmy's chest continued to heave.

"I breathe in, I breathe out," Dr. Cone said in a low, smooth voice, like he was the DJ in a nighttime love song radio show. He repeated the words over and over again as the group breathed in and out. I wondered if this breathing was any different from regular breathing.

"Will Sheba really cut off Jimmy's balls?" Izzy looked at me with huge eyes.

"No." I pulled her off the table and onto my lap. She pushed her head into my neck and I rubbed her back. "She would never do that. She just said that to let him know how angry she was."

Izzy started breathing in and out along with Dr. Cone's instructions, and soon I felt her body melt into me like a warm stick of butter.

"Okay, let's keep this peace." Dr. Cone put his hand on Jimmy's shoulder. "I'm going to walk Jimmy to the beach and send him off. Sheba, you'll be fine and Jimmy will be fine."

"Yeah. Whatever. That's good." Sheba stared at Jimmy like she was daring him on something. "I'll sleep in the sun and wait for you."

"Good. Good." Dr. Cone put a hand on Sheba's shoulder too. He was like a yoke between oxen.

Sheba nodded and then reached up to her head, ripped off the blond wig, and threw it so it landed on the dining room table. Mrs. Cone took off her wig too. She looked toward the table, and then pulled the wig against her chest and held it like she was holding a cat.

Dr. Cone drove Izzy and me to the grocery store. Izzy held all the recipe cards tight in her hand.

When we got to the store, I grabbed a cart and Izzy jumped on the end. "Do we need to find the ratio?" she asked.

"The ratio?" Dr. Cone asked.

"When we go to Eddie's, we count the employees and the customers to find the ratio." I shrugged, embarrassed. It sounded weird and silly when I said it aloud.

"Yesterday it was eighteen to twenty-nine," Izzy said.

Dr. Cone rubbed Izzy's curls. "That's marvelous!"

"I think this store is too big for us to count." I looked up and down the aisles. It was huge, like a warehouse.

"I agree." Dr. Cone turned toward the produce section. I had memorized most of the ingredients on the cards and started putting things in the cart.

"The ratio of the witch is three to one," Izzy said.

"Three *what* to one *what*?" Dr. Cone asked.

"Me, Mary Jane, and Sheba are three. And the witch is only one."

"Well, I'll join your team."

"Then we'll be"—Izzy pointed at me, her father, herself, and then an imaginary Sheba standing beside us—"four! To one. Right?"

"Yup," I said. "There isn't a witch in the world who could hurt a kid in the middle of a four-to-one ratio."

"Agreed," Dr. Cone said. I was relieved that he didn't seem to think the ratio game was weird or silly. And I felt strangely happy that he had been so quick to join our team. Izzy talked about the witch so frequently, I had forgotten that I didn't believe in her.

Before we left the produce section, I shuf-fled through the cards to make sure I hadn't missed anything. "Wait! Artichokes!"

"Fancy." Dr. Cone loped over to the artichoke display. I pushed the cart behind him.

"Do you like artichokes?" I asked. I worried that fancy wasn't good. The Cones seemed anti-fancy, with Izzy standing on the dining room table, peeing on the beach, and coloring penises in her anatomy coloring book.

"I love them. We just never eat them. Restaurants don't serve them." Dr. Cone put his hand on my head and rubbed, the way everyone did to Izzy. It felt so nice, I didn't move for a second, just to sense the vibrations of that touch.

When we returned to the beach house, Jimmy and Sheba were snuggled up together on the living room couch watching *Green Acres*. It had never occurred to me that people who were on TV might watch it too.

"I love this show." I paused, a brown bag of groceries in my arms. Izzy paused beside me. She was carrying the lightest bag.

"Come watch!" Sheba patted the cushion beside herself.

"I have to put away the groceries," I said.

"Mary Jane," Dr. Cone said. "Watch TV. I'll put everything away."

I looked at him for a second to see if he was serious. He and Mrs. Cone were paying me. Was it really okay for me to get paid to sit on a couch and watch *Green Acres* with Sheba and Jimmy? "Are you sure?"

"Yes. Sit. Relax. You work too hard."

"Sit!" Sheba said.

"Okay!" I went to the kitchen, put down my bag, and then returned to the couch. Sheba patted the cushion again. I sat and tucked my feet under my bottom, mimicking her posture.

"I love Mr. Haney," Jimmy said.

"Me too."

Izzy came into the living room and snuggled into me the way Sheba was snuggled into Jimmy. "Why is there a pig in the house?"

"That's Arnold Ziffel," Jimmy said. "He's like their son."

"Why does that lady talk like that?"

"She's a Gabor," I said. "She and her twin sister are very beautiful and they're from another country. Maybe Hungary."

"She's a bitch," Sheba said. "In real life."

"You know her?"

"Yeah. Snobby and mean. Huge boobs. Fake nails."

"But Eddie Albert"—Jimmy pointed to the screen—"damn nice guy. Can drink a fuck of a lot."

"Do you know everyone on TV?" I asked.

Jimmy and Sheba looked at each other as if they were thinking about it. A commercial for Trix cereal came on. The manic white rabbit ran around screaming, *"Trix are for kids! Trix are for kids!"*

"You know," Sheba said at last, "I've been in the business for so long, I do know just about everyone. And Jimmy's toured for so many years that he's met everyone too."

"Yeah. People want to come backstage, they join the tour, they come to the hotel to party. . . ." Jimmy shrugged.

"No more parties," Sheba said. A commercial for Control Data Institute, a technical school, came on. We all watched as if we were ready to enroll.

That first-day fight between Jimmy and Sheba was like a fire hose that cleared away all the debris. From *Green Acres* on, everyone in the house seemed happier and more relaxed than usual. Jimmy and Dr. Cone did therapy on the beach, but it was intermittent and brief. They had a spot between two sand dunes that they called "the Office." They'd laid down a bedsheet there that was quickly half covered with sand.

Sheba and Mrs. Cone and Izzy and I set up chairs and towels and a cooler on the first stretch of dry sand in front of the water, directly in line with the Office. When I turned around, I could see Jimmy eating Screaming Yellow Zonkers, nodding as Dr. Cone talked, or sometimes talking as Dr. Cone nodded. Every now and then he put down the snacks and lay on the sheet, curled up on his side. I got nervous when he did that, but he didn't look like he was in pain, or crying.

Sheba and Mrs. Cone abandoned all wigs, as the beach

really was private. We could see anyone coming from way down it, and whenever we did, Sheba would slip on a pair of sunglasses that covered her face from her eyebrows to her lips. She'd put on a hat, too, to hide all that long, thick black hair. Mrs. Cone often put on shades and a hat when Sheba did. "In case it's someone I know," she said to me once.

Izzy and I dug holes, built sandcastles, and went in and out of the water. Sheba and Mrs. Cone also took Izzy in the water, which gave me time to sit and read my book. I'd found the book *Jaws* on a shelf in the living room of the house. It was about a shark attack on a beach on Long Island, but it didn't make me afraid to go in the water.

Whenever Jimmy and Dr. Cone weren't in the Office, they were on the beach too. Jimmy liked taking Izzy in the water. He'd throw her up in the air and catch her again. Dr. Cone read his book and often napped with a baseball cap pulled down low over his eyes.

Every day, Jimmy went for a walk alone, to clear his head. Before he took off, he pulled out his shorts pockets—when he was wearing shorts instead of a suit—and presented his behind to Dr. Cone to pat. After the pat down, Izzy and I would go up to the house and make dinner. I liked our time in the kitchen. After a day in the sun and water, there was a peacefulness to the warm kitchen, the quiet of the house, the stillness of the air.

I gave Izzy a bath every night following dinner and then put her to bed in our room. Once she was asleep, I joined the adults in the living room, or on the screened porch. They listened to music, or Jimmy strummed his guitar. Jimmy and Dr. Cone each had a cup of tea, Mrs. Cone and Sheba drank wine, and a joint circulated. Dr. Cone, like me, didn't smoke, though once I saw him take a single puff just before he went to bed. And another night, I cleared the teacups and smelled something funny in Dr. Cone's cup. I suspected he was pretending not to drink, so Jimmy wouldn't be the only adult without alcohol.

Jaws was always on my lap at these living room hangouts, but usually the conversation was so engaging that I didn't read. Sheba talked the most. She once named every famous person she'd had sex with and also told us how big each man's penis was and what it looked like. She said one looked like it had knuckles under the skin, one was the size of her pinkie, one smelled like ham and was the color of ham, and one was angled to the right like it was pointing out directions. I had no idea that penises were that variegated. One movie star, an action guy, had a penis so big, Sheba couldn't put it in her vagina. I hadn't known who some of the stars were, but now I'd never be able to watch any of their movies or TV shows without pulling up the image of their penis.

Of the star with the enormous penis, Jimmy said, "I'm bigger than him, but then she had a little surgery to let me in and now it's all good." Everyone laughed at that, so I knew it was a joke.

Mrs. Cone asked Jimmy if he'd made love to as many stars as Sheba. Jimmy took a hit off the joint, furrowed his brow, and looked like he was thinking. Then he said, "You know, Bonnie, I just don't fucking remember. No idea. Drug brain. Before I was with Sheba, the way I'd know I'd fucked someone was that she'd be in my bedroom or the hotel bed or on the tour bus in the morning. Sometimes I'd sense I'd been with someone, so I'd check my back in the mirror. If I didn't see scratch marks, then I'd sniff my fingers."

Everyone laughed, but I didn't get it.

"You remember the girl you lost your virginity to," Sheba said. "And you remember sleeping with Margaret Trudeau."

"Well, yeah, there are people who stand out—"

"You slept with Margaret Trudeau!" Mrs. Cone leaned forward in her chair.

"You didn't forget Streisand," Sheba said.

"No one forgets Streisand." Jimmy winked at Sheba and she laughed. I was surprised she didn't get jealous. But maybe when you were Sheba, and every man in the world wanted to make love to you, you didn't get jealous.

"Miss March," Sheba said, and she put her hands in front of her chest to indicate breasts that jutted out about three feet.

"I think you're thinking of Miss June."

"Miss May."

"There was a run of four Playmates," Jimmy conceded. "I believe it was June, July, August, and September."

"Did you save the issues?" Dr. Cone asked. I thought he was kidding, but I couldn't be sure.

"The only issue he has is the one I was in." Sheba moved from her chair to the ground in front of Jimmy's legs. She wrapped her arms around his calves.

"That's the only issue I cherish," Jimmy said.

I wanted to know what it was like to pose for *Playboy*. If I could summon the nerve, I'd ask Sheba later. And maybe I'd also asked her why Jimmy would look at his back or smell his fingers to see if he'd made love to someone.

On the fifth day at the beach, Jimmy turned his pockets inside out and presented his behind to Dr. Cone, who looked up from his book and waved him away.

Jimmy then presented his behind to Mrs. Cone, who giggled and gave a little slap on each of his back pockets. He went to Sheba next. Sheba was wearing a bikini that looked small enough to fit Izzy. Her skin was smooth and creamy, like she'd been sanded down.

"I need to do a thorough exam." Sheba kneeled at Jimmy's back and felt his pockets. Then she leaned in and bit him. Jimmy yowled and Izzy laughed so hard, her curls shook.

"Your turn." Jimmy presented his bottom to Izzy. Izzy slapped his pockets over and over again like she was playing the bongos.

"Mary Jane has to check too!" Izzy stood and pushed Jimmy toward me.

I slapped his pockets once each. He had swum in his jean shorts and they were damp and sandy. "All clear!"

"Then I'm off!" Jimmy lifted his leg, cartoon-style, like he was winding up to run. And then he did. Run. Away from us and down the beach wearing only those damp, gritty shorts and the leather rope with feathers around his neck.

"What's for dinner tonight?" Mrs. Cone reached out and squeezed Izzy's fleshy leg. Izzy was wearing a red polka-dot one-piece and looked like a cute little ladybug.

"Pizza!" Izzy said.

Mrs. Cone looked over at me. "You're making pizza?"

"No, Dr. Cone said this morning that he wanted to order pizza from some place in Rehoboth, so we shouldn't cook tonight." I hadn't grown tired of cooking, but it did seem nice to have the night off.

"Ah, exciting. I haven't had pizza in ages." Mrs. Cone patted her stomach. Her bikini was as small as Sheba's and reminded me of a disassembled net bag. My mother wouldn't have even considered it a bathing suit.

"What?" Dr. Cone looked up from his book. He'd been completely tuned out.

"Do they deliver or do we pick it up?" Sheba asked. "Maybe we can pick it up and then stop at a boutique and buy a new suit for Mary Jane."

I was wearing the one-piece I'd been wearing all summer. It had started out orange but had faded to a pale almost-pink color. "I don't think my mother will let me wear a bikini," I said.

"Your mother's not here." Sheba winked.

"Oh, let's get a new suit for Mary Jane!" Mrs. Cone said.

"Do I need a new suit?" Izzy asked.

"No, you're a perfect little ladybug." I leaned in and kissed Izzy.

"But Mary Jane needs a new suit?"

"I don't," I said. "And it's a waste of money. We only have two more days."

"It is not a waste of money," Sheba said. "When you run away from home and move to New York to live with me and Jimmy, you can wear it there."

"Mary Jane can't leave me." Izzy climbed into my lap and I kissed her again. I didn't want to leave her. And I'd never once thought of leaving my parents before college. But after Sheba had tossed out the idea of running away and living with her and Jimmy, I was momentarily infected with it. Like a fever that lets you see the usual world through the intensity of the unusual.

Dr. Cone called in the pizza and Mrs. Cone, Sheba, Izzy, and I went to pick it up. Jimmy was home by then, so he and Dr. Cone decided to do some work in the Office while we were gone.

Mrs. Cone drove and Sheba sat in the front seat. They were both wearing black pixie wigs and giant sunglasses. Sheba was wearing a terry-cloth shorts jumpsuit that zipped up the front and had a hood. Mrs. Cone was in her jean shorts that showed the white untanned edge of her bottom, and a tank top that revealed the outline of her nipples. Izzy and I wore jean shorts that did not reveal our bottoms and tank tops that did not reveal our nipples.

Mrs. Cone and Izzy went off to pick up the pizzas while Sheba and I went into the Red Crab Boutique. Sheba circled the store, pulling clothes off the racks without even checking the prices. I walked behind her. I didn't realize she was choosing items for me until she said, "Okay, Mary Jane, in the dressing room."

I looked at the pile of clothes in Sheba's arms. On top of the pile was a black crochet bikini that I immediately loved. But I knew I could never wear it in front of my mother, or even at the Elkridge Club when my mother wasn't there (my mother was always there). Crochet was subversive—it was the domain of hippies and pot smokers, and the Age of Aquarius. I really would have to move in with Jimmy and Sheba if I wanted to wear this suit outside of my bedroom.

I opened a dressing room door, Sheba standing behind me.

"Mary Jane!" I jumped. It was Beanie Jones, coming out of the fitting room next to mine. She was holding a silver jumpsuit that looked like liquid mercury. "I was wondering when I'd run into y'all! And the *out-of-town* guests!" She winked at Sheba as if she were a Cone family insider, and not a stranger to be lied to.

"Good to see you again." Sheba put on her socialite

voice. I wondered if she could remember the name she had come up with when we'd seen Beanie and her husband at Morgan Millard. I couldn't.

"How did you know we were here?" I asked. Dr. Cone had told us that the Flemings, from whom we had borrowed the house, had sworn not to tell anyone we were staying there.

"I saw your mother at Elkridge and she told me you were staying somewhere on Indian Dunes." Beanie Jones waved her hand over the pile of clothes in Sheba's arms. "Are those for you to try on, Mary Jane? That's a sexy little suit you got there." She glanced at me, and then winked at Sheba.

"Here, doll," Sheba said in her make-believe voice. She handed me the pile and nodded toward the fitting room. I walked inside and Sheba closed the door. "Lovely to see you, Ms. Jones. You take care now." There were two footstools in the room; I dropped the pile of clothes on one and started taking off my clothes.

"Should we have cocktails on the beach tonight?" Beanie Jones said from the other side of the door.

"Ah, *malheureusement,* my husband and I are leaving this afternoon. But give my regards to Mr. Jones." Sheba cracked the fitting room door open. I knew she wanted an escape.

"Goodbye, Mrs. Jones, uh, Beanie." I backed against the wall, as I was mostly undressed.

"Well, then maybe we can have a drink next time you're in town?" Beanie Jones said to Sheba.

"Certainly. Bye now!" Sheba said, and then she wedged herself inside the fitting room and pulled the door shut behind herself.

"Bye bye!" Beanie Jones said.

I stood there in my underwear and bra. Sheba and I stared at each other in silence, waiting for Beanie Jones to leave. After a minute or so, Sheba cracked the door open again and peered out. Then she pulled it shut and sat on the empty footstool in the corner. "My god, that woman is haunting us," she whispered. "Try on the suit first."

"Okay." I picked up the suit. Was I just going to take off my bra and be half nude in front of Sheba? If I turned my back, would it be rude? I took a deep breath, pretended nothing was unusual, unhooked my bra, and put on the bikini top. Then I pulled the bottoms on over my underpants.

"Finally something that shows off your gorgeous figure." Sheba made a paddle of her hand and flicked it, meaning I should turn in a circle. Which I did. "You have to get this suit."

I looked at the price tag. It was equal to two weeks' salary. I'd never spent my own money on clothes and couldn't imagine starting with something as expensive as the suit. "I think I should find something less expensive," I said.

"No!" Sheba waved both hands up in the air. "Mary Jane! I'm rich. I'm buying you the suit and anything else you like. No arguing."

"Okay." I laughed with relief. Once I knew I could get the suit, I allowed myself to admit that I loved it. It felt weirdly powerful to wear something so showy. Though I couldn't quite imagine being brave enough to wear it in public.

"Now put this on." Sheba handed me a beautiful yellow sundress. It was sunny. Happy. Something my mother would approve of. I slipped it on over the suit.

"Gorgeous. Next." Sheba handed me a white terry-cloth romper that was similar to the red one I'd seen her in. I climbed into it through the neckline and then zipped up the front. It clung to me like Saran Wrap.

"Gorgeous again," Sheba said.

We went on like this for a while. Between Sheba's assessment of each outfit, she told the story of losing her virginity. She was fifteen and the boy was nineteen. He was the son of a "very famous" actor I'd never heard of. When Sheba's mother found out—she'd walked in on them in Sheba's bedroom—she took a pair of scissors and cut up every article of cute clothing Sheba owned. "The only things she didn't destroy," Sheba said, "were my winter corduroy pants and my thick Fair Isle sweaters."

"Wow," I said. The clothes Sheba was buying me were the first ones I'd owned that I could imagine my mother destroying. "I'm worried my mother will take these clothes away from me if she sees them. I don't think she'd cut them up, but . . ."

"Yeah. Wow." Sheba sighed.

There was quiet for a moment as we both stared at me in a backless tie-dye dress. I was turned, looking over my shoulder at my backside in the mirror. The dress was too long and baggy; it was definitely going in the reject pile.

"Can I ask you a question?" I whispered.

"Yeah?" Sheba whispered too.

I turned toward Sheba and then leaned in close to her ear so no one outside the dressing room could hear. "Why did Jimmy check his back to see if he made love to girls and why did he sniff his fingers?"

Sheba took a deep inhale. I thought she might be on the verge of laughing. It was like I was Izzy and she was me. Even the question sounded like something Izzy would ask.

"Because women scratch men's backs when they make

love to them. And I don't think he really sniffed his fingers, but men make jokes about the smell of a woman's vagina, so he was pretending that he sniffed them to see if they smelled of vagina."

The words *smelled of vagina* clanked around in my head. I had wanted to ask her about posing for *Playboy*, too, but felt too stopped up by what I'd just heard. Did my vagina smell? If it had, I'd never noticed.

The car smelled like pizza. Or was it vagina?
There were four of them in the station wagon.

"We saw that Beanie woman again," Sheba told Mrs. Cone.

"Jesus Christ! I knew we'd bump into someone. Half of Baltimore summers in Dewey or Rehoboth."

"Beanie Jones?" Izzy asked.

"The one and only," I said.

"I heard the Joneses have a house here somewhere," Mrs. Cone said. "Hopefully she'll stay the rest of the summer while we're back in Baltimore."

"Did she give you cake?" Izzy asked. "She makes good cake!"

"No," I said. "No cake this time."

On my lap was a shopping bag full of clothes paid for by Sheba. I had been worrying about how I was going to get any of them past my mother. Even the sandals Sheba bought me seemed sexy; they were made of black leather and had a woven ring that went around the big toe.

"No one knows where we're staying," Mrs. Cone said. "So she won't be dropping in with any cakes."

Sheba sang, *"Beeeanie Jones, Beeeanie Jones, when she enters the room, there are hollers and grooooooans."*

We all sang the line and then Sheba went on, *"Beanie Jones, Beanie Jones, first she grunts and then she moooooans."*

We repeated that line and then Izzy came up with, *"Beanie Jones, Beanie Jones, the telephone rings 'cause she's on the phones!"*

"Good one!" I hugged Izzy and felt a rush of pride.

Mrs. Conc sang, *"Beanie Jones, Beanie Jones, she storms into town like a trail of cyclones."*

"Your turn, Mary Jane!" Sheba said.

"Okay . . ." I bit my lip, thinking. *"Beanie Jones, Beanie Jones, her body is flesh, then there are bones!"*

"Bones, bones, bones," Sheba sang. *"Beanie Beanie Jones. Bones, bones, bones, she hollers then she moans!"*

We all repeated those last two lines, with Sheba taking melody and me on harmony, for the rest of the ride home.

10

At breakfast, Jimmy looked at the last two recipe cards. One was for pot roast and the other was for tomato soup and grilled cheese sandwiches.

"Pot roast." Jimmy slapped the card down in front of Izzy. Izzy had come to the table in her nightgown but removed it when I wasn't looking. She was now eating her porridge naked.

"That's not a summer food." Sheba was in a different bikini than yesterday. This one was white with a crotch so small the fuzzy scribbles of her brown pubic hair poked out along the sides. I was wearing my new suit, but had thrown my new Dolfin shorts and new striped T-shirt over it, as I couldn't bring myself to walk out of the bedroom wearing just the suit.

"But I love pot roast. And I've been so good!" Jimmy climbed off his chair, went to Sheba, and started kissing her all over. She batted him away, laughing. Izzy got out of her chair and ran over to kiss Sheba all over too, so

Sheba was covered by the two of them. I watched, smiling, and wondered what it would feel like to kiss so freely like that.

Dr. Cone came into the room and Jimmy lifted his head up from the kisses. "Richard, what do you think of pot roast for dinner tonight?" He sat at the table.

Dr. Cone looked at me. "Mary Jane?"

"Well, we bought all the ingredients. But Sheba thinks it's not summery enough."

"If we bought the ingredients, let's not waste them." Dr. Cone went to the stove and served himself a bowl of oatmeal from the pot.

"Seriously, Mary Jane. Does your mother make pot roast in the middle of summer?" Sheba lifted her bare legs and crossed them on the table. Izzy settled on Jimmy's lap. She looked over the recipe card and sounded out the letters.

"I copied her recipe cards for the meals she had scheduled this week, so, yes." I wondered if Dr. Cone cared that his naked daughter was sitting on a grown man's lap. No one else seemed to notice.

"You got a hell of a mother," Jimmy said. "The best meal my mother ever made was when she'd buy a brick of cheddar cheese, pull out a sheet of tinfoil, and then melt the cheddar on the foil."

"And then what?" I picked up Izzy's nightgown from the floor and slipped it over her head.

"Then what what?"

Sheba said, "What did she do with the melted cheese?"

"Nothing. That was it. She took the foil out of the oven, put it on the coffee table, and we pulled it off with our fingers and ate it while we watched TV."

I laughed. "What did you call it?"

"She called it 'melted cheese.'"

"How did you ever get so creative and smart?" Sheba recrossed her legs, left over right now. "Your mother was of no help to you."

"At least she was there. Unlike my dad, who was with the macramé lady who lived down the road."

"We did macramé at camp!" Izzy cried.

"Who was the macramé lady?" I asked.

"She sold macramé plant holders outside the supermarket. She had big eyes and big tits. That and the macramé did my dad in. He followed her home one day and that was that."

"Tits," Izzy whispered. I hoped she wouldn't ask what it meant.

Mrs. Cone walked in wearing a breezy yellow sundress and leather sandals. She paused, looked at Sheba, and then slipped off the dress, revealing another microkini. Then she sat at the table.

"Izzy and I made oatmeal," I offered.

"Lovely!" Mrs. Cone clapped.

I went to the stove and ladled out a big bowl for her. "Do you mind pot roast for dinner?"

"What does everyone else think?"

"I think it's too wintry." Sheba recrossed her legs again. Each time she moved them, it was like a flash of lightning that everyone but Izzy turned toward.

"I want it," Jimmy said. "It's better than melted cheese on tinfoil."

"Jimmy's dad loves the macramé lady with big eyes," Izzy said.

"Baby," Sheba said, to Jimmy, "you're right. This time is about you. Pot roast it is."

"Hurrah!" Izzy shouted.

At two p.m., Izzy and I stuck the roast in the oven. It had to cook for four hours. Back on the beach, we decided we'd collect shells to decorate the dining room table.

"Hat." I plopped a purple hat on Izzy's head. Her face and shoulders had been burning and peeling all week long and I wanted to stop the cycle. Everyone but Dr. Cone and Izzy had been slathering on Bain de Soleil tanning oil all week, trying to heighten the sun's effects. Sheba was the darkest, with Jimmy coming in second. Mrs. Cone only crisped and then molted, so she had to start all over again every second day. Dr. Cone was uninterested in tanning, but had been turning brown nonetheless. I looked as brown as a nut and my hair had gone blonder.

"Bucket," Izzy said, and she gripped the handle of her bucket and started marching down the beach.

"We'll be back in a bit," I said, but Dr. Cone—the only one on the beach with us—wasn't listening.

I hurried after Izzy. I hadn't put on my shorts or shirt and felt like there was too much air on my skin as we walked along. Each time I bent over to pick up a shell, I pulled my bottoms out of my crack and checked the triangles of the top even though no one was around to see me.

Izzy started singing a Jimmy song from our favorite Running Water album. Soon, I was singing with her and forgot about my near-nakedness. After each song ended, Izzy paused for what seemed like the same number of seconds as the silence between songs on the album before starting in on the next one in order.

"Look!" Izzy stopped mid-song and pointed at a horseshoe crab shell as big as a serving platter. It was in perfect condition; a mottled, brownish-red, the color of Mrs. Cone's skin just before she peeled.

"Cool!" We'd found half shells, three-quarter shells, and shell shards earlier in the week. But this was our first encounter with an unbroken, completely formed shell.

"Where's the crab?"

"Probably eaten by seagulls." I flipped it around so we could study the underside. "Look at how big this is! Horse-shoe crabs are older than dinosaurs."

"Can we keep it?" Izzy lifted the giant shell and tried to put it in the bucket. It was far too big.

"Yes. But let's pick it up again on our way back."

"What if someone else takes it?" Izzy pressed the horseshoe crab shell against her chest. It covered past her protruding belly.

"We can hide it in the dunes and get it on the way back."

"Yes!" Izzy held the shell high above her head like a boxer with his trophy, and ran toward the dunes. I jogged a couple of paces behind. She climbed to the top of a dune and stopped as if she'd bumped into an invisible wall. When I caught up to her, my body did the same halting bump.

Behind the dune was Jimmy, naked except for his leather-and-feather necklace, and naked Beanie Jones. I supposed they were having sex, but I'd never imagined sex looking like this. Jimmy was on top of Beanie's back; her rump was in the air and his mouth was on her shoulder, like a biting dog. Beanie's face was half on the towel and half in the sand. Her blond hair was fanned around her head and covered most of the exposed side of her face. They were gleaming, sweaty. I was so stunned by this sight that I was silenced. I couldn't move either; it was like I was trapped in mud.

Beanie's eyes flashed open. She said, "Oh!" and then rolled out from beneath Jimmy.

"FUCKING SHIT! FUCK ME." Jimmy stood. His penis jutted out in a way that I'd never seen in sex ed filmstrips or Izzy's coloring book. It was airborne, upright—like there was a string attached to it and someone was yanking that string up.

"Sorry," I managed. Then I picked up Izzy, who was still holding the horseshoe crab, and ran back toward the water.

When we got to the bucket, I put Izzy down and dropped to my knees. I was shaking. Izzy got on her knees and laid her head on my lap. She breathed in deep, her tiny back rising and falling. Neither of us spoke for a minute.

Finally Izzy sat up and looked at me. "Was Jimmy addicting?"

"Yes, I think so." I rubbed her hair. My hands trembled.

"What were they doing?"

"They were wrestling."

"Naked-y?"

"Yeah. Naked-y wrestling."

"Will Sheba be mad?"

"Yes. I think so."

"But this isn't our kitchen."

I knew what she meant. "Yeah, it's not. I don't think Jimmy will break all the dishes here." I wondered how I would have responded to a situation like this when I was Izzy's age. All of it—the kitchen destruction, the beach lovemaking—had been unimaginable until I encountered it. I had to quickly get over my own shock and be the adult—the one who made everything okay for Izzy when the grown-ups messed up in extraordinary ways.

"Maybe we don't tell anyone so Jimmy doesn't get in trouble," Izzy said.

I pulled Izzy onto my lap. Then I shut my eyes and

thought for a second. It seemed important that I get this right. "You don't have to keep secrets from your parents, okay? If it's on your mind, you can tell your mom and dad."

Izzy nodded into my neck. I could feel tears leaking into my skin. "I don't want it on my mind."

"I'll talk to your dad and he can figure out what to do about it. He's Jimmy's doctor. This is his job."

"I'm worrying about Jimmy."

"Don't. This isn't your worry to have," I said. "This isn't your problem. You just be you. We'll make dinner. We'll decorate with shells. Okay? Jimmy's problem is not your problem."

Izzy nodded again. She sniffed and then wiped her nose on my neck.

"Let's go back and make a centerpiece for the table." I put Izzy on the ground and picked up the bucket. She carried the horseshoe crab against her chest with one hand. Her other hand was in mine. I squeezed her fingers and she squeezed back. We squeezed in a rhythm as we walked toward the house.

And then Izzy started singing to our squeezing beat, *"Beanie Jones, Beanie Jones, first she hollers, then she moans."*

In my head I was singing too, *Bones, bones, bones, Beanie, Beanie Jones.*

I plugged the kitchen sink, then filled it with water and dishwashing liquid. Izzy pulled a footstool up and, one by one, placed the shells we'd collected in the water. She put the giant horseshoe crab shell in last.

I got out a cutting board and sliced up vegetables for the green salad. I'd add the lettuce last, just before dinner.

We were silently working like this when Dr. Cone came in from the beach. "Smells delicious." He bent over and looked through the glass door of the oven. Then he went to Izzy and kissed the back of her head.

"I'm washing the shells so we can make the center—" Izzy looked at me.

"The centerpiece."

"The centerpiece."

"That will be beautiful." Dr. Cone kissed his daughter again.

"And," Izzy whispered, "Mary Jane, tell Dad about the sand dunes."

"Yes?" Dr. Cone looked at me. My heart was banging. Izzy turned back to her chore.

I swallowed a walnut down my throat. "Can I tell you somewhere else?"

Dr. Cone nodded. "How about we go onto the porch?"

"I'll be right back," I said to Izzy. "Don't climb off the stool. Just stay here and keep cleaning. Okay?"

"Okay." Izzy's head was down. She appeared to be scrubbing each groove of every shell with her tiny fingernail. I knew she was fully in the task and no longer worrying about Jimmy.

Out on the porch, I took a deep breath. "Izzy and I found Jimmy with Beanie Jones behind a sand dune."

Dr. Cone blinked several times. "Were they doing drugs?"

"No."

"What were they doing?"

"I think they were making love."

Dr. Cone paused for a few seconds. Then he said, "Did you tell anyone else?"

"No. I told Izzy they were wrestling, and I think she

believed me. But she also knows that the naked wrestling was wrong and that Sheba will be angry."

Dr. Cone nodded. "Let's keep this between us for now. After Izzy goes to bed, we'll deal with it. As a family. Me, you, Bonnie, Jimmy, Sheba."

"Okay." I nervously smiled. Until I'd met the Cones, I had no idea that a family would dare discuss something as volatile and embarrassingly personal as infidelity. In my own house, each day was a perfectly contained lineup of hours where nothing unusual or unsettling was ever said. In the Cone family, there was no such thing as containment. Feelings were splattered around the household with the intensity of a spraying fire hose. I was terrified of what I might witness or hear tonight. But along with that terror, my fondness for the Cones only grew. To feel *something* was to feel alive. And to feel alive was starting to feel like love.

Izzy squatted on the dining room table. She placed the horseshoe crab shell, back up, in the center of the table. On the spiny, hard dome, she put the tiniest seashells, one by one. Around the horseshoe crab shell, she placed the bigger seashells, alternating faceup with facedown.

"That's so beautiful," I said.

"It's the centerplace."

"The centerpiece."

"The centerpiece."

Jimmy came into the room. We hadn't seen him since the dunes, though we'd seen Sheba and Mrs. Cone as they'd passed through the kitchen to go to their rooms to dress for dinner. Jimmy was wearing cutoff shorts and no shirt. The leather string with feathers dangled on his neck. It seemed to be pointing down toward his crotch. I couldn't stop myself from seeing his penis again, the way it had bobbed up in the air. My stomach lurched. I was now certain that I was a sex addict. I would have to ask Dr. Cone to treat me. But how would I pay for the therapy? And would he be required to tell my parents?

"Jimmy!" Izzy raised her arms, the signal to be picked up.

"Izzy, baby!" Jimmy lifted her up off the table, twirled her around, and then hugged her close to his chest.

"We saw you wrestling," Izzy whispered.

"I know. I'm sorry." Jimmy carried Izzy toward me, and with her still in his arms he hugged me. "I'm really sorry."

"Um." I didn't know what to say. Jimmy clung to me and the three of us rocked back and forth, Izzy squished between us. I could smell the sun on Jimmy's skin, and his chest hair tickled my face. His penis popped up in my mind again, just as it had popped up in the air.

"I'm really, really sorry." Jimmy held on tighter and kept rocking. I closed my eyes. It felt good to be wedged in there like that. I tried to push Jimmy's penis out of my mind, but instantly discovered that willing it away put as much focus on it as not willing it away.

When Jimmy let go, he stared into my eyes.

"I told Dr. Cone but no one else," I confessed. Tears sprang to my eyes. I was angry at Jimmy for betraying Sheba, and for making love with the married(!) Beanie Jones. But I knew he was an addict. I knew his body was like a teenager's that he had to wrangle into control every day. Until I met Jimmy, I hadn't understood that people you loved could do things you didn't love. And, still, you could keep loving them.

"I know, he told me. It's okay." Jimmy wiped my tears with his thumb.

"Mary Jane, are you crying?" Izzy leaned out of Jimmy's arms into mine.

I shook my head, but tears were spilling down my face. I'd cried more this summer than I had in all the years since I was Izzy's age. And I'd never been happier.

"It's okay, Mary Jane. You didn't do anything wrong." Jimmy leaned in and kissed my forehead and this made me cry a little harder. I inhaled deeply in an effort to suck it up. I didn't want to freak Izzy out.

"Mary Jane." Izzy kissed my face all over. "Don't cry. I love you."

"Everyone loves Mary Jane." Jimmy kissed my head and then he started singing, *"Mary Jane, Mary Jane!"*

Izzy sang with him and I started laughing. Jimmy sang as he went to the living room. He returned, still singing, with his guitar.

As Izzy and I set the table, Jimmy sat on a chair plucking at his guitar and singing. I wished so badly that we hadn't seen Jimmy with Beanie Jones. Or that Beanie Jones had never moved to Roland Park.

Sheba came into the dining room first. She was wearing a long batik sundress with no bra, and was barefoot. She sat right beside Jimmy, watched him for a minute, and then harmonized. They sounded magical together. What if Jimmy and Sheba broke up because of Beanie Jones? What if they never sang together again? What if Sheba went nuts again and Jimmy ran off and did drugs and overdosed? Something was going to unravel and I felt like I was the person who was holding the loose string, about to pull and watch it all fall apart.

Nothing seemed unusual during dinner. If anything, Jimmy was happier and more upbeat than most nights, and Dr. Cone was more engaged. Everyone loved the pot roast and Izzy was thrilled with her centerpiece. Each time someone passed something across the table, she stood on her chair to make sure no shell from the center-piece was disturbed.

After dessert, Jimmy pushed back his chair and said he'd clean up. Mrs. Cone stood and said she'd help him. Like Sheba, she was wearing a long sundress, but hers wasn't batik and looked a little pilled and old. She was barefoot too. Every time someone walked across the kitchen, I said a quick thanks that no glasses or dishes had been broken and there were no unseen shards waiting for a soft, tender foot.

I pushed my chair back and looked at Izzy. "Bath time."

"But wait." Izzy stood on her chair. "We need a polar bear photo of my centerplace!"

"Excellent idea." Dr. Cone went off to find the Polaroid camera as Sheba and I took dishes to the sink. Jimmy and Mrs. Cone had already started washing.

Dr. Cone returned within minutes. Izzy sat on the table near the shells and lifted her hands in a wide V. Dr. Cone clicked a picture and the flash exploded with a brilliant white light that made me see stars for a minute.

"Now everyone with my centerplace!" Izzy said.

"Another excellent idea." Dr. Cone leaned over Izzy and kissed her head. "BONNIE!"

I was surprised Dr. Cone had shouted the way he and Mrs. Cone did at home. The dining room was open to the kitchen. We were looking right at Mrs. Cone and Jimmy, side by side at the sink, chatting and laughing.

"WHAT?" Mrs. Cone turned and looked at her hus-band.

"GROUP PICTURE."

"Oh, we *have to* take a group photo." Sheba was carrying the pot roast platter into the kitchen. She came back with Jimmy and Mrs. Cone.

"I'll do it. Long arms." Jimmy took the camera from Dr. Cone and we all gathered around behind him, Izzy's centerpiece somewhere behind us.

"Say sober!" Jimmy pushed the button, the flash exploded again, and stars swam before me. Jimmy pulled out the photo and lay it on the table next to the one Dr. Cone had taken.

"We'll look at them after your bath," I said to Izzy. I could smell the gluey odor of the fixing agent Dr. Cone was applying to the Polaroids as I picked up Izzy and carried her to our bathroom.

In the tub Izzy sang the Beanie Jones song again.

"Let's sing the rainbow song instead." I'd taught Izzy "The Beautiful Land" from *The Roar of the Greasepaint—The Smell of the Crowd* soundtrack.

We started together, *"Red is the color of a lot of lollipops. . . ."*

When Izzy was in her pajamas, her hair combed, her skin smelling like line-dried cotton sheets, I carried her into the dining room to look at the Polaroids. The grown-ups were in the living room. The smoky eraser smell that accompanied them at night filtered into the dining room.

Izzy stared down at the photos. "We look pretty."

"Yeah, we do." Disaster was looming and yet we did look beautiful. Everyone was smiling. We all seemed relaxed, like we'd just fallen into place. And each body was connected to another body, closely. An unbreakable chain of love. It was the opposite of the staged family photo my mother sent out every Christmas. In Mom's picture, our decorated tree—put up on the first of December—was in the background. My mother and I wore dresses and shoes the same color. Always red or green, with beige stockings on our legs. My father put on the same tie each year: red with a pattern of green Christmas trees. I stood a couple of inches in front of my parents, whose bodies didn't touch. My mother placed her right hand on my left shoulder and my father placed his left hand on my right shoulder. Usually the photo was taken by our next-door neighbor, Mr. Riley. Once, on a family trip to San Francisco, we visited the Ripley's Believe It or Not! museum at Fisherman's Wharf. When I saw the wax people there, I thought of our Christmas photos. I'd always thought that waxy strangers-in-an-elevator look was just because no one in my family was comfortable in front of a camera. But now I wondered if it was because no one in my family was comfortable with any other person in my family.

"I love Mom, I love Dad, I love Mary Jane, I love Sheba, I love Jimmy." Izzy leaned off my hip and put her finger on the photo. On Jimmy's heart.

"I love you." I put my finger on top of Izzy's. Then I picked up the two photos and carried them into the bedroom with Izzy. I dropped Izzy on the bed and then propped the picture of her with the horseshoe crab centerpiece against the lamp base on her bedside table. The other photo I placed on the lamp base of my bedside table. Later I'd ask Dr. Cone if I could keep it.

I was in the middle of the moment, the picture had been taken less than an hour ago, and already I felt the loss of time, the loss of this summer, the loss of this makeshift family. I supposed it was preemptive nostalgia, inoculating me for what was to come. Would Izzy forget me?

Would Dr. and Mrs. Cone remind her of the summer she spent with me? Would Sheba and Jimmy remember this the way I would? Was this summer changing their lives the way it was changing mine?

Izzy fell asleep as I was reading to her. I slipped out of her bed, shut the door behind me, and followed the smoke to the living room. Though I felt tremulous about family therapy this evening, I also wanted it to happen soon, just so I could stop wondering and worrying about how Sheba might react and how Jimmy would respond to Sheba's reaction. My heart hurt for Sheba. And it hurt for Jimmy, too, even though I knew this was his fault.

Dr. Cone clapped his hands when he saw me. "Mary Jane!"

"Hey." I awkwardly lifted my hand and waved. I hadn't been this nervous since the first day I'd met Sheba and Jimmy.

Dr. Cone stood. "Shall we do this in the Office?"

"Let's do it." Jimmy stood and stretched. His shirt lifted, revealing the downy hair on his belly.

"The beach? That Office?" I asked, though of course I knew the answer.

"Yeah, it's really been a good place to open up, Mary Jane. The sound of the waves, the smell of the sea air—it brings you down to the basics. It reminds us that we're alive, just another part of the physical world."

"Baby!" Sheba hugged me. "Is this your first time in therapy?"

"Uh. Yeah." I hadn't really thought of it in those terms. That *I* was going to be in therapy.

"I'm bringing some wine." Mrs. Cone held a bottle against her chest like a baby.

"What about Izzy?" I asked.

"She's too young for this." Dr. Cone shook his head. "But soon."

"No, I mean, what about leaving her alone in the house? What if she wakes up and no one's here?"

"Has she ever woken up since we've been here?" Mrs. Cone lifted the bottle and took a sip.

"No, but what if she does? Won't she be scared to find no one home?"

"We'll leave the doors to the beach open so she knows where to go." Dr. Cone waved his arm as if to indicate the flow of air, the flow of Izzy.

"Mary Jane, Mary Jane!" Jimmy sang, and he walked out the door. Mrs. Cone followed him, the bottle of wine dangling from one hand.

Dr. Cone opened the door to the screened porch and pushed a wicker chair against it so it would stay open. Then he opened the screen door to the beach, and put another wicker chair there. "That should work." He nodded to the side, meaning I should go out.

"Okay. But wait." I wasn't sure if I was really this nervous about leaving Izzy alone or if I was avoiding the pending family therapy. "Are there any animals that might enter the house and attack Izzy?"

"Mary Jane." Sheba spoke firmly. "Take my hand. You're coming with me."

"Izzy will be fine." Dr. Cone smiled at me. "No beach animals will enter the house and attack her. But I do appreciate your concern. You'll make an excellent mother one day."

Sheba pulled me out of the house. The moon was up and stars were scattered across the sky like spilled milk. It was light enough to see our bare feet as we walked through the dunes to the spot where Jimmy and Mrs. Cone waited. They were on the sheet, lying on their sides, facing each other. The bottle of wine leaned against Mrs. Cone's breasts.

I sat cross-legged at Mrs. Cone's feet. Jimmy sat up and crossed his legs and then Mrs. Cone sat up and tucked her legs behind her. Sheba hiked up her dress all the way to her pink underpants and then sat cross-legged next to Jimmy. Mrs. Cone swiveled around and pulled up her dress so that she, too, was sitting cross-legged. Dr. Cone sat between Sheba and Mrs. Cone.

Mrs. Cone took another sip from the bottle. Dr. Cone shot her a quick look. Usually the drinking of wine was more discreet.

"Mary Jane." Dr. Cone looked at me. The whites of his eyes glinted. "This is a place where everyone is honest and open. There's nothing to hide and nothing to be ashamed of. We share our feelings, and we don't judge each other. We accept each other and we accept ourselves."

I nodded at Dr. Cone, feeling even more nervous. Did I have to announce what Izzy and I had seen on the dunes?

"It's all very frank," Sheba said. "But you're smart enough and grown-up enough to handle adult conversation, and to listen without freaking out about issues around sexuality, and childhood traumas we're all still dealing with, our current relationships and all the complications there, of course."

"Okay." I nodded at Sheba now. Did I have to speak? The idea of talking about any of those things, especially sexuality—in light of the fact that I was a sex addict—was as terrifying a thing as I had ever imagined.

Dr. Cone said, "Let's start by going around the circle and just checking in. Saying how we each feel. Where we are emotionally right now."

"I'm feeling a little drunk." Mrs. Cone tilted up the bottle and slugged down the last drops. "And maybe I smoked too much pot?"

"In light of Jimmy's struggles, maybe we could all cool it on the weed, whites, and wine." Dr. Cone looked directly at Mrs. Cone as he said this.

Sheba started singing, *"And if you give meeeeee weed, whites, and . . ."*

I had only recently learned that weed was the same thing as Mary Jane, but I had no idea what whites were. Probably something else Mrs. Cone smoked or drank.

"I'm feeling a little anxious." Jimmy looked right at Dr. Cone. "Today was a bit of a fuckup, and I'm not feeling good about it. But I think my emotions have been pent up inside me, and instead of talking it through, I let my urges burst out in inappropriate ways. So. Uh. Yeah. I'm anxious." Jimmy pulled a joint from one back pocket and a lighter from the other. He lit the joint, took a hit, then passed it to Sheba.

Sheba took a hit. Smoke puffed out of her mouth when she said, "I'm feeling incredible love for Jimmy. And pride, too. I mean, he's working so hard. And I feel grateful for all of you. For this beautiful family." Sheba and Jimmy stared at each other. They were both smiling with their mouths closed. Sheba then passed the joint to Mrs. Cone.

"Mary Jane?" Dr. Cone said.

"Uh, um." I felt like I might throw up. Would Sheba still love Jimmy once she knew about his lovemaking in the dunes with Beanie Jones? Would the Cones fire me if they knew that I was a sex addict? "I feel very worried and nervous."

"Why?" Sheba asked.

"Uh." I looked from Jimmy to Dr. Cone, to Jimmy again.

"It's cool," Jimmy said. "You can say anything."

Dr. Cone said, "Why don't we let the others speak first since this is Mary Jane's first time in therapy?"

"Okay, I'll talk," Sheba said. "I guess I'm a little anxious too. Jimmy and I have been incognito for weeks now and I'm finding that rather than feeling liberated by it, I sort of miss the reaction people have to me. I mean, I thought I hated it. I don't understand why, but I miss waiters falling all over themselves and giving me the best table and I miss girls crying when they see me and I miss the gay men who tell me I've saved their lives."

I wanted to ask Sheba how she'd saved gay men's lives, but I knew it was not the right time.

"You miss your celebrity," Dr. Cone said.

"Yeah. Isn't that weird? I complained about it all the time. But I wonder if I'm sort of addicted to that high of being the person in the room everyone wants to look at or know."

We all were looking at Sheba. She was so beautiful that even if she wasn't a star, I would want to stare at her in a room. I'd want to know her too.

Dr. Cone said, "Let's explore this further. What do you think you gain from *being seen*? Is it emotional? Is there a childhood interaction that is being recapitulated, or an unfulfilled need that is being filled through the act of being seen?"

"Oh, Richard." Sheba shook her head. She pulled on the tips of her bare toes. "You know my mother showed me no love. And she shamed me for my sexuality."

"Your mom's a bitch." Jimmy spoke through nearly closed lips that allowed a thin sheet of smoke to slip out.

"She was. She shamed me for the very things that the public adores about me: my hair, my tits, my ass, my legs. Even my pussy . . ."

I swallowed hard. I'd never heard anyone use that word, but I did know what it meant. I tried to let my brain move past the idea that Sheba was discussing this part of her body; I tried to be the adult Sheba expected of me.

"You've been nominated for an Academy Award," Dr. Cone said. "You're always asked to sing on talk shows. I think it's factual that you are also adored for your many talents."

"But, Richard, no one on this Earth would pay five cents to see my talents if I didn't look the way I do." Sheba threw her hair forward.

"Do you feel any gratification when you're rewarded for your talents, or do you only feel gratified when you're rewarded for your physical attributes?"

"When I was in *Playboy,* I got more recognition, more adoration, more praise than I did for anything else I've ever done. And you know what?"

"What?" Mrs. Cone asked, too loudly, and then she hiccuped.

Sheba and Dr. Cone both looked at her like she'd just shouted during a silent prayer in church.

Sheba turned her head back to Dr. Cone as if he had asked the question. "It made me feel good. It made me feel like I mattered. *Playboy* filled the hole my mother carved out of me when she told me I was a whore and a slut and that I'd never be as good as my brothers."

"Like I said," Jimmy grumbled, "lady's a bitch."

"So you're defying your mother, in a sense." Dr. Cone was nodding. He paused for a moment and then said, "Does this defiance feed you spiritually?"

Sheba thought about this, and I thought about it too. Wearing the crochet bikini Sheba bought me did seem like it filled some spiritual need. When I wore it, it was like I was transforming into the freer, less afraid person I wanted to be. But could I really compare my semi-nudeness in a bathing suit on a private beach to Sheba's total nudeness in a magazine that just about every man in the world looked at?

"It might. Allowing myself to flaunt what my mother wanted me to hide makes me feel like I exist on my own terms," Sheba said, and I understood her completely.

"Let's look at it from another angle," Dr. Cone said. "Is there anything that's worth doing without an audience? Is there any part of you that doesn't need to be seen?"

"When Jimmy and I make love, I feel whole. Complete. Like everything that's missing in me is filled." Sheba reached her arm out to Jimmy and they held hands. He leaned in and whispered something to her. Mrs. Cone sighed so loudly, I wondered if she wanted to interrupt them. Dr. Cone looked entirely calm, like he had no problem waiting for the two of them to finish whatever it was they were whispering, lip to lip.

I heard Jimmy say, "Baby, I just love you so much."

My stomach rumbled again. Sheba had just admitted that her most complete moments in life were when she was making love to Jimmy. And mere hours ago, Jimmy was doing exactly that with Beanie Jones.

When they finally stopped whispering, Sheba said, "I think I need to meditate on how I can feel complete and whole without continuous feedback from exterior sources, including Jimmy. Like, I need to totally chill out and sit with myself, just see what it means to be *me* without the world telling me who I am, or who I'm not, or who I am to them."

"You have given yourself excellent advice," Dr. Cone said. I thought it was neat that he didn't feel like he had to be the one to come up with the advice. And then I wondered if I should see what it felt like to sit with myself without taking into account feedback from exterior sources, even though I usually felt comfortably and quietly invisible, except to my mother, who gave me continuous feedback. Maybe part of my joy in being at the Cones was the joy of not getting feedback from my mother. I wanted to think about this more, but then Jimmy started talking and I didn't want to miss anything he had to stay.

"But wait. I mean, fuck, man, if Sheba's not the super-star sucking up all the attention, then everyone's gonna look more closely at me." He knocked his thumb against his chest when he said *me*.

"So you prefer to be in the background?" Dr. Cone asked. Were all psychiatrists like this? It seemed like Dr. Cone offered very little. Though maybe his questions were designed to help people come to conclusions on their own.

"Fuck yeah. I was never after fame. All I've ever wanted was to make enough money to buy guitar strings and eat. I hate celebrity. If I could do what I do anony-mously, I sure as fuck would. I just want to play my damn guitar and sing. I don't want strangers talking to me or trying to touch me, or even telling me how much they love my music. And I sure as hell don't give a shit what they think about how I look. In fact, I'd prefer they didn't look at me at all."

"Does Sheba's missing celebrity feel threatening to you?" Dr. Cone tapped his fingertips together, his two hands making the shape of a tent.

"Yeah, it feels threatening. Doc, you more than anyone understand that half the reason I love shooting junk is to get away from feeling like a show pony. I do it to get away from the screaming masses and the greedy fucking producers. When I'm high, celebrity doesn't exist. It's just me. Me and my music, numbing out on a level that doesn't take into account the world and what everyone else wants or needs. When I've used, I can hear my thoughts. I can feel my heartbeat. I'm content in just sitting with myself. There's no self-consciousness. None! It's fucking soulful, man."

"No!" Sheba said.

"Jimmy," Dr. Cone said. "Your soul was there before the drugs. Your soul has peeked out since you've been sober, has it not?"

"But junk is a direct line to my soul." Jimmy thumped his heart with his thumb again.

"That's not your fucking soul, Jimmy!" Sheba sat up straighter. "That's fake soul. That's powder soul. That's no more soulful than Captain and Tennille singing at that damn piano! It's an illusion!"

"Celebrity's a fucking illusion, Sheba! We're all just humans: we're born, we eat, we shit, we fuck, and then we die. The fact that random strangers think you and I are better than them is the biggest illusion of all!"

"That's not true," Sheba said. "You have more talent than others. You are better than them."

"I might be better at playing guitar," Jimmy said. "But there are millions of things that other people are better at. Shit, Mary Jane's a better cook than everyone here, and she fucking sings better than most people in the studio."

Goose bumps covered my skin like a sheet that had just been thrown over me. Did Jimmy really think I sang better than some people in recording studios?

Mrs. Cone was vigorously nodding. Then she said, "If

Sheba loves celebrity and you hate it, isn't that hard on your marriage?"

"No," Sheba and Jimmy said at once.

Sheba said, "If we both wanted it, we'd be competing."

"Like I said, she guards me from it." Jimmy leaned over and rubbed Sheba's leg. "She's my smack."

"I'd love to be a star," Mrs. Cone said. "I mean, come on. It's like being the most popular person in school but school is the world." Mrs. Cone hiccuped again. "If I were Sheba, I would pose in *Playboy* too. Hell, I'd pose in *Oui*."

We all looked at Mrs. Cone curiously. Dr. Cone said, "Is being seen like that something you feel you need, Bonnie?"

Mrs. Cone kept talking as if he hadn't asked a question. "Who wouldn't be addicted to stardom? I mean, c'mon. Seriously."

"Well, we're all addicts of some sort," Sheba said. "Part of being alive is figuring out the balance between what you want, what you need, and what you have with what you don't want, don't need, and don't have. I mean, Jimmy, man, you are so not alone here. This whole family, each of us, we're all addicts in one way or another."

"I've grown addicted to pot since you two moved in," Mrs. Cone said.

"You're not addicted to pot." Sheba said it in a way that made it feel irrefutable. "But I am addicted to fame." I wondered, if Mrs. Cone or Sheba had a sex addiction like me, would they openly admit it? Then again, Sheba did talk about sex with Jimmy, so maybe she would.

Jimmy said, "Richard's addicted to work. Shit, Richard, you've now spent more hours talking to me than my mother has over my entire life."

Dr. Cone said, "I may be addicted to work, but you're in high need now, and I want to see you through to the

successful end. I want us all to finish this summer suc-
cessfully."

"High need!" Sheba laughed, and held up the joint.

"Mary Jane's already a success," Jimmy said. "She's
perfect as she is."

"Is that how you feel, Mary Jane?" Dr. Cone asked, and
everyone turned their heads toward me.

"Well." I took a deep breath. It felt like my lungs were
crated in a metal box that wouldn't let them expand properly. "I think I have problems too."

"You do?!" Mrs. Cone laughed. "I can't imagine one thing
that's out of whack for you. Except maybe your parents."

"You're safe here, Mary Jane. We're here to listen.
There's no judgment." Dr. Cone ran his fingers down his
goaty sideburns, like he was combing them.

"Um . . ." My heart was beating so hard, I thought I
might pass out. But if there ever was a chance for me to be
cured of my problem, this seemed like the best place.

"Oh, Mary Jane. Nothing you say could shock us or
make us love you any less." Sheba crawled over Jimmy so
that she was beside me. She picked up my hand and held
it between her two hands. "You can say it."

I took a deep breath and then blurted it out before I
could think it through any longer. "I think I might be a
sex addict."

There was silence. Sheba put her head closer to mine
and stared into my eyes, blinking. I looked toward Dr.
Cone. His eyebrows were drawn together. I'd never seen
him look so serious.

"Have you been having reckless and indiscriminate
sex?" Dr. Cone asked.

"No!" I was surprised he would imagine I had. "I've
never had sex."

"Have you been fooling around with someone?" Mrs. Cone stared at Jimmy as she asked this, as if she expected me to be fooling around with him.

"No! No. I've never even kissed a boy."

Dr. Cone said, "Are you looking at pornographic magazines?"

"No, of course not. I'm taking care of Izzy all day."

"Compulsively masturbating?" Dr. Cone asked, and my face burned hard and deep.

"No, I've *never* done that. But I think about sex all the time. Or at the wrong time. Like, I see penises when I'm making dinner. Or, if I'm grocery shopping, I can't get the word *sex* out of my brain or maybe I'll think *sex addict sex addict sex addict* just because I'm thinking about sex. Or I'll see something that is totally not related to sex and it will remind me of sex." I felt a rush of lightness after having poured all this out. It was like my head was filled with helium.

"Like a zucchini?" Sheba asked.

I paused. "Well, I never thought of that. But I will now. That's what I mean. From today on, I'll think of sex, or a penis, I guess, every time I look at a zucchini." I searched their faces in the shadowy moonlight to see if they were repulsed by me. Or disappointed in me. But everyone was smiling.

"Oh, sweetie." Sheba put her arms around me and pulled me against her. She kissed my head like I was Izzy. "You're fine. Those are just normal human girl thoughts."

"Are they?" I couldn't imagine my mother ever thinking of penises while shopping for zucchinis. And the twins probably wouldn't even think of penises if they were standing in a boys' locker room with abundant visible penises. Would girls who wanted to be president ever think about sex?

"Those thoughts are fully within the range of normal," Dr. Cone said. "And if you were masturbating or looking at pornography, that would *still* be normal, as long as it wasn't to the exclusion of your daily needs and responsibilities."

"Dr. Cone, are you sure about this?" At the beginning of the summer I would have thought this conversation would be impossible. I'd thought I was going to die an old woman with my secret sex addiction. But now, what surprised me more than the conversation itself, was the enormous unburdening I felt. It was like a great wind was suddenly blowing through my hollowed-out body.

"I am certain. You aren't even verging on an addiction."

"Mary Jane! Baby!" Jimmy leaned forward toward me. "I'm the one who's fucking half addicted to sex. You saw what happened! It's not you, baby."

"You're SO fine!" Sheba hugged me. Then she pulled away from me and said, "What did she see? What are you talking about?"

Dr. Cone said, "Jimmy, maybe you should save Mary Jane the discomfort of having to say what happened."

"WHAT THE FUCK HAPPENED?" Sheba stared hard at Jimmy.

Mrs. Cone leaned forward. "What? Wait? What happened? Richard, do you know what happened?"

"Let's let Jimmy talk. And please, everyone, try to reserve judgment and keep your emotions in check until he's had his say." Dr. Cone looked at Sheba as he said this.

"I was walking down the beach today," Jimmy said. "And I ran into that Beanie woman—"

"No!" Sheba said. "That blond-bob housewife can't stay the fuck away from us!"

"I didn't know how to say no." Jimmy sounded pained by this. Like saying no caused him physical distress. "I didn't know how to stop it. I *really* didn't want to do it, but I also didn't want to hurt her feelings, and my dick wanted it, for sure, and then Mary Jane and Izzy saw us—"

"YOU MADE LOVE TO BEANIE JONES!" Mrs. Cone stood. She had the wine bottle in her hand and for a second I thought she was going to hit Jimmy with it. I was surprised she wasn't upset about Izzy having seen Jimmy on top of Beanie Jones.

Sheba said, "What the fuck, Jimmy?!"

"I'm sorry." Jimmy shook his head, like even he was sick of himself.

"How could you do that to us?! Beanie Jones??" Mrs. Cone shouted.

Everyone was silent. Dr. Cone stared at Mrs. Cone. Sheba stared at Mrs. Cone too. Jimmy looked nervous, or confused; his eyes roamed from his wife to Mrs. Cone, back and forth.

Mrs. Cone looked like she was trying not to cry. "It's just, I mean, Beanie Jones?! COME ON! Beanie Jones?!" And then, in a quick semi-collapse, she sat back down. The bottle remained in her hand.

Sheba turned away from Mrs. Cone like she'd had enough of her. "Seriously, Jimmy. Beanie fucking Jones? What the fuck? Every fucking housewife in the neighborhood is going to be lined up at the door to fuck you now."

In my head I saw all the mothers from Roland Park holding cakes and cookies, lined up at the Cones' front door, waiting to make love to Jimmy. Would Mrs. Cone get in line too? Seemed like she'd want to be first.

I thought about how my body felt electric when Jimmy locked his eyes onto mine. His furry chest was warm against my cheek when he hugged me. I'd seen his penis and despite my best attempts, I couldn't get that image out of my head. But when I stopped and asked myself if I wanted to kiss Jimmy, the answer was no. He was handsome, and he had sexiness pulsating out of him like sound waves. But he was . . . well. He was old.

Jimmy was stuttering, blubbering, ". . . I couldn't find my way out of it—the words wouldn't come to me. And once it started, I didn't know how to stop it."

Dr. Cone said, "Jimmy, it's *your* body. You're in charge of it. You can choose not to make love to every beautiful woman who offers herself to you."

"You think Beanie Jones is beautiful?!" Mrs. Cone said. She seemed more upset than Sheba. I had expected Sheba to run into the house and start throwing dishes, Jimmy-style. Her husband had had sex with another woman! But Sheba seemed relatively calm.

"Bonnie, please." Dr. Cone lifted his hands and dropped them, palms down, as if he were dribbling two basketballs.

"We agreed, no fooling around while you're getting sober," Sheba said. I thought about this. Was Jimmy allowed to fool around with other women when he wasn't getting sober?

"And no fooling around with gossipy social climbers like Beanie Jones!" Mrs. Cone said.

"Bonnie!" Sheba said. "He is *my husband*. He has an open marriage with *me*, not you! I agree with you about Beanie Fuckface Jones, but I don't understand what your fucking stake is in this. Are you two making love? Have you been sleeping with my husband?"

The words *open marriage* echoed in my head. What

exactly did that mean? Did Sheba have sex with other people? Did they discuss it beforehand? Did they report to each other what had happened afterward? I could barely admit my sex addiction in group therapy and Sheba had just blurted out "open marriage" as if it were no big deal!

"Of course Bonnie and I aren't making love! That's fucking absurd!" Jimmy said, and Mrs. Cone's eyes flashed like she'd been slapped.

"Bonnie?" Dr. Cone looked at his wife. "What is your stake in this?"

Mrs. Cone dropped her head for a second, like she needed to gather air or courage or maybe just the strength to lift her head. When she finally did, she said, "It's just, God, I don't know. Jimmy and Sheba are *ours,* they belong to us! And . . . and . . . I don't know, I sort of feel like Jimmy betrayed us, too."

"You need to detach," Dr. Cone said. "It's not your marriage."

"And *you* need to not fuck Beanie Fuckface Jones," Sheba said to Jimmy.

"I don't want to be with anyone but you, baby." Jimmy stared at Sheba. "I don't even want to have an open marriage. I only agreed because you wanted it." The idea that Sheba had pushed for the open marriage more than Jimmy knocked around in my brain. I'd always thought men wanted sex more than women. But maybe that was as wrong as the ideas that Jewish people were untrustworthy or Black people should "know their place."

"Oh, baby, I love you so much!" Sheba was tearing up. And then she and Jimmy leaned in toward each other and started kissing. With tongues. Dr. Cone, Mrs. Cone, and I all watched.

Dr. Cone caught my eye and he said, "Mary Jane, are

you okay with everything that's come out here tonight? Do you have any questions about any of this?"

"Um . . ." I did, but I wasn't sure I should ask.

Dr. Cone nodded at me, and then he stared at Jimmy and Sheba until they stopped kissing and looked at me too.

"So. Uh. Does Beanie Jones have an open marriage too?" Was the world full of people whose lives were entirely different than what I had imagined?

"Nah." Jimmy shook his head.

"It's just 'cause it's Jimmy." Mrs. Cone appeared to be talking to the sand. "Women will do anything for the chance to make love to Jimmy."

"Bonnie!" Sheba said. "What the fuck? Are you in love with my husband?!"

Mrs. Cone pulled up her head and stared at Sheba. "What did you say?" It seemed like she was stalling for time.

"Are you in love with my husband?" Sheba said each word precisely, like she had to put air around the syllables and give them space.

"Well, who isn't, Sheba?" Mrs. Cone looked around vaguely, somehow not making eye contact with any of us, and then said, "I mean, I'm not saying I'd fool around with him. But I want your life. I want to spend a month at Cap-Eden-Roc in southern France! I want to go to Muscle Shoals and make a record and drink whiskey in the studio until six in the morning! I want to hang out with Lowell George and Linda Ronstadt and Graham Nash! I want to spend ten thousand dollars on clothes and carry an alligator handbag picked up at the Marché aux Puces in Paris and eat in all the best restaurants . . . and I want—I want—"

"What the fuck do you want, Bonnie?" Sheba's voice had an sharp, impatient edge.

Mrs. Cone said, "I want to be in a marriage where we want to kiss each other like you two just did. I want to be with someone who's so passionate he's bordering on insane. I want to be with someone who will call me *baby* and cry for me and look at me the way Jimmy looks at you. I don't want to be a doctor's wife living in Baltimore. I . . . I just want more than this." Mrs. Cone dropped her head and started crying.

None of us spoke. I couldn't bring myself to look at Dr. Cone. Finally he said, "Are you saying you don't want to be married to me?"

"I think I drank too much." Mrs. Cone stood, turned, and then started vomiting in the sand. Dr. Cone rushed to her. He held her thick red hair back with one hand and put his other hand on her shoulder so she didn't nose-dive as she barfed.

Sheba took my hand and pulled me to standing. Jimmy stood too and the three of us quietly walked away.

I followed Jimmy and Sheba into the kitchen. Jimmy turned on the tap, leaned over it, and took a few dog laps. Sheba sat at the table. She looked at me and patted the chair beside hers.

"Do we have any Zonkers?" Jimmy asked.

"Yeah, in the cupboard," I said. "I'll get them."

"I got 'em." Jimmy opened the cupboard, and I sat on the chair beside Sheba.

Jimmy brought the Zonkers to the table and sat across from me and Sheba. After he took a handful from the box, he passed it to me. I took a huge handful, the size of a throwing snowball. Sheba reached into the box and did the same.

"Shit." Jimmy reached for the box. He took another handful.

"I know." Sheba took the box back from him. She dumped a pile of Zonkers out on the table.

"I mean what the fuck?" Jimmy grabbed the box again.

"What the fuck is right. Poor Richard."

"Do you think Mrs. Cone is going to leave Dr. Cone?" I took the box from Jimmy and poured out more Zonkers into Sheba's pile.

"Who knows, man?" Jimmy reached across the table and pulled the box closer to him. "But even if they don't break up, he's gonna be hurtin' over that little one-act show."

"Can't un-ring that bell." Sheba picked up a nutty chunk from the pile and popped it in her mouth.

"Can't put that toothpaste back in the tube." Jimmy shook the box, letting the last crumbled bits gather in the corner so he could pull them all out in one handful.

"Where do you want to go to college?" Sheba asked me, as if we'd been talking about school and not the Cones' imploding marriage.

"I've been trying to get my parents to take me to New York City, but they don't like New York. So I kinda thought the only way I'd ever see it was if I went to college there."

"I didn't even finish high school," Jimmy said. "I'm not made for school."

"You're still the smartest man I know," Sheba said. She looked at me. "He reads constantly, if you haven't noticed. History, biographies, fiction."

I had noticed. "Did you go to college?"

"I went to UCLA—I had to stay in Los Angeles because we were shooting the show there. But I didn't have a normal college experience. People stared at me and followed me around campus. And I didn't trust that anyone really wanted to be my friend. Even the professors wrote notes like *Let's meet in my office and discuss this.* I always thought that most people just wanted to spend time with the famous girl."

"Kinda like Bonnie," Jimmy said. Sheba and I both looked at him.

"It seems like Mrs. Cone really does like you, though," I said.

"No, I'm sure she likes me. And I like her, too. But it's hard to have a balanced friendship when one person wants everything the other person has." Sheba poked her nail through the pile of Zonkers, searching for the best bits, I guessed.

Jimmy got up, kissed Sheba on the lips, and then kissed the top of my head. He left the room and came back a few seconds later with his guitar.

"How about this?" Jimmy started plucking a song I didn't know. I knew all his songs by then, so it must have been from someone else's album. Sheba sang along, and by the time they started through it a second time, I knew the words and was harmonizing: *"And I'm wasted and I can't find my way home."*

"I like that song," I said when we finished. "Did you write it?"

"Hell no," Jimmy said. "Stevie Winwood wrote it."

"We gotta take you record shopping," Sheba said. She got up, went to the cupboard, and pulled out a new box of Zonkers.

Jimmy started a new song. Before each line, he said the words aloud so I would know what to sing. Sheba stayed on melody and Jimmy took the harmony with me. I could feel our voices vibrating in the air, perfectly balanced like a mathematical equation.

Dr. and Mrs. Cone didn't come in through the beach door, but I did hear the front door open and close. This was late, after the second box of Zonkers was gone. Sheba and Jimmy and I sang through the night—sometimes the same song three or four times just so I could learn it right. Around four in the morning, Jimmy put the guitar down and we went to bed.

Izzy woke up before seven, as usual. "Birds in a nest?" she asked.

"Just come snuggle with me for a minute." My eyes felt like they'd been cemented closed.

She crawled into my bed and I wrapped my body around hers like we were side-stacked seashells.

"Can we read a book?"

"You look at a book and I'll sleep for twenty more minutes. And then we'll get up and I'll make you birds in a nest."

"Okay." Izzy didn't move to get a book. She just lay there, as still and warm as a curled-up kitten. I thought of Dr. and Mrs. Cone with pangs of guilt for not having worried more about them last night. I wanted all to be right and safe in their marriage so that Izzy could grow up in that wonderful house with both of her parents coming in and out. I vowed to do the best job I could taking care of Izzy, to make sure she always felt loved and safe and secure.

"Is twenty minutes up?"

"No. Two minutes are up."

"How long is twenty minutes?"

"Twelve hundred seconds. Count to twelve hundred. Minus the hundred and twenty seconds that already passed." I knew I could fall back asleep if I had only a moment of silence.

"What's twelve hundred seconds minus a hundred and twenty seconds?"

"Um . . . one thousand . . . um . . . one thousand eighty seconds. Count to one thousand and eighty."

"OK. One. Two. Three . . ."

Izzy made it to eighty-five and then rotated in my arms so we were face-to-face. I could feel her warm breath on my nose. I could feel her eyes bearing down on me. She was being so good—saying nothing, barely moving, breathing deeply and quietly. I opened my eyes and stared right back at her. We looked at each other for the longest time, neither of us speaking.

"Okay," I said. "I'll get up now."

Izzy leaned in and kissed my nose. And then she tumbled out of bed, half falling, half cartwheeling, pulling off her nightgown and talking all at once.

It was a long, lazy day. Dr. and Mrs. Cone stayed tucked away in their room. Izzy didn't seem to notice their absence and Sheba and Jimmy didn't seem to mind. By early afternoon, Jimmy put down his book and napped in a chair on the beach. Sheba lay on her back, put on her oversize sunglasses, and sunbathed. Maybe she was sleeping too. I couldn't see her eyes.

Izzy and I worked on sculpting a giant sunbathing couple out of the sand. Izzy heaped mounds of sand for the woman's breasts. I thought about making a penis for the man, then decided to make a Ken-doll lump instead. After last night, I felt confident that my initial urge to sculpt male genitalia didn't make me a sex addict.

"That's a funny penis," Izzy said.

"It's just a mound. We're going to cover it with a bathing suit."

We each took a bucket and walked along the beach collecting driftwood and shells for bathing suits. For hair we collected sea grass.

We were silently working on the seashell bathing suits when Dr. and Mrs. Cone approached, each carrying a chair. Mrs. Cone wore a giant hat and sunglasses. Her lips were orange and waxy. Her bikini covered so little, I wondered why she was wearing it at all.

"Look what we're making!" Izzy said, and they both put down their chairs and came to examine the people.

"Beautiful!" Dr. Cone kissed Izzy's head. She was sweating and her hair gleamed like a new penny.

"Amazing." Mrs. Cone bent over Izzy and kissed her head too. "Everything okay?" She looked at me.

"Yeah. Everything's good."

"We had birds in a nest for breakfast and Jimmy made West Virginia steak for lunch!"

"Oh yeah? What's that?" Mrs. Cone looked at me.

"Skinny, skinny, skinny meat." Izzy went back to placing shells.

"Fried bologna. He said it's what he ate for lunch when he was a kid."

Mrs. Cone looked over at Jimmy and Sheba, who had barely moved. She turned back to me. "I'm sorry about what I might have said last night."

I couldn't tell if she was apologizing to me or just expressing regret. "It's okay," I said quickly.

Dr. Cone settled in his chair and opened his book.

Mrs. Cone forced a smile at me. She rubbed Izzy's sweaty head and then went to her chair beside Dr. Cone's.

Jimmy and Sheba woke up a few minutes later. I could hear Mrs. Cone apologizing to them, too. She claimed she was drunk and didn't even remember what she had said, but that Dr. Cone had told her and "Boy, was it a doozy."

"I've done way worse," Jimmy said. But I thought he'd probably never *said* worse. Jimmy seemed to take good care of the feelings of everyone around him. He was always trying to make Sheba happy first, and the rest of us happy next.

If you'd been watching a film of us that last day, or over dinner that night, or even the next morning as we packed up the car, it wouldn't have seemed that anything had changed. But something had. I felt like an invisible vibrating net had separated us into three alliances. The first was Jimmy, Sheba, Izzy, and me. The next was Dr. Cone, who had always remained outside everything anyway, as if someone had to be the real adult, the one in charge of keeping things aligned. And the third was Mrs. Cone. Mrs. Cone seemed slightly adrift and abandoned. She and Sheba chatted as usual, but their chumminess felt a little more stiff and guarded. Sheba wasn't letting her in anymore. I knew she'd never again mention hotels in Antibes or handbags purchased at the flea market in Paris.

11

The time at the beach had gone quickly, but at the same time, it felt expansive. It was as if a whole season had zoomed by rather than a week. At home in my own bed, I missed everyone at the Cone house. With my mother, at breakfast, I felt like an imposter. Even my clothes were false, as I'd left the wardrobe Sheba had bought me at the Cones' house, and promptly changed into a new outfit each morning right after I arrived. My mother, who had known everything about me since birth—what I ate, when I slept, who my friends were, what music I listened to, and what books I read—suddenly had a stranger at her table. But I was the only one who was aware of the change. I was now someone who had gone to family group therapy for sex addiction and knew the words to both the A and B sides of every Running Water album. Like Sheba in her wigs—I couldn't wait to get to the Cones so I could rip off the false self and just be me. Barefoot. Singing. Cooking dinner. Wearing a bikini. Playing with Izzy's hair.

Dr. and Mrs. Cone acted as if that night at the beach had never happened, but I noticed an effort in their relationship that hadn't previously existed. They almost never touched each other, and when one spoke, the other shut up entirely as if to be careful not to interrupt or correct.

Three weeks after we'd returned from the beach, Mrs. Cone left the house in the afternoon for a hair appointment. Izzy and I were in the TV room, folding clothes. Laundry was one of Izzy's favorite activities: every stage of it, from sorting to putting it away.

Sheba came in eating a Popsicle.

"We're going to iron." Izzy pointed to the growing pile of wrinkled clothes. I'd already set up a footstool by the ironing board and was waiting for the iron to heat up. When Izzy ironed, I stood right behind her, ready to grab the iron if she dropped it, left it too long in one spot, or knocked it off the board.

"Can you believe I've never ironed?" Sheba said.

"Really?"

"We had this Mexican woman who lived with us when I was a kid. She ironed everything. Even jeans and underwear."

"What about in college? Or now?"

"In college I dropped off my clothes at the cleaners every week and they were returned to me ironed and folded. And then after college I hired a cleaning lady who does all the laundry. Toni. She's in the New York apartment now."

"Mary Jane can teach you to iron," Izzy said. "She's good at teaching."

"Okay. I'll try it."

"But you can't have your Popsicle when you iron." Izzy and I had had a struggle over a dripping red Popsicle in her mouth the last time we'd ironed.

"Bossy!" Sheba smiled at Izzy and continued to suck her Popsicle.

"I'll finish it." Izzy went to Sheba and took the Popsicle from her. Sheba got up and stood at the ironing board.

I laid a white button-down open and facedown on the board. "The key is to not linger. You just push firmly and slide it along the fabric."

"One mustn't linger!" Sheba winked at me. She pushed the iron a few times. I watched. Izzy got closer and looked up. The Popsicle dripped down her chin. "Now what?"

"Then you do the sleeves." I readjusted the shirt so there was a single sleeve on the board.

"Firmly. And no lingering!" Sheba raised her voice to sound more like me. She slid the iron around the sleeve, then on the cuff. "Okay. I'm bored."

"Already?"

"Yup. Let's go record shopping." Sheba put the iron on the shirt facedown. I righted it quickly before the shirt burned.

"I wanna go record shopping!" Izzy jumped up and down, waving the Popsicle.

"I don't even know where the record store is." There were no record stores in Roland Park, and none on the regular routes I went with my mother: to the Elkridge Club, Roland Park Country School, Hutzler's for clothes.

"Richard will know. I'll find the keys." Sheba sauntered out.

"Can I get a record too?" Izzy asked.

"Yes. I'll buy you one." I quickly finished ironing the shirt.

"You will? You have money?"

"Yeah. I've been saving all the money your parents pay me. But I'll use some of it to buy you a record."

Izzy ran to my legs and hugged me. I rubbed her head. Then I unplugged the iron and neatly folded the shirt.

Jimmy wanted to go too. He didn't wear a wig and neither did Sheba. They both put on sunglasses. Jimmy was wearing a tank top and a Johns Hopkins baseball cap that must have been Dr. Cone's. Sheba tied a color-block scarf around her head. It covered her forehead and draped down the back of her hair like two red and orange tails.

Dr. Cone walked us out to the station wagon. Sheba got in the driver's seat, and Izzy and I got in the back. Sheba rolled down the window and Dr. Cone leaned on the window frame with his hairy forearms. "You remember how to get there?" he asked.

Sheba said, "Left on Cold Spring, right on Charles, stay on Charles awhile, left on North Ave."

"That's right. Cold Spring, Charles, North Ave. You can't get lost."

"Mary Jane is going to buy me a record!" Izzy said.

"She is?" Dr. Cone looked up from Sheba's window, then came around to Izzy's. He reached in and tousled her hair, then pulled out a folded bill and tried to hand it over to me. I waved him away. "What kind of record?" He tried once more to hand me the money. I shook my head, smiling. Dr. Cone shrugged and stuck the bill back in his pocket.

"I dunno. Mary Jane, what kind of record?"

"What about a Broadway soundtrack?"

"MARY JANE'S BUYING ME A BROADWAY SIDE-TRACK!!" Izzy leaned out the window. I grabbed her waist so she wouldn't fall out. Dr. Cone kissed her and then backed away as Sheba pulled the car from the curb.

"You have fun at the record store!" Dr. Cone laughed at his daughter, who seemed perilously close to dropping onto the pavement.

"Bye!" Sheba yelled.

"GOODBYE!" Izzy yelled, and I tugged her back in before we were moving too fast. Once she was settled into her seat, Izzy started singing a Running Water song. Sheba jumped in on the melody and I sang harmony. Jimmy made instrument noises with his mouth that sounded pretty cool. He could actually make the sound of a trumpet. And for a guitar he sort of said the word *twang,* but in a way that sounded close to a guitar.

The farther we got from Roland Park, the fewer trees I saw. By the time Sheba parked the car near the record store, there were no trees, just pavement, street, sidewalk, stores, and cars. Though I'd lived in Baltimore my whole life, I'd never been on North Avenue. The first thing I noticed was that there were very few station wagons around. Most cars here looked either shinier and fancier—many were the color of jewels—or beat-up and barely drivable. Everyone on the sidewalk was Black and I imagined how uncomfortable my mother would be here. Jimmy, Sheba, and Izzy didn't seem to notice that we were the only white people around.

We walked into the warehouse-size record store and Jimmy took a deep breath. "Fuck yeah," he said.

I examined the store. Signs hung from strings above sections, naming the genre: Jazz, Funk, Rock, Soul/R&B, Classical, Folk, Blues, etc. Along the walls were listening stations that looked sort of like phone booths, but instead of a phone, each booth held a record player and headphones. The people who worked at the store all wore bright yellow-and-green-striped shirts, making them hard to miss.

"Why didn't we come here on day one?" Sheba asked.

Izzy tugged my hand. "Where do we find the Broadway sidetrack records?"

"Over there." I pointed to a sign that said Soundtracks.

A salesperson approached us. He was as skinny as a piece of licorice and had an Afro pick stuck in his hair. I thought it was a clever place to carry the comb, as the comb was too big for his pockets.

"How can I help you folks?" The guy smiled and jerked his head as if he were following a tennis game: Izzy, Sheba, me, Jimmy. "No way, man. No way. Jimmy and Sheba?" His smile grew.

"Yeah, man." Jimmy pulled off the baseball cap, ran his fingers through his hair, and replaced the cap. "I need something new. Some jams that will inspire me, you know. I need a launching pad for my own shit."

"NO WAY!" The guy looked behind him, as if to see if anyone else was seeing this. "Jimmy! I love Running Water! I know every Running Water song by heart!"

"We do too," Izzy said.

"NO WAY! No way, man! I love both you guys! My whole family watched your show, Sheba. For years! YEARS!"

"Ah, you're so kind." Sheba smiled and I could see her sucking in this adoration like gold dust. She was glowing from it.

"My mother is going to DIE! This is UNREAL!"

"These are our nieces." Sheba held her hand out toward Izzy and me. She flipped her sunglasses so they were propped on her head over the scarf.

The guy glanced at us, smiled, then turned back to Jimmy and Sheba. "Okay, okay, okay, so let me help you. Jimmy wants something inspiring. What do you want, Sheba?"

"I just want something fun," Sheba said.

"I want Broadway sidetracks!" Izzy said.

"We got show tunes." He laughed, smiling at Izzy. "We got everything, man. I'm gonna set y'all up. Wait here." He held his hands up like stop signs. "Don't move, okay? Like, not one step. Stay right here."

"We'll be right here, doll," Sheba said.

The guy returned just a few seconds later, a small mob following behind him. The mob was made up of a bunch of guys and one girl. The girl was wearing a patchwork leather cap that I could imagine Sheba wearing on television.

"Holy moly, holy moly, I don't believe this!" the biggest guy said. He stuck out his giant hand and shook Jimmy's hand, then Sheba's, then mine, and then Izzy's.

"We're record shopping," Izzy said, and the man laughed.

"Look at her hair! Look at that cute hair!" the girl said, about Izzy. She was tall and had a face that was a perfect circle.

"Mary Jane is going to buy me show tunes!" Izzy said, and the big man laughed again, and then bent down and picked up Izzy. He looked even bigger with Izzy in front of him, like a giant holding a Munchkin.

The rest of the crowd leaned forward and shook all our hands, and then customers started noticing Jimmy and Sheba. Immediately three of the guys who worked there created a barricade, like bodyguards.

"Let them shop!" one guy said. "Give them some space!"

"Y'all want a snowball?" the girl asked. "My cousin's got a snowball stand at the end of the block. I can get you some snowballs."

"I'm fine, just happy to be here," Jimmy said quietly. I could see that he liked the people who were helping us, but didn't like being fussed over. Sheba, on the other hand, lingered with each person who shook her hand. She asked them questions: *What's your name? Did you grow up in Baltimore?* Each person she talked to looked changed, like they'd been anointed, charged with some kind of power that passed from Sheba to them.

When we moved, we moved as a single mass. The big guy, whose name was Gabriel, was the leader. The bodyguard guys kept everyone who wasn't part of our group back a couple of feet as the knot of us shuffled across the store.

We started in the Rock section.

"My niece needs her world expanded a little," Sheba said about me to Gabriel, who was still holding Izzy.

"She's got a hell of a voice." Jimmy nodded toward me. "You're gonna hear her on a record soon."

"One of yours?" Gabriel asked.

"Oh yeah. Definitely." Jimmy winked at me and I didn't know if that meant he was kidding or serious. I couldn't let myself think about it. I was afraid of ending up wildly disappointed.

Jimmy, Sheba, and Gabriel picked out records for me and handed them to a guy named Little Hank. I soon figured out he was Little Hank because another guy helping us was Medium Hank. I didn't ask where Big Hank was; maybe it was his day off?

Little Hank sidled up to me and shuffled through what they'd picked out. "You're gonna love this one." I looked at the record he held on top of the pile. On the front was a woman with bluish hair, surrounded by a long accordian.

"Is Little Feat the band or is *Dixie Chicken* the band?"

Little Hank laughed so hard, he bent over. "No, man, Little Feat's the band." He shuffled to the next one. There was a photo of a grown man in a very small black bathing suit walking on the beach.

"Boz Scaggs *Slow Dancer*. Is that the band name or the album name?"

"No wonder they're buying you music! No niece of Jimmy and Sheba should be so uninformed. *Slow Dancer* is the name of the album. Boz Scaggs is that guy's name." Little Hank flicked his finger on the bathing suit in the picture.

"A guy named Boz? Is that his real name?"

"Heck, I don't know." Little Hank kept shuffling through the records. He pulled out Steely Dan, who I'd heard of, and Rod Stewart, who I'd also heard of. I'd never heard of Dr. John, but the title of the album, *Cut Me While I'm Hot,* made me want to listen.

In the Folk section, Jimmy picked out John Prine and Gram Parsons. I'd heard of them both because Sheba and Mrs. Cone had discussed them one night. Jimmy handed Little Hank a Joni Mitchell album.

"Hell yeah, Jimmy!" Little Hank said. Then he leaned into me and almost whispered, "She's soulful. I didn't know who she was until I started working here, but Gabriel, man, he turns me on to every kind of music."

I wanted to be Little Hank so I could hear *every kind of music.* Then I realized I already was a version of Little Hank, as he was now handing me—well, not *every kind*— many kinds of music. As much as I liked wandering the record store, I was ready to flee it so we could get home and start listening.

Little Hank and I rushed to catch up to the group. They had moved on to Soul/R&B. The bodyguards backed people away so we could slide into the inner circle.

"He's getting Black music," Little Hank said to me as Jimmy and Gabriel discussed different albums. "That's what real musicians listen to."

Gabriel handed Little Hank a stack of albums and Little Hank shuffled through them so I could see all of the choices.

"I've heard of Earth, Wind & Fire," I said. "I think. Maybe not. Is there another band with a similar name?"

Little Hank thought I was hilarious. He laughed, shook his head, and showed me the rest of the albums: Al Green, Parliament, the Meters, the Isley Brothers, Sly and the Family Stone, Labelle, and Stevie Wonder.

"This guy is blind." Little Hank nodded toward Stevie Wonder, on top of the pile. "And he plays piano. He's cool. Everyone likes him."

I'd heard of Stevie Wonder but hadn't known he was blind. Maybe my mother would like him, since she believed that God had given blind and deaf people extra goodness since He took away one of their senses. A blind man attended our church and Mom always made sure he was seated near the front pew, close to our family, where she could help him in and out.

Sheba handed Little Hank two more records. "These are for me, but you're going to love them, Mary Jane. Let's sing along to these tonight."

"Oh, you gonna be singing loud!" Little Hank said. We looked at the albums; the first was Shirley Brown, *Woman to Woman*. I liked the colors of the album, pink and brown, and I liked the photo, too, because it just showed her: upside down and right side up. Facing herself. Unlike most of the other albums with women on the front, she wasn't posed in a sexy way. That made me curious about her. Next I looked at Millie Jackson, *Caught Up.* The cover showed a man and two women caught in a spiderweb. The back showed just the woman—Millie Jackson, I assumed—talking on the phone with a spiderweb framing her hair. She looked sort of sad in the photo, like she was getting her heart broken over the phone. There was another Millie Jackson album too. This one was called *Still Caught Up.* In the photo she was wearing a big hat and her lips were parted like she was about to kiss someone. It was definitely sexy and I wondered if Jimmy and Sheba knew her and if Jimmy, in their open marriage, was allowed to have sex with her.

"My turn!" Izzy shouted, and Gabriel moved her up to his shoulders. She was riding so high, I worried she'd knock her head on one of the signs hanging from the ceiling.

The crowd gathered in the Soundtracks section. Gabriel smiled down at me. "So what are we looking for?"

"Uh . . ." Would this knowledgeable crowd think I was stupid for liking show tunes? "Just something for Izzy to sing in the tub. You know." I was afraid to say what I was thinking, which was *Guys and Dolls.* What if, in spite of my great love for *Guys and Dolls,* it was actually the dumbest soundtrack ever made?

"Something for the tub, huh?" Gabriel pulled alternately on Izzy's ankles and she laughed.

"We could try *Guys and Dolls*?" I said it as if it had just occurred to me.

"I love *Guys and Dolls*!" Gabriel said, and I exhaled,

relieved. Gabriel pulled the record from a bin and handed it to Little Hank. "What about *Hair*? Wanna try that one too?"

"*Hair*?" I didn't know it. We hadn't gotten it in the Show Tunes of the Month Club.

"Oh hell yeah," Jimmy said. "It's got naked people running all over the park."

"I want *Hair*!" Izzy yelled.

"Is that the name of the song?" I asked Little Hank. "'Naked People Running All Over the Park'?"

Little Hank almost fell to the ground laughing. Gabriel added *Hair* to the pile Little Hank was carrying, and we all worked our way to the checkout counter.

Gabriel slipped Izzy off his shoulders and onto his hip as if he'd been carrying her since birth. "You folks mind if we take a photo or two? For posterity. Never has anyone as famous as Jimmy and Sheba set foot in this store."

"Sure." Jimmy nodded, but his face didn't look happy.

"And we gotta get a photo of Mary Jane before she becomes too famous to speak to us."

"Oh, I would always speak to you," I said, and everyone laughed.

Gabriel took Izzy with him and returned just a second later with a giant camera that had a large rectangular flash attachment. He handed the camera to one of the bodyguards and gave him a quick lesson on how to focus the camera.

Gabriel stood in the middle and hoisted Izzy back up to his shoulders. He let go of Izzy's ankles and put one arm around Jimmy and the other around Sheba. Izzy looked perfectly balanced, her tiny fists knotted in Gabriel's hair. Jimmy pulled me in close against his side, as if to protect himself from the crowd. The rest of the people who had been in our group gathered around on either side, and the bodyguard with the camera snapped off three pictures. Then he stepped in closer, maybe making it so it was only Jimmy, Sheba, and Gabriel, and snapped off another couple shots.

"One more, just to make sure we got a good one," Gabriel said. "And step back so you can see Izzy on my shoulders and the sign above the register."

I turned around and looked up to see what he was talking about. Above the register hung a huge sign that read, "Night Train Music: The Greatest Record Store in America."

The flash exploded when my face was turned away.

"I'm ready to go," Jimmy whispered in my ear, and the flash exploded two more times.

Little Hank rang up the records while Jimmy and Sheba talked to the employees who'd been shopping with us. I pulled out the ten-dollar bill I'd been carrying in my pocket and handed it to Little Hank.

"Jimmy gave me a credit card," Little Hank said, waving the bill away without pausing on the register. His long fingers moved so fast on the keys that they sounded musical.

I leaned into Jimmy and handed him the bill. He bent his head down toward me, glancing at the bill. I could see in his eyes that he wanted to leave so badly, he would bust out of his own skin and abandon his body in the store if he could.

"What's this?" Jimmy whispered.

"I'm paying for Izzy's records. They're a gift from me."

"Okay." Jimmy looked up, with his eyes only, as a woman, a customer, wedged her way into the circle to talk to him. She was in a jumpsuit that was unzipped almost to her waist, revealing breasts that were smashed together like two loaves of bread on her chest. The woman immediately started talking in a run-on sentence, as if she wanted to say everything she could before someone moved her away from Jimmy.

"My babysitter brought Running Water records to our house 'cause we didn't have any, see, and she's a heroin addict now too, just like you, see, and I still listen to Running Water. . . ."

"Uh-huh." Jimmy nodded. His eyes seemed unfocused and fogged over. He reached his arm toward me and I felt a small tug in my back shorts pocket. Jimmy had slipped the bill in there.

One of the bodyguard guys escorted the woman away from Jimmy and then moved other employees aside so Jimmy could sign the receipt. Izzy and I carried the two bags of records as the employee mob walked the four of us out of the store and to the car, the crowd of fans and shoppers trailing behind.

Gabriel laughed when Sheba put the key into the passenger-side door. "You gotta be kidding me, man. Jimmy and Sheba drive a station wagon!"

"Well, we got the kids." Jimmy nodded at me and Izzy and then got in the car and didn't roll down the window. Izzy and I got in too. Izzy rolled down the window and leaned half her body out, watching everyone give Sheba hugs or kisses goodbye.

When Sheba finally got in the car and closed the door, Jimmy said, "Let's roll, baby, roll, roll, roll."

Sheba pulled the car out slowly. The crowd walked behind us, their hands on the back window and hood. It took a long, slow time to get out into the street and finally pull away.

Once we could no longer see Night Train Records behind us, Sheba slapped the steering wheel with her hand. "That place was fabulous. I mean, there was *nothing* missing there. Nothing they didn't have. And Gabriel knew everything about anyone who's ever made a record. He knew *everything* about music."

"Yeah, it was cool." Jimmy rolled down his window and took a deep breath. "If we go back, I'm calling Gabriel ahead of time and we're going in after hours."

"Will he do that?" I asked.

"Oh yeah," Sheba said. "Jimmy and I usually only shop in closed stores."

"I don't think we need more." Izzy slid the records out of one bag and spread them across our two laps. She picked up *Hair* and stared at the cover, at the man with a neon-red-and-yellow Afro that radiated like a burning sun. The green lettering above his head repeated the word *hair hair hair hair hair*—upside down and right side up and sideways. I imagined people singing that word in ten-part harmony. My head felt a little dizzy and full of static, in the happiest way.

Mrs. Cone seemed hurt that we had gone to the record store without her. For the rest of the afternoon, she acted like she was a stranger in the house. As Sheba, Izzy, and I played the new records on the turntable in the dining room, Mrs. Cone sat on a chair at the table, a glass of wine in her hand. She rarely sang along and didn't seem to be enjoying herself.

I was worried about Mrs. Cone, but mostly I was excited to hear the new records. There were so many that we started off by playing only one song from most albums, and two from some. Sheba picked the songs. I thought each one was the best song I'd ever heard, until she played the next one and then I'd think that was the best song I'd ever heard. Izzy requested that we replay "Family Affair" by Sly and the Family Stone three times because she loved singing it and holding hands with me and Sheba. "We have to sing it because we're family," she explained. Once we finished trying all the albums, we went back to Joni Mitchell's *Blue*. Sheba wanted to practice the harmonies in "A Case of You," and she wanted me to memorize it so we could sing it together tonight.

I had the melody memorized after only hearing it once. The words took me a little longer, and I couldn't figure out what they meant. Once I had them down, Izzy and I went off to the kitchen to make baked mac and cheese.

We were stirring the cheese sauce and singing Joni Mitchell when Izzy asked all the questions I'd had about the song.

"What is *a case of you*?"

"I've been wondering that too."

"How do you drink someone?"

"I don't know. Maybe it's about love? About drinking up love?"

"How do you drink up love?"

"Hold the noodle pan still." I poured the cheese sauce over the noodles while Izzy held the pan on either side. She didn't really need to do that, the pan wasn't about to move, but I liked to make her feel like she was involved in every step.

"Could you drink a case of me?"

"Yes! I love you so much, I could drink a case of you." I handed Izzy the bowl of bread crumb mix we had prepared earlier. She sprinkled it over the mac and cheese slowly, as if the pacing were important. When the pan was covered, she dumped the remainder in the middle so there was a small hill of crumbs. I smoothed the hill out with my hand. Then Izzy put her hand over what I had smoothed and smoothed it again. My mother didn't believe in touching the food you were preparing—all contact was made through a third party: knife, fork, spatula, spoon. Even when making a pie crust, my mother pressed it into the pan using two shallow spoons. But since I'd been cooking with Izzy, I'd found that to put your hands in the food, to touch, move, tear, bend, and sprinkle ingredients straight from your fingers, gave you a better sense of what you were doing, and made the doing more effective. It might have been my imagination, but I thought the food I prepared tasted better when my hands had been in it. My fingers knew things a spoon or spatula couldn't.

After dinner, Jimmy got out his guitar while Izzy and I served vanilla ice cream on Nilla Wafers with three marascino cherries on top. He was picking through different tunes when Dr. Cone said, "I know that one."

"Sing it, Richard!" Sheba said. Dr. Cone rarely sang with us. He usually patted his thighs or bongoed the table and nodded with the beat.

"No, I mean I can play it on the guitar."

Jimmy smiled and shook his head. "Doc. Come on. We've been here all summer and you're just now breaking the news that you play the guitar?"

Dr. Cone smiled. "I was in a band when Bonnie and I met."

"No way!" Sheba laughed.

"I played the guitar. And did some backup singing."

"But you barely sing now!" Sheba seemed doubtful that Dr. Cone could ever have been in a band. It hadn't seemed odd when Mrs. Cone told me, but as I looked at Dr. Cone now, hunched over his empty ice cream bowl, I understood why Sheba was laughing.

Mrs. Cone pushed away her ice cream, as if she were done. "I play the flute."

"Get the guitar, Richard!" Sheba took another bite of her ice cream and Mrs. Cone pulled her bowl back and took another bite too.

"And, Bonnie, get the flute." Jimmy kept plucking.

Dr. Cone looked at Mrs. Cone and they smiled at each other for the first time I'd seen since we'd returned from the beach. He got up from the table and returned shortly with a guitar and a small white case, which he handed to Mrs. Cone. I'd never seen the guitar in the house, which meant it had to have been in Dr. and Mrs. Cone's bedroom closet. That was the only space in the house I had never entered.

"Wait!" Izzy ran out of the room and returned with a tambourine. She placed it on my lap.

"No, you play this. You're good at tambourine."

I watched Mrs. Cone assemble her flute. She finally looked relaxed and even a bit happy. Dr. Cone tried to tune his guitar, and then Jimmy put his own guitar down, walked around the table, and took Dr. Cone's guitar from him. In about a minute he had it tuned.

"Okay. Here we go. 'Stairway to Heaven.'" Dr. Cone started plucking on the guitar, his head bent, eyes honed in on his fingers. Jimmy was plucking the same tune, but looking at Dr. Cone. Each time Dr. Cone messed up, Jimmy said the chord, and then Dr. Cone jumped back in. Mrs. Cone picked up her flute and played along. I was surprised by how smooth and pure it sounded. Izzy picked up the tambourine, slapped it once against her thigh, and then looked up at me.

"I don't like this song. It sounds scary."

"Okay. Let's clear the table."

"I think this song is calling the witch."

"Hmm, I don't think so. Witches don't like music. Not even scary music."

I stood and started picking up dishes. Sheba had laid a rolling paper on the dining room table and was filling it with marijuana, half singing "Stairway to Heaven." Izzy and I put all the dishes in the kitchen and then returned to the dining room to say good night to everyone. Dr. and Mrs. Cone were so into playing their music, they could barely look up to kiss Izzy. Sheba was rolling a second joint. The first one was between Jimmy's lips.

"Can we sing songs from *Hair*?" Izzy asked as we walked upstairs.

"Yes. Do you remember them?"

"Yes." Izzy started softly singing: *"Wearing smells from Labradors . . . patching my future on films in space . . . I believe that God believes in clothes that spin, that spin. . . ."* The words were wrong, but I let her go. When she got to the *Let the sun shine* part, I sang along with her.

We sang all through the bath, the wrong words mostly, and then we got into bed. I fell asleep in the middle of reading a Richard Scarry book. When I woke up, Izzy was snuggled against me, her face smashed into my shoulder, sound asleep. I slipped out of bed and silently changed into the shorts and top my mother had bought me at the start of summer.

Sheba drove me home alone while Jimmy continued to play music with Dr. and Mrs. Cone. When we passed

Beanie Jones's house, Sheba lifted her middle finger, as she had every night since we'd returned from the beach.

After we'd pulled up in front of the Riley house next door, Sheba leaned in and kissed me on the cheek. "See you in the morning, doll."

I wanted to say I love you, but instead I said, "I'll make you birds in a nest for breakfast."

"Beautiful," Sheba said. "I've been dying for birds in a nest."

I got out of the car and waved as she drove away.

12

The next morning, when I came downstairs to the kitchen, my mother and father were sitting at the table. Neither was speaking. Neither was moving. The *Baltimore Sun* was in the center of the table.

"Uh, everything okay?" I was worried someone had died. A grandparent in Idaho, or maybe a member of our church.

"You tell me, Mary Jane." My father looked at me with hard eyes. He seemed like a stranger, unrecognizable as he glared and made extended eye contact.

"Tell you what?" I sat across from my father. My mother looked toward the newspaper. I followed her eyes, and then, with a sinking feeling, I pulled the paper toward me.

There, on the front page, was a picture of me, Izzy, Jimmy, and Sheba with the staff at Night Train Music: The Greatest Record Store in America. Everyone was smiling except Jimmy, who was leaning into my ear. The headline said *Sheba and Jimmy Visit Charm City!*

"Well?" my father said.

I looked at the picture again. I was in the terry-cloth shorts Sheba had bought me and a tank top with no bra. I knew Jimmy was whispering to me, but it looked like he was kissing me. The wallpaper tattoo down his arm almost popped off the page in three dimensions. The combination of that tattoo and his mouth against my ear surely multiplied whatever crime my parents were imagining I'd committed.

"Uh," I said. I couldn't catch my breath.

"Beanie Jones called me at six a.m. to ask if I'd seen the paper," my mother said. I couldn't tell if she was more upset about the photo or about the fact that she'd had to hear about it from Beanie Jones.

"Beanie Jones . . . ," I began, then stopped. What could I say about Beanie Jones that wouldn't make this situation worse? If my parents knew Jimmy had been naked with someone while I was babysitting, they'd be even more angry than they were now. Also, I didn't have the appropriate vocabulary to say to my parents what Beanie Jones and Jimmy had done. I wouldn't dare say the words *sex* or *intercourse* or *open marriage*. My mother and I didn't even discuss my periods. (About a year before my first period, a box of sanitary napkins and an elastic sanitary belt appeared under my bathroom sink. After I started using them, the box was replenished each month, as if by magic.)

"EXPLAIN." My father banged a fist on the table and I jumped. I thought of Izzy Cone. How she'd probably never had even a second in her life when she felt afraid of her parents. Fear, I suddenly realized, was an emotion that ran through my home with the constant, buzzing current of a plugged-in appliance.

I figured I'd start with the medical situation. "So, Dr. Cone is treating Jimmy—"

"Jimmy." My father snorted. "You're on a first-name basis with an adult?"

"Beanie Jones told me he's a heroin addict." My mother sniffed, then blinked. I'd never seen her cry, and I was worried she would.

"No one is supposed to know they're in town because of . . . well, because of doctor-patient confidentiality." I was glad I remembered the exact wording Dr. Cone had used.

"Beanie Jones certainly knew!" my mother said.

"Dr. Cone told me I wasn't allowed to tell anyone."

"Why were you with them if Dr. Cone was treating him? And why is a heroin addict traipsing around town with you anyway?" My mother glanced at the paper and then back to me.

"They've been living on the third floor of the Cones' house. Dr. Cone sees him in his office all day and Mrs. Cone entertains Sheba. That's why I'm taking care of Izzy." The truth seemed the least harmful explanation of all.

"What kind of doctor is he? One patient all day long? Is he a real doctor?" my father demanded.

"She doesn't have cancer?" my mother asked.

"He's a psychiatrist. His office is in the converted garage. And she doesn't have cancer." I felt emotion, like the kind I'd been having at the Cones' all summer, welling up in me. Tears started rolling down my cheeks.

My father seemed unconcerned about the cancer lie. "Why is *Jimmy* kissing you?"

"He's whispering in my ear. Not kissing me." I pushed the words out past what felt like a fist caught in my throat.

"Why?"

"He didn't want to take the pictures. He wanted to leave. He was telling me that."

"Why was he telling *you* that? Has this man deflowered you?"

"What? No! What? No, Dad!" That he had even thought of my "deflowering" was a shock. As far as I knew, my father was unaware that I even menstruated.

"Tell us the truth." Dad's eyes were drilling into me again.

"I swear. I've never even kissed a boy." It came out as a whisper: a secret it didn't seem my father—who had never before asked me a personal question—had a right to know. A secret that I hadn't minded telling the Cones and Jimmy and Sheba at the beach.

"And where did you get those clothes!?" My mother sniffed again. Her eyes looked wet.

"Mom. I'm s-sorry." I stuttered and choked on my last word. Then my throat opened up, and I was fully crying.

"Stop that crying. Go to your room," my father said.

That was impossible. I remained in my seat, my back bumping up and down as I sobbed. Instead of deflating me, the crying acted as a pump and allowed me to summon the person I'd become at the Cones. For the first time in my life, I defied my father. "I can't. I won't. I need to go take care of Izzy."

"YOUR ROOM." My father stood, came to the other side of the table, and hovered over me. I cowered.

"But they're waiting for me!"

Like a biting snake, my father's hand was instantly around my upper arm. He yanked me out of the chair and pulled me toward the stairs. I knew there were kids in the world who were actually pummeled by their parents or caregivers, and I knew that what was happening with my father wasn't close to that. Still, it felt as invasive and destructive as I imagined a fist-beating to be. I broke free, as if to save my life, and ran to my room.

Seconds later I heard the front door slam.

I was facedown, crying and shaking from the exchange with my father, when my mother came in. I sat up and looked at her. "Mom! They need me. I can't *not* go to work."

"Your father went down there to talk to them." My mother sat on the end of my bed and stared at me.

"They need me, Mom. They need me to take care of Izzy!" I couldn't have told you what made me cry more: missing the Cones or feeling battered by my father.

"Did that Jimmy person ever do drugs in front of you?"

"No!" I took a few deep breaths, in and out, until I could slow the crying. "Dr. Cone helped him to quit drugs. That's why he's here."

My mother blinked. "Why would the Cones be so careless as to let a known drug addict into their home with a little girl and you?"

"Mom!" I swallowed back the tears that were about to burst out again. "You let me watch Sheba's show on television. You know she's a good person! He's good too."

"How good can she be if she's married to a heroin addict?"

"Sheba likes church, Mom. We sing church songs together." I could feel my body slowing. Calming. Sinking into the bed.

"Beanie Jones said she knew this was going on all summer long. She said they've been smoking marijuana and that other untoward business is happening in the house."

"Mom." I sniffed it all in. Took another deep breath. "Beanie Jones is a nosy gossip and a liar. There is no untoward business. I take care of Izzy. Dr. Cone takes care of Jimmy. And Mrs. Cone entertains Sheba. That's all that happens."

"Were they at the beach with you?"

"Yes." I looked at my lap.

"Why did you go to the record store with them? Why would they take you to *that* store?"

"Because it's the best record store in town."

My mother snorted. "I highly doubt that."

"It is. The people in that store know all about every kind of music. The owner loves *Guys and Dolls,* just like me. And there was a whole wall of classical music and opera."

"On North Avenue? No, dear. Don't lie to me."

"I'm not lying, Mom." I was almost embarrassed for her. Did she think Black people *only* listened to the Jackson 5?

My mother sighed. "What are we going to do with you? You lied to me. Every single day when you left this house, you lied to me."

"I know I lied to you." It had been hard at first, but then it became so easy I barely noticed it. I felt bad about that— that I had become someone who spit lies so quickly they were more an involuntary reaction than a decision. "But really, my days have been spent taking care of Izzy and making dinner. It's been mostly what you imagined. The only thing different is that Jimmy and Sheba were in and out of the house."

"Where did you get the clothes you're wearing in the picture?"

"Sheba bought them for me at the beach. I left them at the Cones' house."

"Dr. and Mrs. Cone don't mind having a summer nanny dressed like a . . . like a . . . dressed improperly?!"

I remembered Sheba saying that her mother had called her a slut and a whore. In her own way, my mother was saying the same thing. But she was wrong. "The Cones don't think about things like being dressed improperly. They just want people to be happy. And comfortable."

My mother shook her head. "You can stay in here all day." She stood and left my room.

I rolled onto my stomach and cried some more. I tried to imagine my father speaking with Dr. Cone. Combed hair facing unruly hair. A shaved face looking at a goaty-sideburned face. Stern blue eyes on clear brown eyes. Would Jimmy meet my father? Sheba? What about Mrs. Cone? Mrs. Cone's nipples were always poking out. Did my father notice things like that? And if he did, would I be banned from the Cone house forever?

At noon my mother came in with a ham sandwich and a glass of milk on a tray. She put the tray on the end of the bed and stared at me. I could feel that my eyes were almost swollen shut. My nose was probably red too. "Well, I hope you're crying with regret."

I wasn't. "Did Dad talk to Dr. Cone?"

"Yes. He informed him that you wouldn't be returning this summer."

"There are only two weeks left. I can't go back for two weeks?"

My mother stared at me as if I had transformed from a girl into a goat. "Of course not."

"But who's going to take care of Izzy?"

"That's not your concern, Mary Jane. Do you not understand what happened? You have, unbeknownst to your parents, passed the summer with hippies and a drug addict while dressed like a girl who . . . like a girl who lives in Hampden!" Hampden was where Dr. Cone took us for burgers at Little Tavern. I thought it was probably better not to mention that.

I was allowed to leave my room to help my mother with dinner. We didn't speak as we prepared a chicken casserole and rice with peas. When my father came to the table, he set the paper beside his plate, looked up, and said, "At least they didn't put it in the evening paper."

My mother sighed.

"I'm sorry." I mumbled. I wasn't, though.

"Do you know how humiliating this is?" my father asked me. "The entire office, every man I work with, every single one, saw a picture of you dressed like a prostitute, standing with a rock-and-roll heroin addict and Negroes in a record store. Do you understand what that does to our standing in the community?"

I thought about what my father had just said. The Cones seemed unconcerned about things like *standing in the community*. It was like they were in a different Roland Park, a Roland Park where people weren't keeping track of each other. Where people were just doing what they wanted, without concern as to how it was seen. Maybe a person's *standing in the community* was an illusion. Like the witch in the Cone house. An imagined evil that created unnecessary rules.

When I didn't respond, my father said, "I asked you a question."

"I'm sorry," I said automatically.

My father put his hands in the prayer position. My mother did the same, then I did too. "Dear Lord, forgive my daughter for her sins and help her find her way to purity. God bless our relatives in Idaho, God bless this family, and God bless the president of the United States of America and his wife and family."

"Amen," my mother and I said in unison. I glanced up at President Ford on the wall. His smile seemed tinged with anger.

My father read the paper during dinner and my mother didn't speak. I wasn't hungry but I ate everything on my plate. After I cleared the table and helped my mother do the dishes, I returned to my room.

I'd heard about depression before but couldn't conceive of what it felt like until that week I spent in my room. I was tired all the time but I couldn't sleep. I couldn't read. I didn't want to sing or listen to music or even watch TV. Not that I could have anyway (the TV was in the den and the hi-fi was in the living room). I wondered if I was a bad person for having deceived my parents, or if I was a bad person for allowing myself to criticize my parents for being racist (and square!). But I couldn't not feel critical. I was unable to unsee what I'd seen of them this summer.

On Sunday morning, my mother came in without

knocking and woke me for church. I had fallen asleep when the sun was already up, so likely had only slept an hour.

"I expect you to wear pantyhose with your dress today." My mother was as upright and stiff as a broom. This was her way of telling me she was still angry and I was still being punished.

"Okay."

"And I want you to stand in the front row of the summer choir. You need to let the congregation know you haven't changed."

"Okay." I had changed. But what would anyone see? That I knew my parents were racist? That I now understood that cleanliness and order were nice, but giving love, feeling love, and showing love trumped housework? That I had seen that adults weren't always right and could be just as confused and make just as many mistakes as kids? That I knew that when people messed up, they still deserved our love and affection? That I had been listening to amazing music made by many different kinds of people? That I was certain that sex wasn't just something to be ashamed of or to hide, and that some people navigated it in ways I'd never before imagined (open marriage!) and that didn't make them perverts? That I'd experienced how good it felt to wear a bikini and feel air and water on my skin? Or that it was okay when I thought of a penis while looking at a cucumber (or a zucchini) and knew I wasn't a sex addict?

"If anyone asks you about the picture in the paper, I want you to say that you were working as the summer nanny for Izzy Cone and just happened to be pulled into the picture."

"Okay."

"If they ask why you were in that neighborhood, I want you to tell them that Dr. Cone had requested a certain record that was only sold there."

"Okay." I couldn't imagine anyone other than my mother asking why I was in that neighborhood, though maybe someone would ask why I was in the photo. The caption below the photo had said that Jimmy and Sheba were "passing through" town, and that they loved Baltimore and loved Night Train Records: The Greatest Record Store in America. No one else in the photo, besides Gabriel, was named, though the caption did list a couple of the records Jimmy and Sheba had bought.

"Do you have a pair of pantyhose with no runs?"

"I've got a new pair of suntan-colored L'eggs." They were sitting in the white plastic egg they were sold in.

"Good. Store them neatly back in the egg when you're done with them."

"Okay." In sixth grade I went to a slumber party where the birthday girl took all her mother's L'eggs pantyhose eggs and handed them out so the empty open halves could be used as fake breasts under our nightgowns. One side of the egg was slightly pointy and one was round, so we swapped until we each had a matching pair.

"And maybe a hat."

"Mom. It's 1975. No one wears a hat but the eighty-year-old ladies."

My mother was unmoved. "We need to restore your reputation."

"You've never worn a hat to church. The only hat I own is that pink one Grandma Dillard gave me and I've only ever worn it in Idaho."

My mother looked at the ceiling as if she were working

this through. "Fine. Pantyhose. And no runs!" She shut the door behind her when she left.

The kids at Sunday school acted like they hadn't seen me for months, though I'd only missed a single week when we'd been at the beach. They were all cute and funny, but I was missing Izzy terribly and would have rather not seen any kid if I couldn't see her.

Mr. Forge, the choir director, was also excited to see me. "Mary Jane! You were fraternizing with Jimmy and Sheba!"

"Yeah." I tried to remember what my mother wanted me to say.

"Did you just happen to be in the record store?" Mrs. Clockshire asked. Mrs. Clockshire was round in every way. Even her open palm looked like a perfect circle.

"Yeah. With Izzy. The kid I've been taking care of all summer." My face burned and my heart hurt. I longed to be back at the Cone house.

The rest of the choir gathered around me. I felt like a fox cornered by dogs, but no one said anything about the clothes I was wearing in the photo. Or the neighborhood Night Train Records was in. Or even that Jimmy was leaning into my ear. They were simply excited that I'd met Sheba and Jimmy.

When it was time for the service to start, I went straight to the front row of the choir seats, just as my mother had instructed. I looked out into the pews and saw my parents. My father was staring off into space. My mother was watching me as if I were a recent parolee with a flight risk. I offered a small half smile. She did not smile back.

When the choir stood for the first song, I started out singing quietly, but eventually let myself go with it. Mr. Forge liked throwing a modern song in every week and this Sunday he had chosen "Imagine" by John Lennon. He changed the words, though, so we sang, *there's more heaven* instead of *no heaven*. He also changed *no religion* to *no warring*.

When the song was over, I looked out at the congregation. Most people had a look on their faces that let me know they loved this song and how we'd sung it. My father was still staring off into space. My mother had no expression. Maybe she was so traumatized by my photo in the paper that getting through church this day was painful for her.

I glanced past my mother and almost screamed. In the back row were Jimmy, Sheba, and Izzy. Izzy appeared to be standing on the pew to see better. Sheba was smiling so big, it was like her face was made up of white teeth. She was wearing the black wig that fell to her shoulders and had bangs, and had on a pair of horn-rimmed glasses, like what the librarian at school wore. Jimmy was in a baseball cap, glasses, and a button-down shirt and a tie, both of which must have belonged to Dr. Cone. The only other time I'd seen Jimmy hiding his furry chest was when we'd gone to dinner at Morgan Millard.

I didn't wave, as I didn't want to draw attention to them, but Izzy frantically waved to me until Sheba pulled her down onto her lap. I winked. I smiled. I blinked my eyes. And then I glanced at my mother, who had turned in her seat to see what I was looking at. I was pretty sure she couldn't see them through the heads in the seats, though. She would have recognized Izzy and known that it was Jimmy and Sheba seated with her.

I sang the remaining three songs as if I were singing for Jimmy, Sheba, and Izzy alone. In my head, I could hear Sheba harmonizing. I could hear Jimmy's bubbling-engine voice. I could even hear Izzy wobbling in and out of tune. I tried not to look at them too much, for fear my mother would get out of her seat and march to the back of the church.

When the service ended, I was the first one off my chair and out the internal side door to the basement where we hung our choir robes. Instead of going back up the stairs into the church, I took the door that went outside. The hot air slammed into my face as I ran around to the front doors of the church. My parents always lingered in their pew and talked with the people who sat near us. I'd have a couple of minutes to say hello to Jimmy, Sheba, and Izzy.

The glossy red double doors were open and people were spilling outside. As I was dashing up the marble steps, Mrs. Cranger stopped me. "Mary Jane, I knew that was you in the paper!"

"Oh yeah! Funny that I was there, wasn't it?" I said without pausing.

But when I pushed my way inside, Jimmy, Sheba, and Izzy were gone. My stomach felt like it did a full rotation. My parents were chatting their way down the aisle, my mother with her hand on the elbow of the blind man, Mr. Blackstone.

I turned and went outside. And then I saw the Cones' station wagon pulled alongside the curb, running.

"MARY JANE!" Izzy hung out the open window, waving her arms to me.

I started to go to her when Pastor Fearson stopped me. He put his two hands over one of mine, as if he were warming my chilled fingers, and then leaned his head in toward me. "Mary Jane! What a surprise to see your picture in the paper!"

"Yes. That was a surprise." I could hear Izzy's little voice calling my name over the murmur of the congregation. People were now filling the wide marble steps that led to the sidewalk. I looked around Pastor Fearson to the station wagon. Izzy motioned for me to come to her.

But before I could move, my mother stepped in beside me and grasped my upper arm. "Mary Jane was the summer nanny for Dr. and Mrs. Cone. They took her to the record store."

"And what a fortuitious trip that was!" Pastor Fearson released my hand. "I don't know who that man was, but I loved Sheba's show. Watched just about every one."

"Mary Jane! Come see me!" I heard. My mother's head jerked toward the Cone station wagon. My father stepped between my mother and me. It was like the execution of a military maneuver.

"Pastor," my father said, sticking out his hand for a shake. "We'll see you next week."

My father set one hand on my lower back and linked his free arm into my mother's. He walked us, chained like that, through the crowd.

A horn beeped twice, quickly, and my mother, father, and I looked toward the station wagon. Sheba was at the wheel.

"Oh no," my mother said.

My father moved his hand up to my arm. "I'm calling Dr. Cone when we get home. He needs to get his patients under control."

We were on the sidewalk now. Walking toward our

house. Sheba rolled the station wagon beside us. Izzy leaned out the window. "Mary Jane! Why won't you come see me?!"

"What is wrong with these people?" my mother hissed.

My father's fingers clamped on my arm. Sheba continued to drive slowly beside us. She and Jimmy were looking straight ahead, as if they just happened to be cruising this same street where we were walking. But Izzy hid nothing. Her arms hung out the window. She stared at us, her mouth open, her eyes wild with confusion.

We turned the corner, and so did the car. Sheba gunned the car so it was half a block past us, and then stopped. Jimmy got out, walked around to the other side, and opened the back door. The engine was still running.

My father squeezed my arm and jerked me forward. My mother gasped.

I looked at Jimmy. He nodded and motioned with his head toward the car

"What do they want?" my mother asked. "Make them go away."

My father yanked me harder. He quickened his pace. My mother's pointed pumps made a clicking sound as she trotted to keep up.

And then, where the sidewalk curved around a massive elm tree, there was a raised buckle. My mother stumbled, and my father let go of my arm to catch her.

And I ran.

"GO, MARY JANE! GO!" Izzy shouted.

I darted toward her voice, toward the open door. The car started moving and I dove in headfirst, Starsky and Hutch style. Jimmy jumped in behind me as Sheba tore away. Izzy tumbled on top of me, squealing and screaming and covering me with kisses.

The car zoomed down the street. Past my house, pretty as a postcard. Past Beanie Jones's house (Sheba's finger in the air). Past the beautiful, messy Cone house.

Out of Roland Park.

Jimmy climbed into the front seat as Sheba got on the expressway. Izzy sat on my lap and I wrapped my arms around her and stuck my nose into her curly hair. I was so happy, I couldn't speak. The window was still down and hot air blew into the car like a torch.

"I missed you all so much," I said at last.

"We missed you!" Sheba ripped off her wig and threw it behind her. It landed on the seat beside me and Izzy.

Izzy turned her head and kissed my cheek. "I cried every night. The family wasn't the same without you."

"It's a family af-faaaair . . . !" Jimmy started singing the Sly and the Family Stone song that Izzy loved.

"It's a family af-faaaaair. . . . !" Sheba jumped in.

And then Izzy and I sang along too.

13

The first thing I saw was my mother, seated on a chair in the Cones' living room. Her thick orangey-beige stockings looked Velcroed together at her crossed ankles. Then there was the even more startling sight of my father on the couch. Beside him, Mrs. Cone was wearing an untucked gold silk blouse. Her nipples tented out from the thin fabric. Dr. Cone stood near the fireplace, one hand flat against the mantel. The house was only slightly messier than I had left it, so either Sheba or Izzy had been tidying up in my absence.

Our Starsky and Hutch escape had only lasted about twenty minutes, so my parents couldn't have been sitting there long. Sheba had worried they would call the police, so we'd returned to the Cones' with the idea that we'd have a quick snack and then Sheba would walk me home and seduce (her word) my parents into a blanket pardon: the escape, the clothing, the lies. We'd even gone so far as to plan the outfit Sheba would wear: a tidy pink sheath that wasn't too short or revealing. I knew the dress Sheba was talking about, as I'd seen it in her closet. It was something my mother would never wear, but it was the only piece of clothing Sheba had brought that my mother might not criticize.

Izzy and I were hand in hand. One of us was sweating; I could feel the wetness pooling in our palms. Jimmy and Sheba stood behind us.

No one spoke for a fraction of a second. Then Dr. Cone said, "Mary Jane, we've missed you!" He stepped forward and gave me a hug that felt both wonderful and terrifying. I couldn't look at my father. What could he think of this grown man, this grown *Jewish* man, touching me?

"Oh, Mary Jane!" Mrs. Cone got up from the couch and kissed me.

"We came back so Mary Jane wouldn't get in trouble." Izzy turned to me and put her head in my belly. I picked her up and held her close against me, her head now deep in my neck.

"Gerald Dillard." My father stood. He walked around the coffee table and shook hands with Jimmy first, and then Sheba. My mother did the same and then sat back down on her chair. I knew my father wouldn't sit again until Sheba did, and maybe Sheba knew this too, as she went to the couch and sat. Jimmy had claimed the other chair, so the only logical place for my father to plant his body was between Sheba and Mrs. Cone.

"Mary Jane," Izzy whispered loudly. "I'm hungry."

"Is it okay if I take Izzy to the kitchen for a quick snack?" I asked. I didn't know who I was asking—my parents? Dr. and Mrs. Cone?—and I didn't know where to look, so I stared at a misdirected whorl of shag carpet in front of Jimmy's chair.

"Oh, that would be wonderful," Mrs. Cone said. "She hasn't had lunch; she doesn't seem to like anything I make for her now!"

Dr. Cone said, "Mrs. Dillard, what an amazing chef you've made of your daughter. Each night another superb dinner!"

My mother smiled, so I took that as a yes and escaped to the kitchen with Izzy still monkeyed on me. We scooted into the banquette and Izzy tumbled out of my arms. There was a chill of cool air on my sweat-damp neck.

"Mary Jane," Izzy whispered. "Are they going to put you in home jail again?" Jimmy had been calling it that in the car. He wanted to know what they fed me in home jail and if I was allowed to go to the bathroom unescorted when in home jail. We had to explain to Izzy what escorted and unescorted meant, and she pointed out that she rarely went to the bathroom unescorted, as she missed everyone when she was in there alone.

"I hope not." I leaned in and kissed the top of Izzy's head. Her loamy, sweet smell and the feel of her curls on my face calmed me. "Let's eat."

I scooted out from the banquette and went to the fridge. When I opened it, I found, to my relief, that it was still clean, though less stocked than I'd kept it.

"Birds in a nest!"

"Okay." I pulled out the eggs. "Who made dinner when I was gone?"

"No one."

"No one?" I got out the mixing bowl and started cracking eggs.

"Hmm, Jimmy made *breakfast-dinner* one night."

"Fried bread and bacon?"

"Uh-huh. And we got Little Tavern."

"Yeah?" I was cracking far more eggs than was necessary for just me and Izzy. Would others come in and eat? Or was I about to be carted off to home jail?

"And I can't remember the other nights." Izzy looked up, thinking. "CHINESE! We had Chinese."

"Good remembering!" I whisked the eggs, then got out the milk. "What else did you do when I wasn't here?"

While I mixed up the pancake batter and heated the pan, Izzy climbed onto the orange stool and talked through her days and nights without me. Nothing particularly exciting had happened, but still I felt that I had missed things in simply not having been part of the daily routine.

Izzy was salting the birds in a nest when my mother and Mrs. Cone came in.

"Oh, are you making eggs in a nest?" Mrs. Cone clapped her hands together.

"BIRDS in a nest!" Izzy said.

My mother leaned over the pan. "You put too much butter in."

"This is how Izzy likes it." I flipped a nest over.

"We love Mary Jane's meals so much," Mrs. Cone said.

My mother's mouth pulled up into a forced smile. "She still has a lot to learn." I saw her look around at the kitchen, the dishes in the sink, the books on the table, the jade Buddha on the windowsill, the unswept floor.

My father stepped into the kitchen with Dr. Cone. "Okay, Mary Jane. Let's go now." His voice was firm and fast.

"Let me just put out the food." I went to the cupboard and took down four plates. My mother's head bopped back just an inch as she watched. For her, letting a fourteen-year-old take over a kitchen was like handing over the controls of a flying jet to a random passenger.

I passed the plates to Izzy, who placed them on the table.

Dr. Cone put his hand on my father's shoulder. "Are you sure you can't join us for lunch?"

"I have something planned," my mother said. "It would be such a shame to waste the food."

I nervously re-salted what Izzy had already salted. My heart ticktocked like a timer.

"Syrup?" Izzy asked.

"Fridge door," I said.

With the red oven mitt that I kept tucked behind the toaster, I lifted the frying pan and walked it to the table. Everyone watched as I slid a bird in a nest onto each of the plates.

"It's much easier, dear, if you bring the plates to the pan," my mother said.

"Mary Jane, aren't you going to eat with us?" Izzy hugged my legs.

"I'm sorry." I put the empty pan on the burner and then picked up Izzy and buried my face in her neck. The urge to cry welled up from my chest to my throat like a wave about to crash. But I swallowed it away and held it down.

I kissed Izzy on the cheek and then took her to the banquette and set her in front of a plate. There was no silverware, so I quickly went to the silverware drawer. I held it open for a moment, admiring how clean it was. Just last week, Izzy and I had removed the silverware tray and emptied the cutlery. Both the tray and the drawer that held it were filled with crumbs, jam smears, unidentifiable seeds, and even dead bugs. I wanted to point out how clean the drawer was to my mother. It was something she might appreciate.

"We need to get going, dear." My mother crossed her arms and stared me down.

Quickly, I pulled out the knives and forks and laid them on the table. I leaned into Izzy's ear and whispered, "I promise I'll be back, but it might not be until school starts again." Izzy looked at me, her eyes huge and wet. I kissed her quickly before I could feel her feelings and double them, and then I followed my parents out of the kichen.

Dr. and Mrs. Cone walked us to the entrance hall. No one spoke until Dr. Cone opened the front door.

"This humidity can kill a golf game," my father said.

"I'm sure it does," Dr. Cone said. "I can take it about fifteen degrees hotter than this when there's no humidity."

"Do you golf too?" Mrs. Cone asked my mother.

"I prefer tennis."

"She's a doubles gal," my father said. "Singles in this heat will ruin her hairdo."

My mother smiled and then patted her stiff hair. "Well, thank you so much for having us in."

"It would be lovely if Mary Jane could come back till the end of summer," Dr. Cone said.

"What a shame she can't," my mom said, and smiled real big and stiff, like she was posing for a picture she didn't want taken.

I stared toward the steps, hoping to see Jimmy or Sheba bounding down. It seemed impossible that I'd walk out that door and simply never see them again.

"Goodbye now," my father said, and then I was on the sidewalk once more, between my parents, moving toward our house. I turned my head back several times, hoping that someone from the Cone house, even Dr. Cone himself, might run out and beg me to return. But no one did.

My mother unlocked the front door, and then the three of us stepped into the sterile chill of the air-conditioning. My father immediately went to his chair.

"Set the table for lunch," my mother said.

I followed her into the kitchen. She took a pot out of the refrigerator and placed it on the stove. "Chicken noodle soup."

I took down three bowls and placed them on the kitchen table. Then I opened the silverware drawer. I had to admire the shiny, organized cleanliness. The spoons were nested, hugging one another. The knives were lined up like canned sardines. And the forks were stacked atop one another in two neat piles. I looked over at my mother, slowly stirring the soup, her mouth in a downward melt. Before I could think it through, I put my hand into the forks and disrupted the piling. Then I did the same with the knives. The spoons seemed to cling to each other, like sleeping kittens. I flipped half of them upside down, and then removed three.

As if to cover my tracks, I paused by the stove. "That looks great." When my mother didn't reply, I asked, "Did you like the Cones? What did you think of Sheba?"

My mother put the stirring spoon on a ceramic holder the shape of a giant spoon and went to the refrigerator. "That entire crew certainly admires you." She removed from the fridge a bag of Wonder Bread, butter in the glass butter dish, and a stack of individually cellophane-wrapped slices of Kraft cheese.

"Do you want me to make the cheese sandwiches?"

"You use too much butter." She put everything on the counter and then went to the silverware drawer and pulled it open. My heart dropped down to my stomach like a boot into a pond.

My mother stared at the disarray for a moment. Quickly, she righted all the silverware, pulled out a knife, sliced off a pat of butter, put it in a frying pan, and turned on the flame.

"I'll try to use less butter next time." My voice was quiet, hesitant.

"And you definitely oversalt." Mom laid three pieces of bread in the pan.

"I can be more careful."

"One should never be careless or haphazard when cooking. Particularly when it comes to butter and salt." She unwrapped the Kraft slices and laid them on the bread.

"Did you like Izzy? Don't you think she's cute?" I felt desperate for my mother to understand the magic of the Cone house.

"How did those people eat before you arrived? They talked about you like you were Gandhi feeding the starving masses."

Was there anything I could say that would shift my mother's focus from disparaging the Cones to appreciating them? Or, at the very least, maybe she could appreciate that I was an integral part of the family? "Well . . ." I paused as I tried to answer the question without betraying the family. "Before I started cooking for them, they picked up a lot of prepared food from Eddie's. And sometimes they ordered Chinese or went to Little Tavern."

My mother looked at me like I'd told her they ate dog poop off the sidewalk. "That poor, poor child." She turned back to the sandwiches. "There's something wrong with that mother."

I opened the cupboard and took down three plates and

put them on the counter near the frying pan. "What do you think is wrong with her?" My curiosity was sincere.

"The way she was dressed. That she doesn't feed her child."

"But she loves Izzy so much. I think she just doesn't want to be a housewife."

"Use paper napkins and fold them in thirds." My mother nodded quickly toward the yellow plastic napkin holder that always sat on the kitchen table. "If she didn't want to be a housewife, then she shouldn't have had a child. And she definitely shouldn't have put that child in danger with those people in the house."

"I was in charge of Izzy." How could my mother not know that? What did she think I'd been doing all summer? "She was never in danger."

"You shouldn't have been in charge. You're a child. You should have been a *helper*." My mother used a spatula to turn the sandwiches over. "I never should have allowed you to take that job."

"Mom." I felt strangely choked up. I wanted to tell her that I was pretty sure that I'd done a really great job being in charge of Izzy and taking care of the house, too. And I also wanted to tell her how much I loved cooking for the Cones. How cooking for people you love feels less like a chore and more like a way of saying *I love you*. And, really, I got that from her, the cooking, the child-rearing, and the housekeeping. My mother had been such a good mother to me in so many ways. She'd taught me so much. And she'd been excellent company. Until she wasn't.

"Mom," I said again.

My mother didn't respond. I pulled out a napkin, folded it in thirds, and put it under the first spoon. Then I folded the second and third napkins. Once they'd been placed, I picked up the soup bowls and took them to the counter near the stove. I was trying to anticipate my mother's directions before they left her mouth.

"Mom," I said.

"Spit it out, Mary Jane." My mother banged the soup-spoon on the side of the pot and then placed it in the holder.

"You did a really good job teaching me how to keep house and how to cook. Everyone was amazed by my cooking and I learned all that from you." I blinked rapidly to keep my eyes from filling with tears.

My mother started ladling soup into bowls, then handed the bowls to me without ever looking up at my face. We were both silent as I walked back and forth, placing the soup bowls on the table, one by one.

"I don't understand why Sheba's with that drug addict," she said at last.

"He's recovered."

"The tattoos look so dirty. I wanted to take a Brillo pad and scrub them off."

The urge to cry vanished and I actually laughed. "It's weird how quickly you get used to that stuff. I don't even see them anymore. It's like Karen Stiltson at school. When she first showed up at Roland Park, she had this lisp, like she said *shoe lay-shesh* instead of shoelaces." I took two plates with grilled cheese back to the table.

"Don't be mean."

"No, I'm not being mean. I'm just saying that I noticed that lisp when she first came to school. But by the end of the year I didn't hear it. My ears just stopped registering it."

My mother brought the third plate to the table. "I hope you never said anything to her about it." She was half scolding me, but her tone was lighter. Maybe I was being forgiven.

"No, Mom." I went to the cupboard, took down three drinking glasses, and placed them on the table. "But it was the same for Jimmy's tattoos."

"I wish you didn't call those people by their first names!"

"Okay. Well, it was the same with the tattoos. I didn't see them after a while. And I didn't see Sheba—Mom, she legally dropped her last name; she doesn't even have one. . . ."

My mother shook her head. She put the frying pan in the sink to be washed after we'd eaten.

"So with Sheba, I forgot she was a big star. She became just a lady. She's super kind and caring, Mom. She doesn't hate anyone, not even drug addicts and not pastors or politicians. She loves singing and she loves the church."

My mother pointed at the table. "Milk for me. You can have orange soda today, if you'd like." Now I knew forgiveness was coming.

I took the orange soda from the fridge and poured two glasses, one for me and one for my father. Then I got out the milk and filled my mother's glass. It was so thick, it looked like wet paint. I thought about the day Jimmy, Izzy, and I had drunk milk straight from the carton.

When I returned the milk to the refrigerator, my mother was standing by the stove staring at me. I could see that her bottom lip was quivering.

"Mom," I said, and now my lip was quivering.

"I just don't understand why you lied to us." A tear ran down my mother's face. My stomach lurched. My body stilled. I wasn't sure what to do.

"Um . . ." My chest rose and fell as I tried to breathe. "I really wanted to work with the Cones. I loved the job and I knew you wouldn't let me if—"

"Exactly, Mary Jane. You knew you *shouldn't* be in a house like that."

"No, Mom. I knew you wouldn't approve of it. But you were wrong. They're wonderful people. It was the best summer of my life."

My mother stared at me and I stared back. We both were breathing hard, as if our lungs were twinned bellows. I had never before told her she was wrong about anything. And until this summer, I had never thought she was wrong about anything.

"Go tell your father lunch is ready." My mother wiped the tear away and re-formed her face into a placid downturn. She sat at the table and I went to fetch my dad.

14

My home jail sentence was to continue, but with fewer restrictions, until school started. I could now leave the house with my mother, though I still couldn't see the Kellogg twins, who had returned from camp. I was surprised by how little I was upset about not seeing them. I didn't feel lonely; I was busy in my head—thinking, remembering, daydreaming. Working out who I had become after spending so much time with Sheba, Jimmy, and the Cones. I figured I'd find my way back to the twins soon enough.

My mother and I did all the usual things: shopping at Eddie's, having lunch and tea at the Elkridge Club, preparing meals, working in the garden, and going to church on Sunday. After our conversation in the kitchen, my mother no longer seemed angry. She filled the air between us with directions, commentary, and general chatter about the house, the garden, the meals, the neighborhood, and the neighbors.

It wasn't until the final two days of August, which I knew were Jimmy and Sheba's last, that I considered sneaking down to the Cones' only so I could say goodbye. I was grieving the fact that this wonderful summer was behind me, would never happen again, and the only souvenirs I had were the thoughts in my head. The clothes and records Jimmy and Sheba had bought me, along wth the Polaroid I'd kept, were still at the Cone house. By now they were likely buried under other clothes, records, dishes, dishrags, shoes, boxes, and junk mail.

Over those two days, I was desperate for an accidental meeting with someone from the Cone house. I scanned the aisles at Eddie's, looked out over the pews at church, and kept my eyes on the sidewalks as we cruised down the roads of Roland Park. My mother hadn't driven past the Cone house since the failed kidnapping. She took parallel streets instead.

When it was time for back-to-school shopping, I knew there was no hope of getting a goodbye moment with Jimmy and Sheba. Izzy seemed just as out of reach, as I assumed Mrs. Cone either didn't do back-to-school shopping or did it beyond the bounds of the northern Baltimore corridor that roped in my family. Still, I searched the shops as we entered, even our traditional final stop, Van Dyke & Bacon, where my school shoes had been purchased each year since kindergarten. My mother was convinced that because I wore flip-flops, which had no restraint and exposed my feet to direct doses of vitamin D, my feet expanded a bit every day in the summer. She liked to wait until this sunshine-growth period was mostly over before we purchased my regulation school shoes (black-and-white saddle shoes or brown oxfords with only three grommets on each side).

At Van Dyke & Bacon there were only shoes, sales-men, and mothers and kids similar to my mother and me. I flopped down onto the red leather bench seat with a weighted sadness over the fact that my summer was now absolutely, and entirely, over.

My mother grabbed a salesman and brought him to me. He wore a green apron and had a mustache that made him look like a walrus. In his hand was the flat silver foot measure.

"Right foot," he said, laying the measure on the floor before me.

I kicked off my flip-flop and stood on the cold metal runway. The salesman outlined my foot with the sliding fins. "Uh-huh," he said. I stepped off and he flipped the plank around and waited for my left foot. "Uh-huh," he said again as he measured.

"She's grown this summer," my mother said. "Did you see how her toes hung off the edge of the flip-flop?"

"I didn't notice." He patted the red leather bench seat. "Sit."

I sat down and he slipped a small nylon sock on each of my feet. His hands were almost as cool as the measur-ing plank.

"It's the sun," Mom said. "She started out with her toes way back there." She picked up a flip-flop and put her finger in the spot where she imagined my toes had been at the beginning of summer. I couldn't remember if she was right.

"Uh-huh." The salesman wasn't interested. "Roland Park Country School, right?" he asked me.

"Yes," my mother said, and he walked away. Each pri-vate school had their own shoe requirements. As far as I'd seen, Van Dyke & Bacon was the only shoe store in town.

Though I wondered if, like Night Train Records, there were amazing, hip, fun shoe stores in Baltimore that my mother would never enter.

"Let's get you new church shoes too," my mother said. "You could wear them to the homecoming dance as well."

"Um, can we get those later?" I asked. My trips to Van Dyke & Bacon in the past had seemed uneventful. It was easy to find shoes I liked. But now that I had been shopping with Sheba, I saw the stock differently.

The salesman returned with two boxes and sat on the the stool in front of me. Just as he was slipping the saddle shoes onto my feet, Beanie Jones entered the store. She was wearing a bright pink headband that pulled her thick blond hair away from her face. The headband was the exact pink of her dress, a honeycomb-patterned shift that fell above her tan knees. Her fingernails and toenails were painted the thick white of whole milk. The pink band of her sandals crossed her bronzed feet. All I could think was *I've seen you naked*.

"Hello, you two!" she said.

"Oh, hello!" my mother said, too cheerfully, I thought. When I didn't respond, she shot me a look.

"Hi, Mrs. Jones," I said.

"Are you getting school shoes, Mary Jane? I hear this is where everyone gets the latest fall styles." Beanie Jones picked up a pair of oxfords on display.

"Mary Jane's at Roland Park Country; the girls there can only wear two kinds of shoes," my mother said. I doubted Beanie Jones was interested.

The salesman double-tapped the back of my calf like I was a horse that needed prodding. I jumped. I'd forgotten he was there. "Stand," he said.

I got up and walked in a circle.

"I remember the saddle shoes I had to wear at Rosemary Hall." Beanie Jones looked down at my feet, smiling. Then she put a hand on my mother's upper arm. "Oh! Did you hear?"

"Feel good?" the salesman said to me.

"Hear what?" My mother glanced between my feet and Beanie's face.

"Yes, perfect," I said.

"Though I don't know why I should be shocked, considering what went on at the Cones' this summer," Beanie half whispered, like she was trying to keep a secret but not really.

The salesman bent down and pushed on the tip of the shoe to see how much space there was between there and my big toe. "Now the oxford." He horse-tapped the back of my calf again. I sat while he removed the saddle shoes. I couldn't take my eyes off Beanie Jones.

"Oh, dear. What is it?" My mother took a half step closer to Beanie.

"Bonnie packed up, took Izzy with her, and moved into one of those dinky little row houses in that Rodgers Forge neighborhood." Beanie shook her thick blond hair as if to let dust fly off it.

"Up." The salesman calf-tapped me again. "Walk."

My head and my stomach felt thick and curdled as I walked a slow, close circle around Beanie Jones and my mother. Beanie Jones pooh-poohed the row house Mrs. Cone and Izzy lived in as well as the idea that Mrs. Cone would leave Dr. Cone *all alone* in that big house. And then she said, "I'm pretty sure there was some canoodling going on between Bonnie and Jimmy."

My mother gasped.

"That's not true." I stopped and faced Beanie Jones.

My face was red and hot. My eyes felt like I'd sprayed perfume in them. "You know that's not true."

"Mary Jane!" My mother jerked her head forward, like a hen pecking corn. "Watch your manners."

Beanie Jones pushed her face into a smile. "Darling, don't be upset." She put her hand on my arm. I wanted to shake it away but was afraid of what my mother would do if I did. "Sometimes the grown-up world is too complicated and messy to understand until you get there."

I thought of Dr. Cone looking for his car keys, with no one to help him out. Izzy suddenly removed from the bedroom that was safe from the witch, the bathroom with the footstool under the sink, the kitchen with the window nook to sit in, the dining room with the records on the floor, the family room with the ironing board, and the living room with all the books we'd so carefully alphabetized. My heart hurt. My head hurt. And my pride hurt a little too, in knowing for certain that after the Starsky and Hutch kidnapping, everyone had given up on me.

"These are good." The salesman was pushing on my toes again. Then he tapped the back of my calf and I sat.

"We'll take them both," my mother said.

"Poor Izzy," I said.

"I heard she's being enrolled in *public school* up there." Beanie Jones said this as if public school in Baltimore County was like special ed for the serial killers in a prison system.

"We reap what we sow," my mother said, and I knew she was trying to end the conversation.

"Have you heard from any of them, Mary Jane?" Beanie Jones ignored my mother and beamed her giant smile on me.

"Oh no, Mary Jane has nothing to do with any of

them now." My mother motioned with her fingers for me to stand. The salesman was headed toward the register with the two boxes of shoes.

"Of course," Beanie Jones said to my mother, and then she winked at me, as if to say she knew better.

I turned and started toward the register.

"Mary Jane," my mother said firmly.

"Oh, sorry." I turned around. "So nice to see you, Mrs. Jones." I pushed my mouth into a big, painful smile. I hoped she would think I was pen pals with Jimmy and Sheba, that a day didn't go by without a fresh letter with fresh news. Beanie Jones was the only person I knew who understood how energized and dazzling it felt to be with Jimmy (and Sheba). She was the only witness to my secret summer. But she was someone with whom I wanted to share none of it.

15

A couple of weeks into the school year, Mr. Forge asked if I would join the grown-up choir, which took over the Sunday services once summer had ended (relegating the children's choir to special performances on holidays). At fourteen, Mr. Forge said, I would be the youngest voice the adult choir had ever had. The only person I wanted to relay this news to was Sheba. I imagined her face, how happy and proud she had looked when she watched me sing at church.

After my first adult choir service, when we were hanging up our robes, Mr. Forge handed me a paper-covered, taped-up box about the size of a brick of cheddar cheese. "This came for you a couple of days ago, Mary Jane. How exciting to get mail!" Mr. Forge clapped his hands twice, I suppose to applaud my having received a package.

The box was addressed to me in care of the church. My heart thudded as I saw that my name and the words *Roland Park Presbyterian Church* were in Sheba's neat, perfect cursive. The address of the church and the return address (no name but a building address on Central Park West) were in different handwriting. An assistant? The housekeeper who ironed all Sheba's clothes? It certainly wasn't Jimmy's giant scribbles.

Mr. Forge stood by watching, as if he expected me to open the package in front of him and share whatever was inside. I looked up, smiled, and then turned and grabbed the robe I'd just hung up.

"Thanks for this. So, um, I'll see you at rehearsal!" I quickly wrapped the box in the robe and held it against my chest. Before Mr. Forge could say anything else, I rushed up the stairs and out the side door to the front of the church, where I stood on the bottom step to wait for my parents. When they finally emerged, my mother was holding the elbow of the blind man, Mr. Blackstone. My father stared off into the distance as usual. It felt like hours before my mother released Mr. Blackstone to the sidewalk with his red-tipped white cane. I leaned in toward her and said, "I'm going to run home. I have to go to the bathroom."

My mother cocked her head to one side like a pigeon. She rubbed her hand over her stomach to indicate a question.

"Yes!" I said. "Can I have the house key?"

"We can walk quickly." My mother threaded her arm through my dad's so they were linked at the elbow.

"Mom. This is an *emergency*."

"What's under your arm?"

"My choir robe. It has a hole I need to fix. Mom, I really *have to go*."

"Give her the damn key," my father said.

My mother unclasped the metal closure at the top of

her shiny, stiff handbag, reached in, and then handed me her enamel Maryland flag key chain. "Leave the door unlocked and put the keys on the piano," she said. I was already running down the street.

In the house, I trotted up the stairs, went into my bathroom, and locked the door. I shut the toilet seat and sat, then slipped my nail beneath the tape and carefully unwrapped the paper, making sure not to rip any of the stamps. Under the paper, I found a white cardboard box. Inside the box was a folded piece of paper. Underneath was an orange cassette tape with a label on it. On the label, in Jimmy's chopstick scrawl, it said, *For Mary Jane.*

I unfolded the paper. The sight of an entire page filled with Sheba's handwriting made me feel something that I could only identify as love. I read the letter once, but didn't take it all in. The simple fact that Sheba had written me was like noise in my head that canceled out the meaning of half the words. I read the letter a second time. Slower.

Hey, doll,

I'm so sorry we didn't get to see you again before we blew town, but we all worried you'd be in home prison for years if we tried to contact you.

Nothing was the same at the Cones' after you left. First of all, Bonnie started cooking, and let's just say she's a lady who needs to find a better use

for her hands. Izzy wanted to remake
everything she'd made with you. Bonnie
tried, and all but the hot dogs failed.
Secondly, we didn't sing as much. It
just wasn't fun without your voice
filling out the melody (or harmony).
Thirdly, that house is a mess! Did
they have a maid before you showed
up? I was too embarrassed to ask, but,
boy, did they need one! Of course, we
couldn't drag any old person in, not
with Jimmy doing the work he was
doing with Richard, and with me trying
to be incognito in your funny little
neighborhood. (By the way, I hope
you give that Beanie Fuckface Jones the
finger every time you walk by her house.
Someone needs to carry the torch now
that I'm gone.)

Jimmy is still sober, Mary Jane,
and this makes both my life and his life
easier. He's been in the studio with JJ
and Aaron and a new drummer they're
calling Tiny Finn. The old drummer

(Stan to the world, STAIN to Jimmy
and JJ and Aaron) has decided he's too
highbrow for Running Water. He told
them he wants to be with someone who
will outlast the style of any particular
decade and is now playing with Morris
Albert. You know who he is, right? That
guy who sings the song "Feelings."
When Stain left, Jimmy fired the
producer, Roger, too. I never liked him
anyway. He has hair like a dirty old
mop, hands like a milk-fed farm girl,
and acts like he's king of the world.
Jimmy's producing the whole thing and
I swear to you, Mary Jane, I think this
is going to be Running Water's best
album yet. Jimmy wanted you to have a
copy of the title song, so he recorded this
for you. Keep in mind, what you'll hear
isn't the finished version, but I think
you'll like it just the same.

     As for me, doll, I'm reading scripts
and I think I found a good one.
It's about a woman who uncovers

corruption in a nuclear power plant.
It's definitely not a glamorous role,
and I certainly won't look pretty in
the dumb worker jumpsuit and the
ridiculous goggles I'll have to wear.
But, you know, maybe it's okay not to
be glamorous or pretty all the time.

I think we did it right those couple of
months, don't you? Great food, great
music, and great fun. Don't ever let
anyone tell you that fun isn't important
because, damn, Mary Jane, if there's one
thing I've learned in my strange life, it's
that fun counts.

I'm sending you love from afar, doll—
tons of it from me and from Jimmy, too,
of course.

Sheba

PS Can't believe I forgot! 1. I left my
nightgown, your new clothes, and your
records hidden in the closet of the room
Jimmy and I used. I hope you can sneak

them all into your house somehow.
2. Richard and Bonnie separated. Poor
little Izzy. Sweet thing. But, really, some
marriages just aren't worth fighting for.
xoxo!

I picked up the cassette and flipped it around to see if anything was written on the other side. My father had a cassette player in his office, though I had no idea why or what he ever did with it. I'd have to wait until he went to work tomorrow to sneak in there and use it.

I placed the cassette back into the box and read Sheba's letter for the third time. Just as I was finishing, I heard my parents enter the house. The stairs were carpeted, but I could hear my mother pattering toward me. Sure enough, in a minute there was a knock on the door.

"How are you, dear?"

"I'm okay." I reached behind me and flushed the toilet.

"I'll get the Pepto-Bismol."

"Thanks, Mom."

"Did you take your temperature?"

"Yeah. It's normal."

There was silence for a moment as my mother thought this through. "Must be something you ate."

I stared at the cassette and letter. I could sense my mother breathing on the other side of the door.

"Did you have something after breakfast?"

"Nope."

"Don't say *nope.*"

"No."

"You didn't eat anything at church?"

I thought for a second. I had become such an accomplished liar over the summer that it was easy to say, "Yes. There were cookies in the robe room."

"Who brought them in?"

"No idea. Chocolate chip. They were really soft."

"Hm. Underbaked, I suppose."

"Yup."

"Don't say *yup*."

"Yes." My eyes were on the cassette. On Jimmy's writing. My name. I flushed the toilet again, and then folded up the letter and placed it back in the box with the cassette. While the toilet was still running, I hid the box in the back of the bottom drawer of the vanity, beneath a plastic container of pink sponge curlers. Then I turned on the water and washed my hands. I didn't leave until I'd heard the gentle *sh-sh-sh* of my mother descending the stairs.

The next morning, after my father had left for work and while my mother was in the shower, I snuck down the hall to my dad's office. Behind the massive desk were built-in cupboards, and in one of the cupboards was a tape recorder.

I opened the cupboard and glanced around. I didn't want to move anything unless I absolutely had to. I stuck my arm in and wiggled past two stacks of documents. My fingers tapped something hard and plastic.

Carefully, I removed one stack of documents and set it on the floor. Then I removed the tape recorder and placed it on my father's desk.

I stuck my head out the office door to make sure my mother was still in the shower, and then returned to the cassette player and hit stop/eject. The clear panel popped open and I shoved in the cassette with a satisfying plastic click. I pushed the door shut (another gratifying click) and hit play.

Jimmy's voice filled the room, so clear it sounded like he was standing beside me. *"Mary Jane! What the hell, girlie, you are missed! Here's the title track of my new album. I sure as fuck hope you like it."* I nodded my head, smiling, as if Jimmy could see me.

I leaned closer to the tape recorder and heard some background fuzziness followed by silence. And then the song began with a simple drumbeat that had a wooden *tick-tick-tick* sound to it. Next a bass guitar came in, strumming a two-four beat. There was anticipation in the music; I could hear it was building to something. Just when I couldn't take the tension of waiting, Jimmy's raspy, throaty voice started in. *"Mary Jane!"* My body jolted at the sound of my name. My skin felt inflamed. I wanted to pat myself all over, like tamping out a fire on my flesh. As the song continued I was no longer in my father's office, standing beside the cassette player. I was in the Cones' kitchen. The smell of birds in a nest on the stove. Izzy's hair glinting in the sunshine that bolted through the window. And Jimmy beside her, his furry chest exposed, playing guitar and singing in the grumble of a low-riding motorcycle.

"Mary Jane!" Jimmy sang. My head buzzed with tiny explosions as I imagined a version of myself that matched Jimmy's throaty words. . . . *"She feeds you, but she ain't never gonna bleed you. . . ."* Soon, the buzzing calmed and it felt like a glowing white light flowed straight out of the

tape recorder and into my veins. I was filled by it. Floating. This song, Jimmy's song, was about the *me* I had become at the Cones'. It wasn't anyone my parents would recognize. It might not have been anyone they wanted me to be. But maybe, I hoped, I really was that person now. The girl Jimmy saw when he sang . . . *"She don't smoke, no*—everything went silent for a beat and then—*"MARY JANE! A voice sweet as honey, SUCKLE, honey, DROPS, honey, DARLING, honey, BABY, sweet, MARY JANE!"*

As the final verse rolled in, the music fell back to just the clicking drums and Jimmy, who grumbled, *"Mary Jane, Mary Jane . . . listen up now, y'all, 'cause I'm talking 'bout Mary Jane."* The music stopped and then Jimmy said, *"Bawlmore. That's how they say it down there. Bawlmore."*

I looked at my arms to see if the goose bumps I felt were visible (they weren't). I put my hand on my heart. It was pounding. My lungs were taking in great gulps of air. As my heart slowed and my breathing calmed, I felt solidified. I was Jimmy's *Mary Jane*! And nothing, not home jail, not my father, not my mother, and not even President Ford could shut down the person I'd become.

I peered out into the hallway again. My parents' door was still shut. I hit rewind and backed the tape up to the beginning, and then I hit play once more. With my thumb on the toothed dial on the side of the recorder, I turned up the volume. Only a little. Just enough so that I could feel the music around me more. This time I sang along quietly so my mother couldn't hear. *"Mary Jane!"*

When the song ended, I popped out the cassette, shoved it into the pocket of my nightgown, and then quickly put my father's tape recorder back.

I met up with my mother in the hall. She was fully

dressed in a plaid skirt and white blouse, stockings and shoes. Her hair had a flip-up curl on the bottom, which meant she'd worn a cap in the shower to keep it styled as it had been for church.

"Why aren't you dressed for school? Is your stomach still bothering you?"

"A little. But I'll go to school anyway." I rushed into my room, trying to escape before there were more questions.

"Maybe you should skip choir practice and come home right after your last class. I was going to change out the planter boxes and put in mums. You can help with that."

I stood next to my bed, staring at my mother. The song was playing in my head. Jimmy's Mary Jane was "brave as hell" and "spoke no jive." I needed to be more like her.

"I'll pick you up, and we'll drive right up to Radebaugh to buy the mums. I was thinking we'd do all white this year. None of those golden ones." My mother had a hand on each hip.

"Mom." I fingered the tape in the pocket of my nightgown. "Mom. I—"

"Spit it out, Mary Jane. No time to dillydally."

"Jimmy wrote a song about me."

My mother got an inch taller as her back pulled up. "Have you been talking to those people?"

"No. Sheba mailed me a cassette tape—she mailed it to me at church. And my song is the title song of Jimmy's new album."

"Must you call them by their first names?"

"It's the title song of Mr. Jimmy's new album."

"Mary Jane, I don't even understand what you're saying. What is the title song of Mr. Jimmy's new album?"

"'Mary Jane.' That's the name of the song."

"He wrote a song about you?"

"Yes."

"What could a drug addict possibly sing *about you*?"

Why couldn't my mother see what Jimmy, Sheba, and the Cones saw in me? Did I hide myself so much at home that I was virtually invisible? "Well, that I cook. And sing. Just . . . you know."

"No. I don't know."

"I kinda . . . Mom. I kinda wish you did know."

"Know what, Mary Jane? Will you make some sense here!" My mother looked at her slender gold watch, as if we were running terribly late. We weren't. We were always early.

I took a breath and got braver. "I wish you knew who I am. Or, how other people see me. I can play the song for you."

My mother lifted her wrist again, as if time were jumping forward faster than usual. "How long is the song? You need to be at school and I need to be at Elkridge for coffee on the porch with the ladies."

"I dunno. I mean, I *don't* know. Maybe two and a half minutes."

"Have you already heard it?"

"I played it on Dad's tape recorder when you were in the shower."

My mother took a breath so deep her entire body expanded and contracted. "This doesn't make me happy."

"I know, Mom. I know. You don't like how I changed this summer. But I do. This song is important to me. It's . . . it's about the me I became with the Cones and Jimmy and Sheba. I like that *me* more than who I used to be. I enjoy being the person they saw." My face burned. I was embarrassed about what I'd just said; I'd always had the feeling that it was impolite and conceited for a girl to actually like who she was. But Sheba clearly loved who she was. And that seemed cool to me.

My mother stared at me like she was trying to bring a blurry blob into sharp focus. "Oh, Mary Jane. I hope I like the Mary Jane those people saw, too." She turned and marched toward my father's office. I followed.

My mother knew exactly where the tape recorder was. She pulled it out, set it on my father's desk, and then pointed at it, as if to direct me to it.

I hit stop/eject, and the plastic door popped open. I slid in the cassette, shut it to hear the satisfying click, and then hit play. Jimmy said, *Mary Jane! What the hell, girlie, you are missed! Here's the title track of my new album. I sure as fuck hope you like it.*" My mother's body jolted. She closed her eyes and put her hand up as if to say *enough.* I pressed stop/eject.

My mother opened her eyes. "You know this language is exactly why you shouldn't fraternize with people like him."

"I understand how you feel about it. But if you can get past the language—"

"And the tattoos. And the drugs." My mother shut her eyes again. She held them like that for so long, I thought maybe she was praying. Finally she opened them and said, "I'd like to hear the song."

I hit play again. Before the first word was sung, I put my thumb on the dial and turned up the volume. My mother watched the way people in movies watch someone cutting the wires to stop a bomb from exploding.

"Mary Jane!" Jimmy sang, and my mother's eyes blinked rapidly at the sound of my name. I couldn't bear to watch her any longer, so I stared at the tape recorder.

It wasn't until the song ended when I finally lifted my

head. My skin was instantly chilled, electric, as I saw that my mother was smiling. Her bottom lip quivered, just slightly.

"Oh my goodness." Her smile broadened and that electric feeling turned into a buzzing that covered my body in something that felt like happiness. I could tell just then that my mother was proud of me.

16

"MARY JANE!" Izzy threw her arms around me and clasped on like a little vine. "I missed you so much!"

I looked behind me at my mother. She was smiling. It was hard not to smile at Izzy Cone's exuberance, her curls, her unbridled affection. I leaned down and kissed the top of Izzy's head. Her loamy smell was so familiar, so close to my heart.

At the sound of footsteps, my mother and I both looked up the narrow staircase, made narrower by the stacks of books and laundry lined up on one side. Mrs. Cone trotted down, barefoot as usual. She was in jeans and a soft orange sweater that showed nothing of her nipples. Her red hair was darker than it had been at the end of the summer, and her lips were waxy and bright with lipstick. "You're here!" she said. Mrs. Cone hugged me, and then she stuck out her hand and grasped my mother's hand more than shook it.

"We have to hurry!" Izzy said.

"Let's go!" Mrs. Cone said. "Izzy and I made cookies. The radio's on already."

The house was narrow with windows only in the front and back. We walked past the living room into the eat-in kitchen that looked out to the tiny backyard. On the center of the round oak table was a plate of chocolate chip cookies, the edges blackened and burned.

"Do you want coffee?" Mrs. Cone asked my mother. "I started to make a pot this morning, then got distracted and never finished." She laughed and my mother laughed too. I think Mom had grown used to Mrs. Cone by now. We'd been coming every week since Jimmy's album was released. My father never asked where we went on Sundays after church. As far as I knew, he was content sitting alone in the kitchen, eating the lunch my mother had left out for him.

"Let me help," my mom said, and she and Mrs. Cone went to the counter and quietly talked while Izzy took my hand and led me to a seat.

A silver transistor radio with a long antenna sat on the table. It looked exactly like the one I had purchased at RadioShack with my summer earnings. The volume was on low, but I could hear Labelle singing "Lady Marmalade." It was one of my favorite songs and I'd recently bought the 45. Izzy turned up the volume and climbed into my lap when Labelle started singing in French. *"Voulez-vous coucher avec moi?"* Izzy sang, and I laughed and hugged her and kissed her some more.

"Do you girls want milk?!" Mrs. Cone shouted as if we were down a hall although we were only a few feet away.

"Yes!" Izzy said.

"Sure," I said.

"I think you're right about the witch," Izzy said. We'd been discussing her every time we saw each other. And last Friday, when I'd babysat Izzy at the Roland Park house where Dr. Cone now lived alone, we searched for the witch using flashlights I'd found in the mudroom.

"She definitely moved out, right?"

"YES!" Izzy pumped a tiny fist. "And I haven't seen her here, either."

"Nope. I told you, witches don't like row houses. She'll never show up here."

"But, Mary Jane—" Izzy turned and leaned into me; her face grew dark and serious.

"Yeah?"

Izzy whispered. "I found makarino cherries in the fridge."

I whispered back. "Your mom put them there."

"She did?" Izzy still whispered.

"Yes. She did." I'd run into Mrs. Cone at Eddie's last week. We'd been standing right at the maraschino cherry jars and I confessed to having told Izzy about the witch who had stocked the fridge with maraschino cherries. She had laughed, picked up a jar, and then put it in her cart.

"So there really is NO WITCH here!" Izzy grabbed a black-bottom cookie and bit into it.

My mother and Mrs. Cone brought two glasses of milk and two suede-colored coffees to the table. They were chatting like any two mothers might. It was nothing like the conversations Mrs. Cone used to have with Sheba, but it didn't sound fake, either.

"Divorce is never easy," my mother said. As far as I knew, she didn't have any friends who were divorcées.

"No, but Richard makes it easier than most. It was such a strange summer, you know. Truly amazing and beautiful in so many ways. But it made me see things about myself. Ways that I'd compromised who I really was and what I really wanted."

"You had wanted to marry a rock star," I said quietly. Then I jerked my head down toward Izzy in my lap. Thankfully, she was tuned out, focused entirely on the cookie that was breaking into rock-hard shards in her hands.

"You remember! Yeah. I did." Mrs. Cone's face looked more freckly in the sunlight pouring in through the window. I could see the younger version of her: fat-cheeked, strawberry-haired, dreaming of tattooed lead singers and a life entirely unlike her own mother's.

"How much more do we have to wait?" Izzy turned in my lap to face me. She had chocolate goo on her teeth.

My mother lifted her wrist and looked at her watch. "Six minutes."

"Six minutes." Izzy shoved the last crescent-moon wedge of cookie into her mouth.

"I've gotta tell you," Mrs. Cone said to my mother, as if the interruption from Izzy hadn't happened, "how relieved and liberated I feel just being me. Not a doctor's wife. Not a Roland Park housewife. Just *me!*"

"Being a wife is a lot more work than husbands ever give us credit for!" my mother said.

"How much longer now?" Izzy asked.

My mother looked at her watch again. "Five minutes."

"WAIT!" Izzy shouted. "I want to tape-record it." She tumbled out of my lap and ran from the room. I could hear her feet clunking up the stairs.

"Oh, Mary Jane!" Mrs. Cone said, "I was talking to Richard this morning and he wanted me to tell you that that key hook you talked him into buying is working wonderfully. He only misplaced his keys once this week."

"That's so great!" I had seen the ceramic placque with hooks on it at Gundy's Gifts around the corner from Eddie's. When I told Dr. Cone about it, he had nodded in a resigned sort of way, but then he drove over there and bought it.

"IS DADDY COMING TODAY?" Izzy shouted from upstairs. As far as I knew, Dr. and Mrs. Cone saw each other several times a week. And every time I was at one house, the other called. I didn't know anyone whose parents had divorced, but still I'd never imagined it was like this. Instead of a drawn-out tug-of-war between two people who wanted to destroy each other, the Cones' divorce appeared to be a gentle rearrangement of housing and time.

"NO!" Mrs. Cone hollered toward the stairway. Then she looked at me and my mother and said, "You know, Richard still gets jealous over Jimmy. Can you believe that? He needs to understand that I wasn't the only person who fell in love with him. That man casts a spell on everyone who meets him."

"I love him, but I wasn't in love with him," I said.

My mother laughed nervously. "Oh, let's hope not!"

Mrs. Cone laughed, not nervously. "No, Mary Jane was the most sane person in the house. She was the adult while the rest of us were throwing temper tantrums, playing dress-up, fooling around. You know." Mrs. Cone shrugged.

My mother took a giant gulp of creamy coffee. Then she said, "Mary Jane is always so reasonable."

Izzy skipped into the room holding a black plastic tape recorder. She clunked it on the table so hard, the cookies shifted on the plate.

"You push here and here and it records." Izzy pushed. "We're recording now, see?"

"Almost time." My mother glanced at her watch again. She was pursing her lips as if she were holding in her excitement.

Izzy turned up the volume on the radio. We waited through the end of "Rhinestone Cowboy" and then Casey Kasem came on, speaking in his nasally, snappy voice. *"A stunning achievement for thirty-three-year-old West Virginian Jimmy Bendinger—"*

"JIMMY!" Izzy whisper-screamed. She sat on the seat beside me. Mrs. Cone was across from me, and my mother was on my other side.

Casey Kasem continued, *"Bendinger dropped out of high school and moved to New York City, where he lived in a warehouse in the Meatpacking District with Stan Fry and JJ Apodoca. Fry and Apodoca had moved to New York from Newport, Rhode Island, where they surfed together and attended the prestigious St. George's School. Fry had just finished his studies at Columbia University, where he'd majored in economics. Apodoca had also been admitted to Columbia, but failed to attend even the first day. The three of them wrote songs while Fry and Apodoca waited tables. Bendinger, a self-described introvert, tried to wait tables but found talking to customers too much of a strain. Instead he wrote more songs, and eventually sold several of his solo efforts to Bonnie Louise, the Suarez Brothers, and Josh LaLange. With money coming in from the songs, these boys bought themselves new instruments: Bendinger an electric guitar, Fry new keyboards, and Apodoca an electric bass guitar. The only problem was, they needed a drummer. When they brought in Stan Fuller, Fry's former roommate at Columbia, Running Water was born. It wasn't long before the hits started coming. Most previous Running Water songs are credited to Bendinger, Fry, and Apodoca. On this new album, Fuller is gone, replaced by Finn Martel of Philadelphia, the former drummer of Kratom Runs. Six of the twelve new songs are credited solely to Bendinger, who might be finding inspiration from his glamorous wife, the starlet of a single name, Sheba. Though the title track of this album was clearly written under the influence of a different girl, a muse, someone whose many great talents and Baltimore roots are hailed in the song. Her identity remains a mystery, however, as Bendinger is as private as he is talented."*

Izzy, Mrs. Cone, and my mother all looked at me, grinning expectantly. I was smiling so hard that the edges of my mouth shook.

A drumroll played. Izzy opened her smiling mouth wider; her eyes were enormous. She reached out and took my hand. I looked to my mother, stuck out my hand, and she took it. Mrs. Cone put out both of her hands and completed the circle so we were all connected.

"Moving up from the number two spot, here is the most popular song in the land, written and produced by Jimmy Bendinger. At number one, Running Water's 'Mary Jane.'"

The drums clicked. The guitar and keyboards joined in. I was biting my bottom lip. My mother squeezed my hand.

"Mary Jane!" Jimmy sang. And the four of us sang along.

Acknowledgments

I am so grateful for all the innovative, industrious, and talented people at HarperCollins and Custom House. Special thanks to Liate Stehlik, Jennifer Hart, Eliza Rosenberry, Danielle Finnegan, Rachel Meyers, Elsie Lyons, Paula Szafranski, Kaitlin Severini, Gabriel Barillas, *all* the hardworking salespeople I have yet to meet, and Molly Gendell.

I have endless love for the following people who offered support, advice, friendship, wisdom, and their faces onscreen during COVID times as I worked on this book: Celia-Kim Allouche; Sally Beaton; Paula Bomer; Fran Brennan; Jane Delury; Larry Doyle; Lindsay, Bruce, and Emily Fleming; Liz Hazen; Lisa Hill; Holly Jones; Matt Klam; Deana Kolencikova; Dylan Landis; Marcia Lerner; Boo Lunt; Jim Magruder; Helen Makohon; Steve, Finn, and Phoebe Martel; Scott Price; the Rende Family; Danny Rosenblatt; Claire Stancer; the Treat-Laguens family; Tracy Walder; Tracy Wallace; Marion Winik; and all the generous people of La Napoule Art Foundation. Also, huge love to my goddaughters, Addie Fleming and Sydney Rende.

And endless love and affection to my hilarious family: Maddie Tavis, Ella Grossbach, Ilan Rountree, Sebastian Rodriguez, Becca Summers, Satchel and Shiloh Summers, Joshua Blau, Alex Suarez, Sonia Blau Siegel, Sheridan Blau, Cheryl Hogue Smith, and Bonnie Blau and her extraordinarily smelly cat, Mookie.

If I could sing, I'd sing to Gail Hochman, the best agent in the business.

If I could write a song, I'd write it about Kate Nintzel, whose genius glows throughout these pages.

About the author

About the book

Insights,
Interviews
& More . . .

Read on

Meet Jessica Anya Blau

Courtesy of the author

JESSICA ANYA BLAU is the author of the nationally bestselling novel *The Summer of Naked Swim Parties* and three other critically acclaimed novels. Her novels have been recommended and featured on CNN, NPR, the *Today* show, and in *Vanity Fair, Cosmopolitan*, and many other national magazines and newspapers, as well as on Oprah's summer reading lists. ∽

An Interview with Jessica Anya Blau

Q: When did you know you wanted to write Mary Jane*?*

A: A couple of years ago, I had been working with a movie star, ghostwriting her memoir. She had offered immediate deep intimacy, which I find very seductive and hard to pull away from. It was an intense, brief relationship where she brought up every morsel of her fascinating life (including naked photos of the many celebrities she'd had sex with) and even let me read her diaries. I wrote, rewrote, rewrote, and wrote over again pages and pages and pages for her, none of which she approved. Though she happily told me all about her juicy, sexy, often-not-sober past, it turned out she didn't want her potential readers to know any of it. In the end, she decided to write the book herself (and, last time I checked, she hadn't finished it yet). Of course, I was hurt by the "breakup" of the friendship and my ego was battered by my inability to write her memoir as she wanted. Maybe five days passed during which I was feeling terrible about the whole thing. And then I woke one morning, and I thought, "Fuck you! I'm going to write exactly what I want, exactly how I want, with no one telling me I'm not writing it correctly!"

Mary Jane poured out of me in the strangest way. As if it were already written in my head. I've never written ▶

anything so quickly in my life. When my editor, Kate Nintzel, read it, she liked all but the end. I wrote a new ending and added two chapters. Kate didn't like those. I wrote another new ending, and Kate didn't like that either. (This wasn't anything like the experience with the movie star rejecting what I wrote for her; with Kate it's a discussion of mood, tone, and where characters are in the end, how they feel.) It ended up taking me almost as much time to compose the ending as it did to write the whole book. Early readers have mentioned how much they love the ending. I don't think they understand how happy that makes me feel. It was worth the struggle.

Q: Let's dive into your portrait of fourteen-year-old Mary Jane, a Broadway soundtrack-loving, highly sheltered teenager in 1970s Baltimore. Was she based on your own experience of adolescence at all?

A: It's funny, but I feel like she's me. When I pointed this out to a close friend he laughed and said, "But you had boyfriends and were drinking beer on the beach in Southern California." Yes, I get his point. But no matter what I was ever doing in my life, I've always felt like Mary Jane. I've never felt popular, or hip, or pretty, or "in." My sense of myself is being someone on the outside looking in at the cool people. I realize, though, that my lived life might point to the contrary.

As far as Mary Jane liking order and tidiness goes, that is entirely me today. I grew up in a house with the disorder, mess, clutter, and chaos of the Cone home. Now, I can't bear to have anything on any of the flat surfaces in my house; I clean the inside of the trash can after I remove the bag; and as soon as I get on a phone call, I pull out the Mr. Clean Magic Eraser and wipe down the floor moldings and light plates while I talk.

I didn't grow up in Baltimore, and my childhood wasn't sheltered enough! There was marijuana growing in my backyard and the only beach my parents went to was the nude beach (a source of deep embarrassment to me at the time). But some of my close friends had families that were versions of Mary Jane's. And after many years and many, many sleepovers, I really feel like

I've lived in those homes, too. I do love Broadway musicals, by the way.

Q: What are the must-haves for any great coming-of-age story?

A: I don't think I'm an authority on anything, but I can say what makes a great coming-of-age story for me. There should be sex, of course. Becoming sexual is such an overwhelming and encompassing thing, it would be strange to omit it. Or, if one isn't becoming sexual, that would be interesting. In seeing the absence of something, you're sometimes seeing it in an even more powerful way. Friendships are intense when we're young (mine continue to be intense as I don't like light or shallow friendships) and the inclusion of the travails of friendship are good in coming-of-age stories. The realization that the way things are done in one's home aren't the way of the whole wide world can be liberating or unsettling. Either way, it makes you feel things. That tension—between the familiar and the newly discovered— might be the backbone of a coming-of-age story, no?

Q: How does Mary Jane experience the tension between two very different family dynamics—her own uptight parents, and the more progressive Cone family for whom she's nannying?

A: For Mary Jane, because she lives in such a homogenous neighborhood (as did I, growing up, but we were the freaky outliers like the Cones), it's startling to find a family, a home, and people unlike what she is used to. It is like traveling for her. I mean, this is why traveling is so wonderful, right? Your mind, your body, your senses, are shocked by the newness, the unfamiliar. You see everything with a greater sense of awareness. Sometimes you like the new flavors and sounds and sometimes you don't. But either way, it's good to be exposed to them and open to them. Mary Jane is at an age when most people are receptive to new sights and sounds. And she gets all of that by being in the Cone house. It's a "trip" of sorts that changes her as it shows her a life she had never before imagined but would like to live in the future. ▶

An Interview with Jessica Anya Blau *(continued)*

Q: Why did you choose to set this novel in the 1970s?

A: There's so much awareness now with the internet and cellphones that it would be hard to find a fourteen-year-old today who hasn't seen porn and listened to every kind of music on Spotify. Not as much was globalized in the '70s, so Mary Jane could go into the Cone house with a believable innocence. I say all this as if I sat down and thought it through. Really, I didn't think about it. I sat down, started writing, and there it was. I think it was '76 at first, and then I later changed it to '75 so I didn't have to deal with the Bicentennial celebrations that were happening all over the country, particularly in the summer. I do love the music and styles of the '70s; it's always fun to write in that time period. I like to listen to music when I write and I listened to loads of '70s tunes. When I was cleaning the kitchen or doing chores around the house, I always put on Billboard top 100 songs of 1975. So I continually had in my head the songs that Jimmy and Sheba knew, and the songs to which Mary Jane was eventually exposed.

Q: We have to ask you about the inspiration for famous rock musician Jimmy and his movie star wife, Sheba, who move in with the Cones. . . . Any clues?

A: Haha! I made them up, though I did have people in my head. In the middle of writing this book, I read Keith Richards's memoir. It's wonderful; he's amazing. A lot of what he said in his book about how he felt and feels about playing guitar, and doing drugs, wedged into me and came out in Jimmy. But Jimmy isn't Keith Richards. And Sheba is just Sheba, though I was obviously thinking of lots of stars from that era. There was the interesting juxtaposition at the time between what America was shown—wholesome family images, people like the Osmonds, the Carpenters, and Liberace—and what was really happening in these people's lives. I liked going into that with Sheba—the personae her family and her mother wanted presented publicly versus who she really was.

Also, I think celebrities are often portrayed in fiction as complete narcissistic assholes. Yes, of course there are many narcissistic asshole celebrities. But there are probably just as many narcissistic asshole lawyers, or writers, or teachers. And just as there are many wonderful, loving, and brilliant people in the world (most people—I happen to like people in general), there are surely wonderful, loving, and brilliant celebrities, too. Jimmy and Sheba are flawed, like all of us. But I think they're pretty amazing people and they are wonderful to, and for, Mary Jane.

Q: Can you share a little bit about the role music plays throughout Mary Jane?

A: Like the discovery of sex, music is another way we break from our family of origin to figure out who we really are through the act of uncovering what exactly pleases us. I love music. Most people do (though I have met people who just won't or don't listen to music). I find it's like reading in that it lets you into another way of thinking or seeing the world. And new music (music that is new to the listener, that is) can really open your mind so that you feel the feelings of other people or get a sense of the place from which the music is created. It's just sounds, really, noise that's been organized. But sounds and rhythms and beats can be so specific to a place, a time, a culture, and the people who create those sounds.

Q: Given all the very adult topics in this novel—addiction, marital problems—why did you choose to write from Mary Jane's perspective?

A: I have to admit that I didn't think much through before I sat down to write. I have written books and many stories where I started in one point of view and then switched to another. (The novel *Drinking Closer to Home* was originally written in first person present tense, then rewritten in third person past tense, then rewritten once more in third person past tense from three different characters' points of view.) With this book, I started with Mary Jane and never thought to deviate. It felt right all along. I think if you took the story from any other character's point of view, it would be too bogged down in the grown-up ▸

7

problems of addiction, infidelity, etc. But to see it through Mary Jane's eyes is to see the people in their entirety—the good and the bad—without getting mired down in the muck of grown life.

Bonus question: When's the last time you called in to request a favorite song on the radio?

A: Ha! People don't think I seem shy, so I'm not going to say I am. But I do feel like I am. I'm afraid of public speaking and rarely raised my hand to speak all throughout school. The idea of calling in a song, when they put you on the air, is terrifying to me. I do, however, remember standing in my elementary-school best friend's kitchen, holding the phone together between our mouths, asking for a song, and then listening forever to see if they'd play it.

Your question takes me back to a tiny stucco house I bought in Oakland, California, with my then-husband. We both were working full-time so the only time to fix up the place was evenings and weekends. I spent a full week painting two coats of cornflower blue on the kitchen cabinets while listening to a late-night radio show called something like "Love Beats" or "Love Jams." The DJ had this smooth, sexy voice; I'm sure everyone was in love with him. Each song he played was called in by listeners, but they had to say who the song was for and why. It was so great because you got an entire narrative, something like, "Can you play 'Use Me' by Bill Withers for Lynn in San Leandro. I love her more than anyone else in the world but she's breaking my heart because she keeps fooling around with my cousin, Martin, and I won't speak to Martin anymore. . . ." You know what I'm saying. So, there would be the preamble, and then the song, which would complete the picture. ∽

Reading Group Guide

1. *Mary Jane* is set in 1975, a very different world than the one we live in today. Despite these differences, though, many of the cultural and political issues Mary Jane grapples with ring true in the modern day as well. What parallels do you see between the 1970s and today?

2. At one point, Sheba tells Mary Jane she reminds her of herself. Do you agree? Despite their very different ways of life, in what ways are they similar? Why do you think Sheba takes such a liking to Mary Jane?

3. How do Sheba, Mrs. Cone, Mary Jane's mother, and Beanie Jones reflect the changing norms for women in the 1970s?

4. One lesson Mary Jane learns is that "adults weren't always right and could be just as confused and make just as many mistakes as kids." How does this make her start to understand and look at the adults in her life differently? Do you remember the first time you realized that adults didn't have all the answers?

5. How did your family of origin's mealtime define your family compared to those of your peers? Were there foods your family ate that no one you knew outside of your family ate? Did you envy the food or meals at any particular friend's house?

6. Even after everything, Mary Jane worries about the Cones getting divorced because she thinks Izzy would be better off growing up with her parents together. Are there limits to Mary Jane's open-mindedness about unconventional families and ways of life?

7. Dr. and Mrs. Cone seem happier and more in love to Mary Jane than her own parents do, yet they end up separating while Mary Jane's parents stay together. What do you think this says about each couple's views on marriage and family life? Do you think things in Mary Jane's parents' marriage are likely to change now that her mother has become more ▶

open-minded and started spending more time with Mrs. Cone?

8. Part of Mary Jane's coming of age occurs through her exposure to new kinds of music, particularly rock and roll, folk, and funk. Do you think finding new music is always a part of growing up? Was there music that changed your point of view, or a musical movement that you took on as part of your identity?

9. Many coming-of-age stories involve characters undergoing dramatic changes to their personalities and lifestyles. But though Mary Jane grows up over the summer and becomes more open-minded in her attitudes, it doesn't change who she is at heart—she never wavers from her love of singing, cooking, and taking care of people. Why do you think it's important that she stays true to herself, and that the Cones accept and love these parts of her?

10. In a review of *Mary Jane,* the *New York Times Book Review* declared, "You can watch the movie in your mind." Who would you cast in a movie version of *Mary Jane*? ∾

Jessica Anya Blau's Playlist for *Mary Jane*

This piece was first published on largeheartedboy.com.

Soundflashes: 1. My parents put on the Beatles and the whole family dances around our California living room, my brother balanced on my hip. My mother playfully bops our heads with a fist during the "Bang! Bang!" parts of "Maxwell's Silver Hammer." **2.** With my saved allowance, I buy my first album, *To You With Love, Donny*. I sit on the bottom bunk in my pink-wallpapered room, singing "Puppy Love." **3.** My high school boyfriend and I agree that it's time to go all the way. I decide that I want Rod Stewart singing "Tonight's the Night" for the event. We end up doing it at the beach without music. I vomit from too much beer in medias res, and the next morning I feel hungover and cheated out of Rod's accompaniment. **4.** In Europe with my best friend from college, we take a train to Rotterdam for a David Bowie concert and work our way, without proper tickets, to the foot of the stage. When Bowie plays "Young Americans" we scream the words, pointing at ourselves, near tears.

It doesn't end there. There is marriage (Chaka Khan), motherhood (Rickie Lee Jones), graduate school (Counting Crows), divorce (Taylor Swift), moving from one end of the country to another ▶

(Prince), relocating to Canada (Sheryl Crow) and later to New York (Shovels & Rope) . . . every chapter in the story of my life has a defining song.

And every book I've written has a defining soundtrack. I search for songs my characters would listen to, and I regularly play the Billboard top 100 of the year in which the book is set. The music puts me in the headspace of the time, the people, and the place (if you turn on the radio in Santa Barbara, California—no matter what decade—you will hit an Eagles song within an hour).

My new book, *Mary Jane*, takes place in Baltimore in 1975. At home, Mary Jane and her mother listen to Broadway soundtracks. At church she sometimes sings tweaked pop music along with hymns. When Mary Jane goes to work as a nanny for a psychiatrist who's housing a rock star and his movie star wife for the summer, she's exposed to everything from funk to folk.

Here's a list of ten from the hundreds of '70s songs I listened to while writing *Mary Jane*:

1. **"Up for the Downstroke," Parliament.** I'd never heard this song until I was searching for early '70s music. Immediately it was one I played on repeat.

2. **"Over the Hills and Far Away," Led Zeppelin.** The tempo change from slow and soulful to head-thumping feels very '70s to me (think "Band on the Run").

3. **"Love and Happiness," Al Green.** One of my favorite songs. Period.

4. **"Rhinestone Cowboy," Glen Campbell.** I love Glen's tangy, country voice.

5. **"Willin'," Linda Ronstadt.** Little Feat sang this song first, but I prefer the Ronstadt version. Is there any song that isn't better when Linda covers it?

6. **"Dirty Work," Steely Dan.** I turned my kids on to Steely Dan and they loved them right away. Since there's really nothing else like this that they've been exposed to, I think their immediate love says something, right?

7. **"(If Loving You Is Wrong) I Don't Want to Be Right," Millie Jackson.** To me, this is the perfect make-out song.

8. **"Hosanna,"** *Jesus Christ Superstar* **soundtrack.** This is my favorite song from the musical. It has a big crowd sing in it, and I love crowd singing.

9. **"Angel from Montgomery," Bonnie Raitt and John Prine.** Their two voices roped together give me the chills.

10. **"Shining Star," Earth, Wind & Fire.** There is no time of day or night when I'm not happy to hear an Earth, Wind & Fire song. I would get out bed at four a.m. and dance if I were woken to this song.